USE

RIGHTS OF USE

SHANNON EICHORN

ISBN 978-1-7324340-0-4

Cover design by Mallory Rock of Rock Solid Book Design (www.RockSolidBookDesign.com)

❀ Created with Vellum

To all those who believed in me.
You've made all the difference.

PROJECT BLACK BOOK

"Reports of unidentified flying objects which could affect
national security... are not part of the Blue Book system."
-Brigadier General C. H. Bolander, October 20, 1969

1

FIRST TIME IN DECADES

Speaker of the House Andrew Rockefeller walked his five o'clock meeting to the door, made his closing remarks, and smiled at the next man waiting. "Senator Stokely."

"Mr. Speaker." Charles Stokely's jowly face smiled back. Smiles that earnest rarely lit his expression and transformed it from the stately visage he wore for official business into something others might consider unrecognizable.

Stokely took his job seriously.

Rockefeller ushered his old mentor into his office, closing the door behind them. "Thanks for making the time to stop by on such short notice."

"It's not every day the Speaker of the House asks to meet."

Rockefeller grimaced. It had been a while.

"I'm kidding, Andy. You haven't needed me for years. It's nice to see how far you've come." Stokely gazed out the window over the desk, which framed a gorgeous view of the Washington Monument stretching into a brilliant blue sky from a stand of steadily-flapping flags. "A bit different from the view you started with."

As one of Stokely's former junior aides, their shared office hadn't had a window, let alone a view. Rockefeller shrugged as he eased himself into one of the wingback chairs in his office's central sitting area. "Back then, I didn't get reminded of what I have to live up to every time I sat at my desk."

"More's the pity." Stokely settled into the chair beside him, angled toward the Speaker instead of the immaculate view. "What's on your mind?"

"I asked you over to get your perspective on this ballistic missile threat. I know you've spent a lot of time looking into defense spending and serving on appropriations committees."

Stokely anchored his elbows on the chair's armrests and steepled his fingers over his lap. He considered the question for a few silent moments then drew a deep breath. "Our country needs a stronger missile defense network to counter the threats currently arrayed against it."

Rockefeller glanced out the window at the peacefully-waving flags and the nation beyond, which hadn't seen war on its shores since the attack on Pearl Harbor. "Do you really think Iran is that much of a threat?"

Quick knocks cut off Stokely's answer, and Rockefeller's aide Tom swung the door open. "Mr. Speaker, your wife is on the phone. She says it's an emergency." Over the last year, he'd watched Tom learn to take a lot of supposed crises in stride, but now his eyes stretched wide and startled on his long face.

Joyce? An emergency? "Thank you, Tom." As his aide closed the door again, Rockefeller hustled to his desk. "I hope you'll excuse me."

He barely heard Stokely reply, "Of course," as he swept up the phone and answered the line.

Joyce's words tumbled out. "Andy, it took Maggie! Something took her right off the cul-de-sac. The police think I'm crazy, but I know what I saw!"

ANDREW ROCKEFELLER WAS young for his station, with dark and full hair and a classically chiseled jawline that televised well. Usually. That slump in his shoulders and worried brow projected the wrong image for a powerful leader.

Stokely tried not to listen to Rockefeller's measured voice answering the frantic tone on the line. If it was going to take long, perhaps he'd best leave the Speaker and spend his time elsewhere.

Maybe, if he left now, by the time Rockefeller turned his attention back to the "ballistic missile" defense system, the Speaker would take his advice to support it without asking what all it might defend against.

And maybe the capital would have a cool, dry summer.

"What took who?" Rockefeller listened to the answer, stiffening.

Time to go. Stokely pushed himself out of his chair and cast one more concerned glance at the Speaker by the desk. Then his jacket pocket rang. As he fished out his phone, it rang for an eternity with ever-increasing, irritating volume, but the Speaker didn't even glance over.

He stepped out of the central circle and faced one of the back walls, trying to keep his voice down. "Stokely."

"This is Colonel Marshall. We made our date."

The Senator plugged his other ear in case the Colonel continued. He had a million questions. How did they know?

Had anyone seen the perpetrators? How were Colonel Marshall and her Air Force subordinates responding? To retaliate or rescue? How did they have what they needed?

But cellular phones weren't secured lines. He bit down on his questions. "Thank you, Colonel."

She hung up.

Stokely lowered the phone, staring at its raised buttons and digital screen.

Alien abductions—for the first time in the decades Project Black Book had awaited them. This time, maybe they could catch the bastards.

After all that money poured into identifying the threat and planning to ambush the source, now they'd face it head on.

"Joyce, keep trying to think of anything else you can tell the police. I'll be there as soon as I can." Rockefeller fumbled the phone back into the cradle, and Stokely turned to face him.

Rockefeller met his eyes. "Someone took my little girl, Charlie. They took Maggie." He swallowed as if he might fix his thready voice. "I've got to go." He flung open the door and rushed out, snapping out a last-minute string of instructions at his two assistants.

Stokely pulled the Speaker's forgotten suit jacket from the chairback by the picture window. He caught the Speaker only halfway through the next room, where his scheduler had mired him in questions.

"Okay, but what happened?" she asked.

Rockefeller shook his head. "I don't know. Joyce said she saw a flying saucer. Something must have happened to her, too."

"Really?" the scheduler asked.

The timing wasn't a coincidence, then.

Rockefeller nodded once then edged toward the exit. "I have to go."

"Andy." Stokely caught his eye and held up the jacket.

He mustered an appreciative grunt, snatched the jacket, and fled, his jerky motions almost masking his trembling hands.

Stokely drew a deep breath and left as well, albeit at a much more reasonable pace. Up ahead, he glimpsed the Speaker disappearing down the stairs.

So Rockefeller's daughter was kidnapped the same afternoon as the first witnessed abduction in almost half a century. The Speaker didn't seem to believe his wife—and why should he? Project Blue Book had long since disproved the validity of UFOs.

Digging his mobile phone back out as he padded down the stairs, Stokely stopped in a quiet alcove off the Crypt and redialed. The Colonel picked up on the second ring, and Stokely spoke softly.

"I need someone read in."

SARAH HAD BEEN AFRAID BEFORE. Like most kids, she'd known the skin-shrinking fear of the bedroom blackness, the lurking presence beyond the outer edge of lamplight. Like her old neighbors, she knew the soul-hampering fear of nature while hunkering under the stairs, waiting for deteriorating hurricanes to rip the roof off or crush the house with a shallow-rooted pine. Like seemingly no one else, she knew the isolating fear of her parents' anger, the lonely nights spent trying not to listen to their arguments, wondering whether they would hit each other. Wondering whether her home would dissolve so soon after they'd moved her away from all her friends.

This fear was different, perhaps the first kind worthy of the name.

Nothing had come from the dark. Nothing had shredded the home. Nothing had split her family. But something she hadn't known to fear had come out of the daylight, from the clear weather, and into the peaceful house and whisked her away.

Sarah squeezed her eyes shut and let the ragged breaths rock her body. Maybe if she wished hard, she'd find it was all a horrible mistake. They'd meant to break into someone else's home and haul out some other teenager.

Yeah. Right.

Her numbing lips tingled on the next hitching breath. She'd heard them search her house and pass up everything valuable until they got to her. Maybe they'd have taken anyone, even her parents if they'd been home.

She held her breath. Her head buzzed. Then she blew out. She couldn't hide like this forever. Holding very still, she counted down to when she'd force herself to face the room. Three. Two.

One.

Sniffling once and swallowing down her queasy stomach, Sarah set her chin on her knee, still hiding behind her folded arms, and opened her eyes. Three men sat with her in the tiny, circular white room.

Two sat out in the open like she did, burly men with tall, elongated heads and square features. Leather armor, scuffed and seared and accented in clinging, deep brown stains, encased most of their bulging muscles. Their dark beards pointed oddly, as if cut with three quick snips of scissors. Both men bore skin only a little darker than hers and greasy, black hair that ended sharply at their chins. One man's face had started to wrinkle around his eyes and mouth, and a scar slashed over his eyebrow. The other man's gaunt cheek-bones stood out over his scraggly beard; it looked like a face made for crime.

Although their relaxed legs stretched halfway across the floor, covering a circular seam around the center, they gave her space and ignored her now. Their low voices filled the room as much as their musty body odor as they rumbled on in a language she didn't know.

Sarah tried to sink further into the white, cushioned floor. It gave minutely.

The third man was older. Color had already drained out of his short, neat hair, and his thick skin sagged on his cheeks. The hanging console he sat behind blocked most of his face, but he occasionally leaned into full view to glance at her, his eyes worried.

About what? And if he cared, why wasn't he doing anything?

When he peered at her again, she ducked her face into her arms. The more attention she avoided, the better, just like at school last year.

Another pang wrenched tight around her stomach. School was going to start again in three weeks. Last year, after moving to the North, the other kids had picked on her so much that she'd quit even trying to do well and just wished to get out.

I didn't mean it! she thought to the void where other people said God was. A mere prayer couldn't change what was physically happening, but at this point, it was worth a try. *I'll work hard again. I'll put up with the bullies. Just let me go home!*

Nothing changed in the tone or volume of the kidnappers' deep voices. Hidden air vents still whispered harshly. Her heels still dug into the floor. Nothing magically changed.

She drew in a shuddering breath and held it. *I'm still here. Maybe I can act like it.* Maybe, for once in her life, something she did could affect what happened to her, unlike arguing about moving, unlike answering the bullies, unlike hiding out while her parents fought.

Unlike trying not to get kidnapped.

I'm still here. She blew out her breath and resettled her glasses on her nose, reassuring herself with their comfortable weight that something remained normal. Like everything else she'd experienced, she'd get through this.

Who was she kidding? She didn't even know how she got there.

She remembered hearing them try the door, then the distinctive, woofing clap when it hit the foyer's parquet.

She remembered listening to them search her house. Furniture screeched. Closet doors slammed. Heavy footsteps clomped up the stairs.

She remembered the younger one finding her in her closet, how she'd kneed him in the crotch, and his calloused hands had pinched tight on her arms.

She'd bit him on the way out, when the scarred man helped carry her, and the younger one had smacked her in reply.

Next thing she knew, they were in here. The men dropped her to the soft floor. She scrambled back to the gray wall—

Pain sparked across her shoulder blades. She lurched forward.

It took only a moment to equate "rippling wall" with

"instantaneous death shock," but then it was a quick lesson: don't touch the wall. She sat well away from it now.

She couldn't have completely lost track of time when he'd hit her; the men's grip on her hadn't changed. It was as if she'd closed her eyes in one place (her front yard) and opened them in another (this little white room). It'd make sense if she'd arrived here on the floor, but in the exact same position she last remembered? If she'd been knocked unconscious, why hadn't the second man dropped her legs? They hadn't just climbed into a car or shifted to a house down the street. Unless Zelienople had houses with shock walls and trap doors. After all, it was down the street from the cemetery in *Night of the Living Dead.*

But she didn't think so.

I'm not in PA anymore. She swallowed against the lump in her throat.

What were they waiting for, yammering on as they were? Something the man at the console was doing? Or was it just a long elevator ride?

Heart pounding in her ears, she inched closer to the gray-haired man to peek at his screen.

The talking stopped and she did, too. She tried to breathe slower to not give herself away. Maybe they hadn't noticed she'd moved much. Maybe they wouldn't mind.

They eyed her warily, and she studied their bootlaces. Aside from getting her eyes off theirs, it let her notice how odd their boots were: round, sickly white cord ran between button holes along the shoes' sides. They looked like someone tried to adapt Roman sandals to Pittsburgh weather. She wished they hadn't.

The men started up their conversation again; she had feigned disinterest long enough.

Sarah sat in line with the console's back. From here, she

had only to lean to see around it. As she did, she caught the controller's fingers darting about the screen—tapping here, sliding there, circling and pinching elsewhere. A little closer, and she'd see the screen, too.

The controller glanced at her and murmured something to the others.

The young one stood.

"No, please!" Scooting back, Sarah caught the controller's stare again and held it. "Please take me back! I just want to go home!"

The young guy clamped down on her shoulders, holding her in place.

"Please, I won't tell anyone." She scrunched down out of his hold and stood up behind him to stare at the controller and his compassionate eyes. "Just take me home!"

The young guy caught her again, pressing down harder and wedging her against him. Right behind his feet, the trap door dropped down—an open exit!

Sarah elbowed his armored gut. He heaved a breathy grunt and bent over, arms flailing after her. She folded her knees, dropping through his hands. Then she dove for the hole's edge.

The room beyond had no floor.

She'd meant to glide through, grabbing the hole's edge to right herself. Instead, she flung her limbs out, catching herself over the impossible pit and wrenching her shoulder.

The room beyond wasn't wider than this one, but it was a hundred times taller. Gold, marble, and opposing green walls converged very far away, and she didn't see a ladder to climb down.

Strong hands lifted her by the armpits and pulled her to safety.

She couldn't catch her breath. Her heaving pants

stressed the grip on her armpits, but it was a reassuring pain this time. She'd almost fallen, almost pitched herself into the abyss—not a good way to get home.

The controller and the young guy both approached the hole and, swift as you please, dropped through—and landed sideways, feet on the marble wall. The scarred man let go and followed them.

What the hell had happened to gravity?

She edged closer, still afraid of falling, only to have the trap door slam in her face. Kneeling, she stared at it, picturing what she'd seen. With the men standing sideways on the marble wall, she could start putting the pieces together.

It wasn't a pit. It was a hallway, seen from a door at the end. With *her* gravity sideways.

Sarah backed away from the hole and kept her distance from the wall. Sideways gravity?

She wasn't in Pennsylvania anymore.

———

Rockefeller wrapped his arm around his wife along the couch back to touch his older daughter's head on her far side. He winced as Joyce's fingers mercilessly tightened on his other hand. The phone rang, so he extracted his fingers and knocked the portable phone on the end table into reach with a tissue box. "Rockefellers."

"Pack a bag for a few days, Andy." Stokely's chipper voice clashed with the gloom of the under-occupied room. "I might know something about your daughter."

Rockefeller sat up, switching the phone to his better ear and uncrushed hand. "Where is she?"

His wife and girls leaned forward, watching his face.

Stokely's lighthearted tone dissipated. "I don't know where yet, but I'm going to find out. You should come with me."

"I'm going with you," Rockefeller finished with him. "Where?"

"Not over the phone. Our plane leaves in the morning. I'll pick you up at six."

Six was hours away! What was he supposed to do? Sit around on the couch?

Rockefeller stood. "Who has her, Charlie? How much do they want?" He stared at his family's reflection in the glass entertainment center door. How much cash could he gather to put Maggie's reflection back beside her sisters'?

"They don't want your money, Andy. Look, I'm your friend, right?"

Rockefeller searched for his voice, unsure where this was leading. "Yes?"

"I'd tell you if you could do something. There's nothing else to be done. Get some rest. We'll talk in the morning. Six."

Stokely hung up.

If not money, what would the kidnapper want? He and Joyce had covered this only hours ago with the FBI. Perhaps political agendas, either in the House or elsewhere in the government, probably something the perpetrator thought the Speaker himself could do.

Notoriety, maybe? Terrorism?

He caught his family's anxious looks and turned back to the phone, dialing Stokely's number from memory. "I'll try again." The line was busy and remained so the next three times he redialed.

The fourth time, Joyce rose and covered the keypad with her fingers. "What did he say?"

He closed his eyes to keep tears from clouding his vision and focused on her skin's warmth where their hands touched around the phone. It took two tries for him to squeeze words past the lump in his throat to relay everything.

Joyce wrapped her arms around him, whether to comfort herself or him, he couldn't tell.

"If I could get through, I know—"

She turned her head to the side, ear on his shoulder, so he could hear. "If he was going to tell you anything else, he would have."

He followed her gaze to the couch: Julia and Chastity sat up where they'd been dozing, blinking blearily and listening.

She hid her face in his shoulder, and the smell of her hair soothed him a little. "Come on. We should rest. There's nothing more we can do tonight."

He watched his other two daughters fall asleep, huddled together in a single bed. He sat at the foot, close enough for them to touch him and reassure themselves (and him) they were safe.

Maggie's room remained empty.

2

BE BRAVE

Alone now, her kidnappers gone, Sarah held her breath and wiped wet palms on her jeans. Tiny vents wafted air across the sweat on the back of her neck, sending chills down her spine and reminding her how exposed she was. When the monsters came back, she had nowhere to hide.

Not that hiding had helped before.

They had broken into her house and brought her all the way to the threshold of this place where gravity didn't work, only to leave her locked alone in this little cabin where the walls bit. She scooted back from the closed trap door and shivered.

What for? What would they do to her?

Either they'd been specially looking for her—

In which case they couldn't afford to hurt her after all the trouble they went through getting her. Maybe they'd left to get an interpreter who spoke English. But if so, why her? Her grades certainly didn't make her stand out. She didn't do anything outside of school except gymnastics and piano lessons, and she wasn't a prodigy at either.

Sarah wrapped her arms back around her knees and tried to scrunch down as small as she could as the fear crashed back in.

Or, more likely, they didn't care who she was.

Normal kidnappers, as far as she knew, took kids for one of two reasons: because they were easy targets for serial killing or for extorting ransom money. She didn't have to be exceptional to die. *Please, not that!* She curled tighter and squeezed her eyes closed on the terrifying hypothetical nothingness.

But if they asked for ransom, her parents had some money. She'd wondered lately if they'd be better off without her, but she knew they'd pay to get her back. Maybe it could be that simple. They'd demand money, her parents would pay for her, and she'd go home.

That made sense for easy targets, but these men had funny-shaped heads and didn't speak English. They had to come from far away. Africa, maybe? Eastern Europe? How many cities had they passed up on their way around the world?

These guys couldn't be normal kidnappers, even without the sideways gravity.

Were they worse than serial killers?

Terror clutched her heart, squeezing until she thought it would stop the frantic pumping any moment, anything to eject her soul free from these monsters' plans.

No, she must have seen it wrong. Sarah gazed at the trap door, picturing how she remembered the room beyond. Maybe it wasn't really that deep but had mirrors set up to make it look dangerous. That way, anyone they took would think twice before jumping out, like she had. The mirrors' angles had made the men look like they stood on the walls.

They'd built a whole room to scare people into staying

inside. They weren't taking just one or two people—they must be taking hundreds.

For what?

Bulk discount parts?

Her fists balled, and she pounded them into the floor. Her hands bounced harmlessly off the padding. How dare they! How dare they take people out of their homes and lives to chop them up for parts! She could've grown up to cure cancer (if she liked medicine) or build Mars rockets or something equally significant. They didn't know, and neither did she.

And now she'd never find out.

She popped to her feet and hauled a leg back to kick the wall. At the last second, she remembered "shock walls of death" and swiveled to kick the control console.

Pain exploded in her foot, but the console wobbled appealingly.

"What is wrong with you!" she screeched at it, picturing the controller and his worthless, compassionate eyes. "Why would you do that!"

Then she broke into sobs, tears blurring the white floor into the gray walls. She might never go home. She might never snuggle into her dog's fur again. Or curl up on the couch with a warm blanket, a bag of carrots, and a good book. Or play catch with her dad.

All because they wanted to chop her up for parts?

The sounds behind her changed from the steady, hissing air to the hollow reverberations of a long hallway. Sarah held her breath, swiped at the tears obscuring her eyes, and spun to face the now open trap door.

The controller climbed through.

She drew a deep, ragged breath. "What the hell is wrong with you! What gives you the right—"

He scrambled up faster, wide-eyed, and jerked the trap door behind him. It closed at its own stately pace while he frantically pressed his finger to his lips for silence.

"No! You dragged me here! I'm not going to be quiet!"

He winced, but he waited for the trap door to latch. He waved her down. "It's okay," his baritone voice assured her, its gentleness an unreasonable counterpoint to her screams. "I didn't come to hurt you."

"You sure didn't come in peace!" She did a double take, checking whether he really was the man who'd sat behind the console earlier. "You understand me?"

"I'm General Donn Marshall from the Air Force. I'm working undercover right now, and I'm not supposed to be talking to you. In fact, I'm not supposed to know English." He knelt on one knee, so he had to look up to her instead of looming over her. "What's your name?"

She hesitated, looking for any way he could hurt her by having her name. Maybe he needed it to set up the ransom. If so, she needed him to know. "Sarah." She swallowed. Undercover with the Air Force and not supposed to be talking to her—maybe he wasn't a bad guy at all. But that didn't absolve him of all the blame. "You stood by and let them take me!"

She threw her best punch.

He caught her fist in his palm, absorbing her energy without even rocking. "They were gathering women from all over the world. The Air Force is coming to take you home. Just be patient. And brave."

"Oh, yeah?" She wrenched her fist from his loose grip. "What do they want with us?"

He rested his arms on his raised knee and leaned heavily on it. "How happy are you at home?"

Not, given the bullies picking on her for her Southern

accent, but that wasn't the point. It was still better than here. "I want to go home."

"Don't you want to be part of something bigger?"

Didn't everybody? But she didn't want a part of whatever he had to sell. "What do they want with us? What do you want?"

He wiped a hint of a smile from his face. "There are bad aliens who want to implant one of their queens in you. It'll control your body and make you do whatever it wants you to."

She stared at him. "Aliens."

He grinned, transforming his face from that of a heartless accomplice to that of someone's uncle. "Yes. Aliens. From outer space."

No. That was crazy. Maybe she was dreaming. Although, with the day she'd been having, she couldn't decide whether space aliens were really unbelievable.

They had to be. Everyone said so, from her parents complaining when UFO documentaries came on to her teachers describing how misunderstandings resulted in flawed eyewitness reports. That had to be it. Aliens were the oversimplified explanation.

He twisted around to face away from her and pointed to his neck. "See this bulge beside my spine?" Now that he emphasized it, tugging on his skin to make it stand out, it looked off. The left side swelled asymmetrically, but his unmarked skin didn't hint at any other mundane explanation. "That's an alien. It's a good one, though, and it lets me be me."

Maybe it was a tumor. Pressing on his brain. Of course, shouldn't that affect something more obvious, like his body movements? He seemed fine.

Mr. Marshall let go, and the bulge blended back into his

sagging skin. "The alien who ordered you kidnapped and his queen aren't like my alien, though. They'll control your body. You will be trapped inside yourself."

She shuddered. "Can't you stop it?" Assuming it was true.

"Maybe. If everything works out."

"And if not?"

He met her eyes earnestly. "Sarah, there are good aliens, too, aliens like the one I host that won't control you. I could swap out the bad one for a good one, so that even if the Air Force fails, you'll be okay."

"And that's it?"

"That's it. I just need to know that's what you want."

A giant lump in her neck? A foreign object, some oozing, living thing jammed under her skin? Behind her, where she couldn't see it?

Ew!

How could anyone want that?

Her empty stomach flip-flopped, threatening to wring itself out over the floor. She backed away until the console pressed against her hips. "You want to stick one of those in me?"

His pleasant, helpful expression fell blank. "Better a symbiont that won't take over you than one that will."

But she had only his word on that, and if what he said was true, maybe she wasn't talking to Mr. Marshall from the Air Force but the little lump he'd pointed out. She shuffled to the console's far edge, keeping her back pushed against it, protected. "I don't want either. If the Air Force comes, I don't have to choose."

"In case they fail—"

"I don't want it!" Her voice snapped into a shrill screech

that even the soft floor couldn't absorb. "You can't make me!"

His face set in the skeptical expression her dad used when he knew he could make her and didn't want to argue. "Sarah—"

"No! I don't have to. I'm not going to do it!"

He pushed to his feet and glared down at her from beneath bushy eyebrows. "Listen to me. My team is dedicated but not very experienced at this. If they fail, if they can't get you home, the bad aliens, the Kemtewet, might choose you for their queen. She will use you like a puppet. She will impregnate you and grow her offspring in your belly. She'll do whatever she wants with your body. And in a few years, when she tires of you, she'll leave, shredding your brain on the way out. If you're lucky, they'll dispose of your body before you finish bleeding out."

He pointed to the lump in his neck. "Are you sure you don't want a Gertewet instead?"

Sarah hugged her arms to her chest and tried not to picture herself lying on the floor, vision going dim as the foreign mass crawled away in tracks of her blood.

She wiped her eyes clear and glared at him. "Go away. Leave me alone!"

He raised his hands to placate her then dropped them as if she weren't worth his time. "Okay, I'm going."

He stomped toward her. She scurried to the room's other side, but he ducked around the console, focusing on it.

She studied him. Would he really listen to her? He had to, right? If he was one of the bad ones, the Kemtewet, if that neck lump controlled him, then he didn't have to ask her permission. If not, if his neck lump was what he called a Gertewet, it didn't control him; she'd talked to the Air Force officer she saw.

He'd asked. Didn't that mean "no" was an answer?

This was all so crazy. How could it even be real?

The trap door opened, and Mr. Marshall crossed to it, his expression grim. Sure enough, he got out and stood sideways to close it. It sealed with a thunk, closing off the echoing corridor sounds.

She tried to swallow the lump in her throat. She'd definitely seen that right this time. At least some of what he said had to be true. Aliens. Space ships. Body possession. Even if it was all true, that didn't mean she had to do what he said.

But what if he was right and getting a Gertewet implanted was her only real option? She'd just missed it.

THIS WASN'T how her day was supposed to be. It wasn't even the worst Maggie had imagined—reality had left *that* in the dust. Those scenarios seemed so simple now.

Possibility one: mission success. Sixteen-year-old crush-since-fifth grade drives her home from an amazing day at the mall, drops her off at her driveway, and since mom's car isn't home, leans in for the perfect first kiss. Probability: low. Mom was definitely going to be home, especially after what her sisters pulled last week.

Possibility two: mission failure. Sixteen-year-old crush-since-fifth grade drops her off at her driveway, where mom is gardening. Mom lets loose with the garden hose through the open passenger's window, ruining his dad's leather seats. Mom yells insults at him, and he vows never to speak to Maggie again as he guns the engine, tripping her on the way out of the car. She falls on her face on the blacktop, and he runs over the mailbox. Mom grounds her for not only the rest of the summer but also the first quarter and decides to escort her everywhere thereafter. Probability: medium. It was too humid to garden fashionably.

Having considered the options, she'd had him pull into the cul-de-sac before hers. He leaned in for a kiss. Her heart pounded.

She'd pictured it before. She'd close her eyes, somehow zero in on his lips, and... Well, honestly, it did look boring in the movies, but there had to be something to it.

She'd had it all right: the perfect date, the perfect guy, the perfect lead-up—and she'd burped. Right into his face. She'd never drink soda again.

Everything had gone downhill from there.

They'd laughed. He leaned away, sitting back in his seat. And as he pulled away, she realized his head had been a wonderful eclipse of her mom standing at the street corner, watching them, toy poodle accessory peeing on the closest stop sign.

Maggie read her lips: "Margaret Maria Eleanor Rockefeller, you get—"

Her fists had balled against the seat of his dad's Lexus. Trust her mother to ruin something good.

No one had seen it at first; they were too wrapped up in the drama. She snatched up her little bag from Claire's, said goodbye, and slammed the car door in the most ladylike manner she could manage. The car only shook a little.

It was after her mother's first demand of "Who is that?" that something blocked the sun. She'd thought it fitting. She'd fumed about the injustice of being caught when she wasn't doing anything wrong, until something lowered into her peripheral vision.

She finally looked up.

At first, she thought it was a plane, then a prank, then something completely incomprehensible: the smooth metal belly of something saucer-shaped hovering over the side-walk. Then she'd done the dumbest thing ever. She stopped to stare.

The pitch of her mother's voice rose, still screaming her full name. The toy poodle yapped. Behind her, the Lexus's door slammed, and someone ran.

Maggie remembered thinking it was too bad she finally saw something cool for herself when she was in such a foul mood. She should have known better. It could only go downhill once her mother found out about him.

The moment she had recognized the flying saucer, someone had pushed her from behind.

"Maggie, run!" Bobby yelled. He got his feet under him, grabbed her hand, and pulled her toward her mother. Then the impossible had happened.

Now, Maggie sat alone in a small, round room with fluid walls. She shook so hard, her muscles all ached. Any moment, the men would be back. They'd flit in without warning, just like they'd left. Just like they'd brought her here. Any time now, in a blink, there they'd be: dark masses in the clinical white room.

Any moment.

She held her breath.

Any instant. Without warning.

Her pent-up breath spilled out, and she gasped through tears.

How could she have been that stupid to stare up at the thing? No, stupid wasn't the right word.

Innocent.

Back then, she couldn't have imagined anything this dark existed. Had that only been this afternoon? Her watch. She fumbled for the pink floral band, shook as she tilted the display her way. 10:38. She was supposed to be home at five, and she was going to be early. So much for that. Her ploy to keep her date secret from her parents had failed, anyway, just like her attempt at a first kiss.

She sniffed and shivered under the cool gust of the air jet. This wasn't her mom's fault or, for once, her sisters'. Maybe this was her own fault, but she didn't think so. Placing blame might not even be relevant.

Maggie shivered harder. Since the barren room had no hoodies or blankets, she started pulling her arms inside her t-shirt. If she let her hair down, its frizzy thickness would shield her from the draft. She jerked the ties from her braids, but her hair stayed in place in crusty statues.

Smearing her eyes clear, she peered at one: something had splashed across it, gluing it in place. She sniffed: a sour, outdoorsy scent tainted with sweat and pond scum.

Right. That.

She'd gotten a mouthful once already.

One moment, she'd been running in the street with her crush. The next, they both ran full-force into that wall of smelly water.

It stung. Everywhere.

They had reeled back as fast as they could, sputtering thick, sour and salty fluid. Crush yelled, and she turned to him, wiping gunk from her face. She blinked her blurry eyes open when dark, thick arms wrapped around his lean body, and both her crush and the assailant disappeared into thin air.

"Bobby!" She reached out, but he was gone.

Another muscle-armed man stood out of reach in the little white room, and she could see one sitting on the floor behind a black screen on a pole to her right. She backed up, now avoiding the wall she'd proven to be liquid, and the first man appeared again, sans Bobby.

Maggie finished undoing one braid and started on the other in short, swift jerks. She closed her eyes and pictured the last moment she'd seen him. If she hadn't had goop clouding her vision, would she have seen a determined look on his face, or had he been scared, too? Had they left him behind, staring up at—

At what?

Her fingers froze mid-braid as she remembered what the shape reminded her of and why she'd been stupid enough to stand there and stare.

A flying saucer.

Really? She was in a flying saucer?

No, that couldn't be right. But she'd seen it clearly, barely higher than the rooftops, her perspective changing as she'd run, letting her glimpse its narrow swell. A flying saucer.

She finished unraveling her crusty braid and fluffed it out. Where did the saucer come from? It couldn't really be aliens, could it? The men inside looked human, even if they did have long, tall heads and amber-gold eyes. They still had eyes, nose, mouth, and ears in the proper places. They were human.

But not American or African or Middle Eastern or Hispanic.

Human aliens.

She should freak out. It was a Big Deal. But it just couldn't compare to the fact that they'd come out of nowhere, grabbed her, and taken her away from her crush and family—and straight out of her neighborhood.

Whatever they looked like, wherever they came from, couldn't overshadow that. She was all freaked out, freak spent, freak-poor, freakless. Freak free.

It still put a new spin on things.

Aliens. She could provisionally accept that. But what

would they want with her? They obviously already knew about humans, since they were. Did they want to study the differences between themselves and their Earth cousins? Did they want her because of her father or because of her gender? And why her but not her mother? They had seen her mother standing *right there*, hadn't they?

Personal safety classes rang in her head, reminding her to stay calm and look for exits. Obviously, the police officer teaching the class didn't expect what *she'd* stumbled into: a place where people appeared and disappeared, apparently using teleporters. If he had, would he have told her to just give up?

No.

She stared at the giant screen her kidnappers had used from the time they brought her on board until they winked out and left her alone. Text in dozens of different scripts filled the screen with fine, gold letters on black. "*Entrez le mot de passe ou de ne pas toucher.* पासवर्ड दर्ज करें या स्पर्श न करें. Enter password or do not touch."

Or what?

Or the teleporter would disintegrate her?

She had to try. Shaking, she tapped the screen in a dozen places, but all it ever did was zoom in on specific languages. It neither zapped her away nor zapped her into pieces.

And that was it.

No doors. No windows. No escape.

Unless she could figure out what buttons to push to beam away—assuming she could get the computer to do anything at all—she wasn't going anywhere.

There was still the liquid wall. There could be another way out underwater. Last time it felt like walking into a giant bug zapper, its electric jolt raking through her skin and muscles. She shuddered. It was an option.

If she could stand to touch it again. If she could stand it long enough to dunk all the way under—and if it didn't keep zapping her. And if it didn't zap her hard enough to kill her.

Maybe not such a good idea.

Fluffing her hair one more time, she finally pulled her arms into her t-shirt for warmth and pulled her knees to her chest.

Nowhere to run. Nowhere to hide. Nothing to fight until the men came back. What were they doing for almost six hours? Surely even adults couldn't argue about what to do next for that long. Maybe alien adults could.

Or maybe they had something to set up. She'd hate to find out what it was, but she didn't see a way out of it.

Aliens. What would it mean if the rest of the world found out? Would everything stop—school, shopping, movies—until people figured out what to do next? Was she missing it? The rest of the world had to know by now; her mom knew, and she'd surely told everyone she knew, who'd told everyone they knew, and so on.

And what would her dad do? Was he in Congress right now, drumming up support for some grand plan for the country? Did he even notice she was gone? Sometimes, it seemed like she came last.

Something clicked in the little white cabin, and Maggie looked up. Nothing had changed, but the air smelled sickly sweet. She knew that smell—chloroform. She held her breath. Her father had made sure they all knew what it smelled like in case of...

Of kidnappings like this.

Not like this. Dad couldn't have anticipated this, not in a million years.

She frowned at the little white room. She couldn't go

anywhere, and she couldn't hold her breath forever. It wasn't like the lessons Dad paid for would do any good in space.

The room winked out.

Another replaced it: a round room, tiled from floor to tall ceiling, where one man stood behind a pedestal facing her. Two more stood nearby, closing in.

And she couldn't breathe. Her chest hurt, and her lungs heaved for more air than they could draw. What had they done?

Then, she didn't care. She saw an exit. Without thinking, she dashed forward between the men for the doorway behind them. If she could just find somewhere to hide—

One man leapt forward and knocked her off-balance—right into the other. He heaved her off the ground, and she screamed, lungs burning.

Whatever reason they'd taken her, she was about to find out.

ALIENS TOOK YOUR DAUGHTER

Rockefeller couldn't sleep. He rose carefully to avoid disturbing his wife, showered, dressed, and folded a spare suit and undergarments into his travel bag.

Questions roiled like smoke in his foggy mind. What was happening to Maggie? Whoever had taken her, were they treating her right, knowing her safety was their lever to money, political action, or whatever the hell they demanded? Would they hurt her? Rape her? Sell her into slavery?

He froze halfway down the stairs, clenching the railing until it groaned in protest. Not her. Not his little girl.

He forced himself to breathe again and keep moving. He couldn't help her without knowing where they'd taken her or why. He'd be damned if that wasn't the most gut-wrenching part of this whole affair: knowing they could do anything to his baby, whom he had a duty to protect, and knowing he could do nothing.

Why couldn't he and Stokely have left last night? What could make waiting more important than finding her?

He dropped his travel bag beside the front door and marched to the kitchen, where he set up the coffee pot far more forcefully than it merited.

As the coffee brewed, he stared out the dark window to the backyard where all three girls used to play. The swing set and play house had stood alone for a couple years already, ever since the older girls became embroiled with boys and Maggie shut herself away with her books.

Gone.

What if she never nested upstairs again, recharging until she rushed down to greet his arrival? What if she never ambushed him with another of the choke-hold hugs her sisters had outgrown?

Rich, coffee-scented steam puffed out with the first spurt into the pot, and Rockefeller took a deep breath. Continuing to focus on the problem never solved as much as focusing on solutions. Only two more hours until Stokely arrived to drive them...

Away from the rest of his family.

He sighed. When the coffee finished, he took a mug upstairs to sip while he watched his sleeping wife then his remaining daughters.

He'd lost the world but still had more to lose.

Not until they'd reached the airport and boarded the private jet did Stokely plop a thick pile of papers into Rockefeller's lap. The Speaker dropped them onto the floor and snarled over the engines spooling up, "Charlie, paperwork is not going to help my daughter! Can't we do something sooner?"

Stokely swirled a glass of either red wine or cranberry

juice. "When you get read in is not going to affect what's being done for her. But you won't know about it until you sign those forms." He took a pointedly patient sip.

"Fine." Rockefeller swiped them back up and read through while the jet prepped, took off, and climbed to cruising altitude.

Nothing in the stunted ream surprised him, since he'd seen it before for other programs: information handling and labeling procedures, responsibilities, suspicious activity reporting, threat of fines and imprisonment for disclosures. Bureaucratic hoops—a tool to control who got what information, as well as engage legal leverage, and intimidate the reader to keep the weak-willed out of sensitive matters.

And waste time.

He signed and dated, signed and dated. If he didn't date so many other pages on a regular basis, this day would be indelibly seared into his memory from the sheer repetition. July 25, July 25, July 25.

Finally, he collected the miniature ream, rebound it, and tossed it at Stokely's feet. The Senator startled, his glass sloshing dangerously close to spilling, and drew back from the window. Lifting the package, he flipped through the signed pages. "That's that, then."

Rockefeller cleared his throat, drawing Stokely's focus. "Where is she?"

Stokely finished glancing through the sheaf. "Out of the country. After I left your office last night, I got on a secured line to Colonel Renee Marshall at Bradshaw Air Force Station in Montana. They're mounting a rescue op for those taken yesterday. We'll get the details when we arrive."

The roiling questions returned with a vengeance, a raging F5 tornado of details he needed immediately. He wet his dry lips. "What happened to her? Is she okay?"

"We don't know. Let's start from the beginning of what we do know." Stokely took one more dark-red swig before setting his glass aside. "In the 1950s and 60s, the Air Force ran Project Blue Book. There were some other highly successful programs before, but Blue Book was the biggest compilation of public and military UFO sighting reports ever gathered."

"Yeah, I remember that crap."

Stokely opened his briefcase on the adjacent seat and traded the legal ream for a hardbound book half its size. This he tossed to Rockefeller. "At the end, Blue Book handed its files to a third party, which independently assessed them and drew its own conclusion."

Rockefeller studied the yellowed cover. *The Scientific Study of Unidentified Flying Objects.* The subtitle continued for another three lines. "What's this have to do with Maggie?"

"I'm getting there." Stokely pointed to the book. "That is the basis for modern public opinion on UFOs."

"That they're bullshit?" He held the cover's blurry photo up for the Senator in case he hadn't noticed.

"Essentially. They found conventional or natural causes for the vast majority of cases. For the remainder, they couldn't dredge up enough information to make a determination."

Stokely stared down at his glass. "But the introduction contains a curiously astute statement. The university was told the government withheld nothing, that 'all essential information about UFOs could be included in this report.'"

"You're saying it wasn't?"

Stokely shrugged. "Flying saucers had already been specifically identified and a means of tracking them conceptualized. They no longer qualified as UFOs."

Rockefeller studied the cover again as if he might find a blurb labelling it the Gag Gift of the Year 1969. Then he thumbed to the copyright page, just to check that Acme Products hadn't published it. University of Colorado, just as the cover said.

Could the entire country really have had its beliefs swayed on the technicality that flying saucers weren't unidentified? Surely, they had to know more truth than that. Stokely had to be feeding him a line.

"You're saying a UFO took my daughter."

Coincidentally, exactly what his wife had told him, but Stokely wasn't screaming incoherently.

"Andy, aliens took your daughter," Stokely corrected. "Probably."

"What is that supposed to mean?"

"It's conjecture, but we got calls only minutes apart. If Maggie's disappearance isn't connected to the Air Force project I keep tabs on, I'll eat my hat."

Not that he wore one.

Rockefeller turned to the window, as if he expected to catch a saucer pacing them to prove Stokely right. Instead, orange sunlight illuminated the thick clouds below, casting long, cavernous shadows between incipient storm cells. The old man had guided him through some ridiculous ropes on the Hill, but this? Perhaps Stokley needed a nice rocking chair on a quiet porch or a constant hug in a long-armed jacket.

He tapped the book against his knee. Scientific study. Right. What kid hadn't loved the glamor of UFOs? But he grew up and watched the Apollo moon landings—with real spaceships and real spacemen. UFOs weren't real.

Stokely sighed with the disappointment of a man who knows he's not getting through. "Project Black Book came

online in the 70s with some close-range gamma ray tele-
scopes, a chunk of Big Sky, and a clear purpose: to track the
damned saucers and blast them out of the air the next time
the bastards flew through."

Rockefeller snapped around to face him.

Normally, Stokely's placid facade hid his biting wit and
scorn for incompetence. Rarely did anything provoke the
old Senator to a more lively response than a well-reasoned
discussion. Now, though, his eyes lit with fury, focused on
some remembered foe.

And he swore.

What brought on *that* ire? Best to play along.

"So, the Air Force shoots down aliens. Then what?"

Stokely glanced over, fury melting, then shrugged.
"They didn't. The aliens stopped coming."

"Until now?"

"Until last year." The Senator lifted his drink again,
swirling the dark fluid. "We finally got one. The wrong one.
It absconded with the general running the program, who
returned only long enough to bring us a ship and show us
how to run it."

Rockefeller tapped a staccato rhythm on the armrest.
"And it took my daughter, too?"

"We'll find out, but I don't think so." Stokely's eyes
searched across the seat backs in front of them and beyond.
"This is much more like the classic abductions that
prompted Blue Book's propaganda in the first place."

Rockefeller's head ached. He just wanted his daughter
back, not the rest of this nonsense. Stokely probably
wouldn't intentionally lead him on a wild goose chase, but
that didn't mean that he was right. "Wait, so the Air Force
has been investigating aliens since the 60s?"

"Forties."

"Okay, if they found out they were real in the 40s, why didn't they do something until last year?"

Grimacing, Stokely polished off his glass and dropped it back into the cup holder. "It was a phased program. In the 40s and 50s, they identified the threat. In the 50s and 60s, they found a way to detect it. They covered over the whole thing with disinformation. In the 70s, they deployed the detection capability, and last year, they struck gold.

"That's when they found out there are two kinds of aliens."

"What?" Rockefeller searched his old mentor's face for that tension in his left jowl that gathered when he lied. No sign of it. He was ready for the funny farm for sure. "That's ridiculous!"

"Personally, I find it remarkable there aren't more." Stokely opened his lap belt and pushed himself to his feet. "But the alien they captured spoke some broken English and explained that while both alien kinds use humans as hosts, its kind—"

"Say that again?" Because it certainly hadn't made sense the first time.

Stokely froze, thinking, then nodded. "Right, I forgot that. The aliens—all of them—live inside human bodies. Even the one Black Book captured, though its human body looked pretty strange. The aliens can manipulate their hosts, control them, make them speak and do things."

Rockefeller swallowed. "What kinds of things?"

"What do you make your body do?"

He ate. He dressed. When he could fit it into his schedule, he ran. He courted his wife. But what might someone else do with his daughter? All the same things? How grotesque would it be to see something else making Maggie run, let alone anything else on his list? And if it controlled her body, could she not even scream?

"Maybe they don't have her."

"You said your wife saw a flying saucer."

"Maybe it was a hoax like all the other sightings that got dismissed." He held up the thick little book.

Stokely reclaimed his seat and leaned forward, elbows on his knees. "You know, Andy, I hope you're right. I hope you read through all those forms for nothing, because Joyce tells you about the kidnappers' demands as soon as we touch down. This Black Book business can let you in on a whole new realm of nightmares. But if I'm right, if they have her, wouldn't you want to know what she's going through? When the Air Force recovers her, won't you want to be able to help her?"

What father wouldn't want to help? But just hearing the possibilities threatened to burn his heart to ash. When she came home from this—if she did—how could she look at him with the same careless cheer she always used to? For her, then. In case this alien insanity had any substance. He nodded.

Stokely sat up. "According to the alien that possessed the General, there are two kinds: Kemtewet and Gertewet, neither of which are allowed near Earth. The Kemtewet rule all the other human-populated worlds, taking new hosts by whim—"

"Other worlds?"

Stokely rolled his eyes. "Yes. A bunch of them. Focus, Andy. The General said the Kemtewet must be the ones Black Book was charged with defending the country against. He said the thirty-person abductions noted in the 40s are very much their style."

Rockefeller's head swam. "And the others?"

"Gertewet, like the General's alien, oppose the Kemtewet. They say hosting shouldn't be imposed; it should be a choice." He shrugged. "That's what he says, but none of us can see as how the General got a choice."

"So, Maggie might have no choice or only the semblance of a choice." He shook his head. "What am I saying? She might have a chance to just say no!"

"Andy, I think if they were going to give her a choice, they'd have done it before taking her off the planet."

"Then what's the point of these Gemtewet? Do we have a deal with them? Are they going to bring her home?"

"We're still getting our feet wet. We haven't had a chance to negotiate with either the *Ger*tewet or the *Kem*tewet. We don't know how to bring them to the table." Stokely regarded the window, avoiding Rockefeller's eyes. "No one's ever been brought back."

"Why tell me all this if you can't help her?"

"I didn't say that. This is the first time the Kemtewet have taken anyone since the General and his Gertewet dropped off a saucer at Black Book and showed us how to use it." Stokely turned back from the window. "Maybe this time, it'll be different. It has to be. This time, we're at least trying to do something about it."

"I don't want you to try, damn it! I want you to bring her home!"

Stokely's voice dropped an octave. "Them."

"What?"

"Your daughter wasn't the only one taken. There are at least a half dozen women and girls missing. Whatever happens when we get there, you have to remember it's not just for Maggie."

"Of course." As soon as he knew Maggie would be safe.

4

LITTLE WHITE LIE

The Gertewet could win once and for all. After all this time, they could beat the Kemtewet and free the galaxy's humans to rule themselves.

Vinnet kept telling herself that. It was the only way to bear the isolation. This was day one hundred and twenty-four. She hadn't had a host for a year. No wonder she was so sick of the tewet environment in the *Kaxandepet!* There were only so many times one could swim around on the wet side of the force field that surrounded the central, human habitat and check Every. Single. Solitary. System.

All of five inches long and limbless but for a pair of fine tentacles alongside her belly, Vinnet swam to the brink of the towering force field between her environment and the open air of the lifeless human cabin.

One of the Kemtewet queens had made a mistake, giving the Gertewet a lucky opening. Since Vinnet was the best qualified operative without a host, the Gertewet Coordinating Council had sent her to take advantage. Her and Kitchell and his host, Marshall. Until she had a host of her own again, she needed someone to move her between this ship and any ground-side symbiont environments. She needed him to get her in place.

But he hadn't checked in for over a day. If anything happened to him out in enemy territory, she'd never know. Only he knew where she was. How long should she wait before admitting she had no way down?

She flicked her tail out of the gel, into the open air, and shook off the sting of the gravitational discontinuity. The gel's surface stretched so far away that it reminded Vinnet of standing within arm's reach of the homeworld's tallest buildings, dwarfed by their height.

Her blood vessels pumped slower in dismay. In some hosts, she'd had to duck when standing in a kaxan's human side. In most, she'd wanted to. A space that short shouldn't feel so tall! In every host, she forgot she was so tiny.

And vulnerable. Nothing was stopping any of Banebd-jedet's mothership crew from barging into her ship. They had access to turn her life support off from the human-side control console, just as she had access to turn it on from the tewet neural interface. Which would reveal her presence if they noticed.

There were some saving graces. Motherships docked hundreds of kaxan, and Kitchell had stationed this one on the engine deck, which had the fewest human crew and the least traffic departing the mothership. He also habitually closed the hatch, influencing the light traffic to seek other, open kaxan first. And even if they used hers, most human pilots knew only enough of the controls to arrive at their destinations. With a little extra training, they learned elementary use of the teleportation controls. Nothing to do with the symbiont environment.

But if they did. And if they noticed her. They could tele-port her into open air and leave her to wriggle helplessly until her skin dried out and cut off her oxygen. Mummified symbiont.

Then who'd save them?

Was there time to get another operative in place before the queen took her next host?

This had to work. With only a few thousand Gertewet left against nine billion Kem who had hosts, they never had good odds. But since the Kem seemed to believe the ruse that the Gertewet had already died out, there'd be no better time to try anything as risky and potentially effective as impersonating a queen.

They had only two more hosts' lifetimes left until the operatives not killed in action succumbed to old age. It was excessively risky, but it might actually end generations of war. They might actually win.

Vinnet swam the perimeter of the human cabin, glancing inside. Each time, she hoped a host would be there, waiting. But no.

It was irrational, but then, before the last hundred and twenty-three days, she'd had constant company for over three hundred years. Other Gertewet knew her for her level-headedness, although she certainly wasn't acting like it now. She would again.

As soon as she had company. As soon as she had a host.

MAGGIE SCREAMED. She thrashed. She tried ramming her elbows into the man carrying her, and she kept trying until he dropped her in a little wooden closet and shut the door.

She sat on the floor, winded, crying, and desperately searching the four open corners around her for any signs about where this was or what they might do next. With her arms inside her shirt for warmth before the teleportation and struggle, she had half of it up around her head. Berating her stupidity and indecency, she resettled her shirt where it belonged.

A different door opened, and she jerked toward the wall. Beyond a wooden lattice door, a giant stone hall stretched with rugs and clusters of furniture, to end in a towering wooden tidal wave. All lifeless.

She waited another minute to ensure no one was going to spring out from behind the little vestibule's own walls. Nothing.

Gulping, Maggie crept forward and checked around the walls to the hall's hidden corners. No one. A large buffet, piled high with bright fruit and pastries filled the back wall.

She stepped farther out.

The room's unnatural emptiness tore at her nerves. Only the faint crackle of flaming torches whispered in a room that should have been filled with hundreds of people snacking and talking and celebrating. Why had they put her in here alone?

The door smacked closed behind her.

Shrieking, she sprinted away.

Certain of something chasing her, she ran halfway across the room. Then she glanced back. Nothing. Nothing but a closed door.

She edged toward a high-backed sofa and slowed. Checking around and under it and the surrounding furniture, she stopped behind it, heart hammering.

Was this someone's idea of entertainment? If so, who was watching? From where? How could they see her if she couldn't see or hear them?

She crouched lower, peeking over the sofa, and watched the still scene by the strangely steady firelight. It looked like a reception, but for whom? Her? Had they taken more like her? If so, maybe someone would know why.

But it didn't look like it.

Then maybe it was for whoever wanted her, not the men she'd encountered, who'd hardly even looked at her when they weren't hauling her around. Maybe it was for whoever they reported to.

Someone else.

Someone worse.

She sank to the floor, shuddering and alone, not even sure what she could hope for.

A clack echoed through the room.

Maggie peered around the sofa, back at the lattice door. It had swung open again, and someone lay inside the vestibule. White-haired but still solidly built, she wore jeans, a t-shirt, and a worn leather jacket. Normal clothes— she had to be from Earth. Maggie wasn't alone!

Maggie launched out from behind the sofa and ran to her. As the woman lay still, a disturbing thought flashed to mind: what if she'd died? She hadn't moved at all.

Maggie slowed and noticed the woman's steadily-rising chest. She breathed. Then she groaned.

Maggie dropped to her side. "Are you okay?"

The woman rubbed her face. "Um. Where am I?"

On another planet, probably, but she had no proof. "Looks like a reception hall. Are you okay?"

The woman opened her eyes, and her gaze latched onto Maggie. She stared for a second then bolted upright. "Oh my God! Someone grabbed me straight off the tarmac." She swallowed. "Who are you? What do you want?"

Maggie put a hand on her shoulder, partly to reassure the woman, partly to make sure she was real. "I got kidnapped, too. Right off the street by my house. My name is Maggie. Maggie Rockefeller."

The woman grabbed her, hugging her tight. "You, too? But there was the white room and no one else—"

"And they left me alone for hours."

"And it had these walls, I guess you could call them."

Maggie pushed back to look in her face. "The ones that shocked?"

"Yeah, that! You were there, too? How long have you been here?"

"Just a couple minutes." Maggie stood with her. "I think we were in identical rooms."

"No way. No way would they have that many weird rooms."

"Uh-huh." Like there was any other explanation. They hadn't been in the same place at the same time.

The woman stepped out into the reception hall. "What is this place? What do they want with us?"

"I wish I knew." Maggie followed her out. "Whatever it is, it's not going to be good."

The door slammed behind them, and they both jumped. Maggie glanced back. "It did that before, when I came in."

A few minutes later, the door opened on another woman, this time a strong-featured woman in a blouse and skirt who spoke with a thick German accent. They muddled through. After her, a mother and daughter from Canada, a woman from Mexico, and a woman in a deli apron. Mostly, they appeared in the vestibule, one at a time, until a group of four from a college swim team. Maggie tried to help them inside as quickly as she could. Some clung to the first face they saw. Some didn't. The swim team took to searching for non-obvious exits.

They'd all seen the little white room.

They'd all been taken at about the same time.

And they were all women.

Maggie started putting pieces together. Every one of them had been brought by a flying saucer on an almost-six-hour trip, thanks to human-looking aliens who snatched a bunch of woman all at once, across multiple countries.

That was bad.

The door opened on the nineteenth, another girl who looked about her age. Maggie stood up to help her.

IT TOOK THE ENTIRE FLIGHT, but Rockefeller finally found the chink in Stokely's story as the jet started its final descent toward the rugged Montana terrain. "They can't be aliens."

Stokely straightened, rubbing his eyes, and craned toward the window to check their progress. "Hmm?"

"Your guys couldn't have shot down an alien spaceship." Rockefeller clapped his hands together. "A real spaceship has to deal with stuff in its way. Rocks and asteroids, space debris. A missile isn't going to take it down."

"It did."

"No, look, in order to travel between planets in reasonable times, a spaceship would have to be travelling fast. Really fast. At those speeds, an asteroid collision could be fatal, so they'd have to have some kind of shields."

"What are you saying?"

Rockefeller shut his mouth. If the vehicle shot down wasn't an alien spacecraft, aliens didn't have his daughter. Stokely wouldn't lie to him. Not about this. So, someone was leading the Senator on. What kind of person could pull that off after all the bullshit they dealt with in Congress?

The plane dropped among the hills and touched down

beside a handful of buildings, a hangar, and an expanse of broken pavement that used to resemble a parking lot.

"Did you figure out the whole asteroid thing?" Stokely plucked his briefcase from the seat.

Standing, Rockefeller pulled on his jacket and straightened his tie. "How long have you known the people calling the shots around here, Charlie?"

"A while longer than I've known you, Andy." Stokely clapped him on the shoulder, grinning, and marched forward to the steps.

These con men had skills to run such a long game. How disappointed they'd be for him to end it now, so he could get off the wrong track to finding his daughter. Too bad.

Rockefeller followed Stokely out of the plane to meet their reception party. Two scrawny airmen flanked a brunette officer in dress blues, complete with uniform skirt and service dress hat. The Senator sent a respectful nod to the ranking officer, who looked particularly uncongenial with her formal attire and impassive face. "Andy, this is Colonel Renee Marshall, the commanding officer of Bradshaw Air Force Station and Project Black Book."

He shook her hand perforce. Her firm, professional grip released so quickly, he'd have thought his hands leprous.

"I'm sorry to meet you under these circumstances."

He got the impression she would have meant the same without the last three words. "Mr. Stokely leads me to believe you may have information on my daughter's kidnapping."

The Colonel raised an eyebrow. "What we have is conjecture. Senator Stokely tells me her disappearance sounds relevant to our project."

"That's not much to go on."

"We're rarely afforded the luxury of abundance." She

held a perfunctorily inviting arm out toward the hangar. "Gentlemen, we can discuss the situation inside."

As the Congressmen followed her across the runway, Stokely squeezed Rockefeller's shoulder. "It's going to be okay. We have a man on the ground—well, in place, anyway —with your daughter."

"He's not our man," Colonel Marshall grumbled.

Stokely stopped in front of the door. "He contacted you, didn't he?"

"Doesn't mean he's on our side," the Colonel argued.

"If he weren't, he'd let them all get taken, and you'd never know where they went." Stokely held the door open for them.

Colonel Marshall led them inside, handed them each a visitor's badge, and indicated an open binder. "Sign in here please."

She continued as they filled in the form. "Normally, we track kaxan by their gamma ray emissions. Since there were none this time, the raid would have come and gone without our knowledge, had the General not contacted us."

"Makes you wonder how many times they have." Stokely finished his name and set the pen down with a thwack.

Rockefeller clipped his badge to his lapel. "Or whether they do at all."

Rolling her eyes, the Colonel slammed open the inner door.

Beyond, an office corridor ran the length of the hangar's eave. The most anti-climactic high-secrecy, high-security facility he'd ever imagined, it bore scuffed white walls and floors, accident-pocked ceiling tiles, drip-buckets, and a burned-out light at the end. Even the office doors repelled civilization: of all he could see, only two featured actual nameplates. Hand-written printer paper labeled the rest.

Colonel Marshall waited for him to step through. "We're a research facility, not the Ritz, Mr. Speaker. We do work. It's not that shocking."

"Of course." He followed Stokely into the deserted hall. "You're not exactly Area 51."

"We don't need to be. You've never heard of us." She let the door slam behind her.

Stokely beelined for a set of recessed double doors. "Here goes. Don't say I didn't warn you." He pushed.

Rockefeller stopped cold in the doorway.

DONN MARSHALL and Kitchell sealed the kaxan hatch and sat at the controls, where Vinnet could study them. When they'd activated the hatch, she'd shifted her virtual focus to the small camera built into the human-accessible control panel, allowing the image, recorded in the human-visible light spectrum, to transmit directly to her optic nerve. Similarly, a microphone filtered sound through the kaxan's computer into her brain.

A steady frown topped off her visitors' tense posture, and she guessed Marshall, the host, had control. Kitchell's undercover persona tended to save his frowns for underlings.

Vinnet accessed the screen and cleared a space to post a message to him. "What's wrong?"

"Nothing." He forced a smile. "We found you a host."

"One of Banebdjedet's Earth girls?" Her tail twitched in annoyance, pushing her tighter against the neural interface.

"Anjedet obviously wanted a host from Earth; you're going to have to choose one of them."

Her tail swished harder. Ger and Kem didn't agree on

much, but they both had explicit policies forbidding interference with Earth. Which, of course, only made Earth hosts
and the languages they brought all the more fashionable,
despite the ready supply everywhere else. Fashionable but
not accessible. Vinnet couldn't name anyone else, Ger or
Kem, who'd ever occupied one. "They all need to go back.
Just because Kitchell got a host there doesn't mean I
should."

His brow furrowed, and he leaned forward. "What
planet I'm from is not going to influence what Banebdjedet's
going to make available for his queen. Who you'll be impersonating. Besides, this is probably your only chance."

"Let me assure you how eager I am to rehash all the
trouble you caused with the Council."

"There won't be any. Anjedet would use someone from
Earth even if you weren't here. In fact, they'll have grounds
to be upset if you don't take one of them. That alone might
compromise your cover."

"Not if they escape first."

He held his hands up. "I think Black Book is coming. I
won't get in their way. If they succeed, we'll see what to do
afterward. Banebdjedet and Anjedet would have to recover,
too."

"Supposing Black Book succeeds—?"

"Let's assume Black Book fails." He glanced at her
message and shrugged. "There are only three real options
Anjedet would consider if she intends to spawn in this host.
The rest are too old or too young." Old enough that they
might have had children or young enough to not be capable
yet, which would delay the queen's next litter. "There are
two brunettes, one tall with short hair, the other short with
long hair. And a short blond with glasses."

Vinnet's tail swished. "So? I can't decide on that basis."

"Of course not, which is why I talked to the blond." His eyes shifted elsewhere on the screen. "Well, the tall brunette, too, but she wouldn't speak. The blond's name is Sarah. She's from the same country as me but the east side instead of the west. She's scared, but she agreed to host you."

"You told her what we do?"

"Of course. Explained it all."

"And she agreed?"

"Like you said, only if Black Book fails. Then she's got someone else standing between her and the Kem."

"Or her and the fields." If the queen rejected a girl as host, Banebdjedet might kill her to get her out of the way.

Donn stared into the camera, meeting her "eye." "Either way, she'll be okay. She'll either go home, or she'll have you. You can relax."

"Not yet."

He rolled his eyes. "Whether or not you will, you can."

"I hope your team succeeds." Then the girls would all go home. She wouldn't be messing with humans outside the Empire, humans who didn't even know they could be raided for hosts, and she could head off any of the Coordinating Council's concerns. There'd be no point in reporting in for the intelligence for her upcoming mission, only to get side-tracked with whether she should have taken her new host.

"I hope Katorin's mission succeeds," she added. The key to getting in the final word in a discussion with Marshall, she'd found, was to change the subject before he continued; otherwise, he would argue all day.

His brow furrowed in confusion. "Why Katorin? There are a dozen operatives on Sais, all to make sure your next mission succeeds."

"Not that part of her mission. She's looking into where

another operative left off investigating the ISC recruitment changes."

He winced. "Sounds dangerous. Couldn't they have sent Chryson?"

"No, because Chryson excels at following orders and keeping a low profile." Her sarcasm wasn't immediately apparent in the text interface he saw, but they both knew Chryson.

Marshall shrugged. "I'm just saying that I'd rather not see her get hurt. Poking around the ISC is a fool's errand. Hopefully, she'll make it home safe." Shaking his head, he stood and leaned down to put his face in the camera's view. "Vinnet, any host you end up with is going to have to be a feasible choice for Anjedet. Whoever she is, she'll probably be from Earth."

"Keep your head down," she answered, purposefully not acknowledging his statement. She didn't want a host as young as Anjedet did, and she didn't think getting tied up with the forbidden planet would work out as well for her as it had for Kitchell.

As Marshall and his implanted symbiont slipped back out of the kaxan and she cleared the screen of her side of the conversation, she supposed she would never want the same host as a Kemtewet. That simple fact might make this mission more stressful than she'd anticipated. Her host for the next few centuries could be any ditz the queen thought pretty.

5

AIR FORCE IS COMING?

The longer Sarah sat alone in the room, through crying fits, screaming fits, and bouts of silence, the more she believed what Mr. Marshall had said—at least, some of it. She'd for sure seen him standing sideways out in the hall—and everyone behind him walking on the same orientation. Earth didn't have tech like that—she'd have seen it on the internet if they had—or at least in a lot more scifi. Sarah pushed to her feet to pace the circumference of the death shock wall, pointedly watching her feet instead of it.

Fact one: she'd left Earth, which led to...

Fact two: aliens existed.

She stopped. She used to lie out on the trampoline behind her best friend's house and stare up at the stars, listening to the crickets in the adjacent field. She'd wished so ardently for aliens to exist, to experience the thrill of first contact in her lifetime, that she'd thought her heart would burst from her chest.

So much for that idea. She took it back. Yet another thing she'd gotten wrong.

She squeezed her eyes shut, trying to unsee Orion cart-wheeling over her friend's house, and scraped the latest tears off on her shoulder.

Fact, no, hypothesis three: aliens lived in humans. Some-how. Despite originating on different planets. For that matter, how was it that humans, funny-looking though they were, kidnapped her? Had they all been taken and implanted?

Or did that disprove that they'd left Earth?

Sarah balled her fists and collapsed into the floor. Why couldn't this be any more straightforward? Hadn't she had enough, what with being kidnapped and threatened with implantation?

Implantation.

The tiny, gleaming ceiling lights blurred in her vision.

What was it like? It had to hurt to get something shoved under your skin, stretching it like plastic wrap. If the bad ones controlled you, they had to do something with the brain, where one wrong move would end you. Her forecast: pain with a chance of instant death.

She rolled onto her side and curled up tight, lacing her fingers together over her neck.

Under her skin. Where stuff just did *not* belong. It could infect her with some alien disease, trailing germs no one had heard of before straight past her first line of defense. Any dirt it tracked in would mix with her blood, turning into gory sludge.

And what if her body rejected it as much as her mind did? Then she wouldn't just be injured and possessed but dying, too. Some comeuppance that would be. *You took my body, but the joke's on you!* What a victory: death by yet another route.

Sarah curled tighter and squeezed her burning eyes shut

as if it might stem the hot tears streaming out and rolling across her face to drip into a puddle on the padding.

The thing had to eat, right? Would it tap a straw into her spine and slurp away?

She sucked in a long, shuddering breath.

What was she supposed to have done? Tell him she wanted the creepy, slimy, no-good neck lump? Why? Worst thing ever! How much better could it really be to have a "good" neck lump over a "bad" neck lump? He'd said what the bad one did—controlled people, impregnated them—

She shuddered. Who used the word "impregnate," anyway?

Ew. Stupid *Miracle of Life* video.

He'd said the bad ones were really bad, but he never said what the good ones did, just what they didn't. They didn't control you. So what *did* they do? Take up space and signal the bad ones that someone's neck was already taken? Okay, that didn't sound so bad.

Ew!

But she'd already told him no. Emphatically. Would she go back and change that if she had the chance?

She tried. She honestly did. It was a simple sentence: "Mr. Marshall, can I have one of those good—"

But even her mental voice choked halfway through and started sputtering.

She wasn't done, wasn't ready to leave everything. Was. Not. Ready. To. Die. And it didn't matter.

She screamed her next sob, which hitched into softer moans. She sucked in another breath, but it jammed in her throat.

Her heart jumped. Her sight flashed gray through her closed eyes. A cold, hard floor pressed against her cheek, and voices and scraping furniture echoed in the distance.

Like falling off the balance beam, she couldn't catch her breath. Her normally content lungs ached in rebellious protest, refusing to fill, no matter how she panted. It was as bad as she'd experienced before. Except that in gymnastics, she could go home and rest afterward.

And floors didn't randomly change.

Holding stock-still, she listened. Maybe whoever was there wouldn't see her.

Big, calloused hands hauled her up and carried her in this new place like they'd carried her out of her house. She twisted and kicked, trying to wrench free before they shoved anything into her neck.

With a shriek, she wrestled her hands loose and twined them together at the base of her skull.

"No, stop! Don't kill me! Please don't kill me. Don't kill me." She didn't care if she whispered or screamed. Her voice was going hoarse, and she started to do both.

The men slung her onto the floor and shut the door. Panting in short, shallow breaths, she pushed up and scooted over to press her back to the side wall, fingers clamped tight over her neck. It was a tiny room where yellow light flowed in through a hundred diamond holes in both the door to the hall and in the back wall. They'd left her alone again.

What was this? Going from one holding cell to another? The Air Force would still be able to find her, right?

The back door clicked, and Sarah groaned. Not something *else!*

With a pop, the lattice door swung out, wide open, so anything could come in with her. The first thing she saw: a girl's face, a girl about her age.

She wore jean shorts and a tank top, both crusted over with something that looked like icing, smelled like pond mud, and flaked as she crouched. Brown hair frizzled over her shoulders and around her forced smile. "It's okay. The rest of us are from Earth, too."

Sarah stared.

Others from Earth? They were here? Mr. Marshall had said so.

The girl reached out, offering her a hand up. "You're the nineteenth so far. Let's get you up, so they can bring the next person in."

Sarah let go of her neck and took the girl's hand, surprised she felt real. She stood, letting the girl guide her out.

"No one knows where we are or why we're here, but—" The girl glanced back at her. "—it doesn't look good."

They stepped out into a cavernous, firelit chamber. Stone pillars extruded from the walls, each artfully blended into a towering figure. The figures' sandstone hands clutched the bases of blazing, bronze torches—the room's source of light. The glowing, flickering flames revealed a line of the largest rugs she'd ever seen, which ran down the room's center, blanketing most of the floor space but for a fifteen-foot border. Clusters of upholstered and elaborately carved furniture peppered the rugs and sheltered what she'd least expected—other people, dressed in mostly normal clothes. When had she last seen someone in jeans and a t-shirt, or slacks and a blouse? Okay, it couldn't have really been longer than a day since she'd watched her parents leave for work, but it felt like an eternity.

Three small, straight-backed groups nervously perched on the furniture's edges, talking in low tones or sitting in silence. One group had a business woman, someone in a lab coat, and a woman in a grocery store apron. The next had a woman with a white tab on her black, collared shirt talking to two women who stood with a girl younger than she was and a girl about her age. Three other women maybe her mom's age sat together in silence; one of them worried the frill on a threadbare poncho. In the far back of the room, four young women and an older one looked like they were searching the base of a remarkable wooden replica of a crashing tidal wave.

What was the chance the Air Force would find this place? They were supposed to be coming, but would they really arrive? What if they didn't? Then their captors could start sticking aliens in people—the bad (well, worse) aliens. Maybe Mr. Marshall was wrong. Maybe they wouldn't pick her. There were all these other people; the aliens could take one of them.

What if they had a neck lump for them all?

No! There had to be a way out! A hole in the—

She scanned the walls between her and the wooden wave. Every foot between the torch-carrying figures was smooth, exposed and unbroken. Maybe a trap door in one of the figures themselves? Or maybe when—not if—the guards came, she could run between them and find some-where else to hide. She hadn't tried running yet. She might be faster than they if she had a chance to run, and at the very least, she could fit smaller places than they could...

If she could get by them.

This wasn't going to work.

She hugged her arms and sniffed her running nose.

Beside her, the girl checked her watch then stared at the anteroom. "They're late."

"What does that mean?"

"I don't know. Maybe that's it. No one else is coming. Or maybe the next person isn't coming straight here."

Was someone else getting an alien implanted? She tried to feel sorry for them, but really, she was glad it wasn't her.

The girl forced a smile again and held her hand out. "I'm Maggie, by the way."

Sarah shook her hand, even though it seemed out of place, as if they'd sneaked it in against their captors' wishes. "Sarah. How come you're so calm?"

Maggie bit her lip and stared at the anteroom doors. "I'm not really, but if I keep busy, I don't have to think about it. That's what the swim team's doing."

She pointed a thumb at the women searching the far end of the room.

"I wish I had something to keep busy with. All I've had is a visitor."

Maggie froze, staring at her. "No one else did."

Then why her? Because she was the one he picked up? Did he feel guilty about his involvement after all? He should. "He worked the controls in the white room. He came back after everyone left and said he was undercover for the Air Force."

Her eyes widened. "The Air Force? They can get here?"

"You thought they couldn't?"

Maggie lowered her voice, even though no one was nearby or watching them. "That little white room?"

Sarah nodded.

"I saw it from the outside first. It's a flying saucer." Maggie waved at the others. "They don't believe me. Nobody else saw it. But I did, and that makes this place a lot farther away than I thought the military could go."

"Well, General Marshall did tell me he's working for aliens." If Maggie believed her, then Sarah would believe herself, too. Should she tell her about the body possessions, as well?

"I knew it!" Then her eyes widened, and she glanced around. "They can get here?"

"He said they could." Of course, he wasn't sure about anything after that.

Maggie leapt forward and hugged her. Then she turned around and shouted, "Hey, everyone! The military is coming to rescue us!"

Her voice didn't reach very far; only the closest groups looked over. Some shook their heads and turned away. Others wandered closer.

A tall girl with short brown hair bore down on Sarah. "You saw something different?"

"Well, no, I was in the same ship as everyone else..."

"She talked to an Air Force officer here," Maggie explained. "They're coming for us."

"Who did this? Who took us?" an older rotund woman in a floral blouse demanded.

Sarah and Maggie traded wary glances before Maggie answered. "Another country."

An alien queen, Sarah corrected. She shivered. If they got rescued and went home, would the queen go after them? Attack Earth for revenge? Had they already, and that's how the military knew how to get here? What if Mr. Marshall's alien was the enemy trying to sneak back to Earth?

But the fact that eighteen other women stood here with her suggested the aliens didn't have to do much sneaking.

"Why? Did he say why we're here?" asked a woman with a middle-school-aged child in tow.

Maggie turned to Sarah.

How could she explain what she didn't completely believe herself? Especially after Maggie copped out on saying anything about aliens. She shook her head.

Maggie stared at her a second too long.

"Where are we?" someone else clamored, raising a chorus of agreement.

"We're not in the U.S. anymore."

The woman in the blouse pointed to a small group halfway down the hall, the one with the woman in a poncho. "Not everyone here is from the U.S."

"So we come from all over." Maggie shrugged. "We don't know any better where we are."

She studied Sarah as if psychically adding, *Unless we do.*

"I didn't even know that was a flying saucer."

The growing crowd burst into babble; everyone had a comment for that, mostly skeptical and derisive.

Sarah tried to follow everything but got distracted watching the girl patting her mother's arm and looking away. "Mom. Mom! Look! There's someone there!"

Sarah followed her gaze to the tidal wave at the front—and the four men now standing atop it. Three were dressed in the leather armor and rough-sewn shirts of her kidnappers, including Mr. Marshall, who stood closest to the fourth.

Sarah adjusted her glasses to make sure she saw the fourth man right. It shouldn't have been so hard, since he stood in front, looking out on the gathered women, but she didn't believe he had four arms.

The man gazed at her and the others, his second pair of arms raised as if to show off his bulging biceps. If that wasn't unusual enough, he wore a long red cape with green accents over black clothes.

Maggie leaned in close. "Did that general tell you anything about this?"

"No, but that's him there beside the guy with four arms."

"He doesn't really have four arms, does he?"

If he did, he'd get deodorant all over his lower shoulders.

She watched him and Mr. Marshall pointing to women around the room, and more and more, she doubted the authenticity of the raised arms. They only ever moved when his shoulders did and were shades darker than the skin on his face and gesticulating hands.

"I think they're fake," Sarah murmured.

"Why bother?" Maggie grabbed her arm. "Uh… Is he pointing at us? Why is he doing that?"

He was.

And the reason would be…

"No way." Sarah edged back, shaking. "No."

Casting one final glance at the men on the wooden wave, Maggie stepped in front of her and held both her arms. "What's wrong?"

"I lied," she whispered. "I know what they want. I told him no. Absolutely not. I won't do it!"

"Do what?"

Sarah shook her head. It was too much to explain. Then she leaned around Maggie to scream at Mr. Marshall, "I'm not doing it!"

The men regarded her, distant and unmoved. The four-armed man said something to Mr. Marshall, who glared at her before responding as they filed out.

But the women nearby studied her, aghast.

Maggie captured her arms and got in her face. "Sarah, what's going on? What are you not doing?"

Sarah stared into Maggie's wide brown eyes that didn't look scared enough. "They need a body. For an alien."

GENERAL DONN MARSHALL stormed down the balcony's narrow steps. Fuck Banebdjedet's sense of urgency.

Everyone knew you had to let folks settle down before you started sorting through them. That's what made the Sais supply chain work: entire orientation sessions and training academies structured to introduce unwilling abductees to their new, glamorous life on the Kemtewet capital world. All they had to do was wait to be accepted into a sponsor's household.

He knew. His symbiont Kitchell had worked that orientation before finding him on Earth. It was supposed to be an easy way to replace Kitchell's elderly host—until they copped out.

And here Banebdjedet wanted to start immediately. Damn ignorant low-ranking lords! He'd been counting on that delay to give the Black Book team a chance to arrive.

He hit the bottom of the stairs and strode along the holding room's length, as if fetching one of the girls. The teleport controls were nearby; with luck, he could pop up to the mothership, pick up Vinnet, and take Sarah up with him when he replaced Anjedet. Simple.

What the fuck is keeping my men? With the same equipment and nav programs, the only difference in arrival time should have been the time it took them to scramble. Plus, they hadn't needed to wait in orbit for all the scattered raiders to return. They should have been here by now.

We knew there could be problems. That's why we have back-up plans, Kitchell reminded him. Get all the girls home or get a host for Vinnet? If anything, Vinnet's mission took precedence in the symbiont's mind.

Donn gritted his teeth. *We have a chance to fix something the Kem have done. We're going to give it an honest effort.*

As time allows.

He rounded the corner and continued the last few yards into the tiled teleport juncture.

Running footsteps rang from the direction of the banquet hall down an intersecting corridor. "*Kommandant!*"

What now? If he didn't skedaddle up to the kaxan to fetch Vinnet now, the time between his departure from the balcony and the first host candidate's arrival upstairs would look suspicious.

A young, scraggly-bearded guard stopped on the tile and leaned over to catch his breath.

"You don't have to run everywhere, Guerin."

Nodding, he straightened. "Sir, we caught two people trying to enter the banquet who weren't dressed right, no one recognized, and can't speak an intelligible word."

Major Patrick and her team? "They came in through the front gates?"

"*Jawohl.*"

Idiots. He rubbed his hands together. They'd finally made it. Now for the next play, and hopefully it wouldn't arouse suspicions. If Donn had a subordinate as ineffective and sloppy as he was acting, he'd haul that airman's ass to his office and ream the man a new one.

"Let's check them out and see if we can put them with the others." He nodded to the palatial holding room.

"Of course." Guerin set off toward the banquet hall at a power march, and Donn followed in his wake, glad Kem technology had cured his creaking knees.

Thanks for running everywhere, kid, so you could tell me about my team. Keep it up!

In less time than it should have taken, they reached an area of the service corridor tucked around the banquet hall. A cluster of local guards pressed a BDU-clad man and woman against the walls, hands empty and splayed flat against the plain stone. The man's face had filled out since he last saw Lieutenant Fairfeld, and it had even started to collect the weathering that marked him as an established adult. And Major Patrick... Still as striking as he remembered, even if she wouldn't win any beauty pageants. He grunted. At least they'd made it.

"Show him," Guerin told the others.

One guard held up a pair of pistols.

"Oh, great!" Donn lifted them free and turned them over. "Celebratory noisemakers from El Fadyir!"

Without exception, the guards shot him the long-suffering expressions such a lame cover deserved. Hopefully, they only thought his enthusiasm was missing the point.

He regarded the prisoners. "Did you find anything else of interest on them?"

Another guard held up a pair of radios; a third, their utility belts. He couldn't pocket it all. He tucked the guns into his belt and motioned for a radio. Making a show of examining it, he "happened to" check the talk button by clicking it three times. Then he tried the power knob next: all the way up then all the way down and off. Studying the belt clip, he "figured out" how to attach it to his belt, too.

He turned to the prisoners. "Too bad they won't make it to the party. I'll take them for the queen's consideration. Get back to your posts and keep an eye out for any more intruders."

A couple of the guards started off but hesitated when the rest didn't follow. Guerin shifted from foot to foot. "Are you sure?"

"These pallid wimps?" He rested a hand on his machete's hilt. "They won't be a problem."

"We'll get back to it, then." Guerin motioned to the others and led the guards away.

While they were still in sight, he drew his machete and

used it to motion the prisoners to walk ahead of him down the hall. Like good captives, they locked their fingers together behind their heads. Experience? Couldn't be.

When the natives' footsteps faded, Major Patrick glanced back the way they'd gone, then dropped her hands. "Having fun, sir?"

"Bailing my subordinates' asses out of their own stupidity? I live for it."

"We don't work for you anymore, sir. Technically, you're AWOL."

He could hear the unspoken continuation of that thought: *You abandoned us.*

I'm trying to be your man on the ground. While the coast was clear, he handed the pistols and radio back. "I don't think I can get the rest of your gear. Remember, Kümmel still had a radio on. Stow them better this time."

"Yes, Dad." Lieutenant Fairfeld tucked his service pistol into a deep cargo pocket.

"I'll be sure to remember my bra holster next time," Major Patrick added, because that would work well with the old steel 1911. Donn tried not to picture its sagging weight. "What's the plan?"

"You don't have one?"

"Relying on our specialist here."

Right. As she should. "After I put you in with those we took, I'll send Guerin to let you out while I tell Banebdjedet he has more options. Can you get home from the ground?"

"Yeah, we're parked in the lot on the next hill over."

Motioning for silence as they neared the teleport juncture, he drew his machete again but carried it loosely at his side.

Lot on a hill? It took a moment for his brain to shift into gear for Earth-isms. Gertewet, like Kemtewet, spoke a myriad of languages, most of which they'd picked up with hosts from Earth, but with the Kemtewet's somewhat monolithic culture, Earth concepts often didn't translate. Parking lot?

Banebdjedet's local kaxan pool!

They passed the teleport operator without comment and continued straight on for another three latticework panels to the half-disguised door into the holding room's foyer, where he let them in.

"I'll send Guerin to let you out shortly. Just have to tell him Banebdjedet found you all unsuitable." Of course, then he'd have to ensure Guerin told no one. If Banebdjedet knew he was letting all the abductees escape right when he was supposed to take one up to the queen, the lord would think him a bumbling incompetent at best, and at worst...

He'd better not give Banebdjedet a chance to think it through.

"Got it, sir. We'll be ready."

He fixed one last image of his old subordinates in his mind. For a year already, memories of their dedication had helped keep him going when he started wondering whether he and Kitchell were the only ones working against the Kemtewet. He nodded to them. "Get these women home safe. Godspeed."

They saluted, and he closed the door.

6

ASTEROIDS

K atorin stared out at the cityscape, picking out the lit towers like checkboxes standing out against the twilit sky. A few blocks away, limned green by bioluminescent tubes, the Culinary Design Center nestled amid the crush of buildings.

Khonsu had established himself there first when he arrived on this planet, Sais, the capital of the Kemtewet Empire. So he had informed the Gertewet Coordinating Council, and so she had confirmed from other employees who remembered him. He'd hoped to encounter Central Palace workers who interacted with the Information Security Corps and could speculate about the motivation behind recent policy changes.

The past few months, she and her host, Setira, had pieced together how that had gone: not well.

Her gaze shifted to the glow on the horizon, beyond Tranquility Bay—the heart of the capital, the sprawling Central Palace of the Empress. It was almost a city in its own right the way a kaxan could almost be a host: technically, it met the definition in its cold, heartless way.

Khonsu had left culinary design abruptly, with his superior's blessing but without his coworkers' knowledge. His first mistake, she suspected, unless his disappearance indicated his success.

Maybe he had actually infiltrated the ISC.

And not told anyone.

It even made a certain kind of sense. The ISC had tighter security than anywhere else in the Empire. It *was* Security. If an operative ever infiltrated it, he'd have no hope of unmonitored communication.

Surely, he would have the sense to deposit whatever information he knew for the rest of the Gertewet to analyze before he went in.

The Council thought so, too, or they wouldn't have sent her in to look for any information he'd left. They had specified they weren't sending her to find him, only his gathered intelligence. They expected he was long gone by now.

She hadn't found anything.

Nothing at the Culinary Design Center.

Nothing here in his lodgings.

Nothing at the perimeter of the ISC headquarters.

With the physical evidence, she could almost believe he'd never come at all. She replayed conversations with the culinary engineers, in case they'd miscommunicated whom they'd conversed about.

You didn't dream it up. Her host Setira thought back over it. *Shiv described his host Amal even more exactly than the Council did. What other Kem would've requested to transfer to the ISC so soon after starting his self-professed "dream job?"*

Anyone who had to work around Paul. Thinking about the Kem she awaited, Katorin refrained from rolling Setira's eyes here. In enemy territory, someone might realize her host had her attention. She kept up her careful study of the district's dazzling lights, in case anyone watched her without her notice. *Or anyone who realized what an opportunity the ISC's new lowered requirements provide. Khonsu had Shiv convinced.*

I had Shiv convinced that morning you slept in and I covered for you.

Sou desu ne. One morning after one exhausting evening with Paul, and Setira would never let her live it down. Katorin scanned the rest of the cityscape: the shopping centers interspersing the research and development complexes. *Khonsu was here, so why can't we find his cache of intel? Wouldn't he have wanted us to find it? He wouldn't have left us nothing. I hope.*

He left it at Mute's house, Setira joked.

Katorin glanced up at the passing stream of aircraft in lieu of rolling her eyes. *Of course. If it still existed. Since it doesn't, we have no leads.*

She heard him before she caught his reflection in the glass; his hard-heeled shoes clicked confidently against the fake marble floor. His black hair atop his tall, narrow head was cut short and boxy; he didn't have much in the way of style. He stopped beside her and casually ran a finger down the back of her neck, along the left side of the spine, where most symbionts nestled.

She hated that custom of theirs.

The symbiont Katorin shuddered as she felt the pressure of his finger against her serpentine body, but she turned her host's head to smile at him. "Hey."

"Hey, Beryl." He returned her smile and rested his hand over hers on the railing. "*Ves káti d'interessant tam?*" he asked, wondering what she was looking at.

"*Heta jda mooi!*" she whispered in awe, including a

harmony of raised seventh chords in her voice. She widened her eyes and focused intently on the sights and continued speaking to him in the jumble of languages all *tewet* used. "How can you ever get tired of the city at night, the lit signs and the reflections on the traffic?"

Above the buildings, a cloud of kaxan darted from departure to destination, their smooth metal bellies throwing back the city's lights.

"Give it a decade or less. You'll be tired of it." With one finger, he scooped the top layers of dust from the onyx-like railing and held it up for her examination. His own harmonics turned flat. "See? Everyone gets tired of it."

"I guess." She turned to face him, pulling his hand with hers away from the window. "Come exploring with me, Paul. Maybe you'll see something new."

Maybe she'd see something new. Even someone as simple as Paul could utter one innocent key phrase and jog their minds onto the right path.

He wiped the dust on his pants and rested his free hand on the part of the rail she'd cleared. "Beryl, I need to talk to you." His harmonics shifted toward a more negative sound but nothing as overt as a minor key; he probably hadn't discovered her true identity.

"Is something wrong?" Her host's heart pounded in their ears. What now?

"Your vassal, Beryl. You need a new one."

She blinked, genuinely hurt. "Lights up," she commanded loudly. Suddenly, the atrium became as light as a summer afternoon, and the reflection on the window multiplied. She leaned forward to study her human host's face. Beneath Setira's black-painted eyelashes, bright green contacts stared back at her. Deep wrinkles streamed up from the corners of her mouth, despite her focused frown. Katorin liked them; she had never had a host who smiled as much as Setira. Despite her age, tight, bright-red curls framed her face. Because they were Setira's favorite feature about herself, Katorin had preserved the color as long as possible. Gray strands had appeared since the last time she'd really looked.

Katorin turned back to him. "What's wrong with my vassal? She's well-proportioned, fit, strong..."

He raised an eyebrow. "Look, you're on the same continent as the Empress. You don't have to keep your vassal until she dies." He pointed to a blazing block of neon and holographic signs that dimly shone through the lit window, marking a popular shopping center. "Value Vassal is even having a sale this month for the Kings' Ball—it ends the day after tomorrow."

She looked at herself again, hoping Setira's end wouldn't come too soon, knowing that every end came sooner than she liked. "Lights off." The simulated sunlight faded off, leaving the dim lights of the city to illuminate the atrium.

"Don't be mad at me," he cooed. "I wanted to let you know. Before Shiv did." Shiv, their research team leader at the food engineering plant, certainly had the lack of tact needed to say such a thing to their sensitive apprentice. "You aren't attached to her, are you?"

She didn't answer. As a Gertewet, of course she was. And it wasn't unheard of for some of their Kemtewet enemies—especially the young ones—to feel that way, either. Just embarrassing. In their culture, human hosts were little more than long-term clothes, an exterior they conquered, subdued, and exchanged on a whim. She made sure Setira's wrinkled cheeks blushed.

"Oh, Beryl, look. The first time's always the hardest. I'll go with you." He ran his hand over hers and drew it back.

"I'm going out." She spun, heading for the stairs.

"I didn't mean it like that," he called after her, heels scuffing hesitantly in her wake.

Cube head, Setira thought, watching the stairs as her symbiont bounded down them on silent soles.

Despite herself, Katorin smiled. *Fitting name.*

"Beryl, wait!" His heels clicked after her, a syncopated metronome until he skidded beside her and caught himself on the rail.

Wiping her jovial expression, she conjured her best glare for him.

He shrank back. "Look, I'm sorry. Let me make it up to you. I can show you something exciting."

Her eyes wandered south, and she raised an eyebrow, still glaring.

It took him a moment to catch on. Then his eyes bulged. "Hell no! Not that!"

Straightening, he checked up and down the empty stairs before leaning close and whispering, "You know the cleaning bots at work?"

I know where this is going, Setira complained.

Katorin crossed her arms and relented. "What about them?"

"You know how they're locked into their closets during the day?"

Conspiracy theorist.

"Yes...?" Katorin tried to sound interested. Really, she did.

"Did you know they're locked in from the outside? Want to know why?"

She tapped her foot.

He backed down a step, conveniently both retreating and leading her onward. "It's built overtop where they killed the first Gertewet."

"What!"

His grin widened. "Back before the Culinary Design Center, before this whole area was built up, they executed the first Gertewet right on the ground under our building—it's not marked or anything, because Empress Neith, in her benevolent wisdom, didn't want to commemorate it. That's just how it's always been. We always get them in the end."

Shivering against Setira's spine, Katorin tried to muster an interested front.

If it fell as flat as it felt, Cube Head didn't notice. "I know! It's great! But she was wrong—it does haunt us. It possesses the cleaning bots and attacks people, still intent on tearing apart civilization."

His words echoed in their minds. The first Gertewet death? That was the first Gertewet, Mute, the one who'd spawned all the rest, including the queen who bore Katorin. Her grandmother, of a fashion.

Did he even realize what he was saying? As her first act as Empress, Neith had her troops pull Mute from her house into her own front yard and had her executed. As an example of how not to be: compassionate to all and respectful of the planet's other major culture.

Mute's house.

Setira gaped. *Khonsu would know that.*

He's wrong. They both are. Katorin shoved her shock away and scrunched her face at Cube Head. But it was still a lead. She had to see it through. "Bot possession? Dead Ger? You're full of it."

"I'll show you. Come on!" He snatched her hand and tugged her down the stairs.

She tugged back.

Katorin, no. This is our only lead not directly connected to Khonsu but to his passions. We have to go.

It's folly.

So? It's Khonsu's folly. He chose to insert himself there at the center. He must have heard this rumor, too, years ago. True or not, it's exactly the kind of place he'd have chosen to stash his intel —somewhere everyone else would dismiss as meaningless.

Setira was right. It didn't have to be the place Mute actually lived and died, as long as it was closely enough linked in Khonsu's mind.

She picked up her pace in Cube Head's wake.

She'd stared out at Khonsu's buildings long enough and had it narrowed down to one. Khonsu had employed a handful of tactics, and now she, too, had her next one. Like her hosts from simpler worlds, she'd caught a bite on her line. Now to reel it in and see if it was worth keeping.

ROCKEFELLER COULDN'T BELIEVE IT.

The hangar housed shiny, silver flying saucers.

Razor sharp on the edges and as thick as a small business jet in the center, they sat atop spindly landing gear as tall as he was. Between those skinny legs, he saw more identical legs than he could count, filling the hangar to its far wall, except for the space occupied by one small aircraft and enough clear space for another row of glistening saucers.

"What are those?" Decoys, part of the Air Force's cover story. They had to be.

"Exactly what they look like," Stokely answered. "Alien spaceships."

"They're called kaxan," Colonel Marshall added.

Rockefeller stared, gaze wandering from gleam to gleam on the orderly reflective hulls. If these were real... If real aliens had taken Maggie... He ripped his eyes away from the field of impossible spaceships to face Stokely. "Simulacra like that could be made anywhere."

"Not like this." Unfazed and grinning, the Senator stepped through and led them to the nearest silver disk's open belly hatch and up its built-in ladder. "Tell me what you think, Andy."

He already had. It wasn't like some glass cockpit was going to change his mind. But Rockefeller mounted the ladder anyway, giving his mentor one last chance to prove his sanity. Colonel Marshall stayed on the ground.

Rockefeller emerged into an admittedly unusual room: no pilot's seat, no throttle, no yoke, no bank of meticulously labeled controls. Only a gigantic computer screen with an intricate screensaver hanging in the middle. "There's no way this flies. There's nothing to control it."

Stokely shook his head. "It runs on autopilot. You select a destination, and it takes you."

He glanced back at the screen, easily picking out Egyptian hieroglyphs, cuneiform, Arabic, and German. "Nothing here looks alien to me."

"Then look at the walls."

Rockefeller did. Aside from the section behind the screen where the floor's padding extended to the ceiling, the rest of the circular room's wall was a rippling gray surface he'd assumed to be a projection. For confirmation, he reached out to brush his fingertips against it.

Pain shot up to his wrist, and he jerked his hand away. "What was that?!"

"That was a force we don't understand holding back a goop we can't make." Stokely withdrew a pen from his sport coat's pocket and poked it into the wall, avoiding getting shocked himself. "It keeps all that from flooding in here, but you can pass right through it on this side. Where else have you seen that?"

Rockefeller racked his brain, determined to come up with something. "One-way mirrors," he answered lamely.

Stokely grinned. "This doesn't look like a mirror to me."

The wavering walls mocked him. Could he believe this and still count himself sane? Defying gravity with an invisible, permeable shock wall was beyond the next step of technology he'd been expecting. Aliens or not, it hadn't developed from the science he knew.

"Fine. This craft didn't come from here. Aliens or... something made it." Just as Stokely had said. In keeping with everything Stokely had said. Except for his last hope. "Asteroids. How did you shoot down a craft that has to deal with asteroids?"

Stokely tucked his pen back into his pocket. "Andy, I don't see how it matters. That's what happened."

"Humor me."

"I know," Colonel Marshall called from outside.

As they clambered down the ladder, Rockefeller again glimpsed the orderly rows. One craft after another with shiny hulls, impossible walls, and puzzlebox computers. Out here, he could almost picture another identical number dashing away with Maggie inside, his wife dumbfounded in its wake.

He pushed the image away. "Well, Colonel? How do we backwards humans shoot down a flying saucer?"

"With Sidewinder missiles. The General's alien told us once. The missile interfered with the kaxan's magnetohydrody—" She frowned. "In atmosphere, the kaxan projects electromagnetically controlled plasma airfoils. The missile didn't disrupt them for long, just long enough for the low-flying craft to lose altitude and impact the ground. Hence his ability to fly away afterward."

"Oh."

7

THE THREAT'S NOT OVER

How sensible. How orderly.

How terrible.

Had Maggie bled on that pristine, white interior? Was she hurt? What were they doing to his baby girl?

"Andy?"

Tears clouded his vision, threatening to spill over where others could see. As if it mattered. As if anything, living or not, had leverage on him compared to the hole in his heart.

"Let's get him somewhere to sit."

"I'm fine."

Someone took his arm.

Someone else had taken his daughter, someone from a race he didn't know and a place he'd never imagined. What did they look like? Did the cities of Earth's future have interstellar idols to look up to? Those who took her could have beat children or raped them, married them young and isolated them from their families. Some societies on Earth did.

Instead, they had a new way to violate her body.

"We can go to the conference room," Colonel Marshall

offered. Escorting him on one side, she helped prod him along.

Stokely steered him into the hall and left, toward the entrance. "How about somewhere neutral? Your office?"

Kidnapped by unscrupulous, body-possessing aliens. She'd been gone twenty hours. Had they already erased her? Or did Black Book still have time for a rescue? How long did it take to implant an alien? If it required surgery, it could take a long time with a lot of intricate, delicate work, but if the Air Force found her in the middle, would they be able to bring her home? Would interrupting hurt her even worse?

He vaguely noticed Stokely crouching down in his field of vision, and Rockefeller looked up. They'd planted him on a padded chair in a windowless office. Shelves of thick books, dense files, and sparse memorabilia lined the walls around and behind an excruciatingly ordered desk. The Colonel's office.

"Andy?"

Rockefeller locked on eye contact. "Maggie is in terrible danger."

"We know." Stokely stood and hid his hands in his pockets. "We're doing everything we can to get her back."

"Will they be fast enough?"

Stokely traded glances with the Colonel. "No one's ever done this before. But the Black Book team is in pursuit, and in the meantime, the General is in a good position to run interference. I'm sure he'll do his best."

"What if his best isn't good enough?"

Stokely looked away, jaw tense. Lying. "He'll take care of her."

Rockefeller drew a deep breath. He'd pushed Stokely to the point of placating him. If he wanted to dig into the truth instead of convenient lies, he had to focus. He had to understand the implications and take control. For her.

Somehow, over forty years of his life had passed without anyone telling him that UFOs might be real, that not only might alien life definitely exist, but the United States could be in contact with it. As much of a news junkie as he was, he'd somehow missed out on the biggest story in the history of mankind. "Who else knows?"

Stokely raised an eyebrow. "Well, we haven't exactly flashed it on the evening news."

Rockefeller mirrored his expectant expression.

"Air Force higher-ups, a few other Congressmen, a couple former Presidents and the current one, and an oversight committee." Stokely backed up to the desk and hitched a hip over it.

"CIA?"

"No."

"FBI?"

"Nope."

"NASA?"

"What, tell them that we got a five-finger discount on a working alien spaceship? It'd break their little hearts."

Rockefeller paced the three steps across the office and back. "What about other countries? You said this isn't affecting only America."

"The British and the Russians both conducted investigations that we know about, but they never released any positive findings."

"And neither did the Air Force." Colonel Marshall shrugged. "But we have confirmed that there are no other kaxan transponder signals on Earth. Without that, I don't see how anyone could know what's going on."

Rockefeller rubbed his burning eyes. "You're telling me

we have no international allies to go up against an extrater-restrial threat, because we brainwashed everyone into thinking this wasn't a problem?"

Stokely and the Colonel traded sheepish glances. "They thought it best at the time."

"Why wasn't I told?"

Colonel Marshall found her voice first. "Need to—"

"Know?" he finished with her. "No, I don't need to know about a particular operation. I do need to know about the war. How can the House do anything without being informed of the issues at hand?"

"What do you think you can do that I haven't already tried?" Stokely snapped. "You mention this to anyone worth knowing, and on a good day, they'll laugh you off. After having your daughter taken? They'll say you've cracked. You'll never get anything done. Your career will end."

Rockefeller stared into Stokely's eyes, unwilling to concede the point. But he could think through it, too. Without declassifying all of it—including the Air Force's disinformation scheme—even those aware of the situation could hardly act.

"Maybe not."

He and his mentor both turned to the Colonel, who gazed down at the lowest bookshelf.

"The Project got a boost after the first incident with Kitchell. Command deemed it worthy of more notice, which was why I was assigned here." She paused, grimacing. "One of the things impeding further support, aside from—" She bobbed her head indecisively. "—conditions here, was the lack of a persistent threat. They assumed it was over."

But yesterday, more people, more American children, had disappeared. Rockefeller nodded. "It's not."

She nodded back. "There are three kinds of people:

those who don't know Black Book exists, those who know and believe in what we do, and those who know and scoff at us anyway. You're not going to change the ignorant into supporters just by explaining our work. You'll need a critical mass of support from those who're already aware."

"Now that we can show the threat's not over," Stokely added, "that should be a lot easier. This raid could be the best thing that could've happened for Black Book."

"Don't you dare turn Maggie's misfortune to your own gain!"

"It's not just Maggie. Andy, Black Book is here to defend everyone—you, Joyce, and your other daughters, too."

Rockefeller glanced from the charismatic Senator to the stone-faced officer. "If that's so, why do you have the third type of person?"

While Colonel Marshall tried to glare him into the vacuum of space, Stokely only sighed. "Let's show you one more thing."

———

"WHAT'S SHE TALKING ABOUT?" the adults demanded of Maggie when Sarah wouldn't answer their questions. "What's she mean, 'they need a body?'"

Sarah shook—her head and whole body. She'd seen Mr. Marshall point her out to the four-armed man, despite everything. Despite that she'd told him no. Despite that he'd taken some risk to tell her what was happening and ask about her wishes.

And when it came down to it, when she might have gotten overlooked, he'd gone the extra effort to point her out.

That creep!

"Give her some space!" Maggie waved the others back then recentered herself in Sarah's gaze. "Sarah, you lost me there. Tell me again. You said you know what they want with us?"

She gripped Maggie's arms, as if the other girl might float away. "They need to stick an alien in a body."

"Oh my gosh, that's why we're all women!" The reverend in her clerical collar turned away, pale. "Uteruses."

"That's crazy talk." The gaudy dresser beside her pulled a cigarette from her rolled sleeve. "There's no aliens. She's scared. She's making stuff up. She don't know more than the rest of us."

But Maggie believed her. It was there in her eyes: the tension of knowing they were so far out of their league. Of knowing they'd never go back, not to the way things were and, honestly, probably not home, either.

"We have to get out." Sarah could barely hear herself over the mounting arguments, but she thought Maggie heard her. "We have to get out now before they come back."

Then a hush swept through the crowd, and everyone froze. Sarah held her breath. Voices came from outside the group—from inside the anteroom. The door popped and swung open.

They were here! They'd come to take her away. She launched toward the back of the room—

—and stopped when Maggie jerked her arm. "Look!"

Two people entered: a man the age of her younger teachers and a woman who could be her mom's peer—both in soldiers' uniforms, their thick-soled combat boots treading silently on the marble floor.

The Air Force? They'd made it in time! Mr. Marshall must have known that when pointing her out to the four-armed man. She shook the hand Maggie still gripped. "We're leaving!"

Maggie grinned back.

The black-haired woman finished surveying the room. "Lieutenant, get me a head count and let me know if we're being monitored."

The young officer didn't salute but drifted to the side to count the gathered women.

"Hello, everyone!" She waved her arms over her head, drawing the attention of the last of the abducted women. They all gathered to listen to her. "I'm Major Patrick. This is Lieutenant Fairfeld. We're here to take you home."

An excited murmur swept through the crowd. Sarah closed her eyes. The others didn't even know what they were escaping: something jammed under their skin. She shuddered.

But they were going to get out!

"Nineteen of them, three of us," the Lieutenant reported, his voice softer than his superior's, not meant to carry to everyone. "We're going to need three more *cash-on* and another pilot."

"*Kaxan* will be easy." Her lips tightened in a frown. "If we can't grab the General, we'll all just have to jam in."

"For six hours?"

"For six lives."

Major Patrick turned back to her audience and fixed a broad, thin-lipped smile on her face. She raised her voice again. "The Lieutenant is going to count you off for vehicles. He'll tell you to go with me, him, or Myers, who's watching our rides. Don't forget who's flying you home."

She pointed to the closed anteroom. "Now, when that door opens, we're all going to walk quickly out of this castle and book it about a half mile to the vehicles. Got it? Any questions?"

"Where are we?" someone shouted.

"Mexico. Next?"

Mexico? But hadn't Mr. Marshall said they'd gone to another planet? Maybe he'd only said the bit about aliens existing. Or had he been messing with her?

"Who took us?"

Major Patrick traded glances with her lieutenant. "He's a head of state involved in the international sex trade."

"Oh, come on!" Maggie leaned over. "Do you believe this?"

"No, you?"

"I saw a flying saucer from the outside. They beamed my boyfriend and me aboard, and I watched them beam him back out." Maggie shook her head, swinging her frizzy hair.

Sarah answered slowly, choosing her words carefully. "Mr. Marshall showed me where the alien in his neck was, but he never said where we were or why they wanted to live in a body, only—"

"What?"

She swallowed. "He did say they wanted to get someone pregnant."

"Ew!"

Sarah nodded. "But I saw his neck lump, and gravity was sideways outside the saucer. Even if we're in Mexico, there's more going on than they're telling us."

"Let's ask."

Major Patrick clapped her hands. "All right, ladies. Hang tight. The doors should open any time now."

As the assembly, now clustered in the back of the room, burst into excited murmurs, Maggie and Sarah crept forward out of the rough line Lieutenant Fairfeld was working his way down. They caught the Major before anyone else. Maggie tapped her shoulder. "Excuse me, ma'am."

She faced them, smile plastered in place but still not reaching her eyes. "Yes?"

"Sarah talked to a General before they put her in here." Maggie crossed her arms. "And based on what I saw and what he said, your answers don't make sense."

The Major's smile faded to concern, and she regarded Sarah. "What did the General talk to you about, sweetheart?"

"He wanted to implant an alien." Maybe she'd know what he was talking about. "A Ger, Gertewet."

The Major's eyes about popped out of her head, and her expression hardened. She recognized it, all right. "The General's retired, because he's crazy. We'll get you out of Mexico and back home in no time flat."

"In more flying saucers?" Maggie asked.

"Just because they're silver and have a blended wing-fuselage design—"

"And transporters." Maggie crossed her arms.

Major Patrick sighed and patted her shoulder. "Fine. Aliens. UFOs. You keep thinking that, and we'll talk when we get home." Major Patrick checked her watch. "What is taking him so long?"

"Maybe he's not lying through his teeth like you are," Sarah ground out.

The door cracked open, showing a stranger in the same leather armor as the kidnappers. A bolt of panic struck Sarah. Others ran.

"Let's go, ladies! Man's holding the door open!" Major Patrick's voice shot through them, and the crowd swayed into motion for the exit. "Fairfeld! Make sure no one's left in here!"

Sarah and Maggie waited to follow the Major until she saw them and shouted, "Go!"

They shouldered into the crowd and pressed through the doors on either end of the foyer.

The stranger in the hall pointed down the dim wooden passage away from the tiled room, and the crowd widened to fill the space.

Mexico. Tatooine. Wherever they were, it didn't matter. They were going home! The military made it in time, and she'd never have to get one of those slimy creepy tumors stuck in her neck!

Home free!

Sarah pushed toward the front of the crowd, leaving Maggie behind. She'd catch up. Anyway, with the Air Force officer and the armored angel at the back, how were they supposed to tell where to go?

Someone pressed urgently up through the column, and Sarah rushed forward to pace her.

Him.

The guard. He reached the front and turned down a darker stone hall to the right. Voices and sounds brimmed in this one: snapping sheets, clattering dishes, laughter. They passed curious, staring women and men in thick aprons. Then their guide turned right again and pushed open a heavy wooden door.

Sunlight and fresh air rushed into the cold hall and gusted over the first heads passing into it.

This was it! No more aliens, no more body-controlling, no more bad guys! The whole nightmare was coming to a close. The crowd sped up, and she ran a couple steps into the light.

The sweet smell of fall, moldy leaves, and the dusty foot-path blew with the cool, crisp air into her face, the warmth of sunshine on her skin. Freedom.

It was all over. Major Patrick just had to drive them home.

"Look lively, ladies. We're not out yet!" called Major Patrick from up ahead.

Sarah frowned. They'd already gotten out.

8

NEW HORRORS

S arah reached the top of the hill, where the women ahead of her had stopped to stare at a giant, open field of flying saucers at the top of the next hill. Maggie was right. Those weren't just new airplanes but real flying saucers. She'd be an idiot to think anything else.

The closest few saucers had trapdoors folded down from their middles, like inverted submarines, and a red-headed man in the same green uniform as the Major and Lieutenant stood beside one. From here, he looked like an action figure.

"Major!" Lieutenant Fairfeld's voice quivered. "Major, they're coming!"

Sarah turned to look down the path they'd taken here. The lower part of the castle extended over the valley's river, and the door they'd left through was at the bottom of this grassy hill. Two men were down there now, following their path: unmistakably the four-armed man and Mr. Marshall. Behind them, other big men were filing out of the door.

"Run to the waving man! Hurry!" Major Patrick pointed once and led the front of the crowd.

The back of the crowd pressed forward. Everyone ran, even the big women, their hair bouncing, clothes and flesh bobbing, chests heaving. They jammed up at rocks on the edges of the trail. Sarah took off, fast and agile enough to dodge between the older women, around the trees to the side of the path, and over the rocks the path skirted.

She made it to the front of the crowd when someone shrieked beside her.

Maggie.

Sarah turned back to help, but the jostling herd behind bowled her over. She smacked into the ground.

The others thundered by. All Sarah could hear were smacking footfalls, heavy panting, and garbled complaints. She wrapped her arms around her head to avoid getting kicked again. Behind her, Maggie cried out with every kick or trip that landed. The crowd thinned, and suddenly, a shadow didn't hit her.

She peeked up.

Lieutenant Fairfeld hauled Maggie to her feet, distracted as he watched over his shoulder. Then he righted her, too. "Major!"

"Get to a kaxan and get them loaded in!" Major Patrick shouted back.

He sprinted ahead.

Sarah took a couple steps to follow, but stopped when Maggie fell again as she tried to put weight on one leg.

"Come on! We've got to run!"

Downhill, the four-armed man and Mr. Marshall—and their backup—were getting closer.

Maggie saw, too. She pushed Sarah away. "Go!"

Sarah took another step but stopped. Maggie knew she wasn't getting out; their captors were now closer than the saucers—they'd have to sprint uphill faster than the long-legged, unhurt men to even arrive, let alone climb in.

But they had to try.

She scooped an arm under Maggie's and steadied her on her better leg. Sarah's own legs throbbed, but she'd been ahead of Maggie, sheltered in the lee of where the crowd had broken around her.

They didn't get far.

The big men's breathing was quieter than the women's, but their steps hit harder and faster on the path's loose stones.

A dark hand closed on Maggie's arm at Sarah's back, ripping out some hair as he whipped her away. The imbalance threw Sarah right into Mr. Marshall's sweaty hands. He turned with her to face the four-armed man.

Waiting for directions.

Mr. Marshall was working for the four-armed man? Had he lied to her? Instead of good aliens and bad aliens, were there only tricksters trying to suppress her protests and gain her cooperation?

She'd decided wrong again. They were all going to die by slimy neck lumps.

The four-armed man whipped Maggie around by her upper arms, heedless of her cries or inability to support herself. He watched the reinforcements closing in. His barked commands sliced through the air. "*Halt sie! Halt sie!*"

Mr. Marshall and the four-armed man turned to watch the reinforcements pass and gain on the out-of-shape women running uphill.

Sarah watched in horrified fascination as the armored men closed the gap. In the front of the pack, Major Patrick and the college girls made it to the top and climbed into the saucers. The stragglers, still only halfway up, were the larger women.

Gunshots rang from the hilltop, echoing in the valley, each explosion making Sarah jump in Mr. Marshall's unperturbed grip. It didn't last long. Major Patrick's voice carried down, something about not hitting civilians. If that wasn't worth the risk, did it mean this wouldn't be so bad?

How could it not?

The four-armed man stepped closer and offered Maggie's battered form. "*Nehm es!*"

Mr. Marshall shifted his sticky grip on her, and she saw it wasn't sweat but blood. Whose?

Marshall hung Maggie's slim body over his shoulder, finally taking the weight off her legs. She didn't seem to mind; she'd passed out.

Sarah shivered. This was bad. Real bad.

Whatever happened next, whomever they chose to host the alien queen, they'd choose from a smaller pool—and Mr. Marshall had already picked her out. She'd have even less of a chance than Maggie and everyone else.

Mr. Marshall and the four-armed man still watched their goons chasing the straggling women.

This is my only chance. While everyone watched the other women, no one watched her.

I'm sorry, Maggie.

Sarah swung her arm around Mr. Marshall's wet grip, breaking free. And she ran. Past the four-armed man. Past the place where Maggie fell. Her toes dug into the dirt path's errant scree through her socks, and it cut further into her feet. She didn't care.

She had to run.

She aimed for smooth rocks and mossy patches, weaving

like a mountain goat. Mountain goats beat creepy men up paths to flying saucers, right?

She passed the first goon walking down the woman in the apron. He lunged for her, and the woman broke free. Sarah heard her footsteps scrabbling behind. Then her scream. A wrench of cascading pebbles.

Sarah kept running. Three more men to pass.

The next didn't even try. He kept his meaty hands clutched tight on the woman in the floral blouse, but his dark eyes fastened on her. He yelled ahead.

Uphill, the crime-faced guy from her saucer turned around. He sneered and spread his scrawny, long arms, blocking the whole path.

Half off the path anyway, she vaulted onto a big rock and steered wide.

Just a little faster...

He hit her back, plowing her into the dirt. She slid. Scrambling to right herself, she elbowed him in the jaw and wriggled out from under him. She got to her feet. She pushed off. He caught her ankle, and she slammed back down.

But that was okay.

Up on the crest, three silver flying saucers retracted their landing gear. The next minute, they darted into the sky and winked into the distance. Gone.

The Air Force was supposed to save her, was supposed to save all of them. They'd sure saved themselves.

———

Rockefeller crossed his arms when Stokely stopped him outside the hangar's conference room. Right down the hall from Colonel Marshall's office, it didn't seem worthy of being shown off, but Stokely had already proven him wrong today. He raised his eyebrows and fought back his assumptions.

"Remember, Andy, it was over twenty years between the last sighting and when they shot down that Gertewet's kaxan. It's easy to lose focus in that time."

"Not with the right leadership," the Colonel grumbled.

"Regardless of leadership."

"I'm remembering. Open the door, Charlie." Over the years, he must have seen dozens, maybe hundreds of conference rooms, some shabbier, some chic-er, all sharing a certain plain mutability designed to aid focus. What was one more? Stokely clearly thought it had meaning, so he tried to keep an open mind.

Stokely opened up a game room.

To call it anything else denied the mere existence of every single piece of furniture and decoration present. Beyond the barstool-lined ping-pong table, a flying-saucer-themed pinball machine inhabited the corner in front of him. Movie posters filled the back wall over a line of spare barstools: *Close Encounters*, *ET*, and *Independence Day*. He took a step inside and discovered a kitchenette along the right wall, complete with counter space, sink, and refrigerator.

His gaze settled on the duct tape tracing out boundaries on the ping-pong table. "This is a room for serious meetings?"

"This is a room for a lot of things." Stokely crossed to the refrigerator and extracted a can of Diet Coke that he held out to Rockefeller. "This room has always been used for the project personnel to gather and exchange ideas, so, yes, it's for 'serious meetings.' But the project ran for over twenty years without detecting anything, and in all that time, the crew waited for craft that their friends, families, and fellow airmen didn't believe existed." He waved his empty hand at the whole room. "They dealt with the stress creatively."

Colonel Marshall intercepted the ignored drink and stashed it back in the fridge. "And invited derision by doing so. NFI-Com wouldn't give us half the trouble they do if they took us seriously."

"Who's that?"

Apparently unfazed by the banned beverage, Stokely settled atop one of the barstools, where the cushion had been split and repaired with red duct tape. "The National Freedom of Information for the Preservation of Constitutional Rights and of Citizen and National Security Commission." He paused for a breath. "They were charged by Congress to provide oversight on matters pertaining to the extraterrestrial threat. They report out on Black Book's activities."

Torn between the unorthodox seating and his own unprofessional inclination to lean against the game room's wall, Rockefeller crossed his arms and planted his feet. "Why haven't I heard about them?"

"They only report to those of us who are already read in." Stokley counted silent names on his fingers, reaching an impressive total of three. "I guess there aren't many of us left."

"You haven't missed anything. They're not the most wholesome people." Colonel Marshall settled herself onto a seat a couple barstools over from Stokely.

So, they were a tarnished pipeline feeding information from a moldering project to a declining coterie of old men. Did none of them realize how vital this work was? To impede it by restricting information was criminal. If it were fixed so the right people had access to the right information, how would that change everything? What could Black Book do with distinguished personnel and a professional environment?

"Colonel, you're in charge of this base—"

"Station," she corrected.

"Station. Whatever. Why not fix the décor?"

She heaved a heavy sigh. "I almost have. Every three months or so, I look into it again. But the table is a couple hundred dollars, the chairs are a hundred each. All the quotes for removing the kitchenette and painting the hall are over five grand." Her eyes coursed over the space. "And every time, I think, 'We're not ready to face the Kemtewet. We need to focus on detection and defenses.' So the money goes to better use. We have to have a way to combat the Kemtewet here on Earth before they ramp up their activity."

Her arm rested casually on the table, but her fingers clenched the edge in a death grip. "We might be out of time."

"Why? What do you think they're going to do?"

"Whatever the hell they want if we can't detect them."

Rockefeller paced around the ping-pong table, thinking, trying to ignore the pinball machine's bright colors and cartoon aliens. "Do they want anything besides the thirty people a year?"

"They might. Thirty a year was the baseline estimate established in the 40s and 50s. They quit coming after that. The pattern changed. Who knows what they want now."

He stopped with his back to the pinball machine. "What do you think they might do?"

"Maybe they decide they want three hundred a year now. If we can detect them, we can shoot down the ones within our missile range and contact other bases to address other areas."

"Once you stop them from taking people," he said, facing Stokely, "how do we stop them from coming?"

Stokely froze. "You want to open peace talks with them?"

"The only wars that ever ended without discussion were ones where the losing side got eradicated. That's unacceptable. Senator, what pressure can we leverage to bring them to the table?"

Stokely sat back, and his eyes focused beyond his surroundings on the hypothetical. "We'll have to establish communication first. Once the team brings our abductees back, maybe we can send them out with a message."

Colonel Marshall screwed up her face. "'Stop taking our people or we'll tell Mommy'?"

"Advanced technology or not, a nuke is nothing to laugh at," Rockefeller reminded her.

"Unless it is. Maybe the same technology that keeps human passengers alive in an accelerating kaxan can stanch a nuclear blast. We don't know that." She pushed to her feet and leaned toward him over the table, pushing down on it as if grounding her aggravation. "You're talking about escalating a conflict with an enemy of unknown capabilities. You don't escalate something until you know you can finish it."

"We can't just do nothing."

"Of course not. Now that we have kaxan, we've been trying to expand our intelligence on the Kemtewet. Once we do, we'll know ways to hinder them, maybe stop them completely."

"What if we backed their enemies? The General's alien must already know how to fight them."

"That's great." The Colonel crossed her arms. "Except they need bodies, too. While we defeat our enemies, how are we going to defend ourselves from our allies?"

"The same way they do?"

"By already having a brain-sucking worm?"

"Colonel." Stokely shot her a reproachful glare then swiveled on his seat to face Rockefeller. "Andy, we don't know much about how they fight, except that it seems to involve a lot of subterfuge. I don't think there are battle-fronts like in traditional wars."

She nodded. "They're not fighting for territory; they're fighting for philosophy. That changes everything about how a war is run—we saw that in Vietnam."

Rockefeller turned to pace in front of the movie posters and pinball machine. "We're going to need their help one way or another. We might as well admit it early and figure out how to deal with them."

He stopped, staring at a fleck of crud on the grisly carpet. "Where do they even come from?"

Rockefeller looked up to find them both staring at him as if he were insane. "What?"

"They come from another planet; what more do you need to know?" Stokely spread his hands helplessly.

"That's the problem." Rockefeller shook a finger at him as if the Senator embodied the topic. "They're from another planet and the human body is ridiculously complex; how do they take it over if they didn't even start here?"

"We don't know. That's why we need to get out there exploring." Colonel Marshall stared into his eyes as if she could bore into his soul. "If we found out what planet they started on, maybe we could learn more about their biochemistry and, if we knew more about their technology, find ways to defeat them."

"You really think you can do that? Deconstruct an advanced alien race and find out what makes them tick in time to do any good?"

The Colonel straightened. "I know we won't if we don't try."

"Then why haven't the Gertewet already done it?"

"Why wouldn't we release polio against the Nazis?" Stokely answered. "Because in the end, it'll hurt us, too."

Rockefeller nodded and redoubled his pacing. "We're not Gertewet."

"Thank God," Colonel Marshall breathed.

"Maybe we can work with them closely enough to find their weaknesses, and then take them all out."

The Colonel smiled.

Stokely stared at them, mouth agape. "Are you crazy? First off, that's cruel. Pure, unmitigated genocide. Secondly, that's not how you keep allies. What if you succeed and find you need their help with some bigger, badder alien? And third, how? General Marshall and his symbiont only pop by twice a year, if that. That's not enough to keep in touch, let alone discover a brain sucker's Achilles heel and then kill them all off."

"What if we studied it, the General's alien, next time he popped by?" Rockefeller scuffed his shoe on the grimy utility carpet. Not that he wanted to dissect a potential ally of the moment, but if it could help, he'd push for it.

The room fell silent. Rockefeller caught Stokely studying the Colonel out of the corner of his eye. She avoided their gazes.

"It's your uncle," Stokely murmured.

"Was." She shook her head. "I just can't figure how we'll keep him here. He knows everything and everyone on this station—and then there's the Gertewet's ruthlessness. And, yes, an ally has seemed more important than a study subject, but how much of that was the alien influencing us?"

"Maybe we can have both. The General as an ally and a second to study. He can't be the only one out there."

"Just the only one that comes here."

"Then we'll need him to take us to the rest."

"Or bring another here." Stokely frowned. "Maybe we can offer them something so tempting, they have to come."

They all met each other's eyes, thinking the same thing. Earth had one resource the aliens clearly wanted.

Colonel Marshall stood up. "No."

"We don't have to give it to them!" Stokely promised.

It felt dirty to even consider handing over human beings for alien possession. "They'll want a sample in good faith."

"We only need one alien. After they find out we took their guy, they're not coming back, anyway. We don't have to give them hosts."

"Then how will you keep the ally?"

"Family." Avoiding their eyes, Colonel Marshall settled onto her barstool. "If there's anything left of my uncle, he'll keep coming back either to visit or because he assumes he can order me to let the other Gertewet go. Either way, he'll be back."

"Great." He clapped his hands together. "Once you bring Maggie back, you'll try to catch an alien for study while still maintaining an alternate information source. Then we'll see how to approach them about leaving us alone."

Rockefeller shook his head. Listen to him. He sounded crazy!

But if this was the rabbit hole Maggie fell down, he was going in all the way. "What can I do to make sure you get her back?"

9

TOO SOON

"Come back!" Sarah screamed at the vanished saucers. "You promised! Come back!"

The goon's iron clamp pulled, sliding her across the rocky shards and poking scrub. She kicked and screamed. She had to break free! Her fingers tore into the loose soil, but it broke off in chunks, hardly slowing her.

Then he had her. With an arm wrapped around her waist, he pulled her off the ground.

She tried everything: she kicked at his knees, shrieked in his ears, clawed at his face. She couldn't go back! Not to that dark, cold room and *not* to the certainty of a body-possessing alien!

One of her fingers caught in his mushy eye. He screamed. His arms tightened painfully, forcing her breath out. He pressed his face into her back, where she couldn't reach.

Keeping a secure grip on her, he plodded downhill.

The rocky path stretched out before her hanging feet, leading straight back to the four-armed man, Mr. Marshall, and Maggie. More guards joined them now, prodding along other Earth women: the one in business clothes, bleeding through ripped stockings; one with her burgundy apron twisted half around; and the woman in the floral blouse. One stumble, and her assailant would set them both tumbling down the jagged path. She could do nothing to keep him from tripping.

But she could swing him off balance.

By the time they rolled to a boneless stop at the others' feet, she'd be such a bloody mess, no one would want her body.

One good rock against his grip ought to tip him off his toes. It even made sense: a good, solid way to keep the aliens from wanting her body when they had four others in mint condition, or better than hers, anyway.

Frozen, she tried to watch his every step while she made up her mind. Her ribs ached. From here, she'd land face-first. It'd hurt, but it had to be an improvement over certain doom.

She whipped her torso forward in time with his next step.

He rocked, his feet skipping on the slope, and toppled. She squeezed her eyes shut. His vise grip pinned her against him, and they landed on her arm and rolled.

Rocks scraped against her cheek and chin, then her other arm. They bounced and slid to a stop. Her arms and face stung, and her ribs burned with every breath, but the guard still clutched her tight, his armored back turned downhill toward any more attacking rocks and twigs.

He panted as hard as she did, but he pushed up to his knees with his elbows, then to his feet. He staggered down-hill with her still clamped in his arms.

Shaking, she scratched at his arm and sobbed, "Let go! Let go of me!"

As they got closer, she caught the four-armed man glaring at her and clammed up. He looked as if he thought it her fault the others got out. Mr. Marshall barely looked at her. "*Die Königen hat noch fünf Wahllen.*"

Wait a minute! Now that he spoke slowly, it sounded like German, at least according to what she remembered from the four-language sampler class she'd had to take in seventh grade. What in the world was he doing speaking a normal language? If this was an alien planet, shouldn't they have an alien language?

Five. He'd said something about five. She counted while the goon set her on her feet and held her wrists clamped behind her back. The three adult women, her, and Maggie made five. What was he saying about them?

The four-armed man glared at Mr. Marshall. "*Du sagst, sie braucht nur eins. Bist du sicher?*"

One. One what? Only one alien after all? Only one person they'd want to use? Her?

She tried to wrench free. Instead, the goon pulled up on her wrist, straining her shoulders until she stopped.

The four-armed man led them all back along the path. Pain flashed up her legs on the first step, making her stagger, and Mr. Marshall said something. Next thing she knew, the goon had her swung up over his shoulder, weight off her raw feet, face pressed against his smelly armor.

Mr. Marshall waited for him to pass and started walking where she could see him. He caught her eye, winked at her, and ignored her again.

What was that supposed to mean? Was it a normal wink, meaning everything was going to be okay? Or a creepy wink, because he still wanted to implant a neck lump?

She beat on the goon's back and screamed until they got back to the building. There, they passed a body lying on the ground, hands loose at his bloody neck: the guard who let them out.

She lost her voice. How could he be dead? She'd seen him alive only minutes ago. He'd been nice; he'd let them out. What happened?

Mr. Marshall's bloody hands.

Mr. Marshall killed him.

She started shaking. Mr. Marshall killed people, people who were on her side, helping her. Did Major Patrick know? Was that why she hadn't wanted to talk about him and the Gertewet?

Now what?

Sarah craned her head to see Maggie slung over Mr. Marshall's shoulders the way Sarah was over the goon's. The last four guards herded the other three women, who shuffled along, downcast and beaten. The final man closed the door, shutting them out of the sunshine.

The service staff they'd passed before were silent now. Had they heard these funeral processions before? Sarah's tears streaked down the back of the goon's armor where her face pressed against it.

All the guards and the four-armed man marched them into the center of the stone room they'd escaped. The goon and Mr. Marshall slid her and Maggie onto a divan.

The instant they stepped away, Sarah scrambled over and grabbed her hand. "Maggie! Maggie, wake up!"

Groaning, she nodded.

"Maggie, they killed the guy who let us out!"

She opened her eyes and glanced around, and Sarah did, too. The men escorting the women stood behind them, still holding them in place. Mr. Marshall and the goon flanked their couch, and the four-armed man watched them all, fuming. She looked away.

"*Es gab so viele.*" The four-armed man spoke in the near-whisper of a man about to explode.

Sarah clutched Maggie tighter. Whatever happened, it'd be the two of them against all the looming guards.

"*Die altere drei sind zu fett. Beseitig sie!*"

The woman in the ripped suit and hose went ballistic, trying to run through the guards behind her. Before Sarah knew what was happening, the woman fell onto her back. A knife hilt pointed from her rib cage toward her toes. Her eyes were wide. She looked startled and like she was still trying to breathe. Dying. Her blouse grew red and wet around the hilt.

The smells of rusty blood and sour sewers hit her with a jolt. Sarah grabbed Maggie and pulled her up from the couch. They slipped between the furniture and the goon and ran for the wooden tidal wave. The woman in the suit had heard him order their deaths.

Maggie's wrist slipped in her sweaty fingers, and Sarah clamped tighter. They had to get away! Her torn socks slid on the rug, but both girls stayed upright.

Behind her, a pair of screams. A meaty stab.

Faster!

A sharp crack.

Sarah couldn't count right now, as she dragged the girl past the four-armed man, but she knew there weren't many others left. She kept pulling and pulling the poor girl as fast as she could across the rug.

At the far wall, in the shelter of the wooden wave, she realized the men were faster than she. They should have caught up by now. She glanced back.

One man wiped his knife blade off on the first woman's suit. Another used the floral blouse to catch blood before more dribbled out of the other woman's open neck onto the rug. Mr. Marshall and another man carried the aproned woman out. Her head leaned too far back.

Everything stank of sewage and blood. As they cleaned up the corpses, the men ignored her and Maggie. It didn't seem like they would come after her.

She held Maggie and shook, heart pounding in her ears.

Two of them left. And two options: Mr. Marshall's Gertewet and the Kemtewet queen. Were they working together?

The four-armed man watched them, and Sarah stared back. The instant he started toward them, they had to run. In this big room, it should be easy to avoid any one person.

The men must have known that. They didn't come until they'd taken the bodies out. Then they lined up across the room and marched forward, leaving Sarah nowhere to run.

She held Maggie. "They're coming."

"I don't think I can run." Her voice shook, too. "I think my legs are broken."

They ran anyway. It didn't work.

———

DONN MARSHALL STOOD with Banebdjedet while his men marched down the room to collect the last two girls. His jaw clenched so hard, it hurt.

Now? He wanted to implant one of them now, when he'd just traumatized them? How was that supposed to make sense?

"Run them both through the teleporter, and take the first one up to our queen."

The first part made sense. With almost a hundred colonized worlds for pathogens to develop on, the teleporters in kaxan had been developed and programmed to automatically inoculate any body they moved. As a convenience for long trips, it also handled waste products and reconstructed simple injuries like broken bones and abrasions—which Sarah and the other girl seemed to have aplenty, given the bloody footprints staggered along the length of the hall. They couldn't let the queen take a host like that.

But if he took Sarah up now, he wouldn't have a chance to kill Anjedet and leave Vinnet in her position. "Would you like the dark-haired one?"

Banebdjedet slit his eyes. "The other, as we discussed before."

"*Jawohl.*" He bowed and straightened in time for the others to arrive with the struggling girls. He pointed to Sarah. "This one goes to the queen first. Send them up to the kaxan and back down beforehand. I'll go with them to keep them steady."

This might work.

Under Banebdjedet's watch, he had Kümmel pass the dark-haired girl to him. He hefted her over his shoulder and nodded to Sarah. "Pass her to me just before we go up."

He led them into the hall, out to the teleport juncture, and Davon passed Sarah over. Donn took her arm to pull her close, and she bit him. He sucked in a hiss.

Then the teleport activated.

"Ow!" He dropped them both in the kaxan's clean, white interior. Screw them hurting him when he was trying to help! He checked his arm by reflex, but the teleport computer fixed him, same as them. Open wounds it could handle but not someone with a stretched diaphragm. He smeared her spit on his pants and ignored his aching lungs.

Seconds counted. Ducking around the controls, he set a new transport: himself to Vinnet's kaxan, where they wouldn't look for him to bring him back.

"What are you doing?" Sarah swiped at her tear-lined face.

He shook his head and teleported out. It'd kill his cover when the planetside teleport operator didn't bring him back into the palace immediately.

But he had no time. He had to get Vinnet.

10

HERITAGE

O n Setira's homeworld, as on many other planets, pedestrians shared the street with vehicles of some sort, and the boundary between ground and building accumulated drifts of grime. The Kemtewet had built this city without either the grime or mixed traffic.

Beneath the darting atmospheric flying saucers, a fine metal grid spanned the gaps between buildings, shunting rain, snow, and the debris they carried into the canals underneath. The last time Katorin had visited the Kemtewet capital, her host had been fascinated by watching the grate melt the snow and carry it away beneath his feet. It hadn't rained here in a week; the canal was dry.

Cube Head's frantic rush settled into a practiced stroll where each step launched brief metallic shivers through the walkway. She listened for it under his droning about the secret inner workings of their office politics. She even marveled at the red night lighting panels at the base of all the buildings and how they cast a mesmerizing gradient of shadows on the copper-colored street grating.

The old "It's still there" rumor caught on with the Kem. Save us. Katorin rubbed her temple. *They tore it down to build the design center. They must have. There's nothing left.*

Khonsu has files of the evidence for it. I spent four nights reading through it all.

And it's all circumstantial. He didn't want to cope with the fact that it's gone. Not that she could blame him. She'd gotten some of their progenitor's fond memories of the house, too.

What if he's right? Setira pressed. *You can't flat-out dismiss any of his evidence.*

But it would have to all be true, and the likelihood of that is so minuscule, it's impossible. Katorin forced herself to uncross Setira's arms. *If the design center architect was Ger, and he decided to preserve the house, how did the Coordinating Council lose all record of it?*

Khonsu's right. A lot of records were lost when the Kem overtook Mountains Base. Between that and turnover on the Coordinating Council—who wanted it silenced to stop attracting operatives all to one spot—we could have lost it completely.

And, coincidentally, these are the only files we didn't know we lost there?

We can't know what all was lost. That's why we call it lost.

Cube Head patted her arm. "Hey, are you even listening? I only thought you'd like it because you asked about that guy, and he was into it. Until he left for the ISC, obviously. Can you believe that?"

"He must have been crazy." Obviously. Conspiracy theories aside, entering the ISC barely made sense for Kem. Spend your whole life in the shadows, enforcing the Empress's tyranny?

Not that the Kem saw it like that.

"Tell me about it!" He studied her eyes, and she stared

back, wishing he'd stop. "You're not going to join, too, are you?"

"I'm not diving into that black hole!" Even if the Council hadn't explicitly ordered her not to. She wasn't ready to get caught and killed. "I've got the rest of my life ahead of me."

In reality, only a couple more hosts' lives, not the dozen and change Cube Head thought she had.

He clapped her on the shoulder. "That's right. Look at you, learning the truth about Gertewet spirit possession young!"

She rolled her eyes while he kept talking.

The Ger were almost at the end. *Who's going to carry on when we're done?*

Don't think that, Katorin! We still have time to win.

And if we don't, who will stand up for humans? Neith excels at ensuring the colonies don't have the resources to rebel. The Grand Empire, when it does have ships, doesn't care about anyone else. Neither does Percalli.

The Percallans would fight if we let them.

They'd be wiped out.

They walked on in sullen mental silence, the clanging grating almost competing with Cube Head's jabbering.

Earth's out there, Setira offered. *That's a human planet the Kem don't overshadow.*

There are still occasional raids.

Obviously, but what's the Earth English word for Kemtewet? There isn't one. That's a place the Kem don't really bother.

One. *We let this mess develop. We have to clean it up before we die out.* Which, for now, meant getting to the bottom of these ISC changes. Why the sudden recruitment push? What was the ISC gearing up for? And why wasn't the Kem populace as wary as the Ger?

The ISC has never been desperate before.

They can't be planning to attack us. With the last Ger queen caught and executed a lifetime ago, the Kem had only to wait for the Ger to finish dying off. Didn't they notice how dramatically Ger activity had declined in the last few hundred years? They didn't need to polish off the rest of the species. Hopefully, they didn't think they could.

Unless they knew where all seven bases were. Only fourteen Gertewet did: those who never went on missions. But even then, the slaughter would miss everyone on deployment, and as her current mission demonstrated, no one knew where they were, not even the Coordinating Council.

If the Gertewet weren't worth ramping up over in ages past, they weren't worth it now.

What else? She hadn't heard anything unusual about the colonies. Some unrest here and there, cults formed and quashed while protesting Kem rule. Lynched doctors. Regretful runaways giving their new symbionts trouble.

Unless the Kem Empire had finally had enough of the Grand Empire's purported independence. A self-inflated penal colony locked in a system of limited resources, the Grand Empire shouldn't need to be on the ISC's radar. Sure, it was the loudest system with an aversion to tewet, but the three planets had only a couple dozen kaxan among them and, for the times they could both steal and defend them, never more than a couple motherships. For the ISC, it'd be squashing a bug. A useful bug. A spider.

If it wasn't Gertewet, the colonies, or the Grand Empire, then why bother keeping it secret? Shouldn't the Kemtewet citizens know?

What was so bad the ISC had to build up to an unheard-of level, but no one could know why?

"Beryl?"

Looking up from the enchanting copper grating, Katorin caught the blazing Value Vassal sign. Her fists tightened. "No, Paul, I am not getting a new vassal right now."

"Come on. Trade in now, nice and quick, and it won't hurt as long." He rubbed her arm.

She side-stepped out of reach, but her perverse gaze swept over the storefront. Two men and two women stood in the store windows, modeling well-tailored evening wear that would be sold with them. She couldn't help studying their faces.

The men laughed with each other as if over a secret crush. The women talked business, standing with relaxed postures and using their hands for emphasis. What had they been told, so they would look so calm? Didn't they know what was going to happen to them? Or had they been drugged to elicit the proper emotional display?

They don't even know. Four lives slated to be overwritten on a whim. Setira's hands clenched, driving fingernails into palms.

If she pretended to examine one or two, she might be able to convince them to let her break them out and take them home. She could take out the sales attendant. Cube Head would be no obstacle. She could leave with them.

But no one would stay to investigate Khonsu and the ISC. She started to take a frustrated swing at Cube Head but maintained cover by swinging into motion instead.

Cube Head might still be useful.

"Beryl, you can't put it off. Wait! Beryl, the discount is going to end soon, and you'll only be able to afford the rejects."

The nerve! How could he perpetuate all these deaths?

He ran to catch up and had to keep jogging to pace

alongside her furious march. "I'm sorry, but your vassal is half-dead—"

Am not!

"—and you need to trade her in before something happens. You're new to this. You don't know how fast a body can go from seeming fine to failing."

She stormed around the corner and onto the street the design center occupied. *Lecturing me on hosts, as if I wouldn't know. He's had maybe two!*

Katorin, it's okay. Their throat tightened. *He's right. There are no lifeports here. If something happened to me, you couldn't crawl to safety. You'd have to wait for a kaxan, go through the normal Kem process, wait in line. It is a risk.*

I can't lose you yet.

I know. You won't, not right now. I'm not ready, either, but I'm saying you don't need to be mad at him for trying to look out for you. This is hard enough when you're not worked up.

Katorin stopped to let Cube Head catch up. She had to patch this up, or it could unravel her cover. She forced the bitter words out a few at a time. "I'm sorry. You're trying to help, but I'm not ready. This is the only body I've ever had, and I like it."

There. Done.

He wrapped an arm around her shoulders. "It's okay. It was hard for me, too, but the longer you wait, the worse it gets."

"I understand. Give me a chance to let it sink in. The day after tomorrow?"

He squinted one eye and looked up. "That should work. The sale will still be on."

Maybe she could arrange to be out of town for the rest of the sale and say she didn't have enough money after that. Plan settled, she leaned into his arm.

He took it back and popped ahead. "Let me come. Oh, please, let me come! I can help you pick out the next one."

Over her dead body. She smiled anyway and followed him toward the concrete center's imposing entrance. "Why? What do you want me to get?"

"Well, a female obviously. A young one."

No, not obviously. Maybe the reason he'd rebuffed her so often was that he preferred men. How would she know? Wait. "How young are you thinking?"

"Sixties."

Her eyes bulged. "I can't buy a host in her sixties! I'll never afford it!"

"Right now you might!"

His idiocy knew no bounds. Was that how he could afford a young host who knew English? She'd had to learn it from Kitchell. "I'm done talking about this. Let's pick it up in a couple days. Besides, we're here."

They had a few dozen strides left. Close enough to cut him off.

He lit up, his whole body straightening. "All right! Right below this building is where they killed the first Gertewet, and I'll prove it to you! First, we'll both need to stand on the scale and place palms on the reader."

"Paul, I do that every workday. I know."

"Right, but did you know the Ger spirit reads your weight and will begin immediate psychic assaults if it's even?" Reaching the building, he stepped onto the scale, noted the even reading, and carefully piled his pockets' contents on the grate beside him. The scale ticked down to an odd number. He scanned his palm and stepped inside.

This is going well.

Katorin shook her head and stepped onto the scale. The

displayed number was odd. She scanned her palm and followed him inside with her pockets' contents intact.

The security log will have recorded that, Setira pointed out. *If we have to come back, we should have a better reason why.*

You mean ghost-hunting killer cleaning bots is not an ISC-validated pastime?

The breach in the squat, utilitarian building's exterior opened into a squat, utilitarian lobby with reception, cafeteria, and worker resources, but Cube Head had gone only several paces in—all straight to the right. He stood quivering beside an open maintenance panel.

"On late nights when Kem come in alone, when the cleaning bots arise to wash windows and sanitize control interfaces, it tracks their movements, their weight." His hands traced out expansive, supposedly creepy movements.

She stifled a yawn. Then widened her eyes to play along.

"It awaits only one wrong move, and then—*pow!* Out of nowhere, a possessed bot stabs them in the gut, never to be heard from again!"

"That's terrible," she whispered. *Terrible storytelling.*

"You know how I know?"

"How?"

"I was here both times they found the bodies stashed in the bot closets. They reinstalled the programming the first time and changed out units the second time, but if it's Ger spirit possession, that won't solve it. And then—" His smirk pinched his cheek to a point. "I found the secret passage the bots use to navigate, the one that channels the spirit straight from where it died!"

He turned to the maintenance panel and entered a simple code: four zeroes. The display turned off.

Bots navigate through hallways and teleporters like anyone else.

Katorin, look!

Twisting the knobs at the corners, Cube Head pulled the panel from the wall and set it aside. In its place was a deep open space; at the upper corner sat a single, large port that normally carried all of the inner panel's input to and output from the building's computer.

Cube Head beamed.

She blinked at him. Maybe he earned a right to that triumphant pose, with hands on hips, chin in the air, and hair angled back like a die suspended mid-fall, the inevitable flattening inexplicably delayed. He'd earned a small, limited right.

She slinked over to peer in. The lobby's dimmed lights probed a meter into the hidden passage, revealing a narrow, rectangular walkway to her left with rough, regular walls and floor, unbroken by anything as convenient as a light source.

"You're right!" About one thing: something was meant to travel through here, but probably not a bot. If that was the case, why make it so tall? Why leave the floor too rough for the little wheels to navigate?

Katorin, we have to go in. Khonsu would've exploded to learn about this. If he left intel anywhere, it has to be back there, whether or not it actually was Mute's house.

You're right, too. She started climbing in.

Cube Head hauled her back, dumping her onto her rump on the hard floor. "You can't go in there—they'll kill you! Did you make sure your weight was odd?"

Pushing up, she wiped her scraped hands from catching herself. "I just want to see where it goes."

"Was your weight odd?"

"Yes, my weight was odd!"

"They'll still kill you if you're in their way. Come on, let's go get drinks!" He settled the panel back into place and powered the screen back on.

"Fine."

Setira agreed, too. *Besides, we need an alibi for accessing the building. Time to go shopping.*

11

WRONG RESCUE, WRONG ALIEN

Rockefeller met Colonel Marshall's eyes, silently urging her to give him an actionable answer. He had to do something to help his daughter.

She laid her palms flat on the ping-pong table. "Nothing we do here will affect anything out there. Near as we can tell, even the Kemtewet don't have any communication faster than their travel. We'll have to wait for Major Patrick and her team to return with your daughter."

Stokely recentered himself on his stool. "Actually, Andy, there is one thing."

"What's that?" The words barely left his lips when he finished tracing Stokely's train of thought. "Funding. You want to fix things up around here."

"Well, yes."

Colonel Marshall folded her hands, prim and expectant. "More importantly, we want to improve our detection and tracking, train more pilots, and expand our tools for reverse-engineering the kaxan."

"And that will prevent future raids?"

"It'll go a long way."

"Colonel!" A young officer burst into the room. "Colonel, Major Patrick's team is back in comms range. They estimate five minutes to arrival."

"Thank you, Sergeant. Please open the doors for them."

"Do they have her?" Rockefeller knocked into the table's corner as he rushed around it. "Did they say?"

The Sergeant hesitated in the doorway, eyes flicking to his superior as if to ask who they were talking about. "No, sir, they didn't say much, but the communication's still open. I need to—"

He motioned to the hall.

"Go," the Colonel said.

He took off.

She held the door open for the rest of them. "It'll be easier to sort out on the ground, but we can ask the Major while she taxis down."

"Thank you, Colonel." He rushed into the hall and realized he didn't know where comms was.

Still rising from the table, Stokely waved them away. "I'll catch up."

Good. He couldn't wait. Every second of waiting, even now, following the Colonel back into the hangar, let the questions rush back in. What if they were following the wrong lead? If not, what if the aliens had hurt her? He'd made sure all his girls got self-defense training (even Joyce), but what if Maggie using those skills had drawn additional retaliation from her captors?

He stepped on the Colonel's heel, and she shot him a glare.

"Sorry."

She led him into the saucer beside the one they'd toured earlier. As he finished climbing in, she stepped behind the control screen and pulled it up to a comfortable height for standing. "Major."

"Colonel," the screen answered.

He joined her behind it and found a woman's face already displayed. Short, black hair framed her defined jawline and green eyes. Major Patrick, he assumed. Not what he expected. "Is Maggie with you?"

The woman on the screen frowned, and her eyes shifted away. "Who is that?"

"This is the Speaker of the House, Andrew Rockefeller. The raid took his daughter Maggie. Is she with you?"

The Major leaned out of camera view. "Is there a Maggie here? Maggie Rockefeller?"

Please. Please. Just this one miracle.

Other voices came across fainter. "No." "Oh, she was that girl who—" "—when I got there." "Oh, her! Yes!"

Major Patrick's voice again. "Did you see her get in a kaxan—in one of the vehicles?"

Silence.

Major Patrick settled back behind the control panel. "Some of the women here remember her, but she's not with me."

His heart stopped.

"She could be in with Fairfeld or Myers. We were pursued to the kaxan and left in a jumble." She glanced elsewhere on her screen. "Looks like they're touching down now."

He traded glances with the Colonel, who turned back to the screen. "Thank you, Major. We'll check."

At the first syllable, he rushed to the porthole and slid through, dropping to the ground with a slap that stung his soles. She might be here—she had to be here, somewhere in this forest of flying saucer stilts. But where?

He stepped farther in.

Something flashed. A glint, framed in the picture window of the wide-open hangar doors, disappeared behind the rows of parked saucers. Was that a gap nearby? He ran down the row to an aisle through the hangar's center. The new arrival hovered over the grass, floating with unwavering precision. It shot into the hangar without seeming to accelerate, as if it had stepped up to its moderate velocity and stopped equally abruptly along the aisle. It extended its landing struts to the ground, precisely aligned with all the other spacecraft, and settled into place.

He ran down the aisle. Was that the last one or the first?

One of the other saucers had its hatch open and an Air Force officer already halfway down. He stepped aside, and Rockefeller held his breath. The first shoe down was a flat-soled sneaker good for long hours of standing. Not hers. A woman in a university sweatshirt stepped off the ladder to join the first.

The next foot was a winner.

Colorful athletic shoes stretched down from jeans to reach the first rung. Then the second. By the third, the girl's hips came into view, and Rockefeller realized he'd been mistaken.

A college-aged girl hopped down.

Another uniformed woman and two other college students joined the growing crowd before the ship emptied, and he turned his attention to the one between it and the one he saw land. She had to be here somewhere.

Colonel Marshall stopped beside him to watch the second ship disgorge its passengers. A mother and daughter... A pastor...

Major Patrick dropped out of the third ship, and he tried

to watch both saucers emptying. Maybe Patrick had over-looked Maggie sleeping in her own ship.

"What happened?" Colonel Marshall called to her.

The Major waited until she closed to answer. "The coordinates the General gave us were for a planet labeled, 'Fifth Lord of Green Primary.' We followed the onboard map to the lord's palace, which was hosting some sort of big party. We walked right in, but the guards detained us. The General took us to the chamber with all the abductees and arranged our release, but he couldn't keep them off us long enough. They recaptured several people."

The last ship emptied, and his daughter hadn't appeared. Rockefeller turned to the Major. "Was Maggie one of them?"

"I don't—wait." She closed her eyes and held a hand up an inch shorter than her head. "Is she about yay tall? Long, curly brown hair?"

"That's her!" Should he be excited that she remembered her, or was his dread justified?

"She was hanging around the girl the General tried to recruit." She craned around them to scan the crowd. "Shit! They're not here!"

"How could you not know?" Rockefeller grabbed her by the shoulders. "Where is she?"

"They're still back there." Patrick's wide, round eyes turned to her CO. "Colonel, we've got to go back and get them."

When Colonel Marshall didn't answer immediately, he let go of Patrick and bore down on the new target. "You're going to get her, right?"

She met his eyes and said nothing. A few yards away, Stokely and the first ship's pilot addressed the rescued abductees, over where Maggie should have been standing. He crossed his arms.

"Major, what was supposed to happen to them next? Can you go back safely?"

"Yeah, the General's got himself set up as head of security. Now we've got the lay of the land, we should be able to park closer, slip in, and get anyone who's left." She raked a hand through her hair. "We can't not go back."

The Colonel studied the gathered abductees. "Get some sleep before you head out."

"No way, sir, we can get six more hours en route." She turned and motioned to the two men in BDUs who had arrived with her. "We just need to reload before we go."

Tossing a salute to the Colonel, Major Patrick took off into the hangar's depths.

Colonel Marshall watched her and sighed.

Good, at least there was a ship heading his way. "I'm going with them."

Her eyes latched onto his. "What?"

He crossed his arms and planted his feet. "I'm going with them to get my daughter back."

"No."

She and Stokely had kept him waiting all day, passing along assurances that her team would bring his daughter home. Empty promises for his empty heart. But she wouldn't care. She didn't care, or she'd have Patrick's ass back on that ship posthaste.

He bit back impulsive screams. She'd obviously take his anger in stride, along with everything else. "You let me on that ship to bring my daughter home, and I'll make sure you get the biggest plus-up in funding this project has ever seen."

She stepped up to him, toe to toe. "Are you bribing me, Mr. Speaker?"

"Do you think your team might not be good enough to bring her back?"

"I don't think they need to babysit you while you try to go running off to her rescue."

"They left her behind once. Maybe they need someone to hold their hands the second time."

"Even if they did, you think you'd be that person? With no training, no discipline, and no experience with aliens? You're a liability."

"And you're a stone-hearted—"

"Nice to see you two getting along." Stokely's voice floated between them, and Rockefeller swallowed the rest of his insult before glancing away. Behind him, the abductees filed away, following the Sergeant out into the sea of saucers. "I told Bailey those women would probably be more comfortable in the old barracks until you figure out how to disposition them."

Colonel Marshall backed off. "Thank you. That should be about right."

"Women?" Rockefeller watched the last few turn out of sight.

"That's right. We asked after the ones that got left behind, too—five, it turns out. They're all women."

That weight congealed in the pit of his stomach again. "Is that normal?"

"No." Colonel Marshall's fists clenched at her sides.

Did that mean they weren't looking for just a body? "We can't leave them there. We have to go back and get them!"

"No one's disputing that." Stokely paused to raise an eyebrow at Colonel Marshall then Rockefeller. "So what seems to be the problem here?"

"I'm going with them." Rockefeller stared at the Colonel, who crossed her arms. Then he caught Stokely's dropped jaw.

"Your place is here, Andy. You can't help them out there."

"You don't know that!"

Stokely rested a hand on his shoulder. "Andy, your talents are best spent here on the ground, preventing the next raid. Let those who are trained for it deal with this one."

He swiped Stokely's hand off. "No one's trained for aliens. She's my daughter. I should go."

Rockefeller stuck his hands in his pockets and forced them still. If he looked as desperate as he felt, they'd never let him leave with them. "Let me do this one thing, and I will make sure Black Book is fully funded to expand its capabilities."

Stokely mirrored his relaxed facade, hooking his thumbs into his belt loops. "How are you going to fund it if something happens to you?"

"Your team brought back a dozen frightened women last time. Surely, I won't be a liability," he said, pointedly meeting Colonel Marshall's glare, "while helping them with the last five."

"And if a Kemtewet decides to possess you," Stokely pressed, "while you've conveniently singled yourself out from the rest of the planet? We'll be at even more of a disadvantage if they learn everything you know."

"Then better me than her!" He hadn't meant to shout. Oh, hell. "Charlie, that's a risk I have to take! My baby girl is out there, fighting for her life somewhere she should never have known about, let alone been dragged to.

"Now, lecture me all you like about security risks and

your other perfect-world ideals. In a perfect world, she'd be back-to-school shopping today, not abandoned on an alien planet by the very people sent to rescue her.

"I'm her daddy, and I'm going to bring her home. If you try to stop me, I will have this project ended and replaced so quick, your hats won't hit the ground before the next commander picks them up!"

"You don't have the authority!" Colonel Marshall shouted.

"Watch me!"

He'd found all sorts of ways to do what others labeled impossible. For this, he'd pull all the stops. The right connections already started popping into his mind.

Stokely cleared his throat and nudged her arm. "Colonel, a word?"

He eyed Rockefeller as he led her a few steps away. What was that supposed to mean? Was it reproach or wariness? Rockefeller turned, too, as if he didn't intend to overhear his old mentor's every word.

"He's bluffing," Colonel Marshall objected.

"He's not bluffing. He only bluffs when he's thinking clearly, when he's not tied up in the situation." He did? "You, my dear, could not have pushed his buttons any more precisely."

Not with his daughter's safety involved, no.

"He means it. Don't give me that look. You and I both know if Black Book lost you, they'd be set back twenty years." Rockefeller glanced back to see Stokely put a hand on the Colonel's shoulder. "But if Black Book lost everyone else, too? The project would never recover. It'd be the end of the line for all the careers here, but more importantly, the country would lose its only shot at protecting itself."

And his other daughters. With as hard as it was to

believe it, Rockefeller could see how new personnel might not take it seriously. He recalled the little green men on the pinball machine and revised that thought—they might take it even *less* seriously.

But in his heart of hearts, he still meant it. He'd open hell to avenge her.

"The Air Force conducts itself with professionalism." Colonel Marshall sounded like she was assuring herself more than reminding Stokely. "The project would survive."

"And what if he declassified it and handed it to NASA? Can you imagine what would happen if people found out?"

"Yes," she squeaked.

What? They'd demand the government take seriously its duty to protect its people? What did an honest project have to fear?

"On the other hand, you've got him all fired up. If you let him go now, if you take this chance, you will have his gratitude, and that's a powerful thing. He'll never forget. He's the Speaker now. He can effect changes I never could, and he's still young. What do you think he'll be able to do for the project throughout the rest of his career?

"Once you let him go off world, get his daughter, see what we're up against? What could happen?"

Rockefeller swallowed. That wasn't the promise he'd meant to make. He just wanted his little girl back. The rest could wait for later.

"This is wrong."

He glanced over to catch her shaking her head.

"Finding out I let the Speaker of the House get himself killed will end the project even faster than making him stay."

"I'll indemnify you!" Rockefeller approached them. "Please. I have to go."

Sympathy flashed in the Colonel's eyes before she caught herself and snuffed it out.

Stokely regarded him, eyebrows raised. "Call Joyce. Tell her we all said it's a bad idea. There's a phone in the Colonel's office."

Rockefeller nodded and took off. He barely heard what they said next.

"You played us."

"It's for your own good."

So what? Stokely had backed him up. It worked. One more thing, and he could ride off to his daughter's rescue.

Hang on, Maggie. I'm coming.

"What was that?" Sarah watched as Maggie swiped her arm through the empty space where Mr. Marshall had been.

"Something's wrong." Not only had Mr. Marshall killed someone who was helping them—a sign he was lying about trying to help her—but now he was rushing to do something behind the backs of all the other men.

Whose side was he on?

Was he going to save them or not?

The saucer room disappeared, and she and Maggie stood back in the tiled room. The men descended again. Screaming through burning lungs, she reached for Maggie, but the goon pulled her away, picked her up, and started walking up stairs leading out of the room.

"Maggie!" Sarah shouted.

Behind her, the guards picked Maggie up, too, and carried her back toward the stone room.

She tried biting the goon's ear, but he bounced her

farther back over his shoulder, straining the arm he held and making the blood rush to her head.

Oh, God! What now? They were taking Maggie back and her somewhere else now. Was this it—implantation?

That was why Mr. Marshall was rushing.

He wasn't ready.

They were going to put the wrong alien in her!

"No! Put me down! Let me go!" She screeched so loud, it hurt her own ears.

He climbed faster.

The stairs ended in a dim, narrow hallway. Silver embossed walls passed by her nose, dancing with the mocking reflections of firelight. The patterns swam in her vision, rippling like the surface of water. Her journey across the Styx River, ending when she reached Hell on the other side?

Swinging her legs, she broke one out of his grip but couldn't angle it right to kick him.

He opened a door, and she flailed harder. She wouldn't go! But he slid her off his shoulder anyway and held her with one arm across her chest and arms, the other hand clutching her ponytail.

He pointed her at a headless mannequin in a floor-length silver dress by the back wall, eclipsed in their flickering shadows from the hall's dim lamps.

"*Putz dich heraus!*" He shoved her forward and closed the door.

A spotlight clicked on, illuminating the sparkling mannequin as if with a neon sign that read, "Put this on!"

Sarah retreated to the corner, drew her knees up, and cried.

12

LAST CHANCE

innet watched Donn teleport into the kaxan for the first time since she had occupied it. Not a good sign. "We've got to go. Come on!"

He held his hand out to the gel's surface and fished for the canteen at his belt. Trust him, the operative in the field, or slow him down with questions he didn't need right now?

She posted a message to the screen and activated a chime.

The clear, pleasant tone rang through the human cabin, and Donn jerked his hand from the symbiont environment and spun to skim her message.

"The candidate agreed?"

"Vinnet, they're taking her up right now. If we don't get down there, when we take out Anjedet, we'll have to kill her, too." His earnest eyes focused on the camera she saw through.

Her tail twitched through the gel. If circumstances were an excuse to neglect her responsibility to ensure her host had a choice, then what differentiated her from the Kem? "Did she approve?"

"You wouldn't rather she died than hosted you."

"It's not my choice."

He leaned forward and clutched the control panel's edges. "And what do you think she's going to choose between dying as a Kem vassal or living as a Ger host?"

"I've been turned down before."

"But in the long run, once she understands the stakes?"

She froze.

He couldn't have.

She shut off the current through the symbiont gel, rendering it transparent. Then she blinked her real eyes open and peered at him, hoping to see some nuance in his posture that the camera had missed. When he caught the change in the gel, he turned to face her, that same hard look in his eye and impatience in his posture.

No.

She posted to the screen and turned the current back on. "You didn't tell her."

"What was I supposed to say? She's never even heard of the empire or life on other planets. It'd take me hours to explain, and even then, she might not believe me."

"You didn't even try?"

"I tried! She freaked out." He held up the fake canteen. "And if we don't go right now, Anjedet won't give her a choice."

The queen wouldn't, but if Kitchell and Donn had their way, Vinnet wouldn't, either. At least she had until they got down there to figure out how to change that.

"Releasing kaxan control now." Holding tight to her misgivings, Vinnet withdrew from the interface, reflexively sheathing her muscle-encased neuron tendrils within her hydrodynamic beak. As she swam to the barrier between

the environment and the air, she couldn't shake the prema-
ture shame shadowing her already.

There was no right way to approach this host. If Donn
and Kitchell hadn't explained who they were and why
they fought by now, he was right. They couldn't finish in
time to conform to the lord's expectations of Anjedet's
time table. Especially using the lord's equipment.
Kitchell's descriptions made it sound painfully rudimen-
tary. Once she crossed into the kaxan's human environment, she'd have no mouth, no ears, and no real means of
communication.

This was no way to start a relationship.

She paused at the gel's surface and watched Donn
unscrew the fake canteen's lid and lift the opening to the
forcefield separating them.

Vinnet squirmed in, rubbing her slick skin against the
canteen mouth's smooth sides, and dropped into the
pouch's cushioned interior, which was filled with the same
nutritious gel as the kaxan's symbiont environment.

He screwed the cap in place, activating the electric
current. Knowing everything else kept going wrong, she
prayed to whatever gods she didn't believe in that he
wouldn't accidentally crush her as he killed the queen.

ROCKEFELLER'S FINGERS shook as he dialed his home
number. Colonel Marshall's phone shivered against his ear.
If something happened to him...

He'd always felt he was the stronger, more adaptable
one, despite calling her his anchor and her criticism of his
handling of change. She'd latched onto him more passion-
ately than he had ever dreamed possible. He was her only,

and as horrible as he'd been told it would be, he prayed he'd outlive her. She'd shut down if something happened to him.

If he went out there, opened himself to harm…

She was an adult. She'd survive, because she had to, right? For the girls.

He had to bring Maggie home.

She answered on the third ring, just when he swore the answering machine would pick up. "Rockefellers."

When had his wife ever sounded so drained?

He wet his lips and leaned harder on the desk. "Joyce. It's me. I know where she is; I'm going to get her."

"Where?"

Where to begin? Even if he could tell her the truth, she wouldn't believe him. "Charlie's here. He said I shouldn't go, but I have to. If I don't—" He swallowed. "If I don't make it back, tell the girls I love them. And you. I love you, but I have to find her."

"Where is she, Andy?"

"I can't say. But she's out there, and I need to go get her."

"Okay." He could just picture her nodding, eyes closed to shield her panicked gaze. "Okay, bring her home safe. I love you."

"Love you too." It took two tries to get the phone back in the cradle.

He closed his eyes and breathed. Staying wasn't an option, not with Maggie out there alone and in alien hands. He had a chance. He had to go.

Now.

He stormed out of the Colonel's office, back into the decrepit station's decrepit hall, ready to catch a ride off the planet.

He even caught Major Patrick reentering the hanger. "I'm coming with you."

She froze in the middle of fiddling with a pouch on her belt. "Maybe as far as the kaxan."

"The what?"

"You don't even know what it's called; you're not flying out with us."

She turned to go, but he spun her back with a hand on her shoulder. "It's my daughter you're going to get. The Colonel won't get in my way. I recommend you don't, either."

"Or what?"

This again? "Or I will get you out of my way."

"Is that a threat?" Her fingers tightened on the pouch.

"If it needs to be." He stepped back, out of her space. "Or it can be an offer of an extra pair of hands. The remaining women may not be especially rational after being left behind. I can get them organized and moving in the right direction."

Which you obviously need help with. He met her eyes steadily. *You have one option. Take it.*

Blowing her breath out her nose, she snapped the pouch closed. "Fine. We need two kaxan this time, anyway. You can keep me company on the way.

He was going!

Planting her hands on her hips, she raised one eyebrow at him. "You're going in a suit?"

He gazed down at his white Oxford shirt. He'd worn these so much the last several years—okay, eighteen years—he'd come to think of suits as everyday, all-purpose attire. Would he really face off against alien bad guys in formalwear? He hadn't buffed these shoes for rugged terrain.

"There's no time for anything else." He pulled his tie loose, shucked his jacket, and started rolling up his sleeves. A spare jacket could come in handy, anyway.

She nodded to the hangar. "Okay, then. Come on. Fairfeld and Myers should be back any minute."

And they were. They congregated beside the newly arrived ships.

Major Patrick met the mens' curious stares with an acknowledging nod. "Gents, this is Speaker Rockefeller. His daughter is among those we're going back for. We're starting off with two kaxan this time around: you two in that one, the Speaker and me in this one. We'll park close this time— right outside the back door. Myers, you'll watch our rides like last time, and we'll go in for the five women. Any questions?"

The short-haired Fairfeld pointed to Rockefeller. "Why's he coming?"

Did no one want him along?

She ignored him. "Good. Move out."

He climbed into the saucer with her and stood aside while she closed the hatch and settled behind the control screen, where she could lean against the sliver of solid wall.

He spun around, realizing there was nothing else to lean back against. "Where should I sit?"

She waved at the rest of the empty cabin without moving her eyes from the screen.

Anywhere. No back support for him.

He tossed his sport coat aside, hiked his slacks up from his ankles, and lowered himself to the padded floor. He tried not to sit where his shoes had been, then shook his head. Preserving his wardrobe wouldn't help Maggie. He might as well write this suit off now and replace it once she came home safe.

Patrick leaned back from the screen and drew her knees up. "We're on our way."

"I didn't feel anything."

"It's a faster-than-light spaceship. You're not going to feel it take off." She closed her eyes.

He rested his folded hands over his crossed ankles. "Do you feel it jumping to lightspeed or whatever it does?"

"Never noticed." She tipped her head away from him.

Listen to him, asking about jumping to lightspeed in a spaceship. This was crazy. But he was on his way to bring Maggie home from another planet. If there was anything even crazier to throw in for good measure, he'd do it to help her.

"You saw her. Was she okay?" A lump jammed in his throat as he watched the resting woman. "Major?"

She sucked in a breath and opened her eyes. "She and her friend were too astute. The General must have told them something; they said he wanted one of them to host."

"What!"

"Yeah, I'd like to deck him for that. Then I think maybe it's a backup plan: a Gertewet instead of a Kemtewet. But that's not how he started hosting. Kitchell's a bad influence on him."

"Maggie was okay when you saw her?"

Patrick shook her head. "She got hurt on the way to the kaxan. Fairfeld tried to help her, but we needed him up piloting. We didn't know she couldn't keep running."

His heart tried to tear in two. "How bad?"

"When the General caught up, he picked her up and carried her. She looked unconscious." She fussed with the pack on her far side. "I was focused on loading the women who made it. We had to seal up before the guards reached us. Maybe I saw wrong."

Unconscious. Dead? Injured? What if this whole excursion was futile and they had already left too late?

"I saw her on her feet. I think she'll recover."

Rockefeller nodded. He couldn't give up hope yet in case she still needed him.

"We'll get her this time. The good news is that they won't want to use her body like that. She's probably safer than all the others."

"Really?"

"The Colonel told you what they'd want her for, didn't she?"

"To use her body."

"Yeah, well, they wouldn't want bruises or broken bones, so she should be safe."

Safe. Hurt but not possessed. They'd reach her soon, he told himself, and she'd be there when they arrived.

"How long until we get there?" How long until he saw her for himself?

"It's about six hours." She leaned her head back again. "And I'd appreciate some silence for shut eye. I've got an alarm set for about half an hour beforehand."

"Sure." He scooted out from the wall and laid down, careful to avoid the walls. It made sense to sleep; he had no idea how demanding he'd find the excursion. He should rest up on the way.

If he could stop worrying.

He shut his eyes.

"Why her? Do they know about me? Out of all the children in America, how did they know to get her?"

Major Patrick groaned. "They don't. It's just random. I guess they pick a flight path or a point on a map and see who they come across."

Random.

She continued, "The area they took her from. What's it like?"

"She was down the street from our house. It's a subdivision. Big yards and nice-size houses."

"Not a lot of trees?"

"No." Would trees have sheltered her from this?

"Probably looks obviously populated from the aerial view."

And Maggie had been out on the street, visible and vulnerable. If he never let the girls outside again... But how? Joyce would probably dismiss such a thing.

"What if we stopped them from reproducing?" Again, how? "How do they reproduce?"

"I don't know, Mr. Speaker. None of us do. Now, I'm trying to get some shut-eye, so I can operate when we get there. Please be quiet."

He turned his head and tried to rest silently.

13

END OF THE LINE

W ith the fake canteen anchored safely at his belt, Donn Marshall stepped back to the console in Vinnet's kaxan to pull up the teleport controls. He snorted. It wasn't her kaxan anymore; she wasn't back there, invisibly haunting the machine. He moved his elbow away from his belt to keep from bumping her.

The screen highlighted its default choice: the palace's teleport juncture. Bad idea. If he appeared there, the guards would swamp him with questions and suspicions. He'd never get to Anjedet in time. With the building's heavy stone interfering with the transmission though, arriving within line of sight of the juncture—using the juncture's own projectors—would be safest.

He set the destination to halfway up the stairs to the implantation chamber and hoped no one saw him.

The brilliant kaxan interior vanished into the palace stairs' flickering darkness and narrow confines. This hall was dimmer than the rest of the palace, even with its stamped silver walls—all the better to contrast with a potential host's final destination.

Trying to step softly and avoid unwelcome attention, he crested the stairs to find a guard waiting between the two opposing doors on this level. Were they already too late? He couldn't avoid attention now. "*Guten Tag*, Davon."

Davon snapped to alertness and clasped his hands first in front then behind him. "*Herr Kommandant*, she should be getting dressed. I've been waiting a while, and I'm not sure what's taking so long. Should I see?"

Not too late. Yet. "You want to scare her with your ugly mug?"

His face fell blank. "Say, you were going to hold her and come right back. Where did you go?"

Three more steps. "I remembered something I had to do." No way that could resolve well.

"The recharge cycle—"

Donn elbowed him in the gut then captured the kid's head as he doubled over and slammed a knee into the kid's cranium. Hard. He eased Davon's limp body to the floor. Maybe no one heard that.

Maybe you'd better move fast, Kitchell answered.

He nudged open the door on the left and dragged Davon in by the arm. Stepping from the dim, echoing corridor into the silent implantation chamber's cheery light felt like stepping into the peace of heaven, and he fought the impression by reminding himself of the room's purpose: easing the Kemtewet's effort to imprison its human vassal.

He blocked the doors closed with Davon's body, which would only slow the generally unsuspecting guards.

If the Kemtewet had perfected one skill, it was the use of art to manipulate emotion; the room was built equally around utility and beauty. With high, arching ceilings embellished with precious metals, the implantation chamber could have functioned as a stately ballroom, if only it had an actual floor. Instead, narrow walkways spread out from either side of the platform on which he knelt and traced the circumference of the room's deep pool. Somewhere in the many cubic yards of symbiont gel lived the queen, an amphibious Kemtewet parasite a foot and a half long that used the human reproductive system to bear young parasites. No sane person would mourn her loss, especially given the credibility it would lend Vinnet's cover while infiltrating the Central Palace.

One other object occupied the room: a reclined chair, held at the gel's surface by submerged machinery, with arm restraints and a long opening along the occupant's spine.

"Rise, Vassal, and explain why you disrupt my rest," the queen's recorded voice demanded. Subtle changes in pitch and harmony would have suggested to an unaugmented human listener that obeying would bring him joy.

Marshall noticed the attempted influence with passing interest, glad that Kitchell negated the compulsions in her voice. He paused on the platform, waiting for Kitchell to take control. The whole death sentence thing struck Marshall as a foolhardy waste of time, but if the symbiont insisted, he could damn well do it himself.

When the symbiont had control, Marshall watched as his body knelt at the pool's edge and anchored one end of a long wire below the viscous gel's surface. Then Kitchell straightened Marshall's body, addressing the queen in his own harmonics-enhanced voice while he navigated the ledge around the pool's circumference. "For the unethical enslavement and casual murder of twelve different vassals; for the execution of over three hundred rejected vassals and over twenty-seven hundred servants, both human and

Kemtewet; for the perpetuation of Kemtewet; and for the poisoning of the population of the planet Prónoia in an unprovoked strike against the Mirach Bulk Trade Alliance; for these crimes and others, the Gertewet Coordinating Council has condemned you to death by any available means." He stopped at the back of the chamber and dropped the weighted end of a second wire into the environment.

"This does not please me." Though the recording shouted in discordant tones, Kitchell suspected what she wanted to say had not been pre-recorded.

He touched the wires to a high-voltage capacitor, sending a deadly shock through the conductive environment and the queen's soft, vulnerable body. The cloudy gel flashed solid white. As it slowly cleared, it revealed a long, legless amphibian drifting toward the surface, its neuron tendrils flapping limply in the gel's drag.

Assured that the capacitor had already spent its lethal charge, he twisted off the cap of the canteen-disguised symbiont environment and released Vinnet into the queen's chamber. The six-inch, blue-and-green-striped symbiont splashed into the gel and swam about, stretching, then approached the dead body and nudged it all the way to the pool's edge. Nodding his thanks, Kitchell scooped the dead amphibian from the pool and squished it into the canteen, forcing most of the gel from within it. The queen's body barely fit; the threads on the cap kept it from flopping free of the container.

Replacing the canteen at his belt, Kitchell smiled at Vinnet's small head, which poked above the gel's surface, bobbing slightly as she was treading water. "It won't be long now. I promise."

She couldn't understand his words without the mechanical intervention the queen used; she dove beneath the surface, and he turned back to other problems: an unconscious body and a girl slated to host.

We can still free her. Banebdjedet will find other hosts.

We can't leave Vinnet exposed that long. Kitchell hefted Davon's twig-like body. *Besides, since you admitted guilt here, we have only limited time remaining. It has to be her.*

He peeked into the empty hall and then breezed into the closet-sized dressing room Davon purported to have left Sarah in.

It looked empty: just the dressed mannequin and shoes Anjedet's borrowed handmaidens left here. When the door shut, spotlights snapped on, glinting on the dress, and Kitchell turned to see Sarah scrunched in the corner, frozen, a scared little four-eyed kid curled up impossibly small.

Sighing, he slung Davon into the other corner, likewise hidden from the doorway, and shucked the dress off the mannequin.

———

SARAH HELD her breath when the door opened and Mr. Marshall barged in with her guard, the crime-faced one, thrown over his shoulder. He'd killed someone else now? Where had he gone in such a hurry? Was she next?

He saw her and sighed, then threw the body aside. Stepping to the mannequin, he pulled the dress off and tossed it at her. He didn't look like himself; he looked irritated. She let the dress lay where it landed, half-wrapped around her folded legs.

"Put it on. Quickly. I won't look." He leaned his ear against the door and raised his eyebrows at her expectantly.

"I don't want this! I'm not going to do it!"

He frowned at the door then crouched down in front of her. "Sarah, there is no getting out of this. If you don't dress yourself, it will be done for you. And if you don't take this symbiont, they'll kill you like they did the women downstairs."

He pushed the dress to the floor and put his hands over hers, staring into her eyes. They couldn't have been the same eyes that met hers in the white room; they looked cold. "I can't promise you everything will be okay, but I can promise I've done all I could."

She jerked her hands back and pressed harder against the wall.

"I've got to go." He stood again, listening at the door. Even Sarah could hear faint boot steps echoing in the hall. Then Mr. Marshall nodded at the body. "Dress before Davon wakes up."

He let himself out, and she followed.

Footsteps climbed up the stairs the guard had carried her up earlier. Mr. Marshall walked the other way, which made sense. He obviously had something to hide from them, and so did she—herself.

He noticed halfway down the stairs at the hall's far end. Wide-eyed, he whispered, "What are you doing?"

She wiped her itching eyes. "Getting out."

"They'll kill you!"

She squeezed past him, but he grabbed her arm. She jerked away, but his tight grip pinched harder. "Let go!"

Voices rang upstairs, and they both froze. Somebody heard her.

"Neith burning at the stake," he muttered, and pulled her back up the stairs.

"No, you can't do this! Stop! Let go!"

Two guards came running and met them at the top. Mr.

Marshall shouldered through, dragging her along. "*Ich habe sie gefunden. Was haben Sie getan?*"

And right there, in front of everyone, he shoved her back in the little room, barking, "Dress!"

She hugged herself, watching the unconscious guard for signs he'd wake up. Mr. Marshall's voice rang in her head: "Dress before he wakes up. They'll do it for you. There is no getting out."

Their voices carried on in the hall right outside. Give in to this and get an alien implanted? Or make them dress her and get an alien implanted?

No, just because he said she had no choice didn't make it true. With them outside the only door, what else could she do? Anything besides wait?

She eyed the apparently only unconscious guard, still armed and armored. That was a start.

Steeling herself, she crept up. The way Mr. Marshall said it, he'd awaken in an instant and start trying to rip her clothes off, but she'd never seen anyone snap awake and focus that quickly.

He groaned.

Just kidding. Better be fast.

It took a minute to find the armor's clasps, and she had to move his arm out of the way to reveal that they not only buckled in three places along his sides but also integrated with the piece under his back, tight enough to flex and settle with his lungs. If she wanted to get it off, she'd have to roll him over somehow. It would take forever.

Not so with his short sword/long knife thing.

It slid easily from its scabbard, despite the weird, widening sweep at the end. With a two-handed clutch, she rested it at her shoulder like a baseball bat, ready to swing, and she quivered.

She didn't really want to hurt anyone, but to get them to stay out of her way. Could she hit someone if she had to?

She swallowed.

Then she lined up with the door, angled a bit to aim her blade-sharp bat, and kicked it before she lost her nerve.

A guard swung the door in, so Sarah closed her eyes and swung for his broad belly. He screamed.

Cracking her eyes open and avoiding his gushing arm, she darted into the hall, raising her improvised bat again. With Mr. Marshall to the right, she ran left, back the way she'd come. Besides, she knew how to get out that way: down through the tiled room, left past the lattice door to the stone gathering room, and right through the servants' hall to the exit. After that, she had only to run.

As she pounded down the stairs, Mr. Marshall followed. He started yelling something, cut himself off, then repeated, finishing. To whom?

Tightening her grip in case she needed her sword-bat, she shot down the last few stairs into the tiled room and came face-to-armor with one of the guards.

Sarah backpedaled, swinging.

He sidestepped, waited for her swing to pass, and swooped in. He caught her backswing on his armor and clamped onto her wrist.

If she didn't get out now...

She popped up, folded her knees, and twisted her arm, trying to jerk her wrist from his grasp with all her weight. It almost worked.

Until something caught her under her still-sore ribs. She swung her free elbow back to smack into someone who didn't seem to care. She snapped her head back into a chin and glimpsed Mr. Marshall's gruff face.

As he lifted her off the ground, she kept hold of the

sword the other guard tried to pry from her grasp and kicked out at him with both feet. Mr. Marshall rocked back with her, stretching the arm the other guy jerked.

He peeled her fingers back, and she grabbed the hilt with her other hand. Between the two of them, they pried it from her, leaving her struggling against Mr. Marshall's immovable arms. She tried kicking, elbowing, even scratching his eyes like with the first guy, but these two were ready for it. Mr. Marshall ducked his head and growled out something at the other guard, who caught hold of her feet and helped cart her back up the stairs.

"No!" She screeched as loudly and shrilly as she could manage. She'd gotten so far—all the way downstairs, halfway back to Maggie and halfway back to the white room where she'd first heard of all this insanity. She screamed her frustration and watched the guard with her feet wince.

The guard she'd hit with the sword waited for them in the upstairs hallway, his shirt tied around his bloody arm. Well, good, she hadn't wanted to kill anybody, but...

For a moment, she used the second guard's lock on her legs to push herself up in Mr. Marshall's grasp and smack his chin harder with her head.

"*Das genügt!*" He shouted something at the bloody-armed guard, even as the man shied away, and he captured her hands as they passed and walked with them.

She tried bicycle-kicking as they approached the closet door. She pictured them starting to undress her and tried exploding her limbs out then in to knock them off. They either moved with her or jerked her to a stop. They reached the doors—

And turned into the opposite ones, pushing open the golden doors facing the closet. An oppressive wave of humid air washed over her. They marched her into the room's glaring brightness, where a gigantic pool filled the expansive space. A single, reclined chair sat on a pedestal at the edge, wholly above the water, slit down the center.

Her destination? She kicked harder, screaming, the whole way over.

It took all three to strap her into the chair. The guy from downstairs lay across her legs to hold one arm. Mr. Marshall held the other while the man from upstairs anchored ratcheting metal clamps around her wrists.

She squirmed down and bit his arm as hard as her jaw could close. He jumped back. Mr. Marshall took over, and she bit him, too, for good measure. He ignored her, tightening the wrist strap to an unchallengeable pressure. He held her down while repeating with her other arm.

"You lied to me!" she shouted at him. "Liar!"

He refused to look at her face. The man from downstairs strapped down her ankles and stepped back.

Mr. Marshall drew his own funky sword.

She shut her mouth. The room reflected on the glinting blade. He stepped behind her.

Oh crap oh crap oh crap.

Implantation started with a sword? She squeezed her eyes shut and screamed.

The blade started at her collar and rent the back of her shirt in ginger rips like dull scissors through wrapping paper. She kept screaming, waiting for it to slip and slice into her skin.

It didn't.

Mr. Marshall reached the end of her shirt without cutting her. Then he reached between the arm rest and chair back and tugged at it, pulling the edges apart to leave her spine bare. Open to the air. Open to sight. Open to the murky water.

Sarah blinked her eyes open, and a shadow swept by the pool's edge, under the surface.

"There's something there! What is that?"

Mr. Marshall still wouldn't look her in the face. He grumbled something to the other two, who left. Then his hand slipped down onto her shoulder, squeezing it, and whispered, "You're going to be okay."

"But what is that?"

"Don't worry about it. You're going to be fine." He squeezed her shoulder again and walked away.

Something was there in the water. She knew what it had to be. "No, don't go! Don't leave me in here with that!"

He reached the door without looking back, held it open for the other guards to carry in the mannequin, dress, and shoes, and slipped out.

"Don't leave me here alone!"

They ignored her, set up the clothes just like they had been across the hall, and left. The guy she'd hit glanced back at her on his way out, smug.

The doors closed, and the room fell into an expectant silence; only her panicked breathing echoed back in the dome.

She craned her neck to look into the pool, but she was at the wrong angle and could see only the surface out near the walls. She'd have to turn around and look over the edge of the chair to see deeper—if she could have moved.

She squeezed her eyes shut and waited. Any moment now, it would attack. She tried to get ready for it, but how? She wasn't ready to die.

The chair jerked, and she shrieked. But it was like an amusement park ride jerking as it began to move. It drifted steadily over the pool, farther and farther from the door and the safe, dry walkway, leaving only ripples to indicate its passage. She didn't see anyone controlling it.

The chair stopped directly below the domed ceiling's apex, and the waves it caused lapped against the pool's edges then subsided into silence.

Her ragged sobs echoed in the dome. This was it: her and the alien. Good alien, bad alien. Did it matter? Her back was wide open to it. Her tears dribbled from her face to the chair.

Something moved in the corner of her eye.

14

THE END

They left Sarah here, all alone with the big, empty room and something in the water.

Her spine was uncovered, wide open for it to jump up and attack. Shaking, crying, she twisted her wrists in the shackles and pulled, stretching her joints like they weren't meant to. The edges bit into the flesh of her hand, but she had to get out. She had to! She bent her elbows, trying to pry it open with the lever of her arm bones.

She leaned forward, pulling her back up from the reclined chair and letting her ripped shirt flop free. The way the chair tilted, with her wrists pinned in place, she couldn't sit right, and she had to hold herself up with abs and arms. At least the shackles gave her something to pull against. She took gymnastics, but she hated ab exercises—v-ups were her nemesis. How any reasonable human being could be expected to lie on her back and raise her straight legs and straight arms together was beyond her.

Now, she wished she'd done more. If she'd known this was going to happen, she'd have trained harder. She'd have done v-ups every night before bed. She'd have trained until she could hold it for hours.

Already, the tremors started to course across her stomach muscles. She pulled harder on the shackles, trying to take up the load with her arms. That was her other weakness. Her buff shoulders and strong legs got her through floor and uneven bar routines.

Nightly v-ups *and* push-ups if she'd known.

A tiny head crested the water halfway from her to the wall, far enough out that she could see it comfortably, even if she weren't holding herself up. Her breath hitched.

Here it came. The end.

Any time now, it would dart across the water and rip into her back. She knew she should look away; it'd be easier not to see it coming. But she couldn't. She couldn't help but watch its every move.

It stilled, its limbless body waving gently under the surface, keeping it from sinking. It watched her. Its tiny, black eyes peered out from a snakelike head striped bright blue and green like a neon earthworm.

It was an animal, but Mr. Marshall didn't talk about it like one. She studied its eyes, trying to figure it out. Was it really intelligent? Self-aware? Malicious?

Or was it just an animal? Could she hold her hand out the right way, let it sniff, and go about her business?

Its opaque, sclera-free eyes revealed nothing. It was blank to her in a way her dogs never were, in a way her friends' otherwise indecipherable cats never were. Like a spider or a scorpion, its intentions unknowable.

Except one thing: it wanted a body.

She pulled harder on the arm shackles, trying to get her abs to quit trembling. She needed to be still. Maybe it could only see motion. She held her breath, too, in case it hunted by sound.

This couldn't be happening.

She choked back a moan. Quiet. Try to confuse it. Try to reason around it.

It didn't look smart. It was just an animal, patient and watchful, like a cat outside a mouse hole or an owl above the forest floor. Like a terrier outside a rabbit den. Maybe not that.

It stared back, bobbing while treading water, its mind hidden and unfathomable.

And it was *not* getting her.

It was so small, though. It looked like it could fit in her palm. A little thing like that surely couldn't just jump out of the water and into her back. First, it'd have to cross from the water to the chair—a bigger gap for it than for her—then between the chair and her back. If it stayed in the gap, it had nothing to push against to break through her skin. And if it did squirm in between the chair and her, maybe she could squish it.

It started forward.

She screamed. Her eyes scrunched closed, and she clung to the shackles. Her abs stopped shaking—now she really meant it! That thing was coming, and this was all she could do to stop it.

Not that it would be enough. This was their planet. Everything else they'd wanted to happen had. Obviously, they didn't think this would be a problem.

It was going to get her.

She squeezed in another breath. She screamed louder.

And when her voice ran out, her sobs choked on the incoming air. Nothing else happened. No one else came, and yet she was still okay.

She cracked her eyes open, and the creature was still where she last saw it.

It bobbed slightly closer, but its eyes stayed eerily trained. Pointing. Piercing. Something in the tilt of its neck made her think it wasn't just watching her but signaling—whether to her or to something else, she couldn't tell.

But she definitely held the spotlight of its attention.

It was still going to get her.

Scorching self-consciousness crept up her spine, setting every nerve on edge. What if it wasn't the only predatory neck lump here? What if, while it floated out where she could see it, another lurked beneath?

Another moan escaped her. Her arms started shaking with her abs; she couldn't keep this up forever. Was that what it waited for? Was she really too far away? She kept straining.

And it kept staring. Silent. Intent. Expectant. As if it wanted something else from her, too.

She couldn't take it anymore. "What are you waiting for?"

It cocked its flattened head.

"Can you even understand me?"

It swam closer.

Her heart pounded in her ears, echoing the alarm in her head. This was it. She was done for.

It darted to the side. It swam to the edge of her vision and back along some arbitrary perimeter, as if it wanted to get closer but couldn't. Crisis averted for now.

She leaned back for just a moment. Her abs ached. Her arms were cramped. Her wrists were on fire. Her eyes anchored on the little alien snake, because this was its chance. She knew that. It had to know that. It was fast, and it might be able to reach her before her weary muscles could lever her back up.

It stilled, retreated to where she could see it without straining, and waited.

Was it toying with her? Did it actually care? Was she anthropomorphizing too much? If it was just an animal, its hesitation didn't make sense. If it was intelligent, she still didn't get it.

"I don't know what you are or what you're planning to do." It couldn't understand her; it watched her because she made noises. "Or why I'm even trying to talk to you."

It stared, still blank.

She could stop embarrassing herself. *Serves me right for talking to it. It's not like this is going to get better.*

The silence hung as heavy as the humid air. Without circulating water or humming pumps—or the sound of distant, milling people so constant in the halls—her every breath, every grunt, every cry echoed back, somehow unattenuated in the thick, rank air. No one was coming. No one would answer.

She pushed her hands farther through the shackles, relieving her bloody wrists, and tried to think. It could have come at her by now. It certainly had the chance.

But it didn't. The one time it disappeared, it surfaced far out, like it would have if it hadn't approached her at all, and she didn't think it had. Whatever this was about, whatever was happening, it wasn't dangling Sarah-meat in front of a ravaging beast.

What then?

She leaned toward it, trying to both see and get more comfortable. She could see, at least.

In response, it rose farther out of the water, tail twitching furiously to keep it afloat and balanced. It hung its head over, nose pointing at its belly, somehow still looking at her.

Was that neck lump trying to pull off puppy dog eyes?

Did it expect pity? The nerve! "You think you have it rough? You didn't just watch a bunch of people get murdered. You didn't get carried out of your house and left behind when the Air Force came to rescue you. You're not going to get some alien slug shoved into your neck. It's not like you're never going home again!"

Oh, crap.

That sounded so much worse out loud. She was never going home. She was never going to see Mom and Dad again. Or her dog. She couldn't just hold out for spring break, when it would all be better, because she'd fly back to South Carolina and see Kat and Lindsay again. Whatever happened, she'd be stuck out here, vulnerable, stranded away from everything familiar and safe. Forever.

Her throat clamped up, and tears blurred her view of the creature. She heard a plunk as the first one fell, and she blinked her eyes clear long enough to see it settled back in the water, relaxed instead of pitiful.

It didn't care. What could it know about family? About missing people and being missed? What could it know about needing to belong and needing to stand out special?

And what would she know after it took over her?

Oh God oh God oh God.

Would she even know? If there was any mercy in the world, maybe she could be comatose or unaware in her hijacked body.

Or maybe it wouldn't happen at all. The thing showed interest in her for sure, but it hadn't threatened her yet. Maybe that whole puppy-dog-eyes thing was an apology. It was a good neck lump, and it was going to leave her alone!

It waved its head at her and then swam a slow, wide arc around the front of the chair, past her feet, around the other side and behind her. She twisted to follow, getting visions of it ducking under and gunning for her back.

When it reached the edge of her vision, she snapped the other way and watched it finish its shark-like circle. Back in its original spot, it cocked its head and peered at her.

Its circle and intent focus convinced her it was asking a question. It had maintained its pantomimed distance so far, but who knew how long that would last? Clearly, it wanted to come closer, but it was doing the unthinkable: asking permission.

Why?

It wasn't like she was going to say yes. As Mom always said, school sucked right now, but she'd be free of it eventually. It wasn't worth dying over—or trading her body for. Ew, no. If it thought she might agree, it was as delusional as Mr. Marshall.

Wait.

They were on the same side. This was one of his "good aliens." She couldn't scoff at that now; it could have attacked her a dozen times already, and she could easily picture how other ones would have. What else was an open-backed chair with wrist- and ankle-clamps good for? And what was the point if you were going to ask for permission?

Especially permission that wasn't coming.

Why even bother?

Because it's polite. The answer popped into her head, and she almost dismissed it as not applying to aliens. But darn it, why not? It was her body, and using it without asking was slavery. It was rape. It was wrong anywhere that people *had* bodies, not just in her culture or on her planet. If these things had to use bodies—and they must not, because that one looked like it survived just fine in that water—the one very least little thing they could do was ask—

Mr. Marshall did ask her.

—and then respect the answer.

The thing in the water cocked its green and blue head the other way. Asking permission? Waiting for an answer?

"I already told Mr. Marshall no. I don't want something living in me."

It blinked.

"How come you can ask permission but can't understand me? What good does that do? We're just going to sit here in a stalemate until someone comes along and lets me out!"

How long would that be? A couple hours? Days? Then what? They wouldn't take her home, but maybe they'd let her work in the palace. Being herself as a slave was still better than being possessed, right?

The thing dunked under the water.

Sarah levered herself back up.

Slave or possessed? She honestly couldn't picture herself as either. All she knew was at least as a slave, you still had options. You could still make your own choices and look for a way out.

The alien leapt into the air, and she slammed forward, bent over her wrists.

As it splashed back down, she realized it wasn't attacking; it was right where it had been before. It resurfaced, splashing about like the end of the world.

Something was wrong.

She studied the door, but it stayed closed. The creature swam around to where she looked and kept splashing. Not company, then. Was it something she said? What was that? That all she had to do was wait. If she could just hold out for them to come back...

These people killed three adults after chasing them down and keeping them from going home. Would they seriously put in the effort to show her how to be a palace servant if she weaseled her way out of this?

She focused on the frantic neck lump kicking up froth between her and the door. This was all starting to look even worse.

"Hey! Listen!"

She didn't think it would work, but the thing settled down, regarding her intently.

"Nod your head up and down if the answer is yes." Sarah swallowed. The moment she put this in words, she could never take it back. She didn't want to know the answer, but she had to ask. She stared into its beady, blank eyes. "Are they going to kill me if you don't get implanted?"

It waited a few moments, still staring, then dove back under.

And now she'd said it.

The more she thought about it, the less she wanted to believe it, and the more she thought it true. The four-armed man seemed to kill the adults to spite the others' escape. That was before his queen was remotely involved. What might he do if she thwarted the queen?

Broken neck. Stabbing. Sliced artery. The adults had all died quickly.

The creature resurfaced in the same spot, and she held her breath. Maybe it hadn't understood her. Maybe she was completely off base.

It hung its head, dipping the tip of its nose back in the water. Then, unmistakably, it nodded.

They would kill her.

It looked up, met her eyes, and nodded again.

One way or another, they were going to kill her. And if

losing most of the Earth women had pissed off the alien overlord, losing half of the remainder had to bring out his cruelest side. He wasn't going to just kill her; he'd kill her in the worst way he could imagine. No doubt his imagination outmatched hers in this regard.

She didn't want a knife at her throat. She didn't want to know what it was like to have it slice in and open her arteries. Or what it was like to futilely clamp her fingers over the top and feel her blood gush through. Or worse.

Then again, she didn't want to know what it was like for an alien to jam itself into her neck, either. She didn't want to lose control.

But was it a fate worse than death? In detached words, it seemed like it should be. The nothingness of death had to be better than living possessed.

What if it wasn't? She could always die later, but she'd never be able to un-die.

Damned, stupid alien abduction.

Sarah's vision blurred, and she cried. Sobs shook her shoulders, her body. She didn't want to decide. She shouldn't have to make this decision. She was too young for this. It wasn't fair.

That didn't matter. It just was.

She coughed out the next sob. A river of tears squeezed out and down her cheeks. She felt cold, even in the hot, humid room. Emptiness filled her like a lance to the heart, an all-enveloping hollowness sucking out every piece of her identity.

It didn't matter how well she read or what books she liked. She'd left them all on another planet. And when the thing took over, she'd never be able to decide to read, not after school or over the weekend or under her desk in class.

It didn't matter where she came from. She'd never be

able to prove to her school or classmates that girls from the South could be just as smart and creative as anyone else. That thing would be the only intelligence anyone saw of her.

It didn't matter whether she tried to blend with the popular crowd or stood on her own and followed her own path, like she promised she would. She wouldn't have her own path anymore. Just the thing's—first, foremost, and forever. Everything she ever stood for or believed or wanted would never matter, because it would never come to fruition.

She stopped breathing. How much easier it would be to pop out of existence without actually dying, without actually making a choice. She couldn't do this. She couldn't decide between dying and ceasing.

The urge to breathe took over, so she sucked air in but not out. She couldn't cry like this, and the water in her eyes blinked away. The creature floated closer now. It drifted nearer, saw her watching it, and stopped. It looked sad somehow.

She didn't get it. It was the bad guy. It wanted to possess her, wipe out everything of who she was. Why should it look sad? Why should it freak out that she might die? After all, Maggie was still around. Sarah wasn't the last. It still had another chance, unlike her. Why should it care?

But it did.

If it were just afraid that she would die, all it had to do was take over her. It didn't have to keep its distance. With a chair like this, it didn't have to ask her. It knew her choices were it and death. How bad was this going to be if even it didn't think Sarah should welcome it?

"I don't want to die," slipped through her lips as the

pent-up air escaped. That didn't mean she wanted anything else, but she knew that much. "I don't want to die."

It inched closer and nudged the air, as if raising its chin or pointing at her. Asking again.

If that were all she really wanted, not dying, there was only one way this could go. It knew that. She knew that. She squeezed her burning eyes shut.

Was there a fate worse than death?

A lot of people thought so, or there wouldn't be martyrs. There wouldn't be suicide.

But she didn't believe that.

Not yet.

She squeezed the armrests like she might break them in half. It hurt, but she didn't stop. Not deciding meant she still got to exist, but it also meant the guards might come back and kill her. Not deciding was letting someone else decide—and it wasn't the someone who'd been keeping its distance and hanging on her every word.

"I don't want to die." She rubbed her eyes on her shoulders the best she could and leaned forward, looking down into that little snake face, those beady alien eyes. She tried to sound sure this time. "I don't want to die!"

It started to lean like it would dive, but she shook her head. They were not dragging this out. "Do—" She swallowed, but as much as she didn't like the answer, she'd made up her mind. There was no getting out of this.

"Do it."

It dove away.

She was alone.

Her heart pounded in her ears. Her ragged breaths rang out, magnified here at the dome's focus. This had to be fast, before the guards came back, or there would be no point.

From nowhere, a woman's voice started talking. Sarah

thought it was still in German, like everything else here, but its pretty, soft consonants paired with melodic vowels crooned pleasantly, a lullaby in the form of a poem. No one else was here. The room was empty, but it must have had speakers.

She lay back in the chair as the woman spoke. She'd told it to do this. She couldn't keep resisting until the creature decided she was too much effort and left her to be killed anyway. She had to do this. She had to leave her bare spine lined up with the chair's open slit, exposed and ready to be attacked at any moment. Her nerves burned with anticipation.

And fear. She'd never been afraid of something she knew would happen before. Except moving, but that didn't count. It didn't physically hurt. She'd never been afraid like this, not even when they took her. She kept squeezing the armrests. Her knees bent, pressing her feet against the lower shackles. She couldn't help it.

"I don't want to die."

The water's murky surface turned crystal clear, and she couldn't see the creature. Was she supposed to? Why else would it be clear? She leaned over the edge, trying to find it. She thought she did. There was something bright blue at the bottom, but it was the wrong shape, like one end was split open. Maybe it was somewhere else.

She leaned back in place, trying to be ready, when the chair started sinking.

She was right. The gap was too big.

Here it came.

Was it going to drown her? Her back hit the surface, and the warm water slid up along her spine, up her neck, and stopped below her ears. It soaked into her shirt and jeans and underwear.

She squeezed her eyes shut.

OhGodOhGodOhGod it could reach her. It didn't have to jump. It didn't risk getting squished. It couldn't miss. It could swim right up and touch her.

The woman's voice continued, steady and slow, melodic and peaceful, as if she didn't have a care in the world.

Sarah did. She had exactly one. This had to work, because she did not want to die.

It stabbed into her neck.

The thing wriggled and squirmed for purchase. All she could think was betrayal. It was killing her after all.

Pain blocked out all else. The knife turned sideways and ripped toward her skull. Her skin tugged taut and throbbed. Tendrils split apart and wrapped around her head and into it. More jabbed into her neck, reaching for her windpipe from the inside.

The wriggling shifted.

Her world throbbed into darkness.

15

DREAMS

Residential food-grade micro-teleporting assemblers cost about as much as a down payment on a really cheap vassal. Katorin picked one up to further deter Cube Head from his vassal-pushing tendencies ("No, Paul, I really can't afford it now.") and for its aesthetically-pleasing paperweight properties as she "forgot" it at her workstation until nightfall.

Of course, back inside the following evening, she beelined for the maintenance panel instead. This time, she noticed handles on the panel's back, which were perfect for setting it in place from within the hidden passage.

A weight lifted as she sealed herself and her host into solitude and set up her pocket light. She moaned in relief. *Just you and me now. We can be ourselves. No more Beryl.*

You and me and Khonsu's notes.

Katorin smirked.

The passage was just wide enough for her to walk through and ran along the outer wall of the building, sloping down at a slight angle. As if it were too good to be true and she needed reassurance, she slipped her fingers

gently across the passage's even sides, though the roughness
of the artificial stone caught at her fingertips.

It seemed like she had been walking forever, the walls
sliding soothingly under her touch. If she kept walking all
night, the passage would probably be safe enough to sleep
in. She felt her eyelids droop and her host's rapt attention
ebb.

The wall on the left ended in thin air, the one on the
right at a wall facing her, and she turned to follow the corridor's bend, half hoping that she had arrived but doubting it.

On her next step, her heel slipped out from under her.

Her pocket light bounced free, cracked, and flicked out.

Scheisse!

Her back raced across the smooth floor—ramp? Slide?

Stop. Stop. Stop. She pushed over onto her stomach and
felt seams rushing along her body. She clawed at them,
wrenching her nailbeds and snapping nails. *We're going
to die!*

We're not going to die. Haven't you ever gone down a slide?

Her fingers burned. It didn't work. *Have you ever gone
down a Kemtewet slide? We're going to die!*

Her panicked wheezes echoed back. She laced her
fingers over the back of Setira's neck, trying to protect both
her host's spine and her own tiny body. She curled tight. *I
love you.*

No, this can't— Setira's mind jolted from thought to
thought, never finishing. It settled on *I love you, too.*

They splashed into a puddle at the bottom.

Katorin fought to sit up, even as they slid across a pool of
oil. Finally stilled, she focused on breathing. They could
have died. It could have ended in spikes or venomous
snakes or a flat wall or—

Or cleaning bots.

She couldn't help it. She laughed aloud, monitors be damned. Stupid nerves. They were supposed to be burnt out by now.

This is going well, Setira commented. *No one will ever be able to tell we were snooping around tonight.*

At least they won't know where. Katorin relaxed back against the slide, trying half-heartedly to keep her hair out of the slick goo. She didn't think it worked. *Okay, Mastermind, your age-old companion needs a few minutes off the hook and seeks your recommendation.*

Setira didn't return the sarcasm but focused on one point in their field of vision. *Is that a light?*

Katorin noticed the dim strip a few stories above that resembled light escaping from under a door. With all she'd seen, she doubted the trap's designer had accidentally left such an obvious exit. Sighing softly, she carefully pushed herself to her feet and navigated to the wall below the light. When she tentatively placed her hands against the wall, she found one of the last things she expected: the wide rungs of an easy-to-climb ladder waited to rescue her from the goop.

Can we not go that way? Setira pleaded.

Whoever designed this, I don't think he was the violent sort. Katorin mounted the rungs, taking extra time to make sure she had a solid grip on each one.

What will they say of us if we die by walking into a fellow Gertewet's trap?

Considering they won't know what happened, they'll probably say we died bravely in battle. In Katorin's experience, that was what they usually said, disregarding how rare battle was.

But I'll know.

And who are you going to tell?

I'll tell you that you decided to ignore the designer's bright, flashing warning signs.

As she neared the top, Katorin rolled her eyes. When her hand settled on the ledge over the ladder, a large section of the wall above slid aside to reveal a relatively well-lit maintenance closet, half-empty of the nocturnal cleaning robots. Hip-high and squat, two of the machines flanked the door, floor-scrubber laser sensors crossing her path. Each blew out a continual breath of filtered air by their midsection grills and, on either side of the window-buffing top extension, held its high-pressure surface spray arm and empty fixture maintenance arm at the ready. The latter was especially startling, as the red lighting glinted off the extension's sharp, slender, metal digits.

They were just bots. Every attachment had a designated, rational purpose. They cleaned. They fixed. They couldn't be possessed—by dead Ger or even living Kem.

Katorin imagined that the red glint on the sharp maintenance extension had become blood slicked across its polished surfaces. She suspected the rogue killing bot problem hadn't been solved.

Glad she'd climbed only high enough to peek over the edge, she withdrew her hand, and the door shut, leaving the tiny strip of faint light. She leaned forward to examine it, wondering why she couldn't see the floor on the other side. Then she noticed that the door did, in fact, lie flush with the floor; an extra lighting filament was embedded in the ledge. Too obvious indeed. She climbed back down.

And so she lived to fight another day and to maybe trust her host's intuitions.

Maybe. But it hasn't happened yet. As she placed her weight on the bottom rung, the lubricant her shoe had left earlier caused her foot to slide out from under her. She scraped her chin on the wall on her way down, but caught herself on her elbows in the slimy goo.

Setira cringed as the lubricant seeped into her clothes. *Yup. No one could ever guess we did something out of the ordinary.*

Then think of an out-of-the-ordinary reason for our appearance, and while you do, I'll keep looking for any sign of Khonsu. Deciding she had nothing to lose while she was already goopy, she ran her fingers along the slide's bottom and then started feeling the sides. She struck gold near the opposite wall, on the half of the slide that began her deceleration. A small portal in the slide opened moments after she applied a light pressure around the rim.

Here we go again, Katorin thought, stepping through. She passed the edge of a ramp formed by the open hatch, and it closed behind her, tripping a circuit that turned on a single light that faintly touched the far walls of the cavern.

The metallic curve of the slide jutted out from one of the cavern's four straight, regular walls. Artificial walls, built around the prize ahead of her: a freestanding building in the artificial cave in the food engineering facility's foundation.

Staring up at two stories with solar panels and small, round windows, Katorin collapsed to her knees, breathless. It couldn't be. It couldn't still exist. But there it stood, preserved exactly the way she remembered: a window on either side of the door, three windows unevenly spaced upstairs. And a tiny front deck big enough for the hostess and two guests.

Khonsu's prize—the house where the Gertewet began.

KITCHELL EXCUSED himself while the suspicious guards focused on Sarah—first to snap Davon's neck, now that he'd played his role with Sarah, then to move the other girl to safety.

Couldn't we have traded her for Sarah?

Why? Kitchell hit the bottom of the stairs at the teleport juncture, nodded to the operator, and blew through toward the holding room. *She has no less value than Sarah. We've contributed to this either way, and we'll have to live with that. At least Sarah had time to adjust to the idea.*

They'd found her crying in a corner before trying to run away. *You call that adjusted?*

Of course not. He opened the anteroom. *She hasn't finished.*

Neither have I.

Please. There's a distinction between facing a change and continuing to develop a relationship.

The anteroom's inner door opened to a deserted space. There was no sign of the other girl between the entrance they stood in and the back wall, where his men had cornered her and Sarah. Perhaps around the sides? Behind furniture?

"*Herr Kommandant?*" The teleport juncture operator stopped behind him. "Are you looking for something?"

"The girl who was left here." Kitchell rested Donn's hands together at the small of his back and regarded the sandy-haired youth as if the answer barely mattered.

He shrugged. "Kümmel took her up to the mothership in preparation for our queen's departure."

"Already?" Kitchell half-closed Donn's eyes, as if the news hadn't spiked his host's heart rate. "I thought she was going to celebrate with us longer."

"A courier came in while you were traveling. You know what that means."

The Empress had felt the need to directly involve herself on one of the lords' planets, which she had explicitly farmed out to two other levels of management. She tended to respond aggressively enough to dissuade similar problems in the future. That was all well and good for her and the oblivious capital, but not as much for the locals.

Kitchell blinked away his surprise. "The queen can't go back yet. She's—"

"Not reincarnated, I know." The operator eased into the doorway as if trying to fill it. "Lord Banebdjedet will protect us, right?"

Did your mother breastfeed you on propaganda? Kitchell checked that no one else was within sight and dropped an amiable hand on the boy's shoulder. "Some things even Banebdjedet can't protect you from. The Empress's wrath and the queen's…" *Insanity.* "…intensity are among them."

The operator blanched.

"Our lord won't risk his holdings." *One hopes.* Patting the controller's shoulder, he withdrew his hand. "He'll comply."

If he does, it may not help Vinnet. Donn thought of her upstairs with Sarah. Were they alone yet? Had Sarah started hosting her? Were they mobile? *We need to know what timetable the courier demanded.*

"Who received the courier while we were traveling?"

Even as the operator said it, he knew. "Setite's steward."

Of course. Who else managed the planet while the lord traveled? Who else maintained continuity on a world amid the chaotic flux of upstarting and deposed lords? "He should be at the banquet, right?"

"If not now, then soon."

"Perfect. I'll find him and see if he needs help."

Kitchell edged past him, but the operator caught his arm. "*Herr Kommandant*, you said you were going to come right back with the girls, but you didn't. You didn't even come back by the teleport juncture."

"Of course, I did. You must have blinked." Kitchell shook him off and pushed through. *This is getting untenable.*

THE REALIZATION MADE Vinnet's blood run cold.

This was bad. The girl didn't know about Gertewet. She didn't know Kitchell and Vinnet were undercover. She didn't know they weren't like the Kem.

Did it matter?

Vinnet was about to take her from everything she loved. She was too young. Vinnet needed hosts old enough to understand the consequences of their decision. She needed hosts old enough to be grounded in their conviction to fight the Kem.

She always had before.

But she'd never taken a host undercover.

The lord's crude setup had almost no means of communicating with the host. No anesthetic. No way of stepping through how it should go or the most common complications. It was primitive: a framed neck. Have at it.

Stranded here alone, Vinnet could do nothing but her best. She tried to show the girl what she wanted. She tried to show her she didn't have to, but the girl picked up on the truth. She did have to if she didn't want to die. As much as she hated it, Vinnet couldn't change it, either.

As she started Anjedet's recording and lowered the girl into the symbiont gel, Vinnet's blood pumped furiously, shaking her.

The girl didn't want her.

She didn't want to fight the Kem.

She only wanted to not die, and in a perfect world, she could have all three. If the Gertewet had finished eradicating the Kem, she could, but they hadn't.

She couldn't let her die, now that the girl had explicitly asked for Vinnet's involvement, but it wasn't going to be easy. No one should start an intimate relationship as a last resort.

Someday, no one would have to.

Vinnet set a timer for the restraints and the door, since she wouldn't be able to control them from the new body. *This is the right thing to do. This is the right thing to do,* she repeated, still not believing it. Tewet were fashioned as predators to humans; it was her responsibility to take hosts respectfully. This girl didn't want her. By all rights, Vinnet should leave her alone.

But Vinnet couldn't let her die, even while she only paid lip service to wanting to host. Even though Vinnet was only a last resort. Vinnet was at peace with that. She could be here for the girl when no one else was.

Vinnet swam up to the pool's new ceiling: a youth's smooth, healthy spine framed between the halves of the chair. The girl had trouble staying still, and Vinnet couldn't blame her. The symbiont certainly couldn't stay still. Not right now.

She didn't need her whole back; Vinnet wasn't a queen. She needed only the neck. She paused under it, collecting her inner self, her rushing thoughts. This was going to be hard for them both, but it had to improve on the current situation. The computer had caught Kitchell whispering that it would be okay.

Vinnet wished the girl had listened.

Because it would. As soon as she got this over with.

Sarah's unconscious state held sensations but not her normal dreams. It started with a bright blue flash and a deafening buzz. Three words surfaced like breaching whales, swimming out of the depth of her mind to burst forth in dazzling clarity: safeguard, impetuous, ardent. Her rattled brain couldn't decide the origin of these words or their pertinence to any experience in her life.

Nor did it have time to decipher the puzzle before her entire skin began tingling, yielding a sensation of floating in the immeasurable depths from which the three words came. The tingling faded as suddenly as it began, ending in a sharp jerk.

Sarah felt the nonnegotiable grip of the ankle and wrist locks. Her eyes blinked open for a fraction of a second before consciousness slipped away again.

The scent of peanut butter filled her dream. Nightmare, rather. It was everywhere, pervasive and unyielding, the one scent she took such care to avoid. This time, though, her breathing felt fine, her airways clear and unconstricted. She didn't feel smothered and panicked.

As the stench faded, the dream world settled, its darkness shifting to a teal-green haze accompanied by a low, constant tone. A chill swept across her body, and the sweet taste of the most decadent chocolate, rich and creamy, filled her mouth.

Then something entirely new happened.

Sarah felt as though she were looking down into a pond. The water's smooth surface reflected a girl like her, but whereas Sarah stood still, the other girl worked busily, putting things away. She paused in her work, smiled and waved, and turned back to her business.

When the girl set her next item on the shelf, a wave of relief crashed through Sarah. The emotion wasn't hers. What did she have to feel relieved about? But she felt it nonetheless. She felt sure her situation had finally settled, was about to turn back to normal, but she knew better than that. She wasn't home, and nothing was going to be the same.

Finally, the dream returned to the pool. The girl under the water, still cheery, placed a dusty old video tape in a VCR and held the TV up for Sarah to watch.

16

TREASURE HOUSE

Khonsu was right. The house still stood.

I don't get it. Setira stared at the house, in tune with the symbiont who controlled her eyes. *Why would the Kem build around this? Why keep it?*

Why build around is easy. Katorin had to focus to think past her excitement. *It was common practice when the support ring for the Central Palace expanded out. Because of the permafrost, they were already building infrastructure like the storm sewers, the water and power systems, and the tewet maintenance ducts at ground level. Then they built the street level and new cityscape on top.*

Katorin continued, *At monuments like the first settlers' houses and the Scientific Symposium, they built around and over them like this and opened them for public tours. Mute's role as adviser to the leadership councils would have made her house a good candidate. Maybe one of us closed it to public tours. I imagine the prison where the Empress's first host lived has long since been demolished.*

I can't believe they didn't demolish Mute's house, too.

Maybe the reasoning was lost in the Mountains Base files, too.

Shaking her head, she pushed onto her feet again. *Mute's things could still be in there.*

We're not here for Mute. She's dead. We're here for Khonsu, so the rest of us don't get killed, too. If Khonsu stashed something here—oh, look, what's that by the hatch?

Katorin rolled Setira's eyes in response and turned back.

Nestled next to the curved wall of the slide was the back-pack-sized box of a teleporter assembly, its darkened interface screen facing her. On top, clearly visible under the flood lamp, rested a portable light, a neat stack of folded clothes, and a closed box.

Fighting the urge to grab the light and rush into the house, she reached for the box first; like the light, she might need it inside. The box contained the kind of plastic writing sheets that would last ages, several filled with a handwritten four-symbol Gertewet code.

With so many languages compressed into the same writing system, Katorin had to whisper it aloud to relate the words to their meaning.

"Khonsu: Operative:

"I have not yet fulfilled my mission. It seems only the ISC knows why the ISC does anything. I have encountered hints at plans to infiltrate the Gertewet, but I don't see how it could be done. We know our own, our hosts' faces, and the locations and security of only one base each. How they could expect to succeed escapes me."

A shiver ripped down both host's and symbiont's spines.

"En masse, they can't succeed, because they can't find us all at once. As individuals, they cannot, because we will easily identify that they do not belong.

"I must investigate further to discover what measures Neith intends to employ if, in fact, this is her plan. If she did succeed and, somehow, slipped an unidentified operative into our midst, a Kemtewet would have direct access to the Coordinating Council. We must prevent this at all costs."

Katorin lifted the page, but that was all. Khonsu left no other notes. The next page, in different handwriting, gave instructions for temporarily deactivating the cleaning robots in case the transporter batteries had died. There was enough energy for a single transmission.

She leaned down and pressed the battery check button, and nothing happened; Khonsu must have used it.

Which left her to face the "possessed" killer cleaning bots. At least she had instructions. *They must be our design after all. If they killed nosy Kem, the Gertewet really did have a hand in "haunting" the premises.*

Setira didn't care. *Strand it, Katorin! He went harrowing off on another old rumor like it had any meaning! He joined the ISC —signed his own death sentence—as if the Kem could actually do it!*

Katorin dropped her grin.

How could he be that stupid and still be alive? I thought only the best of us had survived this long.

Katorin turned back to stare at the house she'd been so sure had been demolished. Khonsu had been right about that all along. *He knew the risks. Only he could assess the credibility of what he heard. Obviously, he thought it concerning.*

Then why not report to the Council, like anyone else would have?

She could picture exactly what the Council would say when *she* told them. *There's not enough here to respond to. Based on this, there's nothing to do besides what we're already doing. If Khonsu knew someone thought it possible, he had to find out why before reporting it, or the Council would still have nothing to act on.*

They still don't.

True. Katorin stared at the house, itching to go in but trying to mull over the status of her mission.

Against all odds, they'd found Khonsu's intel, but it had shed no light on the ISC's up-staffing, only this old idle rumor she'd encountered once every three or four hosts. Yet Khonsu's last crazy rumor had panned out; here she stood at the very place where Gertewet had begun to criticize Kem practices, back before they'd even earned their names.

Logical fallacy, Setira reminded. *Just because Khonsu was right about one thing doesn't mean he's infallible on something else.*

Katorin nodded.

Mute had walked through that door after having surgery to implant the alien augment. In the living room beyond, she'd argued with her son about whether it had made any difference. A century later, in the same room but new hosts, they'd argued whether anything remained the same.

Fine. Go in. Get it out of your system.

It's not as if we'll have anything solid to report out if we don't. She snatched the pocket light from beside the pages and headed in.

Fine dust swirled around her feet and billowed into the air as she crossed what had once been a wide lawn, thick with hardy, lush grass and fond memories. Mute had hosted Landing Day parties here, before she'd lost the hearts of her people. She and her guests had stood in front of the house and watched the rippling aurora borealis.

Katorin glanced up and pictured, somewhere in the darkness above, beyond the slide, the layers of the Culinary Design Center. The offices and cleaning bots and meeting rooms where she and others had carried on for years, unaware of the treasure down here, mere paces away. It felt like another world. Another time.

She stepped onto the deck. The front door lay in the entryway, its hinges and latch ripped out of their places in the otherwise intact frame. That must have been from the forces breaking in to apprehend and execute Mute.

Katorin stepped through.

Inside, the house bore hardly any resemblance to the home Katorin's mother remembered. Amid the lumps of threads and shards that may have been furniture at one point, skeletons of scavenging mammals littered the floor, intermixed with the fluffy plastic fibers they'd used for bedding. Wood fibers had collapsed. Rubber connections had crumbled. Any magnetic or crystalline data had been erased by entropy. The upper level wouldn't be safe, nor would the ground level. She hadn't come for safety.

For guaranteed safety, she'd have to avoid all non-Ger worlds. How dismal.

To the right, a shelf full of books and trinkets had filled one wall. It must have been shattered when the door hit it during Mute's arrest.

A bitter smile tugged at her lips. At that point, Neith thought she had only one Ger to contend with. She didn't know a second queen and her other offspring had fled the planet to set up a new stronghold. They couldn't prevent Neith's rise to power, but they could oppose her afterward.

Katorin crouched among the scattered remains of the shelf's treasures and picked up one of the trinkets. It was a carved image of one of the gods of the plains farmers who had lived on the equatorial continent. A pointy beast whose spines formed into fire, it fit snugly and uncomfortably in her palm. Obviously, a farmer had given it to Mute, but she didn't remember why or what Mute had done to earn his respect.

Sifting through the debris, she withdrew a charred and

half-melted sphere that must have been hit by a laser rifle during Mute's arrest. It had been a sixty-pointed spherical star that represented the heights to which science had taken their civilization. She wished she could have found it intact; it had always been Mute's favorite.

Tucking both into her satchel, she started toward the back of the house.

She turned once around the kitchen, trying to connect its broken, dilapidated state to the cozy home her mother remembered. Time and again, Mute had counseled youths while preparing breakfast or dinner. The next queen, Dea Mute, had even sought (and rejected) advice in this very room. Now, cabinets threatened to collapse, their contents already spilled across the floor, shattered. The intimate table lay dashed aside in pieces, as if something—or someone—had been thrown against it. Mute?

Katorin tensed, as if she might save her ancestor from her violent fate. If she'd been there, could she have made a difference?

Maybe this is why the Council left the house lost, Setira told her. *Why are you doing this to yourself?*

Katorin closed her eyes, blocking out the corrupted kitchen to focus on her host. *I wanted to see it.*

The way you remember it, it's gone. Whatever you're looking for, it's not here.

I just want to look.

She struck gold in the upstairs bedroom where Mute kept her files. Hidden from UV and enclosed with stagnant air, they were still legible and meticulously organized. The front half addressed the sundry details of daily life, but the back folders held names of the people she'd tried to help. Recent files bulged with details; older ones had been trimmed or removed. The last ones held names of her children and, at the back, thick with information, Neith.

Katorin shook as she reached for it.

That's too important. We wouldn't have forgotten anything in there.

Pulling it out, Katorin swallowed. *What if we did?*

The top page covered Neith's promotion from adviser to chairman of the leadership council—the promotion in which she gained power to attack Mute directly. The article outlined the planned policy changes that ultimately enslaved the planet's human population.

Her stomach clenched. *This might have been a bad idea.*

She flipped to the back and found the beginning: Mute's first contact with Neith.

Mute: To Neith, respectfully:

It is with heavy heart I must inform you of the passing of the entire cult you amassed among the farmers. They did not bear well the news of your sentencing. Feeling as if we owed them kindness, in light of your crimes, I informed them myself only days ago, alongside their estranged clansmen. I'd hoped they could begin to reintegrate into their own religion. When we visited again today, we found them killed en masse. The last two to perish appear to have stacked the others' bodies. How horrific!

You and I have had our differences regarding proper etiquette of interactions with farmers, but you clearly spent much time with these people.

I thought you deserved to know.

My condolences.

Neith: My arrogant Mute:

Did I not tell you my return was in their best interests? Now, you see I was right. They needed me.

If I ever again see life outside this barren tundra, I trust you'll remember this incident and leave my devotees to my care.

Their lives were meaningless without me. It's not as if farmers—or most intellects, for that matter— have experience determining direction for their own lives. They value the satisfying simplicity of having it handed to them. Left to their own devices, they make their trinket-gods and we our knowledge-gods, but neither speak. How much more sensible to yield that right to an intelligent being capable of reason and speech and accept direction from her?

With my voice lost to them and no other enlightened intellect to replace it, of course my people withered. After seeing I had a grand purpose for them, they couldn't return to their clansmen's hollow idols. They felt they might as well die. And they did.

Perhaps next time, you and the Council on Ethics won't cling to such limiting ideals.

To a bright future.

Neith: To Mute, friend to the forsworn:

You must be aware of the discoveries on the nearby habitable water world Depth. I'm told Depth's sea creatures have a stunning neuron density, especially the parasitic amphibians, tewet, that take over their mammalian fellow sea creatures and swim them around in new schools. You must know the geneticists and psychologists are overeager to adapt these animals into auxiliary brain space for human hosts, which might allow most of Keidem to achieve a minimal intelligence.

But do you know they plan to test one on me?

Mute, stir up that compassion you so often waste on farmers and call up your sycophants in the Council on Ethics! Tell the geneticists to run their experiments on volunteers. My brain is fine. I need no augmentation.

End this nonsense before it gets out of hand.

Mute: Independent Neith:

I was aware of the tewet discovery, among others on Depth. I did not know of their intention to begin human trials so hastily. I have implored both the Geneticists' Council and the Master Warden to reconsider, but each time, they answer the same: this technology can be adequately tested only through human trials. As a prisoner sentenced to life and responsible for the death of that entire farmer community, you have forfeited your ability to decline participation. I asked them to think it through, to admit to themselves that forcing your involvement in these trials is no different from your coercion of those farmers' suicides. They have not acceded.

I will continue to push for participant consent in these trials on your and the others' behalf.

Mute: Desperate Neith:

I am so sorry. They found too few volunteers and resorted to you and your fellow prisoners. I'm told you're awake and ambulatory. Are you well?

Mute: Mending Neith:

I'm told your health has not suffered from the augmentation and that you are testing well. How are your spirits?

Neith: Most befuddled Mute:

Of course I am well. The implant did nothing but add a bulge down my spine. I test well, because I always tested well. These dimwits forgot to take a pre-implant baseline as extensive as the data they want post-implant.

Except they say my memory is sharper. Surely, I'll prove it to the next farmer village I encounter when I leave.

Mute: Silenced Neith:

I was saddened to hear of your death today. Writing to you posthumously does you no good, but perhaps it does me some.

Had we continued correspondence, I would have informed you that my son convinced me to accept one of the commercial implants. They gave me the first production queen, just as you had the first trial. You would have laughed; I'll be like you the rest of my life.

Your augment outlived you. They'll try it on a new prisoner, one empty of mind and quick of violence. I suspect you'd be jealous of its chance to infest a new mind and body. Luckily, you aren't here to try.

Good riddance.

Kellina and Mute: To the test subject who received Neith's augment:

I know you're still there, Neith. You're not going to fool me. I took Mute's augment. I know it's not just memories that got preserved—I've got that damned nanny yapping at me all the time. I just know you're there, too.

They concluded you're safe to pass outside the detention facility when this host expires. Dupes. You can hide from the analysts, but I know better. When you do get out, Mute or I will be here waiting for you.

We won't let you kill again.

Mute: Neith:

I see you've reclaimed your name now that ninety percent of intellect society has accepted third-generation augments. I still don't understand why they let you remain free now that they can see to connect your crimes to you. Your transgressions are no less egregious now than when we kept the farmers separate, perhaps more. Surely, as you've said, what you've done with one group of people, you would gladly do with more.

Please step down from your advisory position. It suits you poorly, and I will continue to object to your placement.

It's for everyone's benefit that you would resign.

Office of the Cultural Advisor: Honored Mute:

Thank you for contacting us with your inquiry. The Office of the Cultural Advisor declines to make a statement at this time.

Neith: Most arrogant Mute:

I only recently learned your letter was rejected without consulting me. How deplorable!

Regarding your request, I do of course decline. The people of Keidem elected me to this position when they realized how much more secure our lives could be with farmer and intellect societies integrated. Together, we can provide for us all. I shall fulfill my commission to the best of my abilities.

You may not have noticed the truth, but the people of Keidem have. Each successive host changes us symbionts. I am not the same Neith that Mute counseled on the loss of a farmer village, just as you are not the Mute who counseled. Those were humans, dim and unaugmented. We are greater, destined for more, as are the humans aligned with us.

That is what Keidem wants. More. More knowledge. More culture. More security. More augmentation.

Speaking of which, did you hear I'm pregnant? If this works as it does with wild tewet, queens like you and me will be able to sustain production. We won't need to continuously modify wild tewet. We could even support human population growth, spread out to other colony planets. Surely, if production is just reproduction, then given the long lives of tewet, we could even go back and augment the humans left on Earth, elevate them to our level—

———————————————————————

Katorin reread the line: "augment the humans left on Earth, elevate them to our level."

This is it! Her stomach churned.

The buildup of ISC forces, now that the Ger were rumored to be extinct. The new offer of retiring from the ISC after three hosts' lives. Neith hadn't joked about Earth.

She had plans for it.

Katorin scraped together the pile of plastic memos, dumped everything else from her satchel, and settled them in, padded with folders for the long-dead Gertewet. She put the trinkets back in and took off back downstairs.

This was all Khonsu had needed for his mission. If she were caught with it, it would be her death and their intel delivered straight into enemy hands.

Don't get caught.

By Mute, I hope not.

17

THE BEGINNING

S arah's mind raced, hampered by the cloying memory of the dreams it had to wade through. She fought back to her last moments watching the blue alien and the pain of it plunging into her skin.

Shrieking, she reached for her neck. Touch shot pain clear to the bone, and it felt swollen. Her fingers came back with dry flakes of blood. She shook.

It was in her. Oh, crap, what now? Wasn't it supposed to be over? Why had she awakened as herself?

Or had it attacked her and saved implantation for later? Was there worse to come?

Her mind flashed to another memory: swimming through the pool's gel to her own back.

Why can I remember that? I didn't...

That's my memory. The thought came slowly, lazily, as if the part of her brain that generated it hadn't woken to a shot of adrenaline. *You can review them all, now that you're hosting me.*

Sarah squeezed her eyes more tightly shut. No, that

couldn't be it. *That is by far the weirdest thing I've ever thought to myself.*

Sarah Elaine Anderson, wake up! This is your symbiont, Vinnet.

She shook harder and whispered, "You're... You're in my head?"

The voice didn't answer at first, while emotions washed over Sarah in waves: relief, pity, fury, empathy, fear. It was the weirdest sensation. Like feeling a concert's bass drum resound in one's own chest, its emotions resonated in her mind. Lord knew she had no reason to be relieved or feel pity. Its driving beat settled into timid uncertainty, and Sarah fought it. She wasn't uncertain. She was angry. It had no right to drag her through this!

You're not dead. Hopeful uncertainty accompanied the words like a bass line to a melody, giving it context. It wasn't her. *That's what you said you wanted.*

If things were different, Sarah might have even thought in second person like that. But not in a hopeful way.

She hadn't thought that, but that was what she wanted. She'd said so, time and again, and she whispered it now, "I don't want to die."

But it had become an out-of-place footnote, a chord in the wrong key. That thing was in her head now, possessing her, controlling her, keeping her from whatever future she used to have. It was all over. She'd made her decision, and the creature executed it.

Now, she was trapped. She didn't even get to be unconscious, as she'd hoped.

What?! Disgust and revulsion flooded her mind, and she fought to remind herself that was what she'd wanted only hours ago.

The sense of someone else made it hard to think, like a jostled elbow or a shout in a library. Why had unconsciousness made sense? She knew it had—because then she wouldn't have to live with a constant reminder of her lack of control. What was the terror of being trapped if you didn't know you were?

More emotions rolled into her mind, confusion and disgust, and she was now certain they weren't hers. She knew exactly what she said, and on the surface, it made complete sense. The confusion came, because the neck lump had emotions, and she was as up close and personal with it as it was with her. She could read its mind. She even started discerning its emotions from hers.

And both were just plain weird.

She tried to stop thinking, as if she could protect the sanctity of her thoughts.

It responded with cautious amusement. *I haven't come to judge you. You also aren't trapped.*

Oh, yeah? Then how come I can't— Her arms whipped free of the wrist shackles, and she studied the meaty gashes on the back of her hands, proof that she hadn't always been free. Her hands opened and closed and turned when she told them. She was indeed in control of her own body. She swallowed. *Then what do you need me for?*

It was worse than she thought. It had to be. Somehow.

Its thoughts floated in like hers, as textured as a voice but with the silence and immediacy of an instant message. *I will* share *use of your body with you. I also seek your companionship.*

You know nothing about me. Why would you want me as a companion?

For now, because you are human, and because we both want

out of Banebdjedet's stronghold alive. Loneliness poured off it, along with fear that their time together might be cut short by violence or...

I can still refuse you?

It twitched, shooting pain through her neck and along her spine. *When we're safe, preferably when my mission is done, I can try to leave you such that you'll still be alive. I won't be here for redundant neurological functions; you'll be on your own to recover from the resultant brain damage.*

Back to the bad choices: life half-trapped with a brain-sucking alien or a chance at life with massive brain damage. The more the creature's reality sunk in, the more certain Sarah was that the brain damage had to be massive. It could read her thoughts and emotions—connections there. It was going to control her motor functions—connections there. It knew her memories—connections there. How much more did it connect to?

Much.

How easily could it leave her as a vegetable?

Quite.

She sucked a deep breath. *What's the mission? What are you trying to do, anyway?*

We will wipe out the Kemtewet, those who systematically enslave humans. Its hatred faded a smidge. *I'm impersonating one of the Kem queens, so we can infiltrate the Central Palace and take out the highest ranks. As of when he sent you up here, Banebdjedet knows for certain that you host his queen. We need you until I can replace other queens and kings.*

You need my face. Nothing in its mental plans included a specific role for Sarah, the person.

Until I know your strengths, I cannot be more specific. I can say that I've never regretted my host's company. Impressions of a dozen different people, its past human bodies, flung through their minds. *And I have never found my humans useless.*

Sarah focused on the cheery cherubim painted on the dome's apex, just for something external and concrete. Because this was weird. This thing was *thinking* at her. She felt its emotions. She recalled its memories.

She'd always felt safe in the privacy of her own thoughts, where she had to yield to no one. Despite all appearances, in her mind, she could remain unbroken.

Not anymore.

What has changed? It was honestly confused.

She gingerly rubbed across the back of her neck, careful on the tender skin. She wasn't especially familiar with the shape it was supposed to be, but it felt huge.

Yes, it's swollen. It will heal. Less enthusiastically, it added, *There will be a bump. I'm not flat.*

Physical deformity was one thing. But it was invading the only sanctuary that could ever be truly hers.

She got the impression that if it had lungs, it would huff. *We monitor each other's thoughts. Why does that horrify you?*

Policing my thoughts, you can turn me into whatever you want. I didn't agree to that.

It started to object but subsided. *You're correct. I'll be honest with you, Sarah: if I shape you, I want you to be brave and cunning and compassionate. And alive at the end of this mission. If that bothers you, describe what you would prefer, and I'll attempt it. Note this, too: you have all the same opportunities to shape me.*

It had a point. And what it wanted her to be wasn't bad. What more did she want from it? Before it could even talk to her—think at her or whatever—it demonstrated that it listened to and respected her.

What more could she want from her very own neck lump?

She wanted to go home.

When this mission ends, we can go to your home. I can't fight for your humanity and require you to abandon your family.

Promise?

I promise.

They both knew the condition: they had to make it out alive.

MAJOR PATRICK'S beeping watch jerked Rockefeller from his worry-wracked doze. He stretched his legs out until his soles hit something. Pain sparked on his feet, and he jerked them back. Shock walls. Right.

"You okay?" Major Patrick's voice sounded groggy. How long had she been active? Six hours there, six hours back, and six hours there again, one would think she'd had plenty of rest.

"Peachy." Rubbing his face, he sat up. Almost there. They'd arrive and find out whether Maggie was okay. Soon. Anxiety gnawed at his stomach.

A food bar landed in his lap, and he tracked its flight back to Major Patrick.

"It should be open and shut. Walk in, get them, walk out. But if it isn't, this could be our last meal for a while."

He broke into the package, tested the flavor, and repeated her logic to himself before taking another nibble. "When we talked earlier, it sounded like you knew the General before all this."

The wrapper on her bar crinkled extensively. "I did. We

were the last two of the original staff left at Black Book. Everyone else got relegated there instead of being discharged. Except the Colonel, of course. Command wasn't taking us seriously either, until Kitchell swooped down and flew away with Donn...with General Marshall."

He scooted to where he could see her face around the screen. "You said the alien changed him?"

"Yeah." She chomped a large bite of her bar and chewed slowly, stalling. It didn't dissuade him. "They're patronizing and evasive. Donn wasn't like that before—that's what made Black Book work, even with the rejects—don't tell them I call them that. He always set his standards, laid out where he was flexible, and stayed open to compromise. He didn't talk down to people.

"Now, I can hardly tell when we're talking to him and when we're talking to Kitchell. Neither one will fill us in on everything. It's like that part of him, that trust and faith in his people, is just gone." Shaking her head, she sat straighter against the wall. "I shouldn't have told you that. It doesn't matter now."

"It will if they take Maggie's body."

"But they won't. Even if Maggie weren't hurt, it was her friend that Kitchell was grooming for a Gertewet. She's the one we really have to get back there for."

"Was she older?"

"Looked the same age to me." Major Patrick crumpled her wrapper and tucked it into her pack.

"And you're okay with that? Them using kids?"

"I'm not okay with any of it, but I know we're getting back there as soon as we can. We'll bring them home." She checked the screen. "Let me give you a quick rundown before we land. We're going back in the way we came out last time, except this time, we'll park right against the building. The back half of the palace is u-shaped. They're holding them in a room in the center. We'll land next to one of the wings and head left..."

18

NEW RHYTHM

S arah rubbed the sand from her gummy eyes and stared at the tiny granules. It hurt too much to think. If she let herself start, the new litany wouldn't pause.

It's in me! Get it out! Ew! What had it done to her? It had no right! But she'd told it to. *Get it out! Get it out! Ew!*

It hurt too much to give the anger free rein and know she could do nothing about it. She had decided. The alien had acted. The start of implantation seemed like it happened either ages ago or a half hour ago. How long had it really been?

Most of the night, if not longer. We were exhausted.

We. She shuddered.

But it had a point. When had she slept last? She had to think back. Before trying to escape, before the big stone room, before the flying saucer, before the kidnapping—and that had been late afternoon. She'd have been a zombie if she weren't so freaked.

Good. I need us at our best for what's to come.

For impersonating the queen? She froze. She didn't see how she could impersonate someone she'd never heard of. Was this, like, the Queen of England? Had Sarah ever seen pictures of her?

Less important. The Empress keeps a tight rein on the other five queens through the kings, who jealously guard them. They're generally your stereotypical maidens locked away in towers, rarely permitted to see the worlds. They have no overt influence on their kingdoms. Their primary role is reproductive.

Sarah jerked up out of the gel and shuddered as her wet back met the cooler air. *Will I have to—*

Peace! Tewet queens self-impregnate. No one else is involved.

Freed of the wrist shackles, Sarah scooched lower on the chair, where she could balance upright and out of the gel. One less horror to face right now; she couldn't deal with expectations of sex on top of everything else.

Actually, sex is a perfectly valid spy technique.

Sarah's eyes bulged.

That we will not utilize until you're comfortable with it.

She slumped in relief. The shreds of her t-shirt slipped down from her shoulder, and she clutched it as if it had materialized from another dimension. A memento from her first shut-in with the new youth group, it tied her to her life, to home, to a church serving three small towns in Pennsylvania.

And it was cut in half.

Her fingers tightened on it, and its ugly orange fabric brushed against the scabs from her shackles. When she'd put it on—this morning? Yesterday morning?—she hadn't even liked it but had been running low on clean shirts. Now... She pressed her face into it.

We should dress.

It didn't smell like home anymore. It smelled like sweat and body odor—like the locker rooms before all the girls learned about deodorant. But it was still from Earth. *Can't we take it with us?*

I lament we'd have nowhere to put it. Besides, Anjedet wouldn't keep your mementos; neither can we.

Sarah's fingers clenched. *You don't care about it.*

I know you have dozens more you prefer that await your return. Let this one go.

Sarah rubbed her thumb across the ugly fabric.

We'll be safer without it. Kem who have an image to maintain take care to differentiate themselves from their hosts. Like Anjedet and the other fealty and, actually, most Kem.

And the purportedly human-friendly Gertewet of course had to do the exact same thing. They had no choice in the matter at all.

Fine. Sarah lowered her arms, realized she wore only a bra underneath, and pressed the shirt back to her chest. She glanced around the wide-open room where, she realized, even Vinnet felt exposed.

The symbiont fought its own impulses with logic. *The doors will remain locked until we open them from the inside. No one will bother us.* So it thought, anyway.

Sighing, Sarah slipped her arms from the t-shirt sleeves, bunched it up, and held it to her chest. Open water stretched between her chair and the platform. *Now what?*

If you'll permit me control, I can expedite our egress.

Her stomach knotted. There it was: the first time it would take over her. Maybe that was really the last step to wiping her out.

Of course not! I need you intact, or I'll be alone. Vinnet thought that with the same gravitas it might use for getting caught by Banebdjedet, even though it had been alone yesterday and for months before.

Just now, that didn't sound so bad. At least if Sarah were alone, she wouldn't have something trying to control her.

It's not bad! Please, Sarah, you have no training and little idea of the situation here. Let me handle this. When we're safe, I'll yield your body back to you.

You can do that? Give it back? After seeing Mr. Marshall, she should have understood that, but it always sounded so final. Losing control of her body and never getting it back. Could Vinnet screw it up? Would it feel right?

Absolutely.

If its memories didn't answer in tandem, Sarah might not have believed it. But it had trusted its hosts in control on missions where it only advised, as it had so far.

And if you do, afterward, you'll take me home?

We'll check in with those concerned for my safety and then those concerned with yours.

Finally, she'd get back to the safety of her house with the comfort of her bed and room, and this time, she'd have an alien insurgent who could fight off any evil invaders. She could hug her dog and lean into her parents' arms. They'd know just what to say to make it all sound better...for a day or two.

And no Kemtewet thugs.

That couldn't start until they'd finished their "mission," and that couldn't start until the neck lump controlled her. Sarah closed her eyes. All this over again—the dread and waiting and capitulation.

She breathed faster.

Why did this just keep getting worse? Just when she thought she'd hit rock bottom, and it was all better from here, the next crappy news broke.

What the heck? How much longer could it nosedive?

Fine. Do it.

Vinnet didn't dare think anything back, but Sarah felt its resolve to move forward.

What would it feel like? Would she be able to think? What if she needed to jump out of the way of something but couldn't move?

Her eyes opened.

What if it hurt?

Vinnet exuded relief. Sarah didn't see why; it hadn't taken control yet. Her legs pushed out on the ankle restraints and, freed, stretched.

Then she toed the shackles all the way open.

Why did I do that?

You didn't. I did. The chair rose from the gel and drifted toward the pool's edge.

Are you sure? Nothing feels different.

Sarah's body sighed. *You sense my thoughts as though I were an external entity. Your brain processes them like anyone else's speech. My control of your body is simpler and uses only your preexisting neural networks. Because of this, the responses that tell you that your body moves correctly when you control it also tell you it moves correctly when I control it.*

Proving its point, Sarah's arm rose up and, on the second try, pulled the glasses from her face. Sensing Vinnet's intentions, Sarah meant to stop her arm but with the same results as if she hadn't tried at all. *You can't! I need those to see!*

I know what they're for. Even Banebdjedet has the technology to fix your eyes.

But everyone will know something's different when I go home!

They'll be right. Vinnet opened Sarah's fingers, dropping the glasses with a plunk into the gel, where they drifted out of sight. *The Kem and their technology aren't secret. We'll fix your vision and tell your family all that's happened. Except me. We can't tell them about me unless we move them to safety.*

Which was somewhere away from Earth and outside the Kemtewet Empire and, given Vinnet's sense of foreboding, not all that safe.

Fine. We won't tell them. Not that they could say aliens had kidnapped her, either, or fixed her eyes. They might as well say nothing, which would have been easier with her glasses. Lost in the pool's depths, she'd never get them back, even if they needed them in the next five minutes. Another part of her gone forever.

The chair reached the pool's edge, but despite its plans to get up, Vinnet didn't move. *These things mean that much to you?*

I know they shouldn't, but... yes.

Nodding, Vinnet found the shredded t-shirt's shoulders and held it up.

No, wait! Sarah fought to pull it back in to her chest, but her hands stayed poised, arms straight.

What? You can't be squeamish about your body with me. I'm in your head.

It bothered Sarah that she couldn't shudder. *No, wait, you said you're not a queen. You don't have offspring. Does that mean you're a boy?*

Her face smiled, the corner of her lips tightening in a way Sarah never held them. It felt weird. *Since I'm not a queen and the queens self-inseminate, I'm neither boy nor girl. You're female, and my last host was female, so that is how I identify.*

Sarah focused on a far-away point in her vision—the wall—trying to keep the thing that controlled her from seeing her body. *But you identified as a boy once?*

Vinnet folded the shirt into a neat triangle and held it

against Sarah's bare stomach. *Don't wear yourself out with questions now. There will be plenty of time later.*

The alien—she—made Sarah's body stand and step onto the platform. As with her glasses, Sarah knew Vinnet had control, but if she stopped thinking about it, she wouldn't have noticed. Like going through the motions while showering or pounding down the stairs on autopilot, there seemed no meaningful difference between her body doing something and her doing something. And there hadn't been until now.

Vinnet set the folded shirt neatly, almost reverently, on the seat. Then she unbuttoned and dropped Sarah's jeans and stepped free. She folded them, too.

Sarah willed her eyes up away from her body, but they wouldn't respond.

Vinnet paused and closed them for her. *I understand. I do. I'm not welcome. You don't want me. But if we're going to get through this, you must trust me to take care of your body.*

What about the rest of me?

I will do my best. In time, I hope that will suffice. She flicked Sarah's eyes open then forced them shut again. *You're used to protecting your body from assault and ridicule. You're safe. You've lived through the worst I will ever do to you; from now on, my duty is to protect you.*

And she took it seriously. *But it's not your only duty.*

No.

She had her missions, too, which involved her leaving this room as someone she despised, in a role that risked them both. Some safety net.

You're safe from ridicule with me. I've been old enough times, I can have no complaints about your body. She considered the aches and frailty she'd left behind with her last host. Her love for the dead woman and her sense of loss surged, taking Sarah with it.

Which made no sense. Sarah never knew her. They'd never stepped on the same planets. Why should she feel anything for the alien's dead friend?

Apologies. Keeping the eyes closed, Vinnet sighed. *I'm grateful to have met you.*

You're grateful to have me.

Yes. Vinnet bobbed the folded jeans in an exasperated shrug. *What more would you like from me?*

Nothing. Nothing more than for Vinnet to take her home and disappear.

Nodding, Vinnet opened her eyes and stacked the jeans on the t-shirt. She slipped off the bra and socks and settled them on top, leaving Sarah's body with nothing but panties in the wide-open room.

Anyone could see her.

There's no one here.

There could be cameras.

There are, and there's no one on the other side. They tie into the underwater controls.

That's where Vinnet was supposed to watch from, Sarah realized. With access to the cameras and microphones and soothing recordings, she never had to show herself. She never had to swim up and portend doom. She only had to wait for Sarah to lie back, ignorant of what lurked below.

Instead, she explained it all the only way she could.

And now she made Sarah walk around naked.

Vinnet pulled the silver dress from the mannequin and rushed to slip it on over her head. *There. Your breasts and undergarments are covered. This will all progress more easily if you would only relax.*

Ohmygosh, it goes down to my belly button!

Her fingers traced the thick, cold piping running just under the bottom mark from her sports bra. *It's nowhere near—*

Oh, man, it's even lower in the back!

Vinnet traced the back's piping around the open spine all the way past the edge of Sarah's underwear. She reached up and folded them down. *You associate this style with your celebrities; what horrifies you so?*

I can't wear stuff like this! I'm not allowed. And I don't have the boobs for it.

Now Vinnet looked down at the stretchy fabric clinging tight over Sarah's almost-flat chest. *You have no idea what a gift—*

What's the point?

Shaking her head, Vinnet crouched back at the split-back chair, working free something attached to the bottom. *The point isn't your voluptuousness. It's access for the queen. Speaking of which, I'll need to replicate the marks she would have made.*

Vinnet pulled out a small kit and withdrew a powered hand tool. Lining it up beside Sarah's spine, she flicked a switch.

It felt like falling down stairs. The little thing hammered where Vinnet swept it down the gap in the dress's back.

Ow! Stop! What the hell, Vinnet?

She finished and put the tool away.

You said you were going to protect me.

This is protecting you. If you don't look as if you're hosting a queen, we'll be caught. I've done this for many lifetimes. Trust me. She picked up a fine-bladed knife.

What was that for?

This is the kind of thing we really need to talk about first before you go cutting on me.

Vinnet dropped her hands into her lap as if the knife were no bigger deal than a pencil. *You have an entry wound and cutaneous distress along my length.*

With her free hand, she traced gently from the base of Sarah's skull to the base of her neck. Even the light touch set the whole region throbbing. It felt like her dry fingers might catch and rip it wide open again; Sarah tried to jerk her hand away.

Instead, it traced down to the gap's bottom at the small of her back, where only the hammer had assaulted her. *The queen would have started far lower. If I don't proceed, anyone can see we aren't who we pretend. I promise I'll be as quick and gentle as I can. It won't hurt much.*

Hurting her to protect her seemed like a twisted philosophy, but Vinnet's memories backed her. The spy had a lot of experience not getting caught, but she had been once—and there the memories stopped like a brick wall on a highway. Sarah couldn't catch any details, but a wave of intense dread washed through her. Whatever happened, the little cut Vinnet proposed didn't compare.

The symbiont waited for her, hands folded.

Not so bad, Sarah reminded herself. *Okay, I'm ready.*

Vinnet's idea of "not much" didn't match Sarah's, but it was quick, shallow, and afterward, no worse than the throbbing discomfort already in her neck. Sarah's body drew deep, slow breaths, steadying them both.

The blade had a smear of blood when Vinnet set it back in the box and reached for something else.

Are you kidding me?

Relax. It's only makeup. She opened the applicator and brushed mottled black and blue down her back.

You actually cut me when you were just going to cover it with makeup anyway?

Sighing, Vinnet finished and put it away, too. *By the time it wears off, the bruises will blend together and look less regular.*

Of course there was no other way. It's just a human body; you can always get another.

Vinnet stopped. *You must know I don't think that. Truly, all we have to do is run through a teleporter. I usually do, but this state is a point of pride among Kem. They revel in it. I had to extend it.*

'Cause aliens can't make prosthetics that look like cuts.

Too much time and effort to blend behind your back. Also, they tend to peel at inconvenient times. This way was best. Vinnet dumped the box into the pool, where it vanished with Sarah's glasses. Standing, she smoothed the dress and gathered its excessive length regally in her left hand, preparing to leave. *Please trust me to do my best for us.*

It's not like I have a choice.

19

BANQUET

When Major Patrick opened the kaxan's hatch, she slid through and landed on her feet. Rockefeller used the ladder.

Outside, a rambling stone castle engulfed the area they'd landed in, and as he stepped out from under the spacecraft, he picked out crenelations atop the rough-hewn structure. True to Major Patrick's descriptions, they'd landed against one wall of the u-shaped courtyard, which opened out to a swift creek and a swelling, craggy hill. At first, he wondered why grass on such an otherwise undeveloped landscape would be so well-manicured, but he traced the same green to the ground he stood on: moss.

"Did I tell you it was clear?" Major Patrick demanded. Sparing a glance at Lieutenant Fairfeld dropping from the ship tucked beside theirs, she swept her gaze and the gun's muzzle around the lifeless landscape.

He pointed up. "Why are aliens using Earth architecture?"

"Analysis later. Silence now."

Knowing why they did things could guide his approach

to the enemy in any encounters inside. It wasn't rocket science, just psychology, and it wasn't frivolous. Rolling his sleeves tighter, he kept quiet and took a deep breath. The smell of wet, earthy soil and sewer vapors assaulted his nose, recalling the inside of the kaxan shortly before they landed. (He would have expected a spaceship to have restrooms, but it didn't.)

This was an alien planet? Not that alien yet. Nor threatening, so why couldn't Patrick bring Maggie back the first time?

They had no time for accusations. Maggie was here, somewhere beyond those stone walls. She had to be.

Fairfield and Myers dropped from the other ship's belly. Myers took a steady grip on his sidearm and waved the Major off. Nodding back, she started for the door with Fairfeld closing in.

It felt too exposed, as if they'd parked on the street for a jailbreak and, entering the front door, should be swarmed by police at any moment. Terrestrial police carried firearms. What would castle security have? Laser guns? Broadswords? The latter would certainly fit the theme.

Seriously, a castle?

What was this, a theme park? And why hadn't he thought of all the right questions when he'd had time to ask them? Of course, he needed to know about Maggie, but he should have known what armament stood in his way, too.

Major Patrick tromped through a tiny puddle in a moss divot, and the sun glinted on the red-brown surface. Was that blood? As she reached for the pull handle and Fairfeld positioned himself to cover the door, Rockefeller noticed the brown splatter that almost blended with the door's dark grain. Someone had died here.

Maggie?

With a lump in his throat, he skirted the puddle and followed them in.

In minutes, they opened the door to the room where Major Patrick said his daughter was held. It was empty. He stepped inside to check around the corners. She had to be here somewhere!

"Damn it!" Major Patrick snarled.

"Where is she?" No one hid out of sight near the door.

"They moved them all. We need to find the General. Maybe you should head back to the kaxan."

"Like hell." He crossed his arms. "I'm here for my daughter, and I am not leaving without her."

"Shh." The Major backed into the anteroom's corner in time for a sentry to peek in and find them.

"*Was machen Sie hier?*"

German? That explained the castle, but not why so much here borrowed from Earth.

Major Patrick straightened her uniform. "We, uh, need to see your *Kommandant. Herr Kommandant.*"

"*Was wollen Sie mit ihn?*"

"*Herr Kommandant*, uh, *bitteschön.*"

Up close, the sentry looked young and a little out of place, as if he'd strapped on his father's leather armor this morning before skateboarding in. He glanced them over, then nodded toward the hall.

Major Patrick fell into step and waved for him to follow. He did, standing straighter and rolling his sleeves down to look more respectable.

What had happened here? Were they too late?

The back of his head answered, *Certainly.* Major Patrick's six hours to Earth and their six hours back were simply too long. But what did that mean? Were they dead? Moved? All possessed?

The sentry led them along the side of the empty holding room and then beyond, around another large hall, this one roaring with voices and laughter. They turned a corner and found a man in a buzz cut posted by the banquet hall's main entrance.

The sentry exchanged some remarks with him, and the buzz-cut man sent him away. His eyes coursed over the bustling lobby before turning to Major Patrick. "You're lucky he doesn't remember you."

She shrugged. "I've been told that after bar hopping."

His gaze stuttered on Rockefeller. "Who's your friend?"

"A parent with connections. Look, we came back for the last five, but they're not in the holding room. Where are they?"

The man, presumably the General, lowered his voice further and angled away from Rockefeller. "Banebdjedet had the adults killed and disposed of already. He went ahead with implantation."

Rockefeller closed his eyes. These brutal aliens hadn't just taken people; they'd killed them, too, but maybe they'd missed Maggie. Maybe she faced something worse.

"I got my colleague in place in time," the General added.

Some consolation. For this, it'd be worth capturing one for study. Any kind of study.

"Who took it?" Major Patrick pressed.

"Sarah, the blond girl."

Not Margaret. He let his breath out. She was safe from that.

"Last I knew, anyway. They've been up there all night with the door locked. I don't know what's wrong." The General's low voice strained with achingly familiar tension.

Good. You should know what the rest of us have been going through.

"What about Maggie, the other girl Sarah's age?" Major Patrick prompted.

The general turned back, glancing at Rockefeller as he put two and two together. "They put her up on the mother-ship as a spare."

"Spare what?" Rockefeller growled.

"Spare host."

A spare body. Because subjecting one girl to that horror wasn't enough, they wanted to keep Maggie just in case— his whole, beautiful daughter reduced to the alien equiva-lent of a tire in the trunk? No one deserved that, especially not his daughter.

The General caught sight of something in the crowd and ushered them deep into the archway connecting the lobby and the banquet hall. Then he headed out to meet the threat.

"They can't do that to her!"

"We'll get her." Major Patrick refused to meet his eyes and instead scanned the crowd.

"We can't leave her here."

"I know that. We're not going to."

Rockefeller took in the long, narrow hall. Hefty benches filled this half of the room, brimming over with men in layered garb. They drank, toasted, carried on, and spilled foul beer in their bushy beards. An orchestra filled the room's middle, and beyond that, upon a dais, a man wearing two extra arms sat enthroned, a second, empty throne beside him.

He nudged Major Patrick. "Who is that?"

She followed his gaze. "If I had to guess, I'd say Benny-J, the one who ordered all the women kidnapped."

The enemy.

Rockefeller tried to study him further, but he saw little

from here: a black goatee, short hair, and a penchant for dramatic gestures. He looked like an easy man to hate, his recent crimes notwithstanding.

In light of those crimes... "Earth would be safer if he were dead."

"He'd just be replaced," the General answered from behind him. "The lords will be worth taking out when we're done with the Empress and kings."

Maybe, but the Empress and kings hadn't taken his baby girl.

"What was that?" Major Patrick nodded at the man the General had spoken with.

"One of the guards from upstairs. He said the queen banned him on her way down." He stared at the front of the hall. "Here we go."

Light glimmered in the deep shadows, and a flat-chested girl in a sensually cut silver dress strutted onto center stage. The crowd around them roared.

Everything about her came off subtly wrong. She dressed glamorously but wore no makeup. She walked provocatively, but her long hair hung unfashionably crumpled, the bottom half wet and clinging to her shoulders. The girl was Maggie's age, all right, her face still round with youth, but even his older daughters didn't walk with that sensual grace. Hell, even his wife didn't, not across stages.

General Marshall actually relaxed, the bastard. He patted a bulging canteen at his belt, as if it reassured him of something. "They're okay."

"What?"

He even smiled. "They're both okay—host and symbiont."

She turned to take her seat, flashing her back to the audience and shocking some of the locals into silence. Ugly cuts and bruises stretched all the way down her spine from what her hair covered past the small of her back.

The General's smooth leather armor had nothing to grab him by, so Rockefeller smacked his fist into the General's chest. "Tell me how you think that is okay!"

"She's fine. It will heal." The General pushed his fist away. "She's fully mobile and unharmed."

"She's infested!"

The General glowered at him, and he finally thought to wonder whether he was talking to the human, as he assumed. Could the Major even tell? "You want revenge for this? For the women who escaped and the three who didn't? She's the one who's going to get it. Now, if you don't mind, I need to warn her of some things that came up while she was indisposed."

The General turned to go, but the Major grabbed his arm. "Sir, we need to take Maggie home."

Sighing, he glanced at Rockefeller again, then gazed up at the stage. "Fine. We'll get another spare."

Rockefeller shuddered. The General missed the point so casually. No one should be reduced to a backup body.

Whichever it was, General or alien, led them around the room's perimeter to another exit, but before leaving, Rockefeller caught him gazing at the stage. He knew that look too well.

Like a parent afraid to leave his child.

———

Overtaken and out of control.

It was both so much better and so much worse than Sarah expected. The creepy neck lump didn't wipe her out, and it wasn't even going to control her all the time. One point to her having a future! On the flip side, she apparently didn't get to have any privacy from it, and while it professed to want to take care of her, it had no problems intentionally cutting and bruising her. Two points to the end of her world.

Her eyes rolled. *The situation will look better in time.*

Vinnet pushed the pool room's—*implantation chamber's*—doors open and stopped short at the waiting guards—the one whose arm Sarah had hacked and the old, scarred man from her saucer.

Both bowed. Sarah checked whether anyone was watching; no one had bowed to her before.

"Congratulations on your rebirth, Queen Anjedet!" one stammered. He still spoke German, but Sarah understood through Vinnet's comprehension, as if reading invisible subtitles. Okay, that was a perk.

This man mocked you when they left you with me? Vinnet focused on the man whose arm she'd cut.

Yeah?

Allow me to be petty. Vinnet waited for him to straighten and pegged him with a glare. "Why was my vassal not fed? Why does your queen awaken to new life on an empty stomach?"

He squirmed, glancing to his buddy for help. "It was not my duty..."

"You should have seen to it that the others' duties were not overlooked. You are dismissed!"

With a shallower bow, he scurried down the hall the way Sarah had been carried up.

Sarah stared after him. *Why would you do that?*

Because he made you uncomfortable, and because I can. He was out of line to mock you. An implantation isn't payback for his cut arm, and it's not a joke. She faced the remaining guard and raised an expectant eyebrow.

He jerked his eyes off his fleeing friend. "Lord Banebd-jedet would be honored by your presence at the feast."

With her nod, he led her down the back stairs.

Sarah scraped her wits together. *You just ditched that guy, and he listened to you!*

The stairwell led into a second latticework hallway. *You and I have both felt powerless since we arrived. Now, they believe we outrank everyone on this planet. A moment's self-satisfaction will do no harm.*

A little indulgence for Sarah. Vinnet might even have felt more satisfied than she. *I've never had anyone stand up for me like that.*

No one?

Not the other kids on the bus when she got asked to say words that sounded strange to the native Pennsylvanians. Not the teachers when she got ridiculed for high test scores. Not her parents, who kept asking her to fit in and then complained when her grades matched the other kids'.

No one.

Except, this one time, someone who wasn't even her species.

The right wall flowed into an archway of carved wooden flowers, and as Vinnet passed her escort, all her attention shifted to whatever they'd find on the other side.

Man, if that was how the symbiont felt about someone who made a face at her, what was she going to do to Mr. Marshall?

The floral archway melded into a few yards of ornate, mahogany tunnel that emerged onto the dais at the front of a deep banquet hall. Two unnecessarily large chair backs blocked part of their view of the dense crowd filling the room; two stiff, bronze arms extended beyond the right throne's edges, so Vinnet stepped to the left.

The moment the crowd caught sight of her, cheers erupted throughout the entire gathering, startling butterflies from the evergreen decorations at the front of the dais. Their bright wings fluttered up to join the swarm between the high-set windows.

Beside her, Banebdjedet stood, his black mustache wrapped around a smile of perfectly ordered, bleach-white teeth. He reached out, and Sarah tried to jerk away. Immobile in Vinnet's control, her body stayed put, and he stroked the back of her neck. Throbbing pain sparked across her neck and down her spine, and Vinnet flinched away. He moved his hand to her cheek.

Oh my gosh, get him off me!

I can't. So much for Vinnet as unconditional champion. Her mental presence emanated sullen reluctance to reciprocate, but she reached up and felt the bulge to the left of his spine. The fine, bony ridge of a second spine felt especially surreal.

We're not slugs; we're vertebrates, too.

He stroked her cheek with his thumb and then stepped back, facing the audience.

With a grateful sigh, Vinnet settled Sarah's body on the plush, green throne. *I don't think he'll do that again soon.*

The intimate moment kept replaying in Sarah's mind. *He doesn't know me; what gives him the right?*

I'm sorry. He must have known Anjedet well. I didn't expect that.

Banebdjedet raised his actual arms for attention and settled the crowd into an expectant silence. "Citizens of Setite, the Queen of Green Flame, your Queen Anjedet, has arrived. Let the feast begin."

Beaming at her, he returned to his seat and settled the bronze arms in the gap in the cushions.

The way he looked at her, he might try to touch her again, the creep. She had to get her mind on something else. *Wait, we're supposed to be this "Queen of Green Flame"? What's that mean?*

The orchestra picked up, filling the spacious hall with semiharmonious music, while fleets of servers filled the banquet tables with food.

The Empress has five kings, each of whom has five lords. Lord Banebdjedet answers to King Uatschnesert, whose title is the Green Flame. That makes his queen the Queen of Green Flame.

Why was it so complicated? Aliens were always simpler on TV. *But this isn't Uatsch... Green Flame Dude. It's Benny-J. Why does his queen have the same title?*

Because she's the same tewet. Though the answer sounded simple, Sarah felt confusion play through the symbiont. *How did Banebdjedet merit his king's queen?*

More servers brought out personal dining tables for both her and Benny-J, piled them with food, and retreated, leaving the two tewet alone on the dais. Sarah's stomach growled at the smell.

Vinnet had torn into half of a roasted chicken when the creep spoke again, his voice now pitched to address only her, its harmonies light and pleasant. "I missed you, Anjedet."

She stopped stuffing Sarah's face and swallowed. "I finally made it." *Banebdjedet can make of that what he will.*

He shrunk. "I apologize for the delay. I thought you would want a selection of vassals from Earth."

"I did, but the Empress will not be pleased." Vinnet cut a piece of chicken and savored not only the food but also the act of eating. *A year is a long time to forego eating.*

He conceded her point with a nod. "I'd thought we could disregard the Empress's petty opinions." Tentative chords filled the undertones of his voice. "You are pleased with your vassal, aren't you?"

She nodded. "You know me well."

He hesitated, his forehead furrowing in confusion before he resettled his smile.

He was probably disappointed he couldn't choose from among all the others, but if he thinks he gained Anjedet's favor, he won't press the issue.

Now that she mentioned it, the suggestion that Sarah wouldn't be Vinnet's first choice seemed insulting. Even if the only reason she was here was because Mr. Marshall had happened to be assigned to the team that broke into her house. *Who would he have wanted?*

Vinnet took a last, large bite of chicken, and Sarah felt her recent memories playing through the symbiont's mind, like watching a familiar movie in a stranger's living room while standing on the street. *The woman in the tight clothes, high heels, and leather jacket who was in the group to your left would have been a fair match for some Kemtewet with female vassals. For me, most of the women would have been fine, though if I'd had the time, I would have talked to several of you before-hand and chosen based on personality.*

But instead, you're stuck with me.

Vinnet closed Sarah's eyes, deliberately cutting off her host's vision and forcing their attention inward. *I'm honored to have you.* Then she reopened her eyes and continued dining. *Kitchell saw that you could excel in this lifestyle. So you're not elegant like most vassals. You're not done growing, either. Anjedet may have chosen you anyway; one of the other girls your age had short hair.*

My age? That didn't sound good.

Vinnet finished the last of the corn on her plate. *Your*

physical maturity: mostly grown with an unutilized reproductive system.

Okay, that's creepy.

Vinnet settled back from the meal with Sarah's teenage stomach full and satisfied. *It's a fact of anatomy that that is helpful for tewet reproduction.*

A server traded her plate for a crystalline wine glass.

"Your plan worked." Banebdjedet gazed beyond the crowd. "The Empress had Uatschnesert executed last night for losing you."

Uatsch... *Green Flame Dude? The queen had wanted her king dead?*

"Ah, good," Vinnet breathed.

"Teni filled his place, and the other lords advanced, but my position is undecided; the Empress knows you're here." His voice softened. "She also had your doppelgänger executed."

"Oh." A chain of reasoning flicked through Vinnet's mind, ending at *We're in more danger than I thought.*

Why? Run that by me again.

Doppelgänger. Twin. But if he only meant twin, he would have said so. Anjedet must have left her vassal's twin in her place. She needed a new host not only because she needed to not be recognized but because she left the Central Palace through a host quarantine. Vinnet's memories provided context: the servants' exit killed the host, but let the symbiont pass through. *This isn't a tryst or a sanctioned reward. It's a coup. She's trying to oust the Empress by building alliances with lords. Usually, they ally with kings, but the Green Flame must not have joined her.*

If this is a coup, and you're trying to kill the Empress anyway, are you going to finish what she started?

If she had a good plan and left notes. She sipped the foul-smelling wine and blinked at it in surprise.

Banebdjedet rumbled on, "You said that between the Kings' Ball and her other developing plans, the Empress would be distracted. She wasn't distracted enough. An Imperial Herald arrived and demanded your return before the Ball's end, or the ISC would be dispatched to wipe out my holdings."

Like Alderaan? The entire planet?

Or at least their capitals. A colony is a large investment. She blinked at him, her nonchalant posture making Sarah wonder whether it was really a big deal. "And?"

No, that wasn't right. *Vinnet, those are people! You can't let them die.*

Watch him. He will do everything to stop that by himself. We need not defend them.

"And?" he repeated, his face turning red. "You never said this would cost me my appointment. I've put a lot of work into managing these colonies."

"And you'll put much more into managing a kingdom." Vinnet assumed that's what Anjedet had offered him. What if she was wrong? "Now is no time to cave to that cow's demands."

"*The Empress* will destroy me. If we have neither power nor stealth to work with, I have no choice. The Ball ends tomorrow. You will be back in time."

Anjedet's plan is through. Vinnet whipped the wine glass into the floor on her left, where it shattered into tiny, glistening gems in a field of red. Servants rushed forward to clean. The orchestra stopped, and conversation hushed.

"Spineless pawn!" Jumping up, she stormed into the dimness of the mahogany tunnel and emerged into the latticework hall's firelight.

The Gertewet's acting felt too authentic. *I thought you wanted to go, but you're not acting, are you?*

His timetable is too short. If we follow through, we won't pick up the latest intel from the capital. We'll go in blind. She smacked the wall with a fist. *And you'll have no time to get acquainted with me. This isn't how we're supposed to begin.*

With abductions and murder? That's not your usual MO?

The eyes Vinnet controlled narrowed. *With us as practical strangers.*

Hard soles clacked behind them, and Vinnet spun as the lord caught up. "Have you changed your mind?"

He caught her head above the tender entry wound and kissed her. His moist, warm lips pressed against hers as if he owned her.

Ew! No! Sarah tried to jerk away. His breath crawled across her face, its feet the mustache prickling her lip. *Ew! Wrong!*

Vinnet jerked Sarah's head back and gazed into his dark eyes. *He initiated intimacy with a queen! Did she let him do that?*

The hand on Sarah's head moved to her cheek, stroking. *Get him off me!*

Her body pushed up on tip-toe and returned the kiss, lingering. His other hand pressed on the small of her back, trapping her uncooperative body against him.

My first kiss. Worst ever.

Her lips worked against his, pulsing the fleshy mass, and her hand traced his bony jaw.

What are you doing?

Acting. Her body dropped down, breaking the appalling moment. Freeing Sarah. "Perhaps Teni will be more cooperative than Uatschnesert. Try to draw him in."

"Then how will I become king? You said—"

Vinnet silenced him with Sarah's finger on his sloppy lips. "There are *five* kings. You can outrank him without disposing of him."

Or Vinnet could kill them all and keep their dirty mitts off her body forever. That would be a start.

Her finger caressed his lips once more, and Vinnet pushed out of his arms.

Benny-J couldn't take the hint. He caught her hand and squeezed it. "The mothership will be ready to depart as soon as we and your belongings are aboard."

Vinnet stopped. *It couldn't be as easy as taking a kaxan.* She started walking again. "I will meet you in orbit."

Oh, joy.

20

EVOLVING PLANS

General Marshall led Rockefeller and Major Patrick only a few feet out of the banquet hall before turning to them, voice low. "Major, is this man's daughter your only remaining objective here?"

"If the rest are dead, yes."

The General glared at her; they weren't all dead, technically, but she was right. The one with the parasite might as well be. "I'll take him up to find her and get them back to Earth."

"We can help you."

"We're going to be conspicuous enough with a kid in tow; I don't need a posse."

"It's called backup."

Rockefeller coughed loudly, disrupting the developing staring contest. "Arguing in the hall isn't helping. Major, I'll go with him. Clearly, he's the best equipped for this, and if he's concerned about the size of the group, we need to respect that."

Her dark eyes weighed on him.

"Go home, Jo." The General crossed his arms. "Vinnet and I have this covered."

"That's not what you said when you brought us a kaxan."

"You got most of the women home. That's a win. You're not prepared to infiltrate a mothership."

"But he is?" The Major's accusing finger jabbed in Rockefeller's direction.

"He will be an asset in keeping his daughter calm and pointed in the right direction."

Rockefeller nodded. "As I understand it, the last time she saw you was right before you left her behind to fend for herself."

They both glared at him long enough to shut him out. Then the General turned back to his old subordinate.

"I'd lose my shit if they took you as the spare." Clamping his mouth shut, he turned to check the hall behind him, ostensibly for unwanted listeners.

"You're not going to let me do my job, sir, are you?"

Well, this could degrade quickly. Rockefeller set a hand on her shoulder as gently as he could. "Major, our purpose here would be served a lot better by circumventing argument. Good, bad, right, or wrong, the best thing right now is to make a decision and go with it. The decision's been made."

Her eyes narrowed, but she nodded. Sure, she seemed to think she belonged in charge, but she could still recognize he was right. "Fine." She turned back to the General and pointed a thumb at Rockefeller. "Just don't lose him; he's the Speaker of the House."

She stormed off.

"Jo, not like that," the General muttered. He rubbed his

face then, sighing, he raised an eyebrow at Rockefeller. "Speaker of the *U.S.* House of Representatives?"

"Yes."

"Oh, boy. You shouldn't have come."

"You're wasting time, General."

Marshall nodded down the hall and led Rockefeller away. Alone with the body-possessing alien that had full knowledge of Earth's defenses. He hoped this was the right thing to do. For Maggie, but also for him.

"You said she's on the 'mothership'? Where is that?"

Marshall pointed up. "In orbit."

"And we'll fly there?"

"Probably teleport."

Rockefeller stopped in his tracks. "Like *Star Trek* transporters? 'Beam me up, Scotty'?"

The General grabbed his arm and pulled him onward. "Except the proper English term is teleporter. In German, it's *Teleport-Station*. French: *Téléporteur*. Chinese: *Chuánsìng*."

"Why German? Why Earth languages and castles?"

The General pulled him toward a wall before entering the next corridor. "Language, art, architecture... Culture is the most expensive commodity available. Kem cultivate it on the farm planets to sell with vassals."

He nodded toward the next corner. "Now, shut up and follow me."

They were passing an intersecting corridor when someone shouted, "*Kommandant!*"

The General's shoulder slouched as he followed the voice down the hall, where Rockefeller and Major Patrick had first ventured. He waved the Speaker to join him and started deeper into the building again. "*Was ist los?*"

Ahead, at the tiled room in the next corner, the kid in

the oversize armor stood in the doorway with three men behind him who fit their large armor. This didn't look good.

Rockefeller stuck behind Marshall, wishing he could follow the conversation in more than just body language. Why wasn't Marshall responding to the threat?

"*Was brauchen Sie?*" the General asked again.

The men dispersed as Marshall approached, and the spokeskid answered, "*Kommandant, wo ist Davon? Warum haben wir ihn nicht gesehen?*"

"*Er ist plötzlich krank.*" Marshall crossed his arms, one hand resting on the hilt of his sheathed machete.

"*Wo haben Sie gegangen, als wir die Mädchen oben geschickt haben?*"

"*Ich musste etwas im Muuldepet gemacht.*"

A man with hands the size of plates leaned on the wall opposite his speaking friend, flanking the General. Rockefeller backed up a couple steps.

"*Und warum habe ich Sie nicht wiedergesehen?*"

"*Sie haben geblinkt?*"

The man against the wall swiped his machete up at the General, but Marshall fell forward out of the way and spun the kid against his assailant instead.

The thick man in sliced armor swung at the General next, but Marshall parried and pushed him back. The man overextended. Marshall cut into his armpit. The man crumpled, pinned his arm tight to his torso, and pushed back up.

"*Herren, vielleicht sollen wir weiter sprechen?*" Marshall backed out of the room.

Rockefeller checked the empty hall behind them. "What's going on?"

"We're going to be taking a different route."

"I gathered that."

"Go!"

They launched down the hall faster than Rockefeller expected of either of them; his morning runs paid off. Fairfeld was gone from the corner, and Rockefeller missed him and his gun as the first two men caught up. Both bowled straight into Marshall, who collapsed under them and rolled, flinging one off. The other climbed back on and angled an arm toward his throat, ready to choke.

Rockefeller kicked him off.

He glanced up in time to get knocked over by the thick one with the armpit wound. The man pinned him with face smashed to the floor.

Then he heard an ugly crack, and the ham-handed man strangling Marshall fell in front of him, face blank. Dead.

Steel clanged overhead, and Rockefeller prayed it wouldn't swipe his way. He debated whether to jostle his captor off and risk getting caught.

Then the man toppled off, an ugly gash in the back of his skull.

"Move!" Strong hands hauled him up by his belt and shoved him toward the door. Steel rang again, and Marshall and another man grunted at each other.

Rockefeller stumbled outside.

The saucers had been here, ready at this door, but all he saw were green hills and two bright specks in the sky quickly fading.

Marshall bounded out after him. "Just the trainer and the teleport operator left, then we're in the clear."

Sure enough, two more men followed him: the skinny kid and an equally wiry, scarred man.

Marshall smacked the flat side of his blade against his palm, muttering to himself, "What's it going to be, kids?"

They charged.

This pair was different: the old, scarred man and the kid

in large armor complemented each other. When the kid feinted, the elder struck. When the elder swept low, the kid swiped high.

But they didn't compare to Marshall, who parried, dodged, and thrust as if he saw his opponents' next moves a second before they did. Suddenly, he struck out and grazed the kid's neck. The elder's smooth movements hitched in reaction, and Marshall's blade took him at the knees.

He finished them both and stood panting, victorious, four against one—two inside, two outside. The General's attention jumped from body to body, as if one might rise from the dead to stab him in the back.

The General had taken them all against atrocious odds. Rockefeller shuddered but placed a gentle hand on his shoulder. "You won. We can—"

Marshall spun, twisted Rockefeller's arm, and plowed him face-first into the moss.

"What are you doing? I'm with you!"

The General grunted and let him scramble up.

As Rockefeller straightened his torn sport coat and brushed it off, one of the red smears on Marshall's pants stood out. Unlike the others, this one sopped through the surrounding fabric and dribbled down. "You're bleeding."

Marshall noted it, grunted again, and drew a belt from one of the dead men to tie around his leg. He offered the man's machete to Rockefeller. "We can't go back in, so we're going uphill to a kaxan. All you have to do is—"

He sighed as Rockefeller took the weapon, so the Speaker adjusted his grip to be more offensive.

"Just get me to a kaxan and make sure one of us is conscious."

"I'll be conscious."

Marshall tightened his tourniquet one more time. "My symbiont or me."

The General launched up the trail, and Rockefeller caught up to flank him. "You'd better make it. I have no idea how to wake it up. The symbiont."

Marshall shot him an offended glare.

Great. He'd pissed off the old man—and the means of getting to Maggie—twice now. It was time to swallow his pride and stick with his allies for now. Let the faux pas rest.

"What was all that about back there?"

Marshall dismissed it, shaking his head.

"Don't 'It's nothing' me. If I'm going to stay out of your way, I need to know what's going on." Glancing at the blood now seeping steadily toward Marshall's shin, Rockefeller stifled a pang of guilt. Surely, even the veteran could sense the dangers of the Speaker's ignorance.

"Not here."

"What do you mean, 'Not here'? There's no one here, no one listening. You've got to tell me something."

Grumbling, Marshall trekked up the hilly path's loose gravel in powerful, deliberate steps. He waved an arm back downhill without looking. "That is half a blown cover. I screwed it up making sure that your daughter and that other girl were safe."

"You call that safe?"

"Keep your voice down."

"*That's* safe?" he stage whispered.

"Safer than being where they are with Kem."

The girl's infested! He bit down on his mounting outburst, even as her image shot to mind: a little girl, possessed and costumed, overrun from the inside out, slinking across the stage. Diplomacy. Right or wrong, he couldn't afford to lose the General as an ally.

"The other girl, Sarah," the General continued. "Vinnet's not going to leave her unless she dies, and Vinnet will do everything to prevent that. But all the other Kem have to leave your daughter alone in case Vinnet wants to swap hosts. Generally, being a spare is one of the safest positions in the Empire."

"Then why insist that Major Patrick avoid it?"

The General groaned. "Jo's already part of this war. She's doing important work where she is."

"And Maggie isn't? She's got her whole life ahead of her."

"You don't build an army by recruiting within itself."

"She's not part of an army."

"Look." The General struggled with panting breaths. "Jo couldn't have gone. Those dolts back there didn't know it, but a queen wouldn't have a spare that old, not from anywhere like this. She could have had human kids, which would make it harder to have Kem offspring. Best case, they'd kill her."

He didn't want to know, but he had to ask. "Worst case?"

"You saw what a blown cover looks like. Except Vinnet won't be on a farm planet like this with podunk human guards. She'll be on the capital with Imperial Security and special forces. We have to ensure she has the strongest cover possible."

"Why? What's so important?"

The General told him.

KATORIN STEPPED out of the house with a deep sigh and a hand on Mute's files. She had it. The reason for the ISC up-staffing, or at least a conjecture for it.

Earth.

She fumed. The reason they were even on Sais was because the ancestors had left Earth for more space and resources, to flee the more primitive humans' incessant conflicts, and to leave them to their own business. Even on the new world, segregated into intellectual pursuits and more practical ones, the intellectuals were supposed to coexist without imposing.

Neith had undone the segregation on Sais.

Now, Earth, too? They weren't even party to the development of augments; they should be left alone.

In a fog, Katorin reset what she'd found atop the transporter assembly and sprinkled it with the ground's fine dust, as though it had never been touched. If another Kem found his way down, she didn't want him to see that the message had been read.

Reciting the procedures to dismantle the cleaning bots to make sure she hadn't forgotten, she climbed back up to face them. With some agility and knowing the designed weaknesses, she passed through them quickly. The long, nerve-wracking trek back to her quarters convinced her that Kemtewet counterintelligence agents lurked within every shadow beyond the deep-red ground lanterns. Every late-night pedestrian seemed to size her up, scrutinizing her for the slightest sign of wrongdoing.

Just when she thought an ambush would surely spring up in the next block, she arrived back at the living quarters she shared with the other food engineers. Eight flights of stairs were her normal route to her quarters, but she instead took the transporter up to her room. She dropped the robe into a laundry basin and kept Mute's files nearby while she washed the lubricant off.

No sooner had she finished than someone began

pounding on the door and cuing for the computer to notify her of a visitor.

She opened the door and planted a hand on her hip.

With a yowl of protest against her state of undress, Cube Head spun away from her. "Beryl. New vassal. Soon."

"It's three hours until work. What do you want?" she demanded, unmoving. Many Kem were open with their hosts' bodies; she didn't understand why he made such a fuss.

"Minimum clothes, please?" he asked.

"I'm going *to sleep*. Why are you here?"

Keeping his eyes closed, he turned to face her again. "We're off work tomorrow. It's a holiday."

Wound tight from all the day's tension, her stomach launched into a series of flips. "Wow," she replied, keeping her tone and harmonics cheerful. "What's the occasion?"

"Ger execution at the Central Palace. It might be the last one."

How could they think this is the last? Plains Base alone has a couple hundred still. Setira thought of all the friends they saw before they left.

It's a PR stunt. They're saying the war is over and the Kemtewet have won. She forced a grin onto her face. "Sounds historic. Can we go?"

He nodded. "Most people don't pay them much mind, but since you're new, I thought you'd want to know. We could probably get good seats." He started to open his eyes but squeezed them shut again. "Be ready to leave in a couple hours."

"See you then." She abruptly cued the door to close, wishing he had edged inside so it could hit him.

Not that it was his fault someone had been caught. He

was the messenger, and thank Mute for that! So often, they never heard until too late.

We need to rescue him. Setira started forming a plan.

But we succeeded in finding Khonsu's intel.

Which is inconclusive. The only reason to report it is so no one else gets deployed to find it.

And Mute's files. Katorin leaned back against the door. *If we fail, no one will be able to report that the ISC is building up to attack Earth. There will be no second chances, unlike with Khonsu's note; we're carrying Mute's files, and they'll fall into Kemtewet hands.*

Even Setira hesitated.

What could we do different about Earth? Setira asked. *We're already trying to end the Kem as fast as we can. There's just a few thousand of us left. We can't barricade a planet, not against the ISC.*

Katorin sunk onto her heels. *Are you saying our discovery doesn't matter?*

Not unless something changes.

Like militarizing an entire planet. *Not bloody likely.*

We might as well rescue it, Setira persisted. *We can't afford to keep losing people.*

We will anyway. Katorin pushed them back to their feet. *You want to do this, even though the Council specifically told us not to?*

They said not to follow Khonsu into the ISC. We're not. Besides, it's probably not even Khonsu.

It makes sense that it would be. He went missing at the right time—and went straight into the ISC, where he had to have been caught.

So let's go rescue his hopelessly gullible tail.

You realize we probably won't make it.

*Honestly, "We probably won't make it" should be the
Gertewet motto. Let's do this.*

Steeling herself for a sleepless night after a long day, she
dragged herself deeper into the living quarters in search of
clean clothes and a quick, flawless plan.

Pulling a blanket around her shoulders, she sat on her
bed and opened her book of tracing paper. Under the guise
of taking up art as a hobby, she'd stocked herself with the
thinnest, most flammable form of paper available on Sais.

There were four steps to this kind of operation: Get in.
Find the prisoner. Free the prisoner. Get out.

Getting in was easy; she and thousands of others had an
invitation. No one would question her presence there.

Finding the prisoner shouldn't be hard, either. Knowing
Neith, she'd have a policy of proclaiming her own power by
letting the people see the prisoner's plight. If, somehow,
she'd deviated from her usual character, Katorin had memorized the Gertewet's plans of the Central Palace, thanks to a
couple bombing schemes she'd worked in her youth. She
still recalled the most likely prison cells.

She sketched out a route she could try and the most
likely security measures.

Freeing the prisoner would be more of a challenge. He
might be guarded, and she might need to navigate some
biometric locks. She assembled her DNA sequencer bypass
and dropped it into the bag with Mute's artifacts and her
spare symbiont canister.

Weapons components were more unique than lock-
picking tools and hundreds of times more likely to identify
her as a Gertewet upon her arrival on Sais, so she hadn't
brought any. Fortunately, the palace security forces had a
well-known weakness that could yield a convenient weapon.

If that was unsuccessful, she could probably take a guard or two with no weapons and Cube Head as a shield.

She felt fairly confident she could free the prisoner. At least, the symbiont portion. Hosts were usually paralyzed by that point.

Then what? All the normal exit routes would be swarming with security, and all the abnormal routes led into cold storage, which usually had no doors out into the surrounding, barren ice cap. Even if she broke through, the facility's emergency transporters would take her right back into the palace.

Unless you're out of range. And why bother with decently ranged sensors if no one's supposed to be there?

Katorin smiled to herself as well as her host. They might be able to pull this off. Then she circled her favorite exit route on the map, memorized it, and took care to burn the map completely.

21

ONBOARD

y the time they reached the airfield, the General
was limping, leaning heavily on Rockefeller's
support, and focusing on breathing. Rockefeller
didn't mind; he needed the silence to let the ramifications
sink in.

*"If Vinnet succeeds, we'll win. If nothing else, we'll stop the
Kem from reproducing."*

If the General's cohort succeeded, she could infiltrate
and kill the Kemtewet queens—and there were only six.
Well, five now. And that would be it. No more baby evil
body-possessing aliens.

From then on, humans would only ever have to worry
about their purported allies, like the General who'd send
little girls into the thick of the conflict, rather than his own
friends.

Age restrictions on spares, my ass!

On the other hand, the General *was* taking him up to
Maggie in good faith. Crappy opinions aside, he was
working toward freeing her.

Rockefeller hefted the man, adjusting his tiring grip and

evoking a dismayed groan from his guide. Only a quarter-mile left.

The General had to be dealing in good faith, unless they weren't really heading toward Maggie. Unless this was some elaborate scheme to convince him to leave Maggie in their care. Or to trick him to act as Marshall's spare.

Either way, if he thought it was going to work, he didn't understand Rockefeller at all.

They reached the hilltop saucers without encountering anyone else, but it looked hopeless. All the hatches were closed, their hulls as impenetrable as Stokely's faith in Black Book. Or Rockefeller's gullible trust in the General.

He shook his guide. "We're here."

Marshall's eyes peeled open but stayed narrow and unfocused.

"Hey!" Rockefeller jostled him harder. "Don't die on me. We've got a little girl to save!"

Marshall winced and grumbled out some unintelligible phrase.

Rockefeller took a breath to reply, but his vision faded to gray, and when the white saucer interior appeared, he felt like he'd been kicked in the diaphragm.

The General slipped from his grip while Rockefeller fought to catch his breath. In the height of injustice, the older and injured man he'd all but dragged up and down the river valley glided around the cabin with the grace of a decades-younger man; in one smooth motion, he eased across the cabin and behind the control console.

"You faked all that?" Rockefeller barely controlled his voice.

The General glanced up at him, white eyebrows raised. "What? No, of course not. Thanks for the assist. The teleporter patched me up. The pain is gone."

Giving up, Rockefeller supported himself with his hands on his knees. "What'd it do to me?"

The General tapped one more thing into the console then leaned back against the supporting wall. "I don't know. Probably rebalanced the lactic acid in your muscles, gave you a few vaccinations—"

"I didn't agree to any vaccinations!"

"It doesn't care. Besides, it's good for you." The General crossed his arms. "What these ones don't do is make up for blood loss, so I'm not going to be doing that again any time soon. We'll have to hope the suspicions planet-side didn't make it up to the mothership."

"Hope?"

"Listen, we can't be bandying words about up there. There are ears everywhere, or at least, microphones. I need you to follow my cues as naturally as you can, or we won't have a chance to get your daughter. Remember: to everyone else up there, she belongs to someone who rules fifteen planets."

Fifteen planets? Hell, make it a hundred, and it still wouldn't matter. "I'm her dad. She belongs with me."

"Yeah, I get that." Marshall tugged his canteen free, as if he had to get in a swig before they continued toward their goal.

"Can you hurry it up?"

Smirking, Marshall spun the cap off with exaggerated slowness. When the lid popped free, a tail flopped out.

What the hell?

Marshall pulled the rest out by the tail, tugging harder when it jammed, until he held up a mottled beige...snake? Eel? The limp animal hung over two feet long. Marshall waved it at him. "This is the queen we kept out of that girl. You think the way this played out is bad?" He shook the dead creature. "This thing wouldn't have let her stay herself. At least she has that."

Interesting. Major Patrick had said the General wasn't the same. What difference had trading the queen for a Gertewet actually made?

Marshall entered a command on the console, and the hatch swung open. "Here's how this is going to go: We'll teleport to level 4."

He crossed to the hatch and dropped the queen's body through. "The next floor up is the command deck, level 3. Be careful to go up, because gravity switches between levels 4 and 5."

Crossing back to the screen, he closed the hatch again. "When we get in, you will not say or do anything until we ensure that no one else is in the queen's suite. Got that?"

"I understand."

"Then hug your daughter, and keep her close and quiet."

This was happening.

Finally, after coming all this way from DC to Montana to wherever the hell he was halfway across the galaxy, he'd see for himself whether she was safe and whole. He'd take her home from this war she had no place in.

"Come here, and I'll show you the teleporter in case something happens to me."

"Then what do I do?"

The General shrugged. "Look for somewhere safe."

If only it were that easy.

The General stepped him through the indecipherable menus while setting up the connection between their saucer and one of the teleport nodes in the mothership.

"Breathe out, and here we go." The General tapped the final entry button, and the saucer cabin faded.

The smell hit Rockefeller first: ozone and marsh and the

stifling body odor of a young men's dormitory. Breathing through his mouth, he turned in place where they stood between two rows of bunks. One way led to a larger aisle; the other, into a kaxan hatch set into the wall that showed the saucer's light-studded ceiling.

The General nudged him, eyes wide. "Come."

Left elbow. Rockefeller followed, careful to flank the General as instructed. It'd been a while since he was the one escorting, not leading. Was his body language right to all the peering eyes peeking up from rows of bunks? Was he supposed to look subservient? Man, this spy business grated on the nerves when he didn't know enough.

The narrow aisle spanned from what he assumed was one end of the ship to the other, with both sporting simple ladders between adjacent floors. At the end of every row of bunks to the right, a saucer hatch stood either open, waiting for occupants, or sealed, waiting for a ship. On the left, the bunk rows ended in bare wall.

Lean, gruff men with thick beards brushed by them, arguing amongst themselves and casting glares at the interlopers.

An alien mothership, huh? How unimpressive.

They reached the ladder without incident. Marshall checked up and down it, then grabbed on and climbed. Rockefeller cast a cursory glance, too, and vertigo hit him again when he looked up at feet in both directions. Far away, the ladder was only rails and rungs, but where it met this floor, it expanded out to about six feet wide and held a grid of rungs.

Right, the gravity switch. It didn't look fun.

Reminding himself he wasn't going to get sucked down, he grabbed on tight and followed the General.

The next level looked almost identical, but here the

bunks extended to a much more distant blank wall. Downstairs, he'd assumed the long aisle extended down the ship's long axis, but maybe not.

About a third of the way down the aisle, Marshall turned them down a cross-aisle that ended at a door. Napery, ballroom, and queen's quarters, he'd said. This had to be the ship's longer axis. One more straight shot, and he'd see her.

The door led into a room with a telltale sewage odor indicating its purpose, and at the far end, they passed through a hall of linens before entering a massive chamber. At least, where everything else on the ship had been compressed, this bright, airy chamber was not.

Ballroom, then. Just one more door to go, and Marshall aimed straight for one on the far side, one of two with guards. His stomach clenched.

Approaching the guards at the center door, the General sketched a shallow bow, and Rockefeller followed suit, burning with self-awareness. Bowing never felt right.

The exchange was brief.

Bowing again, Marshall led him away to another door with no guard. Rockefeller followed him into the lounge, eyes searching, heart lodged in his throat.

Was she hiding?

"She's not here," Marshall said.

Rockefeller straightened, desperate to heed the nagging sense that he just needed to look harder. "Not here on the ship?"

The General nodded at the quarters they'd stopped at. "She's next door, but they won't let us in there while the queen's away. We have to wait for her to come up."

"How long's that going to be? Can't you take out the guards and get us in?"

"I'd throw two punches and pass out."

"Then make them count."

Marshall glared at him. "This is not the place to be throwing up red flags. All we have to do is wait for our girl."

"How long is that going to be?" Heaven forbid if he had to spend days one wall away from saving his daughter.

"Not long." Marshall dug a watch from his pocket. "If she's not back to Sais tomorrow, the Empress will wipe out all three of Banebdjedet's planets and spend a few years torturing him until he dies. He's a coward at his core, and he's not smart enough to evade the ISC. He'll get her there."

"She's coming here first?"

Marshall waved him off. "Of course. They're not going to let her take a kaxan to the Central Palace!"

Rockefeller drifted to the wall between him and his daughter. All they had to do was wait.

As long as the alien who'd stolen the other girl's body didn't want Maggie's, too.

You let him kiss me.

Vinnet closed her eyes—the eyes Sarah could see through but not control—and breathed out, emptying Sarah's lungs.

You kissed him back!

Please, not now.

The teleporter activated, and the distant mumbles in Banebdjedet's palace changed to cavernous echoes of footsteps and sparse, shouted commands. Rich smells and harmonious notes drifted through from the kitchen and performance hall Vinnet expected nearby.

"The exalted Queen Anjedet of the Green Flame."

Vinnet opened Sarah's eyes to a gigantic ballroom,

where soft-sanded wood flooring stretched from the dining hall's arched doorway on her right to three ornately embossed doors at the end of the ballroom on her left. Scattered throughout, a dozen servants bowed or curtsied wherever they'd been when she appeared.

You kissed him.

You believed it; so will he. You, at least, should know better. With direct access to the symbiont's mind, a host could tell how it felt.

Yes, Sarah could. Vinnet felt no attraction toward Benny-J.

"Queen Anjedet." A man stepped to her right, and while the rest of the servants straightened and continued their business, he bowed.

She caught Vinnet picking out his embroidered vest and polished boots as signs of his station. "Lord's Steward."

"My lord specified the best chambers for you." He held an inviting arm out toward the three ornate doors at the ballroom's end.

She walked with him.

You can't use my body like that.

Do you or do you not want to stop the Kemtewet? Do you want to stay safe here in enemy territory? Vinnet glanced at the servants; the melody of her thoughts played out the theme of how precarious their lives could be and how much more so for a spy caught among them. *This is why we shouldn't take hosts on missions.*

"Your new clothing has been moved in, along with another vassal. If you require additional assistance, any crew member can summon me."

"Of course." Her hands pulled the dress's hem out of trip range, and Sarah's fingers dug into the fabric. *We haven't even acclimated yet, and already, they're sending another human?*

The steward stopped at the door, and Vinnet plowed past him into the queen's chambers. The door opened into a private sitting room done up in soothing pale greens with gold accents. Among the scattering of plush furniture and accenting ferns, another pair of eager servants stood by, and way behind them, Maggie bolted off a divan to her feet.

"Sarah!"

Gosh, when had she seen Maggie last? It felt like years. And she was okay, not slated to get a Kemtewet implanted. Except... She thought back to what Vinnet had thought. *You're not going to switch to Maggie, are you?*

Of course not. I just got you. Spares are for emergencies. Vinnet turned her back on Maggie in favor of one of the servants. "Have my wardrobe woman lay out new attire. I've worn this dress too long."

The first woman nodded and hurried into the bedroom.

Vinnet pointed to Maggie. "Did anyone feed her? If I used her now, I wouldn't want to be hungry."

The second servant, now on the verge of panic, gawked at Maggie. "She hasn't said..."

Vinnet finally turned to Maggie and switched to English. "Are you hungry?"

Shaking her head, Maggie stared, wide-eyed and horrified.

It's okay. Somewhat. Kind of. Except for not being able to decide whether Vinnet was going to protect her or betray her again.

Vinnet turned them back to the remaining servant. "Bring me wine and something for her."

The servant curtsied and scurried into the ballroom,

letting the door slide closed behind her, leaving the two bodies and three minds temporarily alone.

She turned again to Maggie, who backed farther away.

Yesterday, or whenever they'd been in the giant stone room with the other women, they'd become friends. Allies, at least, teamed up against Benny-J and his murderous guards. Now, it hurt to see Maggie afraid of her. *You have to tell her I'm all right! She's scared. She thinks she's next.*

The less she knows, the better she'll perform. But then Vinnet frowned and settled on a divan. "I won't hurt you."

Maggie froze in place and raised her eyebrows. "I don't believe you."

Why would she? You totally beat up my back.

The first servant returned with a click of the bedroom doors. "My queen, your traveling attire is ready. One of the seamsters is preparing a smock for the girl that should be finished within the hour."

"Good. I'll be in when it suits me. Wait for me there."

"Yes, my queen." She returned to the bedroom.

Moments later, the outer door admitted the second servant, who set two goblets and a tray of fruit and rolls on a table beside Vinnet's divan and tucked the tray under her arm. "Do you require anything else?"

"I will call when I do. Await me outside. I do not wish to be disturbed."

Finally, the last servant retreated, leaving them alone with Maggie for as long as they needed. Maggie backed away two more paces until she met the wall.

"I won't hurt you, Maggie."

"Like no one hurt Sarah?"

"Sarah is unharmed."

Maggie raised an eyebrow but swallowed her retort.

Told you so.

If she doesn't trust us, we won't be able to protect her on Sais. Vinnet did something in her brain. *Convince her.*

How? Her eyes fixated on the nearest spotlight shining up through the ferns at the room's perimeter.

Any moment now, you should have control.

Now? I thought you were going to wait until... Hadn't Vinnet said she'd stay in control until they got home to Earth?

We have different strengths. Right now, your strength is your existing bond with this girl and your ability to calm her. Go ahead.

Sarah's gaze shifted to Maggie then down to the hands she turned palm-up. Those were her fingers, her fingernails (the few not broken) long and strong, just the way her grandparents and old friends knew her. Even though Vinnet had been using them, making them move while she ate and...and kissed a stranger—they were still hers.

And if they were still hers, they should...

As she thought about it, her fingers split into the sign for "Live long and prosper." Vinnet wouldn't do that. Just her.

She had control of her body again.

Shaking, she looked up at Maggie, still cowering warily against the wall. Her soft voice shook, too. "Maggie, it's me! I'm—"

What? Alive? In control? Those sounded stupid. Just herself? Wrong. Once more, her fingers curled and uncurled under her direction, exactly as she wanted them.

"I'm okay." A lump that wasn't Vinnet choked off her voice, and tears clouded her view of the green lounge. It might be true. It seemed like it was, somehow.

Yesterday, the world had ended. Today was her post-apocalyptic reality, but now... She wasn't dead. She wasn't controlled. She might have a future after all.

There, in the back of her mind, Vinnet's bass line of emotion resonated with encouragement. Anyone else should think her stupidly emotional. *Take your time. You have every right to your feelings.*

Nodding, Sarah smeared her eyes with the heels of her shaking hands while Maggie watched. "I'm sorry. Hang on."

It took another couple swipes to get herself almost under control. She sniffed, trying to focus again on Maggie still pressed against the wall. "I can't believe it, but I think I'm okay. Did they do anything to you?"

Maggie shook her head.

What was she supposed to be doing, again? Right. Getting Maggie to trust her, or rather, Vinnet. Even though Maggie stood, stiff with fear, as far away as she could. "I saw them take you back to the—" The English translation of the Kemtewet term for the big, stone room sprang straight to her mind from Vinnet's. "—storeroom." Ungh! Really? "The big, stone room. Did they bring you straight here from there?"

A nod.

All that eternity Sarah had spent fighting with Mr. Marshall and the guards and suspended over the pool, unconscious, waking up with Vinnet, and finally through Benny-J's feast (with his disgusting lips), and Maggie had hardly gone anywhere? Lucky her.

She frowned. The feast. "You didn't eat anything in all that time?"

No answer.

"Holy cow!" Leaning down, she swiped a roll and tossed it over. It pelted Maggie in the shoulder and bounced to the floor. "You've got to eat!"

Maggie glanced from her to the roll and back. "You can't

be Sarah. She told me what they were going to do: implant an alien. I saw what you did to her back."

Sarah rubbed her bruised spine, recalling the feel of her fingers gripping the knife against her skin. "It still looks bad? I couldn't see it, but it's feeling a lot better. Vinnet wouldn't have done it if she didn't have to."

A wave of panic blasted her. *Don't do that!*

What? She froze. Was she going to paralyze herself?

Say my name! It's the only thing Kem can use to track me from host to host. Never use it on missions!

Sorry. That was all? Maggie wasn't going to trust her easily. If it took spilling a couple beans, oh well.

Vinnet stewed.

Sarah met Maggie's eyes. "Don't tell anyone her name."

"Whose?"

She pointed to the back of her neck. "Hers."

You did not need to be more explicit.

Do you want her to trust you or not? It was the impossible task. Then again, she'd almost trusted Mr. Marshall until he'd asked her to host. Collapsing on a divan, she considered Maggie. "They're not going to implant anything in you. They brought you up here to be an emergency host for the 'queen.'"

After the air quotes, she motioned to her neck. "That's what they expect of the queen, but in reality, she's not going to leave me."

Just her and Vinnet for the rest of her life. Her breath caught, but she didn't shudder this time.

"How do I know?"

Good question. "You can't; I'm the one connected to her brain. But look at it this way: if I tell you that everyone else we're going to see in the next—"

Several years, Vinnet supplied.

The bottom dropped out of Sarah's stomach, but she forced herself to smile. "—in the next while wants something worse for you than we—" We? Had she really said that? "—do, are you going to risk it to not believe me?"

Maggie wilted and glanced at the fallen roll again. "Who are you?"

Sarah! Not that she'd believe her—or should. "The girl who's telling you to eat."

Maggie thawed a little more, fists clenching at her sides. "Are you telling me I have no choice but to trust you?"

Wow, that sounded bad. "Kind of."

"And they're not going to implant anything in me?"

"Not if we—" Another jolt. "—have anything to say about it."

Maggie nodded, sighed, and slinked forward to pilfer food.

22

REUNION

Rockefeller closed his eyes and leaned his head against the wall between him and Maggie, wondering what would happen if the fake queen did inhabit her. Wondering what was left of the host. "I saw the way you looked at her. Why do you care so much about that girl if she's just a body?"

Marshall, sprawled on a divan, turned his head without opening his eyes. "What?"

"The girl in the dress on the dais, the one we're waiting for."

The General hummed and took a deep breath. "Lots of reasons. Her symbiont is my symbiont's little sister. They've got a long-standing camaraderie."

Little sister. That explained it. All the empathy was for the space slug, not the girl. Made sense, for a fellow space slug.

"And because I was on the kaxan that picked up Sarah. I was the one who talked to her and thought she'd be a good match. She reminded me of when my niece was young."

"Colonel Marshall?"

"Renee was a fiery teenager, too." He checked his watch and levered himself upright. "I told the queen's guard— borrowed guard, thankfully—that we'd been directed to wait in here. He knew I was the ground commander, so he let it slide. Our girl should be up by now; we ought to get going before anyone suspects us."

Finally. Rockefeller was on his feet in moments, ready to go. Was this the second or third or sixth time he'd almost reached Maggie? What could possibly go wrong this time? He tried not to think that too loud and jinx himself.

This time, the guard knocked and led them into the queen's quarters.

And there she was. His beautiful baby girl, sitting on a divan, her chestnut hair an uncontained mess, still in her rumpled tank top and shorts from days ago. Her eyes bulged—

—and so did the other girl's, the fake queen in her glamorous silver dress, pushing invisible glasses up her nose. Blinking, she faced the guard and eked out, "*Dankeschön. Geh!*"

She sounded as if she'd never spoken German in her life and was repeating after someone.

The guard bowed and left.

Beside the girl, Maggie bolted off the divan, but the fake queen grabbed her arm, stopping her. Her eyes studied the General, querying.

"He's her father," Marshall explained.

With that, Maggie was freed to run to him, and he held her close. Her chin dug into his shoulder, and her slight body filled his arms, finally letting him protect her, as he was meant to. He closed his eyes and couldn't mind the rank odors wafting from her. Soon, they'd go home safe, where he'd wrap her in blankets and never let her out of his sight again...until he had to. Never let anything happen to her again.

"You're okay. Are you okay?" he whispered, checking the shape of her head and shoulders. They seemed right.

She nodded against his neck. "I was so scared!"

Me, too, baby. He tried to swallow the lump in his throat. "They didn't put anything in you?"

"No, Dad." She angled to glance back at the fake queen.

But she was in his arms. "You're safe. We're going to take you home now."

Major Patrick had said something about Maggie being hurt. He looked over her, trying to remember, until he saw the vivid green bruises spread in patches across her legs. "Your leg's not broken?"

She looked with him, as if she'd been too busy to notice.

"Teleporter fixed it," Marshall explained. Just like with his stab wound. They needed some of those on Earth.

His little girl, whole and safe. He held her tight, and she squeezed him back.

"Vinnet?" The General sounded uncomfortable. "Sarah? Put Vinnet back in control."

Still holding Maggie close, Rockefeller turned to the other two squaring off across the room.

"Why?" the girl demanded, fists clenching. "Because you can't face me after what you did? You carried me back and left me there alone!"

"I left you there with someone—the only one—who could take care of you. If it hadn't been you, it'd have been someone else too young for it—" Marshall pointed at Maggie, safe in Rockefeller's arms, and the Speaker held her tighter. "—and she's not as good a match as you are."

"Match? You picked me because I was handy."

"And we were damned lucky."

Lucky? Rockefeller shook. Lucky to be spoiled for choices of children's lives to ruin? Lucky to get another body and, after that, a spare to use? Lucky no one was present to stand up for them?

Standing, he faced Marshall, keeping Maggie close. "You did that to her?"

Marshall rolled his eyes. "Come on, people, we're trying to save the galaxy here."

"She's a little girl, not a virgin sacrifice."

"Sacrifice? What do you think we are, Mayan gods?"

Sarah crossed her arms.

You have an advocate. I'm here, he thought to her. Then he set his sights on the General. "You must think so. They're not your lives to direct or throw away."

"I'm doing the best I can, so you and your family and everyone else back home can be safe and not worry about the Kemtewet! You want this to stop? Well, it can't, not until the Kem are gone!"

"Consequences be damned?"

"Enough!" Sarah's voice cut through the shouting match, drawing all eyes to her. She held Marshall's gaze. Her posture had straightened, and she no longer merely accused him but commanded as well. That wasn't the same girl. "We have much to discuss, Donn. The situation was not as you told me."

He looked away first.

Then she caught Rockefeller's gaze. "Check your accusations until an appropriate time, lest they destroy us all. My host's wellbeing is no longer your concern."

Like hell it wasn't. He squeezed Maggie's hand and opened his mouth.

"Save it for later, if you must. At least grant us time to clear the adjacent room."

He considered brushing her off, except that Marshall blanched and fingered his machete. But they'd been arguing in English; what were any of the surrounding German-speakers going to overhear?

And, damn it, that unnerving impostor demanded with posture alone that he heed her. She stood straight, poised, and certain that he should. She hadn't stood like that a minute ago, when Marshall called her Sarah, and she'd launched into him.

Was this jarring difference, from a temper tantrum to regal command, the difference between the human and the alien? Were Marshall and his alien that different? If so, when did they switch?

Could a human regain autonomy?

Someone knocked on the outer door.

Eyes wide, Sarah—Sarah's alien?—signed something to Marshall, who signed back and waved Maggie and the Speaker to follow him into the next room. A sprawling bedroom, complete with massive mirrors and an even more massive bed, sheltered three servants, who popped to their feet. Marshall shooed them through one of the two back doors and closed it behind them. Then he eased his ear to the wall to the lounge.

At a loss, Rockefeller stood beside him. Then he pulled Maggie into another hug and whispered, "You're okay?"

She didn't have one of those things in her. She wasn't suddenly someone else like Sarah was.

Maggie shrugged and held him tight.

Someone spoke in the front room, and sure enough, his voice carried clearly into the bedroom. Rockefeller pulled Maggie against the front wall, out of line with the door.

He leaned over to whisper to Marshall, "That doesn't sound like German."

Marshall shook his head. Not now, or it wasn't German?

The voices continued and suddenly, Marshall snarled at the wall, soft enough it wouldn't carry. "Are you crazy?"

"What?"

"She's demanding another spare, but they can't get another in the time we have."

"So?"

Marshall shook his head, still listening. In a minute, the voices quieted, and the door opened.

Sarah studied them. No, the alien. She said something to Marshall in that other language she'd used moments before. So German wasn't their actual language. What had the General called it? A commodity to sell with the humans.

And what commodities had they meant to get from Maggie?

He shuddered.

The General didn't laugh at whatever she'd said, despite her playful smile. "They can't get another spare here. We have to have already left."

"I thought you were listening." With a hand, she invited them back into the lounge. Either she trusted the door guards more than those bundled in the back room or the suite's outer door and walls had better soundproofing. She closed the bedroom door behind them. "He offered anyone on the ship."

She and Marshall traded a skeptical expression.

"Why? What's that mean?" Rockefeller asked.

"It means he's an idiot," Marshall answered.

"A smitten idiot," she elaborated.

"Any women on the ship will be too old to be good cover in the Central Palace." Marshall crossed his arm and planted his feet.

"Then I'll have to go without one. Surely, queens must

be able to acquire spares within the palace." She shrugged one healthy, young—stolen—shoulder. "It could be a point of disgrace, a way to set the Empress at ease."

"Now's not a time to suck up to her."

"It most certainly is!" She stalked back from the door to face him down, despite barely coming up to his shoulder. "Neith must recognize Anjedet's escape as an attempted coup. We see it as a grace, but not if Neith's first action on our arrival is to kill us."

"She's not going to, right?" Maggie asked.

Rockefeller's heart lodged in his throat as he read the aliens' expressions. They were only hoping for any other outcome. It didn't matter to him what happened to the alien, but Sarah... That was her when they came in—her anger at Marshall, her sense of betrayal. She was just a little girl, daughter to parents who didn't know where she was or whether she was safe, same as he hadn't known about Maggie.

That could have been his daughter about to take a chance on alien Russian roulette.

The alien controlling Sarah's body stepped forward and rested a hand on Maggie's shoulder. "Many people have tried to kill me. I didn't survive this long by obliging them."

Maggie nodded, but Rockefeller saw it for the non-answer it was. No one knew when they'd lose their last fight, and trying to escape didn't mean succeeding.

"You're going ahead with it, then?" The words scraped out of his throat, leaving it raw.

She met his eyes. "When we succeed, no one will ever be forced into hosting."

Damn, if it wasn't the same kind of line Marshall fed him, but her, he could almost believe. The way her gaze pinned the General at the end, he saw she blamed him, too.

Then she hugged Maggie, and his daughter let go of his hand to hug her back. "Sarah wishes you well. May you travel in peace."

"You, too. Don't die."

When she straightened, the queen's impostor nodded to him. "Be well. Heed Donn and his symbiont; they'll get you where you need to go." She caught his skeptical expression. "We're all here for the same end, even Donn."

"Take care of that girl you're in. She belongs home with her family, too." Everything in him shouted that he should be doing more, that he should get her back for her family, but Maggie was still in danger; he had to get her out first.

Frowning, she nodded once. Assent? Feigned assent? Too late to tell.

She opened the outer door and said something to the guards. She pointed at Marshall then to outside, and he ushered the Rockefellers through.

The Speaker clutched his daughter's hand as if someone might try to take her away. The guards had to be watching them. Their accusing stares bored into his back all the way across the ballroom and until the napery door closed behind them.

Letting out his pent-up breath, he jostled Maggie to his right, so he could try to shield her view of the occupied toilets in the next room. "That's it? They'll let us go?"

Marshall pressed his finger to his lips.

THE DOOR CLOSED behind Mr. Marshall, Maggie, and her dad, and Sarah could almost believe that she'd made her body sigh.

She'll be okay. Vinnet turned away and strode into the

bedroom, mind abuzz with plans to change and settle in. *She was the last of the raid victims we could help.*

Except Sarah. Of course, they couldn't help *her.*

You know I'll do what I can. Vinnet crossed to the closet and slid open the door. "Is my dress ready?"

The three servants inside snapped to attention. One whipped a dress from the wall and stepped forward.

Vinnet studied the fold of green fabric. *I assume you still prefer that no one sees you undressed?*

Duh!

Her hands snatched the fabric free. "Excellent. Await me outside the outer door."

All three bowed their heads and scurried away.

In their wake, Vinnet held up the dress, checking it over. Sarah didn't care. She thought the laces up the sides were weird, but the neck lump seemed satisfied with it.

It means we can dress ourselves without servants. This is good. She pulled up the scandalous silver dress, exposing Sarah's body again. *Your home life differs from this, correct?*

Suddenly, the possibility of prying eyes didn't seem such a big deal.

Home.

A two-story house on a wide, wooded lot. Except she didn't live there anymore. "Home" now was a compact little building with a postage stamp backyard, hemmed in by a press of other houses. Where people made fun of her on the bus rides to and from school and half the time in between.

Vinnet had made sure no one stayed to make fun of her here.

Before, she was trapped in a school where she could either fail classes or endure more ridicule. In the evenings, trapped at home with her parents' increasingly intense arguments. Now, she was trapped inside with Vinnet controlling her body.

Her hands put on the emerald dress.

In the long run, who was going to miss her? What good was she to anyone, anyway?

You're good to me. Vinnet settled the dress in place, its faux halter top ending short of pressing on her sore neck.

I'm just a body to you.

Their gaze rested on the closed door to the rest of the ship. *Not just. But because you hosted me, Maggie is able to go home. You being here, your willingness to host, made a difference in her life. How much more so if we can bring down the Kem?*

Sarah didn't want to listen to her. Persuasion was just one more means of control. But...

But what if...

What if her life didn't have to be meaningless? A futile march from boring classes, repeating what she'd learned in the last two grades, to miserable bus rides, trying to find the one seat where everyone would leave her alone? And evenings locked in her room, wishing she had one friend she could reach, aside from her toppling stacks of paperbacks?

Her fingers tightened the side corsets' endless cord, picking steadily through the loops.

She'd been locked on the conveyor belt of school, pressed so tight between what she had to do to fit in and what she had to do to please her parents, her personality would surely buckle under the weight. Going above and beyond to try to be a good person? Try to make a difference in the world?

What a joke.

Any chance she'd have was so ridiculously far in the future, she'd never reach it, even before Benny-J and his goons showed up. She might as well stop wanting to try. Obviously, Vinnet could make better use of her body than she could.

Her fingers stopped Vinnet's rhythmic tightening. *I never meant that!*

Vinnet never had to. It just was. *It's fine. Go for it. Human rights. Rah!*

Hesitantly, her fingers returned to tightening. Vinnet's thought melody replayed over Maggie's fortunate freedom as if it might cheer them. 'Cause human rights.

In all fairness to the neck lump, Vinnet had chosen Maggie's freedom over her own convenience and optimal safety; she could have argued her need for a spare. She could have pointed out that the last major Gertewet mission needed every advantage. But no one could have missed Maggie's relief and joy at seeing her dad, however he'd gotten there. Vinnet honored that.

Sarah couldn't have wished it to happen another way. Not unless she could wish herself home, too.

Going to school, living at home, she wasn't helping anyone. Life stayed on hold indefinitely—until she reached the impossible threshold of "old enough," as if kids had nothing to contribute until they turned eighteen.

This shouldn't have happened. Sarah and Maggie and all the other girls shouldn't have been plucked out of their lives. But at least Vinnet wanted to stop it, had devoted her life to doing something about it, even if it meant risking her life and her hosts, even Sarah.

How did it go? "No greater love than to lay down one's life for another"?

At least it was a purpose.

At least it mattered.

What was more real than fighting for human rights? Or at least letting your body fight for human rights?

TROUBLE CAUGHT up between the rows of bunks on the Command Deck, before Marshall and the Rockefellers even made it down to the level they'd started on: a shout over the crew quarters' soft din.

Marshall turned and caught Maggie's free arm. Rockefeller followed his gaze.

A middle-aged man bore down on them. Wearing linen pants and vest and clean-shaven, he was tidier than anyone else Rockefeller had seen here outside the queen's quarters. He explained something to Marshall, pointing back the way they'd come.

Marshall tried to talk his way out, but the man would have none of it. Rockefeller watched the General weigh his options, assessing the area's suitability for a fight. Maybe one bunk in four was occupied, but it was a big room, and anyone they roused might jump in, if only to restore some peace and quiet.

"*Ja, ja, wir gehen.*" Marshall turned them around. When they'd passed the man, he muttered, "Maggie, tell me when the chamberlain stops watching."

They weren't capitulating! "What's the plan?"

"We don't have to go back to the same deck. We can find a kaxan nearby and keep the hatch shut until we drop down to sublight again."

"What, we'll get 'lost in hyperspace' if we separate?"

Marshall shook his head. "You make it sound like a load of baloney. It's not. Undocking perturbs the course of both ships, and even small perturbations take time to correct.

Every second, we're travelling about two-hundred times the distance from the Earth to the sun—if we're in normal space. Nobody really knows. Hell, I don't. You want to risk it? Or anyone left on this ship?"

Yes. Anything to get away, not that it was a logical outlook. "Fine."

Maggie glanced at them uncertainly then turned back. "He's still watching."

"*Scheisse.*" Marshall turned them back into the aisle toward the ballroom. "Speaker, I'll take her through to the napery and wait for you there. You double back and come get me when the chamberlain is gone."

Leave this smarmy betrayer of children with his daughter when he just got her back? Maggie's wide eyes met his, pleading.

Marshall rolled his. "The chamberlain will recognize her or me. You have to go."

"Can't we just fight him?"

"In the middle of the reinforcements? Just go, you big baby. We'll be two doors down."

Rockefeller squeezed Maggie's hand, stopped, and watched them until they passed into the next room. Then he turned back.

Was that a double cross? If so, it was exceptionally smooth. He'd followed Marshall since parting with Major Patrick, and not once had they encountered the chamberlain to arrange this. In fact, the Major hadn't even warned him they were coming. Had the alien controlling Sarah arranged this when speaking that other language? Then how had she managed such a convincing heartfelt goodbye?

Is that what she meant by years of practice?

Rockefeller reached the intersection with the main aisle and caught the chamberlain overseeing a handful of women climbing up from the ladder. Turning, the chamberlain led the women up the aisle.

So much for a clean getaway.

Rockefeller scrambled back toward the napery, trying to ignore the feeling of dozens of hostile eyes watching him from bunks and sanitary stations. He should be used to that. Out of 435 Representatives and countless aides and visitors, only a portion were his party, and a smaller portion also on friendly terms.

But they weren't trying to implant aliens in his daughter —and maybe him. If only he could take her place.

He found Marshall and Maggie in the napery, as promised, looking busy by folding sheets. Maggie tackled him with a hug, but Marshall only asked, "Is he gone?"

"He's coming back up the aisle with a group of women."

"*Scheisse.*" Marshall glanced between the three doors out and stepped toward the only one they hadn't used yet. "Get in."

They poured through and shut the door before registering the three startled faces in the already-cramped space. The six of them stared at each other in silence before the oldest woman inside stood, grinning, and shouted, "*Perfekt!*"

She fell on Maggie before Rockefeller could fathom what to do. In moments, she'd whipped fabric from the table, slipped Maggie's shirt over her head, and slid the new garment on, chatting to her companions all the while.

The younger woman working inside edged past the cramped table to study Rockefeller's jacket and pants. Her frisky fingers traced from his collar down the front lapels and then the fit of his pants. It took a minute to collect her hands and push them away.

Marshall leaned close. "This isn't going to work. I'm sorry."

"What do you—"

The door opened to not only the chamberlain, but also a man in even nicer dress: a vest with formal trim. It was the other man who spoke. "*Wir brauchen die Frauen.*"

Rockefeller caught that. The women were being summoned.

The senior seamstress frowned. "*Auch das kleine Maedchen?*"

"*Alle.*"

With her hands on Maggie's shoulder, the older woman steered her past, trailing the younger female seamstress.

Rockefeller reached for Maggie, but Marshall held him back.

The General smiled at the chamberlain and said something to ward him off. The door closed again.

As the remaining seamster settled back to his work, the General kept a tight hold on Rockefeller. "It's just a few minutes. You know she's not going to get chosen."

"I know?" Rockefeller shook free. "You planned this."

"Like hell. I thought it was going to be a cakewalk as soon as she got up here. I didn't know her stupid demand was going to start a witchhunt. But think about it: she knows who Maggie is. If she knows we'll be there for her again, she'll reject her again. No harm, no foul."

"How do you know?"

"Look, Kitchell's known her for mill—" He shook his head. "Centuries. Earth years, so centuries. She's not going to change her mind unless something new comes up. And, trust me, nothing new has come up in the last few minutes."

"If you say so." It still felt wrong.

Clanking his scissors down, the seamster looked up and asked, "*Brauchen Sie etwas?*"

MARSHALL LINED Rockefeller against the ballroom wall with the other curious bystanders, all male. It took two rounds of baths and a change of clothes for all the women to be considered acceptable, and even after that, there was a delay Marshall couldn't explain.

All the while, the chamberlain and fancy-vest man surveyed the two hundred or so women gathered together, most of whom looked as angry and indignant as Maggie did nervous. She stood in front, where he could watch her.

Marshall shook his head. "Women don't qualify for mothership duty unless they've had at least three kids. Even the men are probationary until they've done the same."

"Three?"

"How do you grow a population when you're constantly exporting people?" Marshall lowered his voice further. "One of our queens had a human child once. After that, she lost every litter of tewet in that host."

"What?"

"I don't know. Her pelvis was too wide for tewet or something. We didn't really experiment with it. She miscarried every litter until she got a new host." He nodded to the assembly. "Maggie's the only girl out there who can carry a litter of tewet to term. If Banebdjedet doesn't know that, he's a fool."

Rockefeller forced himself to take a breath. "If I were you, I wouldn't talk about getting my daughter pregnant."

Marshall nodded, not even looking at him.

In the end, the lord from the feast glanced over to them, then returned with his "queen." Sarah had changed—or been changed, like Maggie—into an asymmetric emerald gown gathered high in the front and trailing in back. The seamstresses beamed at the dress, even as the queen appraised them.

As expected, she dismissed them all and retreated to her quarters.

The alien lord grabbed one and let the rest disband—everyone but Maggie.

23

INTO THE FIRE

Katorin figured that, at some point, Neith would outfit her security forces in full spacesuits. Until then, they were still vulnerable in the restrooms. After incapacitating a security officer and slipping his plasma stun gun into her bag, she met back up with Cube Head along the public promenade. Behind him, she glimpsed the sparkle of kaxan-taxis outside swooping down to deposit a light stream of spectators inside the atrium. Neith loved redundancy; the transporters' programming normally would not transmit weapons or explosives into the Central Palace Complex. In case they did, however, all visitors had to pass through a security checkpoint manned by her direct offspring. Gertewet practiced acquiring weapons inside.

Katorin and Cube Head turned away from the checkpoint and entered an enormous, covered stadium. Above them, a clear dome had frosted over, its bright crystalline patterns shining against the background of the black, predawn sky. Thousands of padded seats encircled the large pit so many stories below. At center stage, rising up from the sandy floor, stood a pole to hold the accused. Everyone knew the show ahead was overkill, but at least it got them off work for a day.

Instead of taking an escalator down to the front rows, Cube Head skirted along the back wall. "You know, if you want to, you can see the Ger beforehand."

"Really?"

"Yeah, I think it's to discourage us from betraying the empire, but a lot of people want to know what Gertewet look like."

"I'd love to!" She smiled to herself, thrilled she didn't have to talk him into it.

An eighth of the way around, he led her to the ground and down a clean, white corridor. They stopped across the hall from an arched doorway flanked by a pair of grey-uniformed guards. The men stood perfectly still, their faces blank, eyes studying the spectators, fingers on the triggers of their averted stun weapons.

Katorin peeked through the archway as the watching guards expected. A third guard stood at the round room's far wall, as alert to the visitors as his compatriots in the hall. In the room's center, a man was strapped to an upright plat-form. Khonsu's host. Like the wooden stocks some lords used as punishment on their worlds. A single, wide metal clamp locked the prisoner's wrists and neck in place; a stiff, tightly woven barrier covered his mouth. His eyes were closed, as though he were already dead.

We always get them in the end, Cube Head had said. Despite his assurances that no one cared anymore, the stadium looked far busier than normal; Neith's proclamation about the end of the war worked.

Time to change that.

Three guards. She could take care of them.

Taking a step behind Cube Head, she withdrew her stolen gun and shot the guard to the right.

"Beryl?"

Both of the others began aiming their weapons at her, but she shot the second guard in the hall first. Then she drew Cube Head's squirming form closer, fixing him between her and the third guard with a firm pinch around the symbiont's spine.

"Beryl!" His voice quivered.

The third guard took shelter behind the prisoner and let off a poorly aimed burst. She didn't feel anything, so she edged to the right for a clearer shot, pulling Cube Head with her. Her next shot caught the third guard.

"Beryl, what are you doing? Stop!"

The third guard's positioning had lured her into the range of fire for a hidden fourth, whose shot grazed both Cube Head and her; a faint buzz of the electrical component tingled through their near contact.

Cube Head shouted, his mind finally catching onto the fourth's existence. "I'm on your side! Don't shoot me!"

Having spent so much time on the perfect shot, the fourth guard left himself open enough for her to shoot him. The tiny plasma sheet deflected slightly through an intervening gravitation field in the doorway, but when it connected, the last guard dropped to the ground.

Inside, the bound Gertewet opened his eyes and stared at her.

She pulled her companion with her to the keypad beside the doorway, slamming the DNA bypass into place and counting seconds until reinforcements arrived. Grabbing one of Cube Head's fingers, she started using it to enter Gertewet-planted security overrides.

"Beryl?" he asked, voice quivering. "What's going on?"

She didn't answer. As she finished, a red light on the keypad turned green. Stepping forward with the Kemtewet, she waved a hand through the door. When she felt nothing, she was sure the force field had shut off. She pulled Cube Head into the room. Letting him go, she kept the gun trained on him. "Move and I'll shoot you, too."

He stood stock still, back to her, hands in the air. He sounded like he was going to cry. "I turned you in. They said you were young. They said you weren't a Ger."

"And I'm not," she lied, pulling a canteen from her satchel with her free hand. "I just have my own plans for them."

She opened the cover over the host's mouth and whispered into his ear, "Thank you for your service."

Hopefully, her comrade was causing enough brain damage as he left that his host couldn't be revived for information. The host, unfortunately, would be dead by the time the symbiont escaped and, fortunately, dead by the time his public execution took place.

Cube Head turned slowly around, in time to see a short, yellow and brown amphibian slip from its host's mouth into the canteen. "Hades! You're *not* a Ger! You're just taking the tewet!"

Of course she was. Didn't he know all hosts were permanently paralyzed before their executions to make it that much harder for them to escape? She supposed if that knowledge got out, it would make the spectacle of executions considerably less exciting.

After replacing the mouth cover, she screwed the lid on with her free hand and stowed the container back in her bag. "All right, Paul, now that we've established an understanding, listen up. We're going to head back outside as if nothing happened, or I will find a blade to sink into your spine. *Capisce*?"

He nodded dumbly.

Grabbing him by the arm, she pulled him to the doorway, checked the empty hallway, and stowed her weapon. Placing her arms firmly and affectionately around one of his, she pulled him into the hall, heading back the way they came.

THE "QUEEN" had already tried to send her away. Maggie clung to that thought while the chamberlain lined her up with all the ship's women. She thought it when the chamberlain sent women away, and they came back clean and in nicer clothes.

At one point, Sarah walked through, to the chamberlain's obvious consternation. She—or the alien possessing her—met Maggie's gaze and frowned, then caught sight of Maggie's dad and Mr. Marshall against the wall. Then she disappeared into another room.

The "queen" wouldn't choose her again. She'd sounded serious about preferring to go alone, even though Mr. Marshall and others seemed to expect her to have...

A backup body.

Maggie glanced around again at the large crowd of seamstresses, maids, cooks, and crewmembers pulled from bed, all whispering angry complaints at each other. Somebody was serious about her having a backup body.

Sarah (if that was her) said the alien wouldn't leave her to possess Maggie. Would the same hold true for someone else? What if, by going with her, Maggie would save someone else from possession? Would she go? She should.

But no.

She watched her dad. The "queen" wouldn't pick her. She'd promised, hadn't she?

Her dad watched her, too, mouthing reassurances until Mr. Marshall started talking to him. Whatever he said back, she was glad she couldn't hear. It didn't look nice.

Eventually, the "queen" returned from the other room, along with the four-arm man, and surveyed them, pacing slowly past each one.

Maggie's heart pounded. Someone else. Someone else. No one else. No one at all.

She passed Maggie especially quickly. In the end, she chose no one and returned to her chambers. The assembled crowd sighed in relief and buzzed with new discussions. A word from the chamberlain started them flowing away.

Safe.

Until someone grabbed her arm. The four-arm man motioned.

And the room disappeared—the crowd, the wooden floors, her dad.

She faced a green wall beside a doorway, her chest aching as if her heart had exploded.

No!

No, this couldn't be happening!

She was supposed to go home! It was supposed to be over. She was supposed to be safe! Not—

Breath frozen in her chest, she spun slowly, taking in the new room, trying to figure out where they'd sent her now and, more importantly, with whom. None of the walls matched, and many featured crests of different items: wheat, ballet shoes, instruments, and other things that didn't belong together.

The opposite wall also displayed a mural of bones.

Human bones.

Skulls and femurs and ribs in no sensible pattern or order, all plastered in place like 3D wallpaper. Like an empty, grotesque fireplace.

She barely peeled her eyes away to see the black sculpture at the room's end, a table of food in the middle, and a surprised woman with short-shaved hair and a round, friendly face.

But was she really friendly?

Maggie backed into the corner.

"Anjedet?" The woman skirted the table and looked her over. Frowning, she launched into a longer question.

That wasn't German. It sounded more like the language Mr. Marshall and the "queen" had used.

Another alien.

Maggie crouched down, trying to get away. Not again.

INTO THE FIRE. Vinnet blew out a breath, closed her eyes, and waited for the transporters to deposit her and her new host in the coals of the Kemtewet Empire. All her sensibilities screamed that it was too early to take a new host on any mission, let alone one in which she might contact the Empress.

She'd been captured by a king once and tortured until she escaped, and her host died two weeks later. The Empress was so much worse, the Coordinating Council rarely ordered missions that might interact with her; so many ended in death. Rumor said she could see through people, but Vinnet tried not to lend credence to it.

The sounds around her abruptly changed from the

reverent whispers among the mothership's crew to clinking dishes and soft sobbing. Vinnet opened her eyes.

She stood in a corner facing a narrow, green wall beside a doorway, shoulder near a deep burgundy wall. A sculpted trident of green fire against the green wall presided over four other items: a bundle of wheat, a six-stringed lyre, a reinforced-toe dancing shoe, and a bowl of fresh fruit. Exports from the planets ruled by the Green Flame.

Complete with a spare body crouched in the corner. Sarah's stomach wrenched, and Vinnet sympathized. Maggie.

No. This wasn't her plan.

A quick glance around the room showed walls for each of the kings: mirrors for the Eater of Ghosts, recycled bones for the Bone-Breaker, and a gurgling fountain for the Eater of Blood. She couldn't look at the one for He With His Face Behind Him.

A wide-eyed woman tending the refreshment table in the center motioned impatiently to the girl.

Good. They expected Anjedet to help.

Vinnet crouched with her and laid a hand on Maggie's shoulder, catching some of her brittle curls. She kept her voice low. "Be brave."

Maggie looked up, her face streaked with tears for the first time in Sarah's memory since, well, the execution of the older Earth women. Why had Banebdjedet done that? It was wasteful, even by Kemtewet standards. Maggie shook her head. "Why?"

"So I can take you home when we're done." Oh, this was foolish. Another promise? Soon, she'd be crushed in them if she wasn't careful.

Maggie searched her face, as if she'd find any deception.

Schooling her impulse to monitor the Kemtewet

woman, Vinnet met her gaze. The girl must not realize she'd had lifetimes to discipline her body language and make it convey what she intended.

But you'll really do it, right? Take her home?

She's from your planet. If we all survive, it won't be out of our way.

Time to go. Authentically scared or not, they needed to get a working understanding of the situation here.

"Come on. All you need to do is follow me." Vinnet offered her a hand, and when Maggie took it, pulled her up.

As they stood, Maggie started at something behind Vinnet. She turned. The Eater of Blood's token was a fountain of blood sheeting down the center of his long wall. Her host echoed Maggie's shock and disgust.

It probably wasn't taken from anyone living. All the servants in this area dispose of their hosts when they enter and leave. Both the blood and bones may be salvaged from them.

And that doesn't bother you?

The fact that they're killed is far worse than what's done with their parts.

Then why does that statue at the end bother you so much?

This time, she couldn't avoid it. The back wall held no exports, only a statue. She hoped it was a statue. Otherwise, it was actually a young, hairless man, head twisted unnaturally to look backwards, who had been dipped in hot tar. At least she couldn't see his expression.

And that's worse than recycled body parts, how?

If it wasn't sculpted—and I doubt it was—that man was never a host. Otherwise, his twisted neck would exaggerate the gap a symbiont left behind. *See the texture on the side of his head? He was tarred first, then killed.* Probably by someone under orders to touch the hot tar. Probably another human harmed for this "art," since a Kemtewet's discomfort would have affronted his sense of citizenship.

Sarah didn't recognize the statue's symbolism yet.

That's an extremely elaborate representation of He With His Face Behind Him, the king who captured our queen.

She had probably died even more horrifically.

"Queen Anjedet." Apparently satisfied that the spare was under control, the servant approached. Stepping away from the refreshment tables, she kept her surprised harmonics just shy of rude. "My lady the Empress will be pleased to see you've returned safely. Would you like me to take you to her?"

Probably under orders to bring her the rogue queen immediately. After all the independence she'd exerted recently, Anjedet would chafe at the suggestion. "I'd like to refresh myself first."

The servant's vassal had a beautifully sculpted face, especially when she smiled. "There will be time aplenty once my lady the Empress has seen you. Besides, you don't want to miss the execution."

Execution? Hers or someone unrelated? "Who is it this time?" She tried to sound bored.

"The last Gertewet." The servant waggled her fingers teasingly as she passed to lead them deeper into the palace.

"Sure, the last. Coincidentally in time for the Kings' Ball." Vinnet followed her, glancing back to confirm Maggie was staying close. For her to slip away from the King as she had, Anjedet had to flout her irreverence, but Vinnet hoped she wasn't pushing her performance.

The servant shrugged. "I heard she was saving him for three years." She glanced back as if seeking confirmation.

Great. Anjedet was supposed to know things. So much

for pumping palace servants for information. Vinnet rolled
her eyes. Let the girl chew on that for a while.

They wound through the halls, occasionally encountering other servants who stopped against the walls and
waited for them to pass. Eventually, they arrived at the edge
of a narrow, red runner that started mid-hall and extended
clear through the next chamber.

A red carpet? Sarah wondered.

One of Neith's new fashions. From your world, I suppose.

The servant stopped at the edge. "Happy execution,
Queen Anjedet."

Vinnet powered ahead, straightening Sarah's back to its
full length and holding her chin high. This, she knew how
to do. She paused at the doorway, mimicking what she'd
seen at other events on Sais from the public perspective.

"Now announcing Queen of the Green Flame, Anjedet."

Vinnet walked into the room and brushed by the
reporter in the chamber's center. Kings and lords took every
opportunity for interviews. The Empress spoke on special
occasions. Queens seemed to be forbidden. She followed
the red runner to the door at the back of the chamber,
which opened in response and let her pass through.

The next room wasn't what she'd expected, but she
hadn't had many expectations. The public wasn't permitted
many details about the fealty, so she'd imagined the same
sorts of places she'd seen the lords and kings build:
sweeping marble chambers filled with servants and
designed to impress.

This was an intimate space, comfortably full for the ten
milling occupants and their spare vassals lined up against
the side walls. It wasn't hard to guess their number: all five
kings, their matching queens (except Anjedet), and the
Empress. The front wall was transparent and looked

straight out at a post in the center of the execution arena's floor.

The door shut behind her. No turning back.

We'll be fine, right? You've done this a hundred times.

Not this. Not with the Empress. Not even with more than one king, but there was always a first. She hadn't been killed yet.

She turned to Maggie. "Stand against the wall." Luckily, any new spare, not just hers, would need some instructions.

Maggie opened her mouth to reply, and Vinnet turned her back. Out of the corner of her eye, she caught Maggie retreating. There went one worry.

Most of the kings and queens regarded her, but only one approached. The Green Flame wore wide, reflective scales and crossed the room in long, angry strides. With no regard for appearances, his meaty fingers wrapped around her biceps and pulled her to the side of the door. "Where were you?"

That hurts!

Normally, Vinnet would pull her arm free, but she didn't know how queens responded. She knew so little about them. Scowling, she met his eyes. "The Empress knew."

His open palm flew up from nowhere and struck her face with enough force to send her reeling back toward the doorway. He jerked her to a halt before she fell. As she steadied herself, he spoke through his teeth. "You cost Uatschnesert his life. You won't do the same to me."

Subservient or aggressive? She knew Anjedet was Neith's spawn. She stepped in closer and backhanded him, though she weakened the blow as if she weren't an experienced fighter.

In hindsight, it wasn't the best move. He backed her against the wall and held her by the throat.

I can't breathe! Sarah panicked.

Patience. We'll be fine. She hoped.

Sure enough, the Green Flame let up in moments. His thick hand moved down to her collar bone. "Neith will give me permission to kill you."

Vinnet held very still, and not merely to perform her role. As possible successors to the throne, the queens should have been untouchable. Unlike most Kemtewet, they possessed not only the Empress's complete memories at the time of their conception but also the ability to produce more Kemtewet. Professionally, it was interesting that they might be permitted to die. Personally, it was disturbing.

She whispered through gritted teeth, "That will be unnecessary."

"See that it is." He let go and turned his back to her. A closer study of the room showed all the queens standing silently behind their kings. She straightened her burning neck and took up her position, hoping this would be her only blunder.

All the while, the Empress hadn't moved, though she had to have heard the whole exchange. Everyone must have. Neith still stood with her back to the room, gazing out the window toward the empty arena pole. "Anjedet." The tone of her voice, like her servant's, wasn't a question.

The Green Flame stepped aside and regarded Vinnet with raised eyebrows.

First test. Vinnet crossed the room, aware of the others' riveted attention. Scrutiny was never good for a spy, but if she could make it through, if she succeeded, it would benefit every planet for all the future. She stopped at the Empress's left and gazed out into the stands.

"I'm surprised to see you. I wouldn't have returned." The

Empress kept her voice soft, her harmonics casual and enticing.

Even in light of the destruction of three cities. Surely, Neith's attitudes were what corrupted the Kemtewet so thoroughly. Vinnet only smiled.

The Empress studied her and smiled back as if getting in on the joke.

Then something caught her eye, and she nodded through the window. "Do you see them descending the escalator in front of us?"

Vinnet studied the walkway the Empress indicated, expecting not to see anything standing out. Streams of people trickled up and down, some in a hurry, some meandering. Her eye caught on a puff of bright red hair. The red-haired woman leaned against a man in a black jacket and boxy haircut riding slowly down the escalator to the bottom. When she recognized the woman's posture and body frame, Vinnet tensed. *Katorin.*

The Empress angled a handheld screen toward her that showed security footage of a firefight outside one of the prison cells.

She's your friend! The Empress identified her; you have to do something!

Vinnet took a slow breath. "I see them." The statement she'd meant to sound anticipatory came out neutral. *I can't. I love Katorin as my sister, but this mission is more important than her life. If I revealed myself, that would put the three of us at risk along with her.*

The Empress smiled across the arena at Katorin. "Now we begin the endgame."

Be safe! Vinnet watched her and the man crest the escalator and follow the walkway at the top of the stadium, avoiding the gray-suited security at the main exit. She watched them with the Empress until the curve of the stadium blocked their view, trying to shake the certainty that she'd never see Katorin again.

"Are you going to kill her?"

"Not until she finishes." The Empress smiled.

It's a trap! But was this exercise also a demonstration that the Kemtewet had already seen through her cover?

"I will uncover your plan. I suspect I'd like it for my own."

If only.

Yeah, Empress, Sarah added, *go jump off a bridge.*

"For now, you have a lovely new vassal, one you apparently intend to keep for years. You know as much as I do that insubordination cannot go unpunished." For as placidly as she stared into the arena, the Empress might have been discussing rose gardens. "If you could see no reason not to take your vassal from Earth, I ought to kill you where you stand."

Vinnet kept her gaze down and clasped her hands together by her belt. "Of course I see reasons not to, but we both see reasons for it." Besides prestige? The Empress knew the planet where humans originated was still thriving but had never moved to conquer it. Besides the fact that the Empress had forbidden Earth hosts for everyone except herself and a gifted few, why would Anjedet want hosts from there? This line of questioning didn't sound like an inquiry into simple insubordination.

How else could it possibly affect the Empress?

Neith stared out at the arena, her current vassal's smooth jawline profiled against the sapphire window. "Their culture is rich and varied. Our samples show them continuously evolving. If they knew about us, if they collected enough details, they would find ways to defend against us. They would outmaneuver us, and we would have hardly a hope to bring them into the Empire, into their fullest potential.

"It's almost time. They have millennia of history and development completely independent of our own. If we wait much longer, they'll be able to prevent us from reuniting with the rest of civilization."

Chills rippled across Sarah's skin.

This Neith had a lot of experience outthinking not only the leaders she wrested her capital from, but also all her predecessors in name and title. And she thought Earth might best her?

How advanced are you? Vinnet wondered.

Well, we don't have teleporters and spiffy spaceships. I can tell you that.

Then what did Neith know? No, she could analyze later. What would Anjedet say now? "On a planet that size, that heavily populated, all of us here could have a steady stream of vassals and never start to influence them."

"Pay closer attention to your vassal's memory."

Vinnet tried to hide her confusion. *Why? What do you know of them? Kitchell talks to your defenses; has she heard of him?*

We don't know anything! Our idea of aliens is Roswell grays and flying saucers, nothing like any of you. Memory images accompanied her thoughts, and the latter struck a chord.

Your flying saucer myths! Those are our kaxan! She met the Empress's gaze wide-eyed. "They've seen Kaxandepet."

"One mistake, Anjedet, could ruin everything. You won't make a second." She turned back to the window and raised a dismissing hand.

Vinnet bowed her head, crossed the room, and fell into step at the Green Flame's side.

That wasn't so bad. Neith doesn't live up to her reputation for evilness.

She wouldn't in public encounters like this, or she would never have gained control in the first place. Vinnet studied the Empress's placid profile. *Her retribution against Anjedet is yet to come.*

24

ESCAPE FROM THE CENTRAL PALACE

M aggie disappeared. Rockefeller's blood ran cold.

Marshall tugged him toward the exit, even as the alien lord stalked through the emptying ballroom toward the queen's quarters.

Rockefeller clutched Marshall's sleeve. "We can go after her."

"Shut up, or I will knock you silent and carry you out."

They passed through the napery and adjoining room again. They'd come so far to get Maggie. Surely, even Marshall knew it was worth following her to one more place. Sarah's alien would give her up.

They just needed one more try.

Marshall chose the first saucer they passed on the Command Deck. This time, Rockefeller found the screen first and followed the menu choices he'd watched Marshall use before. Only one of the destination options flashed; he picked that one.

Suddenly, the ship disappeared, and Rockefeller found himself in a wide atrium with snow-dusted glass ceiling.

The chamber felt draftier than the cozy kaxan, and its echoes muddled all sound together. All around him, a buzzing crowd drifted in a single direction.

That's where Maggie must have been going.

He let himself get swept along, through a security check-point staffed by a machine and its bored operators, and into a stadium.

This was it? Another alien planet?

If it weren't for the ships and beaming down, he'd have a hard time believing it. Sure, the folks in the crowd dressed funny and spoke a strange language, but he'd been in a dozen other countries like that on Earth.

Staring down across the rapidly-filling stadium seats to the empty ring below, watching the body language tell of the growing excitement for the big game or whatever it was —nothing about it felt truly alien.

A hand clamped on his shoulder. "There you are."

At Marshall's voice, Rockefeller shrugged the hand off. "Here I am. I told you I'd find her."

It was a big crowd, but if Maggie was with the queen, she should be somewhere obvious. Nothing stuck out.

Marshall lowered his voice. "You shouldn't be here. Any one of these Kem would swap hosts in an instant to have somebody from Earth. We have to get you out."

"Not without my daughter." Box seating. The queen was supposed to be be important; she should be sitting some-where special. Did anything stand out as box seating?

"You can't reach her. These public areas don't connect to the feudal areas." But Marshall scanned the area, too. Maybe not so certain? "Perfect!"

"Neith hasn't stayed in power so long by having security gaps," Cube Head warned at a whisper.

"That's my concern, not yours." But it had Katorin worried. She expected Neith's forces to respond by now, but she was glad they hadn't. The plan she'd put together in one hour wasn't all that good. She didn't have the resources she needed to pull off a smooth rescue. Normally, she would pass off her cargo and run for it, confident that three or four others were doing likewise and frustrating the security forces. But she didn't have backup. This wasn't a Council-sanctioned operation. Any other Ger here wouldn't blow their covers before getting vital information to Vinnet for her next mission, the beginning of the Kemtewet's end. She had to finish alone.

She leaned her head against Cube Head's shoulder as they reentered the stadium, calmly retracing their route.

"You certainly put on a show," he remarked softly. "When do you plan on killing me?"

"I haven't decided." Catching the stares of other spectators, she straightened up but still clutched his arm. Already, hundreds of Kemtewet had gathered to watch the execution of the being in her satchel. At least they could still watch the death of his already-dead host.

Cube Head stepped up onto the walkway around the stadium's perimeter. "Are you going to decide my fate any time soon?"

"Are you going to shut up any time soon?" Gray security uniforms started popping up by the exit, so she took a sharp right away from them.

"You know, when I think of the enemies of the Empire, I generally assume they're smart enough to take exits when they leave."

She rolled her eyes but kept him walking. How could he

have missed the swarms of security forces at the main exit? Or did he think he could change her mind about her route?

A familiar face stood out in the crowd, and she looked away, hoping not to cause suspicion about her activities to spread to Kitchell. She raised her voice, so the other Gertewet could hear. "It's too bad we have to leave already!"

He slipped in behind her, tugging along a man with a small head and clothing popular on only a handful of worlds—all with enclosed environments. Or was this another human from Earth? A Kem with a vassal gifted from Neith? Looked like a useful dupe.

Kitchell had decided to follow her. Good. With two Ger and two dupes useful for diversions, her escape just got easier.

She smiled at him. "We can't exit through the atrium; they'll be looking for me."

Kitchell nodded.

"This way."

ROCKEFELLER SEARCHED THE CROWD, trying to identify what had caught General Marshall's attention.

Before the Speaker found it, Marshall latched onto his arm, towing him forward. "Come on!"

"What?"

Marshall didn't answer, but his unyielding grip brooked no discussion.

If this was how his daughters felt when he and Joyce navigated them through crowds, no wonder they put up such a fuss. He twisted his arm, trying to break free. "I've come this far. I'm not leaving without her!"

Marshall wasn't even listening. He stared at a curly

redhead attached to the arm of a sweaty kid who might have been right out of college...on Earth. She glanced toward them, recognition sparking in her eyes, then away. She raised her voice, but Rockefeller couldn't even guess what language she spoke.

Marshall followed her, not even discreetly.

Stopping, she flashed him a short-lived smile, ignored Rockefeller, and said something else, nodding to the entrance they'd come through.

"What is going on here?" Rockefeller tried again to tug his arm free, but he only wrenched Marshall's hand against the developing bruises.

The redhead's companion said something sympathetic sounding, but it still wasn't English.

Still ignoring him, she addressed Marshall, nodding in a new direction. "This way."

Marshall followed, dragging Rockefeller, too.

"What is going on? Who is she?"

Her companion wrenched around the best he could, stumbling a little. "She's some kind of mercenary. She—" He switched into another language. "—the prisoner!"

She elbowed him silent.

Marshall leaned over. "It's going to be hard enough escaping without you making a scene."

"Escaping? We can't leave yet!"

"We have to while we can."

"There's no one even after us!"

"They will be soon." He dropped his voice even further, so Rockefeller could barely hear him amid the din. "She has the prisoner slated to be executed today."

He blinked at her companion anew. Sure, the kid looked afraid, but he didn't seem to be in any rush to leave. Rockefeller shook his head. "Then why are we following her?"

Marshall's jaw worked. "If we don't leave with her now, we may not be able to for another five to seven years. You'll never last that long."

Years. That was a long time. Suddenly, he needed to get home to watch Julia and Chastity grow up. "What about Maggie and the other girl? We could leave with them."

"They might take at least that long, but they're safer than you are. Maggie's only there for show. Our girl should be able to protect her the whole time."

Should. Right. "How?"

"She's spoken for, as a spare."

"Then call me your spare, and let's go get her."

Marshall glared at him. "Only fealty have spares. It usually takes months or years to get set up like that."

Marshall was afraid for him. Rockefeller glanced around the stadium, and it suddenly clicked. The problem wasn't that everyone around him was an alien. The problem was that each of the thousands of people surrounding him in a small sea was controlled by a body-possessing parasite. Even Marshall. Even the redhead and her college-age kid.

How many of those body-possessing parasites would gladly kill their hosts to possess him? How long would he last if they found out? Minutes? Seconds?

Maggie wasn't the only one in danger.

KATORIN STARTED FOR THE ESCALATORS, Cube Head wrenching in her arms to talk to Kitchell's dupe. "She's some kind of mercenary. She extracted just the prisoner."

She elbowed him. If she could have sealed his mouth, she would. Epoxy? Adhesive strips? Needle and thread? She had none. "You try that again, and I will relieve you of your tongue."

She, at least, would feel relieved.

He pouted.

She hung tighter to his arm. "It's not all bad. You'd waited to date for how long? Since I arrived?"

He turned his pout away from her; Katorin was right on target. *You'd think I was a spy or something.*

Just remember one thing, Setira noted. *To pat yourself on the back, you have to go through me.*

But you're doing a great job, too.

They stepped onto the down escalator. Cube Head quelled, but Kitchell's dupe grew agitated, pointing at the feudal areas until Kitchell reined him in. She glanced that way, caught the Empress watching, and closed her eyes, leaning her head on Cube Head's shoulder.

"She's going to catch you."

She shouldn't let him get to her. His was blind faith, rooted in propaganda, not a knowledge of the intersection of her plans and the Empress's resources.

"She's smiling."

"So should you." She caught his lips with hers, felt him tense in protest. If he pushed her away, this would never work. Then he simply leaned into her, as if he'd never kissed before.

He hadn't.

You just realized that? Setira scoffed.

The Empress's direct attention aside, laughter bubbled past her lips, separating her from him.

Cube Head blinked at her then swiped his mouth with his sleeve. First kiss. Of all the universe's ironies!

"She's been strangled!" Kitchell's dupe blurted.

Katorin forced herself not to look at him, but Cube Head

did and followed his gaze to the feudal area. Who were they discussing?

"She's standing with the Empress now, so it looks like a good start," Kitchell told him. It must be Vinnet! Why Kitchell would tell a Kem such a thing disturbed her as much as it cheered her to know Vinnet fared well. It had to be Vinnet. She was the only one getting set up to stand there. What did she look like now? Katorin sneaked in one more glance before stepping off the escalator.

An Earth girl.

The Coordinating Council would be pissed, but it was a tactical choice: high fashion. Vinnet's mission had better work, or she'd be put through the wringer.

Stepping off the escalator, she aimed for a hallway leading out of the stadium.

———

ROCKEFELLER AND MARSHALL stepped onto a down escalator behind the woman and her ungrateful rescue. It was then, trapped in the crowd, that Rockefeller saw the box seating. Right on ground level, with an expansive window separating the sandy court from a catered gallery. Front and center stood the fake queen and a smug woman in a chainmail dress, both of whom seemed to be staring at them.

More importantly, he caught Maggie's puff of hair where she stood in a line with others against the back wall. His baby! She still looked whole and sound—just not safe. Her worried gaze anchored on the girl, the Gertewet.

Just look past them. I'm right here, baby. I'm coming for you.

He shook Marshall's arm and started to point, but the alien smacked his free hand from the air. "I see them. They're watching us."

"But Maggie's right behind her."

"Yes, I know." Keeping his grip on Rockefeller hidden behind the woman's back, Marshall leaned against the rail, angling his back toward the window. "You can't get in there. Servants' vassals are quarantined. You'll either die or...or worse. Let our girl handle it."

Sarah's head looked around, but the shadow underneath moved with it into the light.

"She's been strangled!" The vicious marks on her neck sent a chill down his spine.

"I saw." Marshall closed his eyes. "She's standing with the Empress now, so it looks like a good start."

He got in one more glance of the elegant woman beside her before they reached the bottom and rushed into the smell of nutmeg and vanilla.

Someone had tried to strangle a little girl, and Marshall still thought it was going well? He had to find a way in.

HERE, the air smelled strongly of vanilla and nutmeg. As Katorin and her tagalongs ventured farther in, racks of pastries waited along the walls to be served to the hordes of guests. The few chefs they passed cast disdainful glares in their direction but said nothing.

Following the palace map she'd memorized, Katorin took a smaller hall to the left. Suddenly, she felt Cube Head's arm pull forward and sweep back into her stomach. Letting the air get knocked out, she locked his arm with hers, wrenched a finger free from his fist, and pulled it back in an unnatural position.

He hissed in pain. "Okay, I'm sorry, Beryl. It won't happen again."

Ignoring him, she kept moving forward, pulling him along by his awkwardly bent hand. They were too close now to waste time. She could see the destination, the wide rectangle in the floor that marked the area where goods could be transported into the secondary freezer. She pulled Cube Head in with her.

"Are you sure about this?" Kitchell muttered, stepping in with his dupe.

It was the only workable plan she'd thought of in the middle of the night, but if she'd waited, early morning planning generally fared worse. Shrugging, she smacked the activation button.

The warm, bustling atmosphere of the bakery faded into a small, blue-tinged dome filled with marked boxes and vacuum-sealed bags of food. They'd left the tropical warmth of the Central Palace in favor of the icy conditions of the storage freezer.

Kitchell's dupe panicked, but that was his problem.

"Can I have my hand back?" Cube Head asked as she studied her surroundings, looking for an outside wall.

"No," she answered absently, renewing some of the pressure on his flexed finger. Catching sight of her target, she marched out of the transport rectangle.

Cube Head followed at her side, occasionally trying to jerk his hand away. "It's kind of cold here, Beryl," he whined.

Bracing herself, she stopped at the outer wall and withdrew the plasma stun gun. She aimed at the wall and fired. Thick layers of frost vaporized, as did some of the snow outside; plumes of steam engulfed them, scalding the skin of their faces and hands. Hardly hesitating, she threw her weight counter to Cube Head's jerking form, and they fell into the mushy snow outside. After the heat of the steam, the snow's cold burned intensely. The predawn wind cut through their clothes and down to their bones.

Trying to ignore the painful stimuli, Katorin pulled them along, determined to get away from the freezer's internal teleporters.

Behind her, Cube Head yowled. "Cold! What kind of imbecile thinks the best escape is through the blasted polar ice cap—without a coat?" Staring around the barren snow field, he kicked at one of the wave-like drifts.

"Walk before I kill you." She pointed away from the storage shed, aiming the plasma stun gun at him, and tried to keep her teeth from chattering. It shouldn't be long now, as long as they got far enough away.

Glaring ice daggers at her, he turned away and trudged angrily through the drifts. "You're as mad as Mute herself. Neith curse the day you—"

And without warning, a kaxan-taxi teleported the four of them into its shocking warmth. It worked! Even with Cube Head and Kitchell's dupe's resistance, they'd gotten far enough out. "Destination?" the tewet pilot asked through the text interface.

She grinned.

"My apartment," Katorin replied aloud, swiping Cube Head's captive finger on the scanner.

He jerked his hand from her grasp, and she finally let go. Then he stared at her, wide-eyed and stunned. "You're insane."

"And pilot," Katorin added cheerfully, "have a kaxan meet us."

"Authorization code?"

She answered in the long string of digits for a vacation authorization, a rare allowance.

"Would you like a layover bypass?"

"Yes, please," she chirped.

"En route."

Still nursing his finger, Cube Head glared at her, the skin of his face frosty-white with melting snow. She had it, as well. "Are you done killing me?"

"Do you want me to kill you?"

"Aren't you going to anyway?"

"I haven't decided yet." Pulling her satchel protectively closer, she casually shot him with the stun gun.

ROCKEFELLER LOST the will to fight after the woman shot her prisoner, her gun's steady beam clicking electricity through his body.

They transferred to a ship with a regular ceiling, and Marshall relaxed his hand from covering Rockefeller's mouth. Marshall pulled the collapsed prisoner away from the control console and seated himself behind it.

They'd been so close. Rockefeller had seen her, only a few dozen yards away, less than the length of a football field. Just hours ago, he'd held her. She'd been okay. They'd been on their way home. What had happened? Damn Banebd-whatever-his-name-was! Damn these stupid aliens!

How was he ever supposed to get his daughter back now? He didn't even know where they were.

What would happen to her? Could the "queen" protect her, as Marshall promised? It sounded like one more bit of convenient bluster.

This was Marshall's fault. One last stand, and they could have gone home, father and daughter. Marshall had fought off four others at that damned castle. He could have at least tried something on the mothership. He could have taken out that damned Kemtewet lord loaded down by those fucking arm sculptures!

The woman stood and fiddled with her belt beside the shock wall, nodding to her prisoner. "Is he really out? The stunner shouldn't have done that."

"Fainted or asleep."

She shrugged. "Long day."

Crazy. They were both crazy. Rescue someone only to knock him out? What did they really want with the kid?

Catching her breath and grinning, she unscrewed a canteen from her belt and poured it into the fluid wall. A creature plopped out and disappeared inside.

Rockefeller jumped to the center, away from the walls. "What was that?"

She frowned at him, then at Marshall, realization dawning on her face. "You brought a human into the Central Palace? Were you trying to get him killed?"

"He brought himself, Katorin," Marshall answered. "I just carried him out."

Oh, so innocent? Rockefeller fumed. "My daughter is still in there, and you don't give a fuck!"

Frowning, Katorin turned to Marshall. "Why? Where is she? Not the Central Palace, right?"

"Anjedet's spare."

"Did we get a chance to—" She stopped mid-sentence and glanced at Rockefeller, blanching.

"He knows," Marshall confirmed. "And, yes, Vinnet is there with his daughter."

"Oh, good!" She beamed at Rockefeller. "Vinnet will watch out for her. She takes her responsibilities seriously."

"And sometimes in the wrong order," Marshall grumbled.

She rolled her eyes at him. "If I had to leave my daughter in someone else's care, Vinnet would be top of my list."

"After you," Marshall agreed.

"That's not the point!" Rockefeller shouted. "She should be at home with her family, not standing by a wall behind some alien overlord!"

Marshall wouldn't look at him. The woman wilted, also not meeting his eyes. She stepped closer and placed a hand on his shoulder. "I'm sorry."

As if.

Marshall definitely wasn't. "Look, I wish I could have gotten her back for you. I should have been able to, but I didn't. Now, she's there to enhance Vinnet's cover. If they succeed, we can end this war and stop anyone else from getting taken."

Rockefeller bore down on the top of the console Marshall sat behind. "You could have saved her a dozen times. You could have set her aside for Black Book at the castle or taken her back before she even arrived."

Marshall stood and crossed his arms. "And then we would have had to go get more girls, disrupt more lives, and send somebody else's daughter. Do you want that?"

Yes. More than anything. Let some other family face this crisis. He could be brave for someone else's child. But he couldn't say that.

"Mister, I'm sorry this happened to your daughter and Vinnet's new host." The woman rested a light hand on his shoulder from behind. "And I'm sorry we must seem so callous. But Kitchell has a point. We've been at this a long time. The best we can do is minimize impact now and end the Kemtewet system as expediently as possible."

Minimize and expedite.

Shit, they'd made a business of cost-benefit analyzing human lives.

Not that he could argue with it. Damn it. A few hours, and Maggie was gone forever. "Isn't there another way?"

She rubbed his back.

25

NEW PROSPECTS

W hen the prisoner was brought out and anchored to the arena's central pole, the kings and queens lined up at the window where they were guaranteed the best view of the proceedings. Standing beside the new Green Flame, Vinnet studied the bound prisoner. Supposedly looking out through half-lidded eyes, he struggled weakly against the neck restraint that held him in place.

She was close enough to see that his eyes never blinked.

If he's dead, how can he move? Sarah wondered.

Tiny motors attached to his bones. On her last mission to Sais, Vinnet had worked that detail, spending hours surgically inserting motors, testing their in situ operation, and coordinating with the execution producers to find ways to put on a better show. That time in the Central Palace was what qualified her for her current mission. *The recipients aren't always deceased at the time, just paralyzed. That man may have been lucky.*

Did you know him?

There are seven bases and very limited interaction among them. I probably did not.

A cloud of flying beetles grew out of a hall to the right, regrouping in the arena's larger airspace before finding their prey. Vinnet was glad to watch it from behind solid sapphire for once, instead of relying on the invisible gravitational fields that protected most of the audience. Her hosts had died a few different ways but never by flesh-eating beetle. She intended to keep it that way.

"Teni."

Vinnet and the Green Flame turned to regard the man behind them, a king in a black suit with a high collar and sharp angles at the neckline and shoulders. A similarly dressed queen accompanied him.

"Herfhaf," the Green Flame replied, "to what do I owe the pleasure?"

Vinnet smiled tightly to hide her dread. Left to her preferences, she wouldn't interact with He With His Face Behind Him.

The king smiled directly at her. "I noticed how spirited your queen is. Perhaps you and she would be amenable to proposing that the Empress trade her assignments."

Trade queens? She studied the woman behind him, who glared daggers out of eyes darker than her black dress. Clearly, she had no intention of trading the highest-ranked king for the second lowest.

If the trade went through, the next Gertewet mark could be the king closest to the Empress, not the Green Flame. Vinnet matched Herfhaf's queen's disdain with eagerness, turning to regard him front-to-front and edging closer.

Teni clutched her arm. "You don't want a queen who's fallen out of the Empress's favor. I can contain her."

Herfhaf raised skeptical eyebrows. "Of course, you

could, but I wouldn't say she's fallen out of Neith's favor. I saw no one else Ger-watching with the Empress."

I thought only the Empress knew about Katorin. Did she tell everyone?

It was a trap. Katorin fell for it. Vinnet spent one more moment considering it. *An execution was a perfect match for her compassion. She probably didn't survive.*

"No one else was invited," the Green Flame answered through clenched teeth.

"Details. The view was plenty wide to watch from a distance." He met Vinnet's eyes. "Did it get away?"

None of the queens had spoken since she entered the room, so Vinnet smirked.

Teni relaxed his grip minutely. "See? She can learn control."

Herfhaf's steady gaze finally turned away, refocused on the Green Flame. "You're behind the game, Teni. They never have to learn control; it's innate. You should know that by now."

The Green Flame's face grew beet-red, his vassal's pulse throbbing in his neck. "Petition her. See what it gets you. Happy execution, Herfhaf." He clamped down on her still-tender upper arm and spun her to face the window.

"And you, Green Flame and Queen." His chuckles faded as he found a more distant perch at the window.

Out on the arena floor, the beetles had taken a visible toll on the body. Black birds now swept through to pick off the beetles, along with tiny scraps of flesh. While the animated corpse waved its arms to protect its head and kicked at the birds and beetles, a pair of sandy-furred desert cats were sent in, regarding both birds and body with slit-eyed interest.

Ugh! How can you be happy?

If He With His Face Behind Him's deal passes, it effectively seals the Empress's fate. We'll replace him first, then use his station to draw the other kings to him one at a time, where they will be easier targets. For those, the operation won't need new hosts like I did; I'll be able to verify their identities.

But the execution. He was one of you!

Protesting the desecration of a corpse belies an emotional attachment to an intelligence that is no longer there. For Sarah, she broke her study of the performance to crane around the Green Flame as if seeking He With His Face Behind Him. Her gaze fastened on Maggie, who still leaned against the wall with the other spares, attention riveted on the grueling scene. She saw Vinnet and made a face.

Enough. Maggie was still safe. Vinnet and Sarah were, too, barring whatever retribution the Empress might devise. If they rode this out, they might pull through alive and end the Kemtewet at last.

GONE. They weren't going to do anything for Maggie. They'd rationalized away any reason to. Rockefeller collapsed to the padded floor and rubbed his burning eyes.

"That was too easy," Katorin murmured.

"You had a good plan," Marshall answered.

"I barely had a plan." She shook her head, as if it still didn't sit well. It shouldn't. They'd left behind two girls who had no business being there. "Where are we heading?"

"Earth."

"We can't go to Earth!" She eyed Rockefeller sideways and switched languages. "*Der Rat wird böse.*"

"*Der Rat—*" Marshall eyed him, too. "The Council will have to make an exception. We can't go to Percalli with your

rescue. We can't go home with either of those two." He
nodded to the unconscious kid and then the Speaker. "We're
not going to screw up Earth civilizations by taking Rockefeller home."

"We can't take a Kem to—" Her eyes lit up, and she
turned back to Rockefeller. "You're really from Earth?"

Then her eyes widened, her smile dropped away, and
she stared in some horrified realization.

"Katorin?" Marshall prompted.

Her eyes flicked to him, still horrified, then relaxed into
blankness.

"What's wrong with her?" Rockefeller asked.

Marshall stood. "Setira?"

Huh?

She blinked then turned, anchoring Marshall's head
with her palms on his cheeks, and buzzed away in her own
language.

"Slow down!" Marshall begged. "And English. It's his
planet; he has a right to know."

She glanced at him dubiously.

"He's kind of their equivalent of Cimeran. He should
know," Marshall assured her.

Rockefeller crossed his arms, annoyed at this sudden
show of shyness.

"My English is slower than Katorin's. I not repeated—"
She winced. "—haven't practiced. As much."

"But you are Katorin," Rockefeller pointed out.

"No." She pointed to her neck. "Katorin is my tewet. I am
her human. She worries over your world. Very distracting."

"He gets it, Setira, or will soon." Marshall took her
wrinkled hands off his cheeks into his bulky fingers. "Now
tell us both. Why do you think Neith is going to attack
Earth?"

"Attack?" Rockefeller repeated. "Who's Neith? What have we ever done to them?"

"Nothing. Tewet began long after civilization left Earth, but she wants to go back and add it to the Empire now—that's why the ISC is building up, why they'll let people out. I've got it all in the messages. They'll take thousands more hosts and stop all the culture and language and—" Tears streamed down her face, and Marshall brushed them off.

Rockefeller looked away from the couple. An alien invasion. Earth wasn't ready for this; they couldn't even stop a handful of ships from taking a few dozen people.

On the other hand, what was up with the waterworks, especially after she'd so callously dismissed Maggie? Maybe it wasn't true, just a ruse to get him to jump.

His gaze wandered to the unconscious body as Marshall got Katorin or Setira or whoever wound down. "You have a strange way of rescuing prisoners. He didn't look like he wanted to be rescued."

She sniffed one last time. "Oh, he's Kem. Kidnapped, technically. The one we rescued is the tewet you saw me dump through the wall."

That *thing* was rescued? *That's* what they referred to as a person? Did they need a body for it? He edged toward the center, trying to spot the alien deep in the cloudy walls. "It's not living in me!"

The two conscious aliens with bodies traded confused glances. Katorin answered, "Khonsu has just been through a very traumatic experience. He's not fit for a new host right now."

"What do you mean?"

"Starting to host is hard enough with a healthy symbiont. It'd be terribly unfair to ask someone to handle his—" She petered out.

"PTSD," Marshall supplied. "Khonsu was captured and tortured until the Empress decided he had no further use. He may be crazed. You can't ask someone to deal with that by choice."

This made no sense. One minute, they said human lives didn't matter. The next, that they had to be respected. Which was it? "Do human lives matter or not?"

Setira frowned. "Our lives always matter."

"We just don't have the resources to protect them all." Marshall shook his head. "We have to do the greatest good for the greatest number by ending the Kemtewet as fast as we can."

"I knew it!" a wobbly voice announced from the floor. "You *are* Gertewet! The ISC told me I was wrong. They said you were just young, but I knew better. Ger!"

Setira crouched in front of the drowsy man. "Then why take me sightseeing to your proof-of-the-first-Gertewet tunnel?"

"Because. Um." His shaking arm swept across his rumpled hair. "Because the killer cleaning bots can handle even your ilk!"

"Cleaning bots," she repeated. "They're a great cover for Ger assassinations, aren't they? Then you never realize how close we've gotten."

Shaking her head, she frowned at Marshall. "We're not really taking him to Earth, are we? We could drop him off on the way—"

The kid's eyes grew to saucers themselves, and he bolted up, grabbing a fistful of Rockefeller's shirt. "You can't let her take us to Earth! The ISC—they'll kill us! They'll drip our brains out our ears then string us up for the next execution. Why are we only speaking in English?"

Rockefeller pushed the hands off and straightened his

shirt. "Because that's my language." This goofy idiot was the enemy? The looming threat arrayed against the entire human race? "This is what all your sacrifices for the 'greater good' are protecting us from?"

"Yes!" Setira shouted.

The boy hunched behind Rockefeller. Big, hulking threat he was.

Marshall crossed his arms. "You, Kem."

"Paul," Setira supplied.

"Paul, where'd you get your vassal?"

Rockefeller turned to regard the Kemtewet and keep the kid from sheltering in his shadow.

"Value Vassal. They had a seventy-percent-off deal during the last King's Ball."

Marshall nodded. "So about a third of a year's wages?"

Paul nodded. Then he glanced at Rockefeller. "But, um, it's a reputable seller. They treat all the vassals real well— feed them and give 'em space and such."

"And where did your vassal come from, before Sais?" Marshall pressed.

"Geez, I don't know, man. I don't want to think about it."

"He was from a planet. He had a family and aspirations and dreams. What does he have now?"

The kid with the boxy hair shrunk further. "An apartment and a job and a headache." He pressed his temples. "What does your body have?"

"I am the body."

"Huh?"

Marshall turned back to Rockefeller. "See? He takes over so thoroughly, he can't even fathom that a host's mind would still exist after implantation. That doesn't bother you?"

"Should it?" the boxy-haired kid answered.

"Yes!" Rockefeller and Setira chorused.

Dumb question. Rockefeller pointed at Marshall. "What proof do I have that Gertewet don't do the same but more insidiously?"

No one answered immediately. Perhaps he'd called them on their scheme.

"Ah-ha!" Hair boy jabbed his thumbs at himself. "Might as well be Kem and know what you're getting!"

Setira slapped his hands out of the air. "No, Cube Head. Might as well not. Mr. Rockefeller, you can't be sure of anyone's intent without knowing them. The only way our symbionts can prove themselves to you is with time."

"So you can condemn them immediately." Rockefeller pointed to Cube Head. "But you need time to prove yourselves. How convenient."

"Fine." She resettled her satchel across her shoulders. "Donn, we should drop him and go. Your dreams of Earth reinforcements aren't just bad policy. They're impossible."

"He's one guy having a bad week," Marshall answered. "Try an hour talking to base personnel. Smell a new world. See if the people actually involved can change your mind."

"I'm involved." Rockefeller fingered the holes in his jacket. "After I dragged you to that saucer, you let them take my daughter. I'm involved."

"Excuse me. Talk to the people whose only job is defense of our country."

She frowned. "I don't know that I've ever seen a country."

"Country. Fiefdom. Close enough." Marshall changed something on the screen, and Setira edged closer. "We're in visual range."

Cube Head pressed into Setira's other side to also get a look. "The blue and white one? Are all planets that pretty?"

"No," she answered. "Only the best."

Rockefeller watched the three of them studying his Blue Marble: the man who wouldn't fight, multiple personality woman, and the body-possessing kid. As Katorin let the kid into her personal space and they bantered like friends, he wondered where they drew the line between acting and authentic relationships. Did they even know?

Well, they weren't his friends.

In fact, yesterday, he might have wished for this in his wildest dreams: two Gertewet and a Kemtewet heading for Black Book, one as ally, one to study, and one for bonus. How much could Colonel Marshall and her crew suss out from this group of three?

How much more could someone competent discern? Perhaps the CIA. But would they even believe him?

Setira's voice caught his attention. "You're cloaking on a friendly world?"

Marshall chuckled. "Just seeing whether—"

"Unidentified kaxan, state your name, passengers, and intent." The new voice sounded like someone from Black Book, but he couldn't identify it. "Oh, General, it's you. Do you have the Speaker and his daughter? Who else?"

Marshall's jovial expression withered. "The Speaker, another Gertewet, a Kemtewet captive, and me. No girls."

"I'm sorry to hear that, sir." Not sorry enough. "We'll open up the hangar for you and let the Colonel know you're coming."

"If you have to," he grumbled back. The group started to disperse again.

Weren't they related? Didn't he want to see the Colonel?

Setira beat Rockefeller to it. "I thought you wanted me to meet your old comrades."

Marshall kept his eyes on the screen. "Family's different."

"Oh, your niece."

"What about her?" Rockefeller pressed.

Marshall barely glanced at him while he worked the controls. The saucer didn't have controls. Stokely had shown him that. Worked the menus? What was there to do, stall? "Apparently, getting a symbiont is like visiting Vegas and coming back with a wife. Regardless of how much you've changed or how much you mean it, the family doesn't take it seriously."

Rockefeller blinked.

"Kitchell says that's a bad comparison, but it's the best I've got."

"Well, since he hasn't said anything over the past day, does *Kitchell* have any ideas for rescuing my daughter?"

"Already tried them." He tapped the screen dismissively.

"Have you, now."

"In fact." Marshall pushed to his feet, keeping his head ducked under the low ceiling. "Kitchell says to get over it and leave her to Vinnet, which I wasn't telling you, because I thought it was rude and insensitive. But what do I know? I'm just a 'crazy, AWOL ex-general who's run away from anyone who ever cared about him.'"

He tapped the screen one more time and transported out.

Rockefeller stared at the empty space. Well, then.

Cube Head stared at him, and the woman studied the screen, resetting something. "He didn't deserve that."

Then she frowned. "Do armed guards greet all the ships on your world?"

How should he know? There weren't saucers anywhere else. "Yes? Why?"

He walked around to see the screen over her shoulder showing a thermal image of the space under the saucer and the surrounding area. Men enclosed the kaxan and the General's lone outline in the center, and each pointed a sidearm at him. Colonel Marshall must have remembered their conversation on preventative measures, although in hindsight, perhaps Katorin would make a better free ally than the General.

"Maybe we shouldn't go out there," she suggested.

"No, it'll be fine." He tried to sound nonchalant, as if he encountered swarms of armed guards every day. Maybe he did. He had both yesterday and today. A new habit? "But let's take the ladder and go out slowly."

"I'll stay here." Cube Head sprawled out on the open floor, arms pillowed behind his head.

"Nope. You first." The Gertewet woman wedged a toe under his hip to roll him over. "If they shoot you, I'll teleport you back up, good as new."

"But you're the one who shot me first."

"You'd never been shot before?" she gaped then motioned down his body. "You aren't even hurt."

"I got a leg cramp."

"Really?" Shaking her head, she commanded the hatch open. Then she frowned and looked at Rockefeller. "What is protocol in this situation?"

Good question. He leaned over the opening. "There's three of us. We're unarmed. We're about the climb out."

The General called out, "Roberts. Peterson, keep your sights on the man who isn't the Speaker. He's got black hair, looks about twenty."

"You don't give the orders anymore, sir," someone shouted back.

"He's a Kemtewet."

Slides racked.

"Aw, but Beryl, they're going to shoot me!" Cube Head's doleful eyes might have worked, had they been his own.

"I've got my finger right here over the teleporter control."

Moaning, Cube Head started down the ladder.

Rockefeller leaned closer to her, his voice soft. "It'll really heal him if he gets shot in the head?"

"I only brought him to leave less evidence on Sais." She pulled her hand from the screen and stood; it didn't matter to her whether he died. "It's safer for you if I go next. If they do shoot me, even if it's a head shot, make sure they let Kitchell help me." She pointed to the back of her neck. "They probably won't hit the symbiont, and I'd rather not have to decide between suffocating in Setira's body or crawling across that floor."

She patted his shoulder as she passed. Starting down, she called, "Second one coming. Unarmed Gertewet."

He actually held his breath until she made it down without shots fired. It was so quiet, he could hear her feet touch the ground.

The General announced on his behalf, "The only one left is the Speaker of the House. Do not fire."

"Do not fire unless he approaches you," Colonel Marshall corrected. "He could have been implanted."

"Really, Renee?"

Now or never. He took the rungs slowly, careful not to make any sudden movements and, when he reached the ground, to raise his empty hands. Katorin and Cube Head followed suit.

Colonel Marshall, Stokely, and the other Black Book officers stood behind the ring of MPs. The Colonel, in particular, watched coolly, all business. "Major, check them. Lieutenant, get ready to sweep the kaxan."

Mirroring her CO's brusqueness, Major Patrick slipped through the circle, approaching the General first and reaching for his neck.

General Marshall backed away a step. "Come on. What's this going to tell you? That I have a symbiont? You already know that. It still won't tell you what kind."

As the Major persisted and the General submitted, it dawned on Rockefeller that Colonel Marshall really didn't care what kind. She hadn't seen the night-and-day difference between Sarah and the fake queen, hadn't heard their heartfelt goodbye to Maggie. She hadn't seen the senseless, indiscriminate control Banebdjedet had exerted over the women on his ship.

True, with Donn Marshall and Cube Head thrown into the mix, he couldn't say he thought the Gertewet any better than the Kemtewet, but he knew they were different.

Major Patrick checked the General's neck, declared him clean, found the ray gun, and moved down the line. Rockefeller was clean. Cube Head said nothing, but Katorin submitted only with complaints. "I told you I'm Ger. I don't see why you need to feel me up like that."

Goaded on, the Major patted down Setira's arms, legs, and waistband. "Open the bag, please, ma'am."

Katorin's cordial front evaporated and, clutching the bag tight to her skin, fell into a combat-ready stance.

The General snapped at her, and she launched into an explanation in their language.

"Yes, I know they're irreplaceable papers of strategic and historic significance. Jo is looking for weapons. She'll be gentle with them."

"Unless I see something to be concerned about, you can handle them all," Major Patrick confirmed.

The satchel got searched without incident. All told, the

Major's search produced only the stun gun from the General.

"Please follow me to the conference room." Major Patrick led them away with their flanking guard, while Lieutenant Fairfeld mounted the ladder into the saucer.

Rockefeller felt like he'd been lumped in with everyone else as the "them" in "us versus them." Normally, that wasn't of much consequence, but as the only human traveling with aliens, now surrounded by a unit of other humans, it made no sense.

The General broke the silence first. "New security best practices training?"

The Major shrugged. "You said the magic K word."

Everyone glanced at Cube Head, who caught Katorin's hand and clung to it. She twisted free.

"Then why don't you lock him up?" the General pressed.

Major Patrick shrugged, refusing to look at him.

It was obvious: they considered Gertewet a threat, too. How had the General begun hosting, anyway? How close to fact was his weekend in Vegas analogy?

26

US AGAINST THEM

T he conference room didn't look so outlandishly comical this time. As they filed in, prisoners first, Rockefeller found the absurdity a relief. If only aliens had come in peace like *ET* and *Close Encounters*. If only they could be fought off head-on like *Independence Day*. Even the absurd pinball machine, with its little green men and oscillating, embellished saucers, promised that this dreadful reality wasn't as bad as it felt.

He'd made it back to the familiar.

Major Patrick caught him staring, patted his shoulder, and offered him a can of pop. "Best Coke you ever tasted."

His traitorous stomach growled, and he accepted. He didn't even like Coke, but the cold can felt so familiar. Body-possessing aliens, saucers that whipped between planets in hours, tyrants who stole back girls who'd been set free—they all existed. And so did this room full of enemies, pregnant with the decisions that would launch their futures and the country's, even the planet's.

All because Maggie was gone.

"Thanks."

This time, surveying the room, he noted the people. The General and Katorin conferred in the open area by the movie posters, Cube Head sheltering behind them and keeping nervous watch over the passive MPs flanking the door. Major Patrick stood near Rockefeller; he hadn't realized he'd drifted toward the kitchenette as he tried to see it all.

And he hadn't realized the Major was trying to console him. He squeezed the can tight, its cold lancing his palm. He couldn't think about that now.

"This can't go on."

She nodded once, listening.

Not that he knew what else to say; his thoughts stuck there. Never again. This must end. No more lost children.

He nodded to the room. "We have everything we need. We just have to figure out how to use it."

"The Colonel liked your idea about a second Gertewet. We've been kicking it around, but we weren't ready for you to turn up with one—and a Kemtewet, to boot. She'll be in as soon as we're sure on a go-forward plan for keeping them here."

Something about that felt wrong, but what? Treating that senseless kid like a killer, confining vivacious Katorin— How could there be a problem with either when they made logical sense? "I'd like to be part of those discussions."

"These are temporary arrangements. I'm sure you can be involved for final planning. Besides, she'll be in any minute now."

He squinted at her and the doorway. "Am I free to leave?"

"Yes...but why would you? They'll be in momentarily."

"I like knowing where I stand."

Finally smiling, she looked more like the smart-ass

major who had mouthed off to her superior the first time he saw her. "You're standing in a kicked beehive. This project has never had this much action. Did you know we had to have SFs shipped in from Spokane to make sure all the abductees we rescued stayed put? We had to quintuple the food coming on-station and import psychologists and lawyers with clearances. They're not even here yet; we're using the scientists we have where we can.

"And here you show up unannounced with two aliens we never expected to get our hands on."

"Oh."

"We're getting all sorts of attention from the Brass, just by asking for the resources we need to deal with this, and they can't deny it, because there's a pile of civilians neck-deep in our classified project, and it's not our fault. Because we rescued them. From another planet." She patted him on the shoulder. "This is a good thing."

Except for Maggie.

She nudged him with her elbow. "You said this can't go on, and it's not. They finally have to take us seriously."

"They could have done that *before* anyone got taken!"

She sobered. "This time, maybe. We couldn't do much until the General got us a kaxan. But with more personnel, we'll be able to keep monitoring the kaxan transponders *and* reverse engineer more tech to level the playing field. Next time, we'll be ready."

Footsteps in the hall announced the arrival of Colonel Marshall and Senator Stokely, both wearing their game faces. They stepped inside, shedding their escorts at the door.

"Listen up!" The Colonel's voice would have cut through any din, had she not already gotten everyone's attention. "In about an hour, we'll be moving you to another building.

Until then, I'd like to understand what transpired since the Speaker and Major Patrick separated."

She motioned for everyone to sit.

"Renee." The General leaned on the ping-pong table across from her. "We came to drop off the Speaker and take a look around. Then we're off."

The General shrugged and pointed a thumb over his shoulder at Cube Head. "You can keep him if you want."

"No one is 'taking a look around,' and no one is leaving." Her eyes bored into him. "No one and nothing is outbound until we sort out the present situations."

"I took him to the mothership. We failed to get his daughter. We met up with Katorin, and I brought him home. Sorted."

"Hardly." She chose a stool on the table's long side, and Major Patrick settled on her right, Stokely on her left.

The General, Katorin, and, reluctantly, Cube Head perched on the other side, as if the table itself were the net dividing the room: Air Force (and company) on one side and Gertewet (and company) on the other. Us versus them.

Rockefeller nudged the short end's stool toward "us" and settled.

"Katorin has time-sensitive intelligence to report." The General nodded to her satchel.

"We will attempt to come to a sensible and equitable solution in a timely manner." The Colonel promised nothing. Everyone must have heard that.

"You could do that by letting us leave."

"There will be another arrangement."

The General shifted his focus. "Senator, I'm sure you recognize that letting the Gertewet continue our work is in everyone's best interest."

"Not mine," Cube Head mumbled.

Katorin kicked him.

The Senator's hard expression remained. "General, you must not realize what a great opportunity this is, and you must have forgotten how desperate we are for any advantage."

The General didn't understand at first, but as it sunk in, anger bloomed across his face. As he glanced between Stokely and Katorin, a weight sank in Rockefeller's gut. All along, they'd talked about releasing the General, their first connection, and studying the other. They hadn't known the other might be a playful, sympathetic being like Katorin.

For the good of the planet. To defend their children.

"You can't be serious." The General studied Stokely's unmoved expression then smacked the table and stood, flinging his stool back. "After all we've done for you? After she just risked her life twice over?"

Katorin leaned close. "Why? What are they planning?"

He shook his head.

"I don't understand." She studied the four of them on the Earth side of the table. "Are you afraid of us?"

Terrified. Every time he saw the fake queen using Sarah's body, knowing her movements and words didn't fit the little girl on the outside, his stomach twisted. And he'd never met her first. Was that what Colonel Marshall saw in her uncle? How terrible to watch that shift, fully knowing what was lost.

In fact, every individual on the Earth side of the table, besides Rockefeller, had known the General first. They stared down the alien woman with hard eyes.

Colonel Marshall broke the silence. "What you do to your hosts is unforgivable. Last time, it was the General. This time, a girl from Pennsylvania. Next time, who knows who it could be? Any of us, our families, our friends, our neighbors. That's what we're here to stop."

"Gertewet host-taking is not random acts of violence." The General looked ready to punch someone.

"Tell that to Sarah Anderson," Major Patrick replied, "reported missing at 5:22 Thursday evening from her family's home in Zelienople, Pennsylvania. Police are scouring the countryside, looking for any clues."

"That was a Kemtewet raid."

"That you participated in!" The Major rose, jabbing a finger at him. "You told us that you agreed. Fine. But Sarah agreed to nothing. The other eighteen girls agreed to nothing. You dropped us a memo and did nothing while we scrambled to get them back, and people died. They died without a clue what was happening or why, and you can sit here, worried about when you can leave, so you won't be held accountable?"

Fuming, Major Patrick visibly forced herself to sit. "That's not the Donn Marshall I worked with to carry this project through its dark years." She glanced at Katorin. "So, yeah, I'd say you're a threat."

Rockefeller caught himself flowing along with Major Patrick's emotional appeal, piling blame and blame atop the General. She painted a desolate picture of indelible change, the same insidious takeover he'd mentioned not long before. But what about the General's Vegas wedding analogy? Did it hold up? What changed, simply because there was someone else with some other objectives in the equation?

An airman stepped into the room and reported to the Colonel.

Nodding as he stepped back, the Colonel answered, "Your quarters are ready."

"May we request a few more minutes of your time?" Katorin rested her folded hands on the table, her eyes downcast. "I'd like to try to clarify our understanding of one another."

"What do you have in mind?"

"Um." She glanced at the General, as if she knew he wasn't going to like her proposal. That probably helped her more than anything else. "It seems to me that we make you feel vulnerable. Perhaps you don't realize how vulnerable we truly are."

The General scowled. "Katorin, no!"

She ignored him. "Back on our kaxan, there's a free-swimming tewet."

While Rockefeller shuddered, the other humans merely looked confused.

"What's that?" the Major asked.

"A Gertewet without a host."

The humans leaned uncomfortably away from her.

"I promise we won't let him take a host here. He isn't in good condition." She must have caught their appalled expressions. She held up her fingers. "He can't take a host through the hands or arms. If he seems to act aggressively, drop him."

Major Patrick's jaw dropped. "You want us to hold it?"

"They'll break him!" Cube Head shouted.

"They don't need to see that," the General added.

The MPs at the door, inside and out, looked uncomfortable.

Rockefeller stood and straightened his jacket, heart pounding, until the rabble died down. "I think it's a good idea." He leaned on the table and recalled how their suspicions had already lumped him in with the Gertewet. Time to dispel that notion. "Every vulnerability is worth knowing about, and right now, we know nothing. We're not going to change that by rejecting an opportunity because it's uncomfortable."

Stokely, the Black Book officers, and the General shut their mouths. Katorin smiled uncertainly, and he realized that worked both ways: trust in the Gertewet that their disembodied compatriot wouldn't hurt them, and trust in the humans that they wouldn't hurt it. Who had the greater risk?

"I'll need my canteen or another container," Katorin said.

Cube Head grabbed her wrist. "You're not actually going to show humans how to hurt us, are you? You can't do that. How are you supposed to take vassals, like, ever again? You just can't!"

She twisted her arm until their grips were reversed, his arm pinned to the table. "General Renee, if you are taking custody of this piece of misery, now may be a good time to secure him elsewhere."

Cube Head tried to pull free, but she held fast.

The Colonel nodded. "Major, if you would please escort him to the modified room with a pair of SFs." She looked back. "Sergeant Bailey, a container, please."

———

THE PREDATORS ATTACKING the dead man in the arena progressed through mutated wolves, to two-legged reptiles, to massive snakes. By the end, some of the metallic motors showed through the corpse's torn flesh, and dead predators littered the arena floor.

The Green Flame escorted Vinnet to the doorway of a wing near the arrival hall, where he bid her good night and waited with his spare until she and Maggie passed through the wing's unadorned entrance.

It was like passing from glaring noon to soothing twilight. The bold edges, bright colors, and impressive décor softened into curves, pastels, and plush. As the door closed behind them, their feet landed on padded tiles that absorbed the sound of their passage.

What's it like to live like a queen?

My awareness of the queens comes from the Kings' Ball, so I know very little of their lifestyle. If our experience watching the execution is typical, I can understand Anjedet's desire to escape. If the actions she initiated hadn't been so horrific, I might have felt sorry for her.

"What are we doing here?" Maggie's voice was loud in the hushed hallway.

Vinnet spun and held a finger to her lips. *Don't speak! Please don't speak. The last thing we need is for the Kem to think I talk to you.* Of course, actually talking back would accomplish the same end. With Maggie quieted, she continued along the gently-curving hall.

Come on, Vinnet. She's confused. The hall's deserted. You can at least tell her something.

Is it deserted? Are there doors? Microphones? We're in an unfamiliar and hostile environment. I hate to quote Neith, but one mistake could ruin everything. Vinnet glanced back at Maggie. One of her mistakes could end the mission, too. Maybe Sarah had a point.

"Anjedet, the favorite."

Vinnet stopped and finally saw the black-clothed figure in the cross-corridor she'd passed—the queen of He With His Face Behind Him. The queen stepped forward, followed by a plain-faced, brown-haired girl in a simple black shift.

"Anjedet, the ambitious. Anjedet, the stubborn."

"You're one to talk."

The queen's black-lined eyes narrowed. "Anjedet, the Earthling." This she said in English, and Maggie's eyes widened. The queen skirted Vinnet until she stood between the Gertewet and Maggie, her attention divided.

"What do you want?"

"How generous of you to ask." From that point on, she stuck exclusively to English. "If you're replacing me, I want recompense." She nodded to Maggie. "News from Earth." Meaning: a new host.

No!

"I can tell you anything you want," Vinnet answered, still mixing languages. She'd rather not reveal details of Earth directly to the Kem, but it would be worth the girl's life.

"Not in detail, you can't." The queen reached out and smushed Sarah's face between her palms. "How would I know you weren't withholding the best parts?" Letting go, she sidled up beside Sarah. "We could reminisce together."

Vinnet edged away. "You have a spare."

"I have a wardrobe of them." She pouted. "None from Earth."

"Do you fancy Neith's wrath?"

The queen wound around to her other side. "I did not fetch an Earth girl."

No, Anjedet's proxy had.

Vinnet met Maggie's worried stare. After all these years, she shouldn't have felt so much at a loss for what to do. What would be Anjedet's next move? What would the consequences be? If she'd headed to the base for intel, she might know, but she would never have arrived at the Central Palace in time.

The queen humphed daintily and turned back toward Maggie. "You must be tired after all that standing."

"Maybe." Maggie's voice quivered.

"Come with me, and I'll find you a bed."

Vinnet opened her mouth to object, but Sarah interrupted. *You don't think she's that stupid, do you?*

"I prefer the devil I know, thank you."

"The devil?"

"You all watched that man getting eaten alive. That's horrible! You didn't even try to stop it; you enjoyed it!"

The queen forced a chuckle past her flattened smile. "How plebian." She reached for Maggie's hand. "Come, let me teach you culture."

Maggie evaded her hand and ducked around to stand at Vinnet's side.

"Loyalty in someone who detests you." The queen shook her head. "You could be Empress, Anjedet." She waved to her spare, and they both swept back the way they'd come.

Odd. Vinnet wouldn't have thought a queen capable of either concession or compliment.

If the queens are descended from the Empress, and you said the Empress had to win over a planet...

She'd have to earn respect in public. This isn't public.

Beside her, Maggie gripped her hand. At least they hadn't lost her. Vinnet squeezed back and let go.

You could be Empress. Maybe it was a warning. Maybe it labeled her a target.

27

CONFINEMENT

R ockefeller waited only a few minutes until Major
Patrick, Katorin, and two MPs returned to the
conference room. Katorin maneuvered a
wheeled mop bucket that smelled of the kaxan's fluid walls,
and Major Patrick held her gun drawn and pointing at it.
This was the grand show and tell? In a mop bucket?

A brown lump sloshed in the industrial yellow bucket's
smeared recesses. Unfortunate coloring. Snake-like with a
lumpy head, it had two fine fins tucked against its side and
curled in on itself, as if bracing against the rocking current.

"We need flamethrowers," the Colonel breathed.

Rockefeller couldn't disagree. A close-range shotgun
blast would hit the skinny creature, but with a pistol, one
only had luck.

The General wandered to the Earth side of the table,
stopping near Rockefeller's elbow. "Well, he's an ugly one."

Katorin shrugged and elaborated for the humans, "Most
of us are bright colors. I'm mostly purple."

"Kitchell is green," the General offered.

Stokely pointed into the bucket. "What do you call that?"

"Shit brown."

"No, what's its name?"

The General shook his head, but Katorin answered, "Khonsu. He was captured by the Kemtewet during a mission on the capital world. They tortured him, and he was supposed to be executed today."

Khonsu unfurled and swam to the bottom, nosing at the bucket, exploring it.

"My mission," Katorin continued, "which I need to report in on when you decide it's time to release me—"

The General glared at her.

"—was to finish his mission. My host, Setira, spent a long time studying him before we left. One of Khonsu's favorite pastimes was investigating rumors that the house of the first Gertewet was intact."

They stared into the bucket, mesmerized.

"Is it?" Stokely asked.

"Of course not," the General answered.

"Actually, I found it!" Katorin beamed.

"Impossible!" the General said. "It was destroyed."

The first Gertewet? Ever? Rockefeller crossed his arms. "How long ago was this?"

The General answered first. "Four thousand years."

"Four thousand sixty," Katorin amended. She tugged her satchel. "And Mute's files were still there." She shook herself out of her reverie and reached into the bucket.

It looked as if Khonsu should break into pieces as she pulled him out, but instead, as he rose, stripes resolved that matched the bucket, and he looked quite solid and considerably less lumpy. Lying across her dripping fingers, he did look vulnerable. One squishing twist or a sharp bend like snapping kindling, and he should break.

"I can't hold him out too long, or his skin will dry."

"And that's bad?" Major Patrick asked.

Katorin stroked her wet thumb across its wet body. "We absorb nutrients through our skin—everything from minerals to oxygen. If this membrane dries, no more breathing." She shifted it onto one palm and used her pinky to trace out a seam on its fleshy beak. "This isn't a mouth. This is where the outer sheath separates to release neuron tendrils into a host's brain."

Everyone took a step back.

"Can we see?" Stokely asked. Crazy bastard.

"No." Katorin resettled her hands underneath it. "Two reasons: One, the sheaths are lined with little, sharp bones, and I don't want to get cut. Two, if I damage the tendrils, it will hinder his interface with his next host, if he's ever safe to have another."

"Hinder his interface?" Rockefeller repeated. "Like swapping left and right?"

"More like not able to interpret emotions correctly," the General said. "Or not able to share memories. It's usually a huge problem to the developing relationship."

That's how he saw it—a relationship. Maybe he literally considered it his shotgun marriage. "Do you talk to each other?"

"Oh, yes," Katorin answered.

"Of course," the General agreed.

"Setira kept me sane on Sais. I would have been miserable without her. I don't know how the Kem can stand it. Or you, for that matter. It seems terribly lonely." She shrugged, not looking at anyone but the slimy snake in her hands. "That's one of the worst parts about being between hosts. The loneliness."

"Sounds crowded, having an extra brain." Major Patrick

edged closer. "Sometimes, mine is loud enough for three people."

"It can be, especially in a symbiont's first or second host, before they've learned discipline."

Taking a deep breath and holding it, Major Patrick held her hands out, and Katorin carefully tipped Khonsu into them. He wriggled upright. "Okay, so, um, he's not going to try to, you know…"

"He has to ask first, and he can't, so no. Mr. Rockefeller." She crooked her finger to beckon him closer. When he stepped in range, she stroked the back of his neck. "This is where we need to end up in a host." Then she drew a line up his arm toward his neck. "If I'm looking for a new host, the last thing I'm going to do is burrow up his arm to his neck. I'm not going to start out by hurting him and then have to live with it myself. It's not just an inconvenience; there's no trust."

"You could…crawl." Major Patrick shrugged.

"Sure. If I wanted to give him a chance to flick me off into a wall. Even a host who's agreed is not going to sit still for that."

"They agreed, didn't they?"

"That doesn't make apprehension disappear."

Stokely put out his hands to hold it next, and Rockefeller followed after him. The thing was heavier than it looked, felt cool to the touch, and cast about aimlessly, as if searching for food. It seemed so small. He dug in his brain for one more name. "Is Vinnet this small?"

Katorin's face lit up until she realized what he was doing. "Yes, Vinnet, Kitchell, and I are all this size. Vinnet… Donn, you saw her last. What color is she?"

"Neon blue and green," the General ground out.

Stokely frowned at him. "Who's Vinnet?"

Rockefeller met his eyes, as if he could transmit what he'd seen on the other worlds and the horror of watching a child who wasn't herself. "The Gertewet that took over Sarah, the missing girl from Pennsylvania."

He handed the brown thing back to Katorin, who released it into the mop bucket.

One little, fragile implant had the capacity to destroy lives.

Colonel Marshall peered into the barrel in distaste, then surveyed the two other Gertewet. "I think it's time for you to go."

THE FIRST HINT of direction was the tiny emblem Vinnet caught on the wall: a decal of a transparent face. The emblem itself didn't bother her; she'd seen it hundreds of times before on products exported from the Eater of Ghosts' kingdom.

Bedroom hallways. Of course they each had their own quarters.

A couple minutes of searching revealed Anjedet's down the next hall to the left, marked by a removable cloth banner of a flaming green trident.

In moments, she'd be alone with Maggie to recap the day. Vinnet pressed against the door, slipped by it, and turned her back on the room to see that it closed.

We're being watched. Sarah's mind froze, awaiting a bolt of adrenaline.

Vinnet turned very slowly, giving her eyes time to adjust. It took a couple blinks to confirm she wasn't seeing double; the crowd really was that large.

Flooring differentiated this entry hall into two sections: a Kem area denoted by black marble, and a vassal area denoted by white marble. The black side held a long line of dresses on posing models and a grid of drawers that presumably held more attire. The white side she couldn't see much of for the press of bodies at the border. All the girls in the front stared with big, hopeful eyes. They must have been Anjedet's spares. The Queen of Faces was right. It was a whole wardrobe, a stockpile of single-use vassals. Anjedet had had all this and gone out of her way to disrupt lives on Earth.

We have to do something about this, no matter what it takes. Sarah fumed, raw after the show of the execution, even though she knew the man had already died.

Kitchell was right. She would fit as a host.

Can we free them? Sarah pressed.

Not if we want to maintain our cover.

"Who are they?" Maggie stuck close to her side.

"Others like you."

As if that were a signal, all the girls in front started talking, then shouting, over one another: "Queen Anjedet, pick me!" "I've been waiting for you. Take me!" "I'm right here!" *"Watashi o erande!" "Jiē wǒ!" "Category kula!"*

Ignoring them, she motioned to Maggie and swept into the next room. The safety of privacy!

Except from a dark-haired young woman rising from a desk in the corner.

"Anjedet!" Her wide eyes darted past Vinnet to scan Maggie, and her expression darkened. "I didn't expect you to return."

Frozen only far enough inside to let the door close, Vinnet tried to get her brain moving. Who was this girl? All the other spares stood obediently in the outer room; surely, this one hadn't simply decided to avail herself of vacant space. Had she?

Vinnet struck a stern pose and raised an eyebrow.

The girl faltered, her expression flicking between anger and hope. "I'm sure Neith told you I was dead."

The doppelgänger? Well, this opened opportunities. Sure, she'd apparently had a rocky relationship with Anjedet, but what more valuable resource could exist than someone the queen trained to stand in her place? This one human was worth more than all the intel she'd missed—if Vinnet could entice her cooperation.

Vinnet crossed the room and laid a hand on the girl's arm. "I can't believe it!" Danger nagged in the back of her mind. "She let you live?"

The doppelgänger pushed up her sleeve to her shoulder, revealing a dozen straight, surgical lines sealed with thick, itchy, black stitches. Swollen injection sites speckled her upper arm. "She let me die slowly."

Intentional Itatubian heartworm implantation. Vinnet thought twice before caressing the girl's forearm, but heartworms weren't touch transmissible. This infection was treatable. If a basic teleporter wouldn't correct it, five minutes with a medical teleporter would. If it weren't a trap. Could Vinnet find help in time in this maze? It had to be a trap.

Someone knocked on the outer door.

The doppelgänger watched Maggie, then cast her gaze down and answered the door. After a moment, she turned back. "Serket, the Bone-Breaker's queen, requests an immediate audience regarding an urgent matter."

"I accept."

The corner of the girl's mouth tightened, but she sketched a curtsy. "I'll show her in."

Vinnet pointed Maggie to the wall beside the desk in the corner and moved to stand beside the most opulent chair among the cluster in the middle.

Serket wasn't what she expected. During the execution, she'd clung along the wall, far from Vinnet and the new Green Flame. Between the distance and the cut of her gown, Vinnet hadn't realized she was pregnant. Her waddling steps into the reception room corrected that.

A hundred-some potential Kemtewet, not yet born. She could stop them, if she didn't want to keep her cover.

Serket's vassal's glowing face smiled sympathetically as she waddled closer. "Anjedet, I'm sorry for the loss of your adorable vassal pair, and I'm so sorry you were forced to return."

She held her hands out, and Vinnet clasped them as if she trusted the Kem. Interesting. "I accomplished what I needed."

Let them contemplate that.

Serket pulled her down to sit on adjacent chairs. "I hope that can buoy your spirits, in light of the latest development. The new Green Flame has petitioned Neith to execute your wardrobe."

The hopeful faces in the outer room played in Vinnet's mind. "All of them?"

Nevermind them. Does Maggie count?

Almost certainly.

"Every one that remains in here when they come." Serket's honeyed voice almost softened the blow of picturing the vestibule piled with prone bodies, its white marble floor flooded red. "I don't know how you could stand that after losing your vassal pair, Anjedet, so I came with a proposition."

The kings would kill their own first, under their own control. Would the queens so easily carry out such a directive? What other option could she offer? "Please, go on."

"I can shelter your wardrobe with mine. They'll be safe from whoever the imperial agent is."

Done. For all those in the vestibule, it was a harbor as safe as they'd ever had. But for Maggie?

You can't let her die!

Nor can we let her host a queen; she knows our identity. Vinnet studied the pregnant queen, so docile and harmless with her hands folded in her lap. "Teni petitioned. The Empress hasn't granted it, has she?"

Serket's frown deepened, as if Vinnet had deviated from her expected script. Beyond her, a smile ghosted the doppelgänger's lips; this was a good move for Anjedet. "She will. Perhaps you've underestimated her anger for your breaking out during the high visibility of the Kings' Ball and then returning with not only an Earth vassal, but also an Earth spare. She may not have decided your future yet, but what is your wardrobe to her?"

"What is my wardrobe to you?"

Serket blinked her wide eyes. "I have no intention of killing them. After all the security Neith will implement because of your actions, you can't expect better from the other queens. Anyone with a modicum of sense would ally with the Empress."

"Then have you no sense?"

She hugged her belly. "You know I wanted you to succeed. You've been forced back here and lost both your vassal pair and perhaps the only chance you'd ever have of becoming Empress. I couldn't stand seeing you lose your entire wardrobe, too."

Maybe, somehow, this Kemtewet queen, spawn of Neith,

had genetically mutated to have compassion. Or was this simply a ploy? What would she gain? "When the threat has passed, will you return them?"

"Come now, Anjedet. I'm doing you a favor. You can't have everything."

No.

So what? Vinnet didn't need them; she meant to keep Sarah for many decades. (Although a willing spare could be invaluable, if she could find one.) If the girls would be safer elsewhere, they could go. The only question was Maggie and the potential for her to be compromised. As a prize host, that might not take long.

On the other hand, she'd have an ally in another queen's quarters. A foothold.

"Anjedet?"

"This is a lot to take in. I need time to consider."

The doppelgänger frowned. Oops.

"You don't have time to think! I don't know when the agent will be dispatched. It might already be too late!"

The doppelgänger mirrored Vinnet's consternation. Quite a rush for a benevolent offer! If she wanted the prestige of a double wardrobe, Vinnet could cede her that, especially in exchange for a chance at extending Gertewet influence by replacing another queen.

But will Maggie be okay?

They'd have to act fast. There was at least one other operative in the Central Palace, standing by for just this purpose. Vinnet would need to find him, make contact, and move forward. Would he be ready? Did he know she'd arrived so early?

Surely, Serket wouldn't abandon her litter to switch vassals. There would be some time.

"Anjedet!"

"Apologies. I wasn't ready to part with them."

Both doppelgänger and Serket studied her; when she'd escaped, Anjedet hadn't planned to return to them.

"Again. So soon." Closing her eyes, she took a breath and centered herself. "Take them. I would rather they live."

"Oh!" Serket reached for her hand and squeezed it. "They'll be happy with me. I should go before Neith's agent arrives."

Vinnet walked her to the door, where Serket hesitated, glancing back.

Vinnet followed her gaze: Maggie and the doppelgänger. On second thought, perhaps it would be best to keep them both, or hide them elsewhere. "Both of them?"

Serket shook her head. "We all watched that one be infected."

The doppelgänger. At least Vinnet would still have that source of information. While she lived.

Swallowing through her tight and bruised throat, she met Maggie's gaze and waved her over. All this time, she and Serket—and even the surviving twin—had spoken in mixed languages, but now she used only English, as Sarah knew it, rather than the Sais-distributed dialect. "Come over here. You'll be leaving with the Bone-Breaker's queen."

Maggie approached, wide-eyed and scared. Best not to dissuade that caution. Let her fight anything the other queen tried to do. She craned around to watch Vinnet while obediently falling in behind Serket.

Vinnet couldn't meet her gaze.

Because this is wrong!

It is a risk. But if it works...

She repeated her instructions for the crowd in the vestibule, and Sarah's heart pounded madly while they watched the girls (and a couple men she hadn't noticed before) file out behind the Kemtewet queen.

So many things were wrong here; how did one start to make them right?

28

KILL MAGGIE

"I can't believe you let that slimy wench score off you so easily!" The doppelgänger held her hands as if something had slipped through.

Vinnet's portrayal of Anjedet needed work, then. "They won't all come back, but I'll get some return."

"You're the one who taught me to weigh the probabilities." She jabbed a pointing finger at the door. "Why in all the worlds are you going all in on an unsubstantiated threat?"

Even lords didn't put up with that sort of insubordination from humans. Did Anjedet? Then again, this girl had substituted for Anjedet. She couldn't have done that by being meek, and Anjedet had to have worked with her closely. Maybe this was normal between them. "I was weighing the possibility that they would die."

"So, what? Now you have no spares. What will you do if you're attacked?"

She certainly wouldn't take a random host.

Vinnet, what's she mean, attacked? We're in the middle of the Central Palace. Your memories all say the kings, the lords, and the rest of the planet aren't allowed in here. How is someone going to attack a queen?

"Have you heard of plans to do so?"

She glanced away. "Neith may be after your wardrobe, but the others could be planning more. As you've said, there's no substitute for vigilance."

Watch her. Vinnet couldn't worry about this girl and her standing among the queens and mind other threats alone.

But you have control of my eyes.

Listen to her. Think about her actions. Warn me when you understand what she's doing. That was what her previous hosts had done.

If I had to guess, she's going to attack us.

I read that, too, but then why would she worry about spares?

The doppelgänger folded her arms across her chest. "At the very least, you'll never get your Earth spare back. You know somebody will take her tonight."

"Tonight?"

"Well, they can't have her be influenced by the others; they'll want her experience pure." She narrowed her eyes. "Are you testing me? Aren't we a little past that?"

Vinnet stared at the door as if she could see through it.

No foothold.

No cover.

No way to continue the mission unless they got Maggie back.

Vinnet swallowed. "You're right. My mind was elsewhere. I need to recover her."

Vinnet needed Maggie back, or she needed to kill her. She grabbed the doppelgänger's wrist. "Do you know where they'll be?"

The girl studied Vinnet as if she'd grown a second head,

then shrugged. Smirking, she whipped her hand free and stalked into the next room back.

You're not going to kill Maggie, are you? Sarah's stomach clenched.

It only made sense. They couldn't leave Maggie to host a Kemtewet, or her knowledge would betray Vinnet's cover. She doubted she could recover Maggie without compromising herself and voiding the best opportunity the Gertewet had of defeating the Kemtewet while they still could.

Free humanity from tyranny on the hundred worlds or continue trying to protect this one girl?

The decision was simple, but Vinnet didn't have to like it. She didn't need another senseless killing. Moreso, she didn't need Sarah's anguish added to the raw hurt of her recent kidnapping and their new, precarious relationship.

But there were millions counting on her mission's success, whether they knew it or not.

The doppelgänger emerged from the back room with a katana and a tanto. She presented the larger blade to Vinnet and tucked the smaller into the folds of her dress. "I will be ready."

Her neutral words implied neither support nor opposition. The Gertewet would be ready, too.

A sword?

Vinnet studied the larger blade. Nicks marred the edge and sides, and rust smeared it in places; it hadn't been cared for. As she adjusted her grip on the hilt and took in the doppelgänger's steadiness, the implications unfolded. The queens commonly used weapons against each other? Perhaps this assignment was more dangerous than anticipated; she'd counted on status to inhibit some attacks.

Then again, if the queens really meant to kill each other,

they'd use weapons that created damage a common tele-porter couldn't heal. Was this just another game to them?

Nothing to do but keep moving onward. Switching to a single-handed death grip, she lowered the sword casually out to her side until she didn't mind drawing all attention.

She nodded to the doppelgänger. "Lead."

Vinnet followed her into the vestibule, where the room's surprising depth and stillness only emphasized its empti-ness. Without the press of bodies, she saw clear back to the doorway leading to the vassals' quarters, all lined in white tile.

Harbored with the Kemtewet, the whole assembly was destined to be used and cast off. Their fates hadn't changed, whether with one queen or another.

Vinnet followed the other fake queen into the hall and back into the depths of the queens' wing.

You know Maggie is the only one of them who wasn't already going to die here. Sarah's anger burned against Vinnet's mind.

Situations change. She made mistakes; everyone did on early missions into new territory—like this one.

She hasn't done anything to anyone. If you kill her, you're no different from the Kemtewet.

Except she killed less frequently than Kem, and even that, she hoped, would one day pan out into a total cessation of hostilities. *This must be done.*

No, it doesn't!

Her host would understand in time.

The corridor ended at large, embossed doors with padded benches on either side. Two girls looked up from the benches, one in gray and one in black—spares of the queens of Bones and Faces, separated from their mistresses. Did she need to leave the doppelgänger, who'd pledged her readiness for...something?

The doppelgänger opened the doors and followed her in.

Vinnet took in the room in a moment: a tiled path led to a rippling pool surrounded by cafe tables inside a colonnade, and straight ahead, another hall led even deeper. A cloying scent marked the central pool as a symbiont environment, and Maggie reclined over it, strapped into a replica of the chair Sarah had endured. The Queen of Faces entered the pool beside Maggie, where she required nothing but to swim from vassal to vassal. Serket and an attendant looked on from the patio furniture.

Serket leaned against the table. "You lost her, Anjedet. There's no need to fuss."

The Queen of Faces waded deeper into the pool.

What if Sarah was right, and a peaceful solution existed? What if Vinnet could have it all? She had to try. "This was not part of our agreement."

Everyone there, doppelgänger included, stared at her.

Rolling her eyes, Serket propped her chin on her fist. "Of course it was. I've ensured that Neith's agent won't kill her."

Except killing might never have been the real threat. Who could say that Serket and the Queen of Faces weren't Neith's agents, sent to pettily deprive Anjedet of her Earth prize?

"We've won, Anjedet. Accept it."

The Queen of Faces dove into the water, leaving choppy ripples in her wake.

Out of time.

Vinnet ran.

It took far less time to leave a host than take a host; the queen could be free in seconds and poised to take Maggie.

Vinnet reached the pool's edge.

The dead vassal's body surfaced, streaming blood from neck and back that clouded the nearby gel.

Too late.

Vinnet adjusted her stride to jump in beside Maggie. Her sword slashed at Maggie's neck.

Maggie screamed, "Vinnet!"

The sword splashed in, hitting nothing but gel.

Strand it all! They weren't going to take down the Empress with compassion!

"Vinnet!"

Maggie's voice registered just as Serket's first throwing knife caught in Sarah's hair, inches from Vinnet's true body. Too close. She dove under.

The situation had evolved. There were two enemies: one with knives, one in the water with her. There were also two unknowns in the room: the doppelgänger and the woman in the back. And Maggie had said her real name.

Vinnet had been caught before; the ISC or the Queen of Blood could remember her. They had everything they needed to crack open her cover, with or without Maggie's continued existence.

Then don't kill her!

There'd be no point. Now, she had to keep word from spreading. Did she have three targets or four?

Maggie screamed, and Vinnet cracked open her eyes. A long symbiont, easily a clone to the real Anjedet, struck at Maggie's back, beginning to burrow in. Too focused on its prey, it didn't notice that the sword worked underwater, too. The gel robbed Vinnet's swing of speed, but the blade batted the symbiont out of place in a puff of red. Maggie's blood bloomed.

Vinnet surfaced for a breath. Something whizzed over her shoulder and clattered onto the patio—another knife.

Someone grunted. Over at the tables, the doppelgänger wrestled with Serket, keeping her too occupied to throw any more knives. An ally, then. Three targets.

That left the swimming queen. Vinnet dove under and glimpsed the queen making another attempt at Maggie's back. This time, Vinnet's swipe pinned the queen's long, slick body to the pool's floor, but the blade's edge slipped sideways. Vinnet lost pressure while turning it, and the queen writhed away. Vinnet swiped after her, clipping the end of her tail before she darted out of range.

That was something.

But not enough.

If Vinnet could get Maggie free, maybe the queen would focus on Vinnet—and open herself to attack. Vinnet breached the surface and unclasped one of the wrist restraints. Maggie should be able to get the rest.

But Maggie didn't respond, only stared.

Blood tinted the gel around Maggie and the queen's dead vassal pink, and tiny red streaks trailed in the queen's wake.

It's going to take forever to catch her. Sarah's mind replayed the feel of the queen slipping away.

A waste of time, Vinnet realized.

A dark shape darted toward her, and she swatted at it with the katana, swiping through the tail tip's wispy trail. They had to either kill it or get out now. She freed Maggie's other arm. "Move!"

The girl bolted upright and reached for the restraints at her legs. With her back out of the gel, the queen couldn't get enough purchase to use her. A drone might, but not someone that large.

Vinnet climbed out of the gel.

The woman at the back inched away, careful to not get

involved. On the pool's far side, the doppelgänger danced around Serket, heckling her with the tanto while staying out of range of the knives. Mostly. Both bore small cuts.

Enough. They didn't have time for this.

The doppelgänger scored Serket's shoulder and flitted a step back toward the door, drawing the queen's attention away from Vinnet. Catching Vinnet's eyes and grinning, she kept up her attacks and counters, and most importantly, Serket's attention.

Vinnet crossed the room unnoticed until she drew close. Serket expected her closer and swiped out with a knife.

Vinnet eased to the side and swung the katana.

It sliced open Serket's belly, spilling dozens of tiny eels in a spray of blood. Fetal symbionts covered her slippers.

The doppelgänger let down her guard, as if they'd finished.

Too early. Despite Vinnet's interference, one of Serket's knives caught her thigh.

One more katana swing caught the back of Serket's neck. Her body collapsed on the slew of infant Kemtewet.

The doppelgänger gaped. "You...you can't kill her. You told—Anjedet told me!"

"Can't?" Vinnet pried open the second wound, checking that she'd really caught the symbiont. Fine bones protruded from both sides of the cut.

The doppelgänger trembled. "The Empress won't let us live. She decides if anyone dies, not anyone else."

One more way she'd blown her cover. Might as well leave.

Maggie?

Vinnet glanced back. The observer had disappeared (teleported to safety to spread the alarm?) and only Maggie remained, standing atop the reclined chair and looking for a way to jump free without entering the water. She couldn't; it was too far.

"Jump in and climb out!" It shouldn't take long, and the aquatic queen had nothing to hold her prey in place.

Maggie looked past her and gasped.

Vinnet dropped, and something grazed her back. She rolled away to her feet.

Collecting herself, the doppelgänger readied her short blade. "You still have a spare, Anjedet. Don't worry; I'll put her back in place for you."

What?

The doppelgänger rushed forward, brandishing the smaller blade, but she wasn't well-trained. Vinnet feinted, and she fell for it, leaving her left side open.

Vinnet struck her ribs. She let the girl pass, then hamstrung her.

The doppelgänger dropped her blade, and Vinnet kicked it away. She clamped hands on her side and tried to speak.

But Vinnet cut open her throat.

29

TRIAL BY FIRE

Two enemies dead, one castrated, and one fled. Vinnet and Maggie needed to leave.

Maggie stood frozen, out of the pool, mirroring Sarah's distress. Her wide eyes flicked from the bloody bodies to Vinnet and the sword, and she shook.

Sarah likewise fixated on the blood and bodies; she'd seen the like only once before, in Banebdjedet's palace. Violence was still new to them.

"Look away and come here." Vinnet walked toward the exit, where they could turn their backs on the scene.

How can you be so calm? Sarah focused on the human bodies' blood and stillness, but the dying infant Kemtewet could have been props to her.

One day, she'd see symbionts as people, Vinnet reminded herself. No host started that way. *Ask me when we're safe.*

Maggie caught up and stopped at a distance, dripping and shaking.

Grabbing her hand and holding tight when she pulled

back, Vinnet forced Maggie to meet her eyes. "We're going home. Stay close and silent."

Maggie nodded.

We're going home, she repeated to Sarah.

No one dies like that there. Lies like that seemed to soothe Sarah's dazed mind.

Nowhere was that peaceful.

"Let's go." She opened the door barely enough for them to slip through and found the two waiting spares, their shifts clean and dry. They wouldn't stand out like Anjedet's sopping and bloodied gown. "Give us your clothes. Now!"

Either because they thought her a queen or because the katana still dripped with the doppelgänger's blood, they stripped immediately. In minutes, she and Maggie wore something more sensible and stalked away unchallenged.

When they left the spares out of sight, Vinnet squeezed the katana's hilt. It would be lovely to keep it handy, but for now, they needed stealth more than the weapon. Besides, in other parts of the Central Palace, their opponents would have plasma guns that made swords obsolete.

She set it in one of the side corridors and kept moving, all the way to the entrance where the Green Flame had parted from them. She saw no one. Tugging Maggie forward, she sprinted down the corridor, heaping silent blessings on whoever decided to include sound-dampening flooring: plush, discrete, and stealthy.

Vinnet paused at the exit, glancing back and listening for pursuit. Stealth worked both ways. *Beyond this door is the kings' area, where vassal attire will be conspicuous. The servants there work throughout the palace's restricted areas.*

Won't they recognize us?

Possibly. She scanned the door for traps, and her hopes sank at the sight of two disks, one matte gray and one shiny black, embedded in the ceiling over the exit. Two matching sets were embedded in the walls at the side. *Short wavelength imaging.*

What's that mean?

If they had this system on earlier, they'd have seen me within you and known I wasn't a queen; I'm too short. Vinnet took a deep breath into Sarah's lungs. *They'll know now.* She activated the door and led Maggie through, but no siren blared into the hall's pristine silence. It should have been swarming with people.

What happened? Why didn't it go off?

Maybe it's a silent alarm. Perhaps our runaway observer already set it off. That seemed right. Any moment, security forces would swarm. She pulled Maggie along, their running footfalls reflecting off the hard-surfaced halls.

Sure enough, echoes of other rushing footsteps reverberated ahead of them. It sounded like too many to fight, especially unarmed as she was, and they surely had a visible-spectrum image of her from the checkpoint at the exit from the queens' quarters. She couldn't count on deceiving them.

She grabbed Maggie's arm and activated the next door on the right. It opened into a small, square room with three portals: a door with no access panel, which meant it was one-way—in only; one ahead, at about Sarah's chin level, a dark, fluid-filled port set into the wall; and a trapdoor in the floor with the disposal symbol. An emergency exit. Strand it!

"What now?" Maggie whispered.

"*Into the garbage chute, flyboy*"? Sarah suggested.

The disposal unit is a dead end. It immediately deconstructs discarded bodies dropped in.

How do the servants get out?

This is an interlock. They leave their vassals on this side to fall into the disposal and swim through the port in the wall. They take a new vassal on the other side. She looked at the human-sized door. *That's where the vassals come in when the servants enter. The other side of the passage is in the feudal areas with us, too.* She grabbed Maggie's hand.

How do the humans get in?

By teleportation, as we did. She backed into the hall. "That won't work." Not unless she wanted to leave behind both humans in her charge.

So is that how we'll get out, teleportation?

As when we arrived, we won't have access to the control panel from here. Even as Anjedet, we wouldn't have the authority to command a servant to let us out of the Central Palace. Checking that the coast was still clear, she pulled Maggie back into the hallway through the kings' and lords' quarters.

Is there another way?

Not yet. If not the way servants or fealty left, perhaps they could leave the way normal Kemtewet citizens did after the execution. Except the two areas weren't supposed to connect.

The corridor to the feudal day rooms began at a pair of ornately embossed doors. Vinnet hesitated before actuating them. "If this doesn't work..."

Maggie raised an eyebrow at her.

"*You might want to decide now how you'd rather die*" sounded too callous. She shook her head and activated the door. *It's not as if she'll have a choice.*

IT ALWAYS FELT weird being escorted by humans who knew Katorin was Gertewet and who would happily kill her for it.

She certainly meant them no harm, and anyone who knew her knew that.

They're afraid. Setira had watched silently through most of the show and tell. *You made a lot of progress by showing off Khonsu, but you weren't going to change their minds in an hour. If you'll recall, you didn't change my mind in an hour.*

Katorin swallowed. *It took years.*

And you succeeded.

The humans led them outside, into a world of sunlight and blue skies and blowing wind. She should have enjoyed such beauty, but instead, she could only worry that she and Donn might tip Khonsu's precious gel out onto the cracked pavement.

Are there symbionts uglier than Khonsu?

On Sais, Katorin didn't smile at her host, because she feared others would recognize her interaction. Here, she refrained, because she feared they wouldn't. *Probably not.*

Slinging the bucket between them, they waddled across the near edge of a paved area for the local vehicles until they reached the adjacent building. Inside, the small lobby split into two hallways of identical doors. Except the first on the left, where sawdust and metal chips marked recent construction and a single, distraught guard marked trouble.

Katorin and Donn set the bucket down.

"I don't know what happened, Major. The prisoner said he didn't know how to use the facilities, and since he was funny-looking, we believed him. Sergeant Rodriguez went in to help him."

No. Katorin caught Donn's eye and signed, "I'll go."

After all, his team still seemed angry at him and Kitchell. Maybe they'd work with her. She eased forward until the front guard held out his arm to stop her. She stopped.

From here, she could barely see into the first room's open door and watch as Major Patrick stepped up to study the prone body.

"You killed him?" The Major's voice promised retribution.

"The Sergeant did. He was real upset about it, wouldn't say anything after."

"Where is he now?"

He pointed. "Couple doors down the hall. He didn't look so good."

Setira's heart beat in her ears, loud and distracting. Katorin called over it, "Major, may I look at the body? I suspect you're not going to like this."

The Major's hard eyes studied her, but she waved Katorin forward.

Approaching, she studied the body from shoes to shoulder.

Behind her, Major Patrick shifted her attention. "Are you boys from Spokane?"

"Yes, ma'am."

"Why aren't the local boys here?"

It shouldn't hurt to see Cube Head still and motionless, his boxy hair flat on the floor like a settled die, his slack eyes forever gazing at the wall. He was just another Kem, except...

"There weren't too many to begin with, ma'am. One had to go help the girls next door, and the rest... Sergeant Rodriguez said the other two or three prisoners—I wasn't clear on how many—were more of a concern than this one."

Katorin reached out and touched the flabby pocket of skin to the left of his vassal's spine, where Cube Head himself used to reside. "Major, this is only the vassal. The Kem must have moved into Rodriguez."

"How?"

Donn answered before she could. "Kem learn how to switch vassals like we learn first aid and CPR."

Katorin hadn't realized that before. On Sais, switching vassals *was* first aid. "Let me help. I worked with him as a cover during my last assignment. I know him."

Major Patrick nudged the clueless sentry down the hall. "Which room?"

"106."

Exchanging nods with the Major as she passed, Katorin reached the room first. She tried not to mind the rising pistols behind her.

Three knocks, and she let herself in. Now was no time for cute nicknames. "Paul?"

Beyond a narrow passageway with opposing doors, a dim bedroom sheltered itself behind shades. Barely enough light leaked through to show her adjusting eyes a barrel of Earth's weapon of choice pointing at her from the adjacent room.

She froze. It looked like a passage to room 105, but if so, the swarm of troops outside should stop him if he tried to leave. "Paul?"

"Beryl?" he whispered. The gun didn't move. The new vassal's voice was deeper and raspier. An hour ago, Paul would have been no threat, even with a gun, but the new vassal knew how to use it. "Don't tell them. Please. You showed them, and now they're going to want to kill me."

Anyone who knows you wants to kill you. Slowly, she shifted her weight from foot to foot, getting him used to motion. "No, Paul. Remember when you thought I wanted you for information? That's exactly what they want. If you keep talking to them, they'll be happy you're alive."

Somewhat.

"But now, they think I'm dead, and they'll leave me alone."

As good as any time.

Katorin swiped the muzzle up and tackled him, shoulder to stomach. The gun fired. Something hot bounced into her hair. She should have bowled him into the ground, but he hit a hollow wall with a crack, leaving her short of the position she'd planned. Pinning his legs, she caught his arms before he repositioned and snapped his wrist back. The gun clattered free—but still close.

With one hand, she caught his unbroken wrist, and with the other, she pinched his actual body in the new vassal's still-tender neck.

He froze.

"No one thinks you're dead. Yet. And I'd rather not kill you when they want you alive."

———

By NIGHT, cleaning robots scoured the daytime rooms in the Central Palace that were reserved for the Kemtewet fealty: audience chambers, conservatories, libraries, dining halls, and gardens. Vinnet happened across the first robot when transitioning from a desert garden room to a musical hall.

As the robot finished buffing its area, it spun in a circle, reorienting. Its laser guide swept across the floor, scanned past Vinnet and Maggie, then backtracked. It steadied on Sarah's leg.

"Keep away from it," Vinnet warned Maggie. Maybe she should have kept Anjedet's sword.

You're going to fight it? Let's run!

We can't outrun the whole network. They may be in the public areas, too.

The fixture maintenance arm rose from the robot's pitted crest, looking for all the world like a three-fingered skeletal hand crafted out of knives. The arm canted forward, and the hand splayed. The robot jolted toward them, rolling faster than it looked like it should.

Vinnet picked up a nearby stringed instrument and held it like a bat. *I courted a Gertewet who was on the design team for these.*

The robot closed in. It leveled its gleaming hand at her face.

She backed around a large percussion instrument, luring it toward friendlier terrain: a decorative lip in the floor its wheels could barely handle.

Do something! Sarah insisted.

The robot dropped down the lip, and Vinnet swung.

The string instrument shattered on the top edge of the robot. As the articulated blades clawed into the remaining splinters, the robot tipped.

But not far enough.

Vinnet growled under her breath. *Too weak!* She swung again with the backbone of the instrument then jumped feet-first toward the dome and its grasping blades.

Both struck home.

She pushed the robot to topple up over the lip, but it caught her shin as she fell onto her back.

"Sarah!" Maggie screamed.

A wave of surprise and pain hit Vinnet from her stunned host. *Ignore it!* They didn't have a choice; this robot wouldn't stay immobilized forever.

She pushed herself to her feet as pain seared down her right shin and calf. It didn't feel broken, and she'd certainly had worse cuts. *We'll be fine, Sarah. We must keep moving!* She picked up the last couple feet of the dead instrument's neck and crept toward the robot.

Even on its side, its articulated arm still quested about, seeking a stable enough hold on the floor to push itself upright. Batting its feeble grip aside, she reached toward the shaft at the base of the arm.

Are you asking for more?

Peace. After half a rotation of the shaft, the arm lost power. After two more twists, it came off in her hand. *There: a weapon.* She caught Maggie's eye and nodded for her to follow. As she crossed to the far end of the practice hall, she dismantled the linkages in the robot arm; eventually, it would leave her with three knives and a telescoping pole.

"You're bleeding," Maggie whispered.

"We'll be okay."

"It's leaving a trail. Stop." Maggie caught up and crouched down to look at Sarah's leg. She wrapped it in sheets of stiff linen music then slipped a hair tie over Sarah's foot and into place around her shin. Dark curls from her unbound ponytail framed her face with pouf. "That will help."

Vinnet nodded and urged her along. "Good thinking." But unnecessary; she'd planned to let the Kemtewet's other robots clean her trail.

They wound through a half-dozen other rooms and dispatched one more robot before arriving at Vinnet's next checkpoint: the arena observation room, where they'd spent the afternoon.

"Here?" Maggie asked when the door closed behind them. "I stared around here for hours. There isn't another way out."

"Yet." Vinnet drew two of the scavenged knives and left

the other four tied into her shift. She headed for the window.

"I don't think you're going to break glass with those."

"This isn't glass; it's sapphire. It's much stronger." Vinnet stopped next to the wide pane. On the far side, remnants of the execution still swarmed in the arena—stray flesh-eating beetles; scaled creatures munching them; and two large, black felines with matted manes. If they wanted to get through, they'd have to be fast and careful.

Vinnet stabbed between the base of the window and a vertical edge in the floor. She slid the knife along the seam.

"Then how are you going to get to the other side?" Maggie demanded.

Sarah's thoughts echoed her.

"I have thought this through," Vinnet answered them both. She sawed farther along the window's base. "We have no good means of cracking sapphire."

"If you'd gone back for one of the lasers…"

Vinnet furrowed Sarah's brow at her. "What lasers?"

"On the droids."

She had to wait for Sarah's vocabulary to interpret "droids." *On the cleaning robots.* She sawed harder at the seam. "Those didn't have enough power to blind someone, let alone melt sapphire."

"But if you focused it."

"If you found a lens to focus it perfectly, it still wouldn't output enough energy quickly enough to get us through." She paused long enough to slide the second knife across the floor to Maggie. "Start on the other side."

She'd gone another six feet when Sarah thought, *You're destroying the seal—then what?*

Sealing is an ancillary function. This window is flush with the walls on the outside, and it covers a larger area than can be viewed from this side. She reached the corner and started sliding the knife down from the top. *It was designed to withstand high forces—like an attacking animal—from the other side by overlapping the wall on that side. We're destroying the mount.*

"Can they find us in here?" Maggie had a quarter of the bottom left to go.

"Yes." Not that Vinnet needed a reminder to hurry. If the Empress caught them... The star of the execution could easily have waited three years for his death, and she didn't intend to follow in his footsteps. The last part of the side seal gave under her knife.

She pulled a drink table near the window to stand on, then stabbed into the top part of the seal and addressed both her host and Maggie. "When we get through, we will walk calmly toward the end of the arena to the right. Stay along the wall as long as you can stand, even though it will be easier to move toward the center of the arena than away."

Maggie stabbed the seal on her side, then turned to watch Vinnet slicing across the window's top. "What about the cats?"

"Try not to attract their attention." Vinnet attacked the seal anew. *That should be easy for Maggie with your blood already flowing.*

Can we make it?

She and her past hosts had lived through worse, right? Vinnet tried to recall an example but didn't want to spare the attention. *Of course we can.* Anything was possible, if however problematic.

Let me do it.

Vinnet paused to consider. *But I'm familiar with the animals and the technology.*

And I'm familiar with my body. After four years of gymnas-

tics, I know how to sprint. Or walk, like you said. I won't wobble like you have today.

Vinnet eased Sarah's fingers from the knife, ensuring it would stay lodged in the seal. She eyed the predators stalking each other on the far side of the sapphire. Synchronizing coordination in a new host did take time. *If you're certain...*

30

NOT COMING HOME

I *can do something better than Vinnet. I'm not useless.* Now, Sarah had to prove it.

She stared out the sapphire window at the scaled creatures crunching on beetles in the arena's sand. Bigger than she and rough-looking, they still struck her as the arena's smallest danger. *Lions and beetles and falcons, oh my.* Still, she had to pass them. *When are you going to give me control?*

You have it.

Sarah looked down at her hands as she curled and uncurled her stiff fingers. With a deep breath, she grabbed the knife and continued slicing the seal.

"Are you okay?"

Sarah shrugged. The alien super-spy had doubts about their survival; for her to be "okay" would be a stretch. "Let's get this over with." She finished off the seal, but the sapphire wall didn't move.

Push it. Hard.

She did. Then she smacked it. The window stayed put.

"Do you hear that?" Maggie crossed the room and leaned her ear toward the door.

Vinnet focused on the sound of footsteps down the hall, and twitched in alarm, twinging in Sarah's neck. She relayed what the symbiont gleaned. "They're still searching. They don't know we're in here."

"They will when we knock that out."

The guards on both sides will, Vinnet agreed.

Sarah stared through the window, trying to pick out security forces pre-ambush. Sure enough, she spotted a couple at the top of the arena, patrolling toward the public exit. If Sarah and Maggie turned back now, they'd have to find a king to authorize their exit or Vinnet would have to use the emergency exit and leave the humans to be...atomically disassembled. The only way out was through the sapphire, animals, and patrol.

Of course Vinnet was right.

"Help me knock it out." Sarah placed her back to the door and waited until Maggie mimicked her ready stance. "Three. Two. One."

They burst forth, crossed the room in four long strides, and launched shoulder-first into the center of the wide pane. In a moment of wild panic, Sarah felt herself falling. Then the sapphire slammed against the sandy arena floor with a woofing thud.

Beside her face, beetle guts gushed against the pane, preserved for inspection like a botched bug display.

Get up! You must move!

Sarah pushed to her feet, feeling like she'd been buried in sand after a long practice, and nudged Maggie forward. She tried to ignore the gleaming yellow eyes of the cat beside the executed man's clean-scoured skeleton.

"I don't feel right," Maggie groaned.

It's the gravity.

Sarah pushed her to walk parallel to the wall, her arms and legs sluggish to respond. "It's okay. Keep moving." They edged toward the oval arena's end, growing more and more tired by the moment. Too soon, Maggie slowed and collapsed to her knees.

Something thumped into the sand behind them.

Sarah turned to find the feline only yards away, pulling its face out of the sand. Vinnet grew frantic. *Get up! Move! It's not going to stay!*

Sarah did. One arm jerked Maggie onto her feet long enough for Sarah to shove her hard toward the arena wall. Then she ran, angled toward the center of the arena's end, so she edged out of the most severe part of the gravitational field—onto center stage.

The first lion eyed the lone prey nearby with interest and ignored Sarah. The second didn't. It launched into motion from across the arena.

Sarah had never run like this: lifting her knees toward her chest, stretching out her stride, urging all the power she could coax from her legs, even as pain spiked up and down her shin.

A vicious game of tag. If she stuck to the straight path, she'd never win.

She noted where unlucky beetles had found the gravity field's far edge and fallen. She pushed closer, every nerve screaming that the lion had to be reaching her back. Then she bore left in a wide turn through the mild edge of the projected gravity barrier.

Behind her, giant paws scrabbled in the sand.

As Sarah peeled back around the skeleton, sending disturbed beetles flying, she caught sight of both cats trapped in the extreme side of the projected barrier. The first had given up on Maggie and settled down in the sand, tail flicking sporadically.

It got stuck at five gees? Vinnet speculated. *Maybe three?*

The second simply collapsed, panting shallow breaths.

That one almost got through as it turned to follow us. Nine gees.

With both felines indisposed, Sarah paused, crunching more beetles underfoot. She was gasping, too. She glimpsed security forces filling the feudal observation room, but none tried to follow her into the arena's deadly center. *So how do I get through the field?*

The predator tried to turn in the heavy area. You'll go straight. Fast.

With a deep breath, Sarah pumped her legs again and aimed straight down the center of the arena. When she hit the field, it robbed her burning legs of power. Then her stride broke as her feet met the ground too soon, and it was all she could do to keep herself upright. Her body felt so heavy that she couldn't stand. She collapsed face-first into the sand. Her vision grew dim.

Something pulled on her arm, and her face slid across the sand. And she was through.

Gasping for breath, Sarah looked up at Maggie, who stared down at her leg, horrified. Sarah followed her gaze to a handful of the flesh-eating beetles clustered around the gash on her shin. She felt too tired to freak out, but she flicked them off toward their brethren trapped in the gravity field, where they clicked to the ground and stayed.

The beetles had expanded the gash from the cleaning robot, leaving the edges ragged and bloody. Now that she looked, it burned and throbbed in time with her racing heart. "The music sheets are gone."

Disregard them. From here to the exit, the security forces will see you anyway. Just go!

Easy for her to say; the symbiont wasn't bleeding out onto the coarse sand or sore from the extra weight. Sarah pushed herself to her feet and tried to ignore the dribble down her shin. "Let's go."

"I saw what you did with that panther. It was awesome!"

"It was luck." Sarah pointed at the arena wall. A sheer ten feet high and topped with an ornate gold railing, it towered over her head. "We need to get over that."

Maggie studied it. "That."

"Yeah."

"No problem." And it wasn't. Maggie showed Sarah how to hold her hands for Maggie's feet. Then she climbed up, jumped, and caught the ledge. She reached back down and caught Sarah's hand when she leapt. At the end, both girls collapsed in the front row of stadium seats, panting but off the arena floor.

"How'd you know? How to do that?" Sarah asked.

"Camp team-building activities." Maggie smiled.

You must keep moving! Even this far along, Vinnet's tension hadn't eased.

But no one outside the observation room has even noticed us!

We should depart before they do. If they don't recognize you at once as Anjedet, they will still recognize that you're out of place. You're too young to be Kemtewet vassals.

Sarah studied all the indicators of Maggie's age: her padded cheeks paired with a slight build, a few telltale signs of acne on her forehead and chin. *Too young? I thought they wanted girls our age.*

The queens do, because it's easier for them to reproduce if you haven't had children. But Kem drones want instant beauty. They would have let you finish maturing. Vinnet caught herself, and her sense of urgency slammed back into Sarah's mind. *I can lecture you when you're safe. Move!*

Sarah pushed herself out of the seat, ignoring her protesting shin. Everything still ached from the gravity field, but she'd dragged through enough practices to know she could make it out. After all, she knew—Vinnet knew—the exit was near this end of the stadium, by the top of the closest aisle. She pulled Maggie up, too.

"What is it?" Maggie stood but leaned against the railing. She hadn't recovered, either.

"No one's supposed to be here, and we don't look like we belong. We need to get out of here now." She tugged Maggie onward.

Before, Sarah had watched Vinnet's friend riding down the escalator a third of the way around the stadium. Now, none of the escalators operated, so she took their steps two at a time. *Almost there. Just a little farther. Almost there.* Endurance was all about lying to yourself.

Maggie surged ahead and beat her to the top, then paused. Sarah blew by her, intent on the exit, and then noticed the crowd of security hustling their way from the other side. "Run!" She didn't watch Maggie as she followed her own advice. Sprinting, they might make it; youth and lack of weighty equipment gave them an edge.

They burst around the corner to the exit corridor and found a surprise. They'd beaten the swarm of security to the corner, but another team already waited ahead. The thin line looked up from the checkpoint and readied their weapons.

Stall them, or they'll fire!

Sarah drew an extra-deep breath. "Don't point those at me! I'm a queen!"

Sure enough, they hesitated while she closed on the one nearest the checkpoint's narrow doorway.

It was high-speed, high-stakes Simon Says with a heads-up display. Vinnet identified targets, how to hit them, and what to do next—and Sarah did it.

Your hand to his helmet. Swipe. The helmet slid over his eyelids.

Your far elbow to his stomach. Hard. As Sarah swung around to hit him, she caught sight of Maggie using her distraction to dart between guards. Others in the stationary group swung their weapons toward the girls but had to catch their comrades in the crossfire.

Someone must have fired already, because the oncoming group thinned. Some lay stunned behind them.

Get beyond the threshold.

Sarah darted between the guards she'd hit, through the narrow doorway where security screened incoming traffic, and into a wide, deserted atrium.

She barely noticed the tall ceilings and wide skylights above the marble floors where all general visitors to the Central Palace arrived and departed. She glimpsed the doorways to five other public wings before the surroundings changed in a blink.

The atrium's fractured arctic glare transmuted into the soft glow and cozy confines of another flying saucer, but this one had a clear canopy that featured a peaceful, clear-blue sky.

"Destination?" asked the pilot's simulated voice.

Sarah grabbed Maggie's hand, as if to keep the enemy from having her. *Pilot?*

A free-swimming Kemtewet inhabits this vehicle until it's earned enough to buy a vassal and living quarters, Vinnet explained. She didn't seem to feel any particular disdain for this Kemtewet; it was part of the machine. *This is no time to switch. Tell it we would like to transfer to a kaxan.*

She did.

"Authorization code?"

Vinnet fed her a long string of numbers that she repeated aloud.

"Invalid code."

Vinnet's alarm and dread and fear hit Sarah full-force for the half-second it took until her world winked back out.

Her eyes next opened in the midst of a crowd of security.

IT WASN'T Palace Security from the public areas. The circle of bodies each held a steady plasma gun and bore the plain uniform of the Information Security Corps. Neith's personal, specially-trained Information Security Corps.

Where do I hit first? Sarah asked. Vinnet's host took a step back and pressed her shoulders against Maggie's, releasing the girl's hand.

It doesn't matter.

The corpsmen fired.

ROCKEFELLER FOUND a paper towel in the kitchenette while Major Patrick and the whole contingent of MPs led the Gertewet away.

Stokely's hand rested on his shoulder. "How are you holding up?"

"Let's talk about something we can act on."

"Another rescue mission?"

And that was why they were friends. Once a way had

been made, it was always an option. "I don't know. I didn't get it at the time, but it's starting to sink in that they took her to the capital. And those two, the General and the woman, they can sit here and be mild and patient, but at the capital, they were all business. Before then, I watched him fight through four men at once. They're very capable. And they're afraid of operating there."

"What are you saying?"

"I don't think we can get her back." The realization hit like a punch to the gut. "They know so much more than we do, and they're worried. Charlie, I had her in my arms, and we got separated. I don't think I'm ever getting her back."

Wiping his eyes dry, he caught a whiff of the symbiont water on his hands and thought of the ugly brown lump. Would another one get implanted in Maggie? Would it take over, completely overwriting her, or would some remnant shine through, like it did with Sarah? Could he live with that?

Colonel Marshall approached, arms crossed. "If we can get enough intelligence from our prisoners, we could build a case to send Special Forces. Getting her back from their capital would announce that we are not a planet to cross."

"And if they fail?" Stokely shook his head. "It may start a war we can't fight yet."

Rockefeller pointed to where the bucket had sat. "Today, we learned five ways to kill them."

"When they're outside a host."

"And inside a host, they're human." Rockefeller mirrored Colonel Marshall's stance. "Special Forces can handle humans."

The Colonel shook her head. "Senator Stokely is right. We can't start this unless we get the intelligence to ensure we can win, but we can make that our highest priority."

Major Patrick strolled back into the conference room with Katorin. They'd only been gone fifteen minutes, and Katorin wasn't supposed to return. Major Patrick tossed a badge on the table. "Who are we supposed to call? Edwards, Spokane, or the county morgue?"

"What?"

Katorin slipped onto the stool beside the Major and leaned heavily on the table. "The Kem swapped vassals. Donn is watching him now."

"Not only is the old host dead," the Major added, "but he took over one of the imported SFs. So one John Doe with an actual dead—and funny-looking—body, and...Do we report the SF as dead, too?"

"We'll have to," the Colonel answered. "He's secure now?"

Katorin answered quickly. "Yes."

Major Patrick was slower. "I believe so. Besides having the General in the room with him, our usual SFs are on guard. They know better than to take the Kemtewet lightly. The Spokane guys didn't."

"And why is she here?" Colonel Marshall demanded, gesturing to Katorin.

Rockefeller and Stokely drifted to the short end of the table to listen closely.

"Colonel." Katorin sat straighter and folded her hands. "Major Patrick agreed to bring me back here because of my role in apprehending the Kemtewet."

"Our men could have done that."

"At greater risk to themselves. He grew up on ghost stories of atrocities the Ger commit against Kem and on news sprinkled with violence against Kem on the lords' planets and the Grand Empire. He's concerned, and right-fully so, that you'll kill him, but he doesn't understand why."

"So he killed one of my men?"

"In his limited experience, he thought that would make him safer. Remember: he sees no problem with his parasitic existence. That's the way they are, and that's why we're trying to kill them."

"Then why is he still alive?" Rockefeller asked.

Katorin blinked at him. "You don't take them out one by one. You bring down their society and cease their reproduction. That's what they did to us."

Cease reproduction? "Your entire race is sterile?"

"Can we not get into that? It comes down to this: we're dying out, and we haven't won. You're still alive, and the Empress is planning to take over your planet. Can we please work together?"

Stokely circled the table and sat opposite Katorin. "What Empress, and why does she want to take us over?"

Her jaw dropped. Then she explained the political structure of the Kemtewet Empire and sighed. "I can't tell you everything you need to know. It would take years. What if we could visit, if our leadership allows, and teach you what you need to defend yourselves?"

Rockefeller and Colonel Marshall traded glances. That kind of arrangement would only get them the information the Gertewet wanted them to have. "If that's how you feel about it, what about a permanent liaison?"

She lit up, beaming from ear to ear. "That sounds ideal!" Then she deflated. "We have a long-standing no-contact policy for Earth, but in light of the imminent threat, perhaps the Council could consider a more enlightened philosophy."

This was all well, but what he really wanted was the girls home on Earth.

"Vinnet."

All four people in the room stared at him.

"We want Vinnet as the liaison. If she survives, she'll be in Sarah or—" No, anything but that. "—or Maggie. They should be home with their families."

Katorin's eyes said it all.

They weren't likely to come home.

31

THE GREEN FLAME

Vinnet couldn't blame her host. After the strain of making it through the arena's gravitational fields, then pushing on to the exit through security, the electric shock of the plasma guns' stun setting interrupted her muscle control. Still, Vinnet had to wonder if it would have been different with the more experienced mind in control. Maybe she could have moved faster, taken out more guards, or entered a valid vacation code.

Every optimistic scenario she played through ended with their arrival in the kaxan-taxi, with her choosing an expired code. Her new host had nothing to do with that.

She could only watch as ISC forces in pristine gray uniforms peeled both her host and Maggie from the floor and strapped them onto stretchers. Cold fingers brushed against Sarah's skin as they clamped a padded metal ring around her neck, and as the device constricted into place, Vinnet cringed. To attempt escape now wouldn't just damage Sarah's brain but mutilate her body, too.

How bad can it be? Sarah wondered. Even her thoughts slurred with fatigue.

Vinnet shuddered. Last time, she'd been captured in a regional palace, the Eater of Blood's capital. He had isolated her, given her drain water to drink, cut off her fingers... And he was a king, not the Empress who spawned such creatures.

It was all starting over: the shackles, the questions, the torture.

"WE WANT VINNET AS THE LIAISON." Rockefeller clasped his hands over the duct-taped ping-pong table and tried not to look desperate. "If she survives, she'll be in Sarah or Maggie. They should be home with their families."

Katorin deflated. "In the meantime, I suppose we could ask them to station Kitchell."

"No." The Colonel's strong voice rang in the still room.

"Even if it gave you a chance to mend your relationships?"

How did Katorin not know what kind of land mine she was tap dancing on? If she knew the Colonel's and General's relationship had problems, why did she think she should point it out?

Stokely jumped in. "I think we need a more objective viewpoint to start with."

"Even though Kitchell alone has the tactical knowledge and context of both your forces and ours? That's a unique perspective."

Rockefeller expected the Colonel to cut that argument off at the knees. Emotionally, there was no way for it to fly. But even pained by the prospect, she considered it. "Well, Vinnet—"

"This is only until Vinnet arrives."

The Colonel deliberated.

Rockefeller stepped in. "We'd like a more neutral liaison, someone we can begin building trust with, rather than taking time, energy, and effort to undo distrust."

"I see."

Stokely settled on a stool and cracked open his planner to the notes section. "So far, we're looking at a permanent liaison to Project Black Book: Vinnet, when she's free, and someone who isn't Donn Marshall in the meantime."

Rockefeller leaned over. "We need a more generic term than Black Book, in case the name of the project changes."

"The Air Force, then?"

"How about the United States?"

Stokely frowned but corrected his notes. "So, this is an advisory and informational role. Any specific objectives?"

"Tactical briefings on destination planets," the Colonel provided.

"Kemtewet anatomy," Rockefeller added.

"Kaxan instruction and help with reverse engineering," the Colonel continued.

Stokely scribbled.

Katorin blinked. "Anatomy? Reverse engineering? Why?"

"Because understanding their bodies will show us where they're weak." Rockefeller watched his words sink in and Katorin's gaze jitter from person to person. Presumably, the same information would work on Gertewet.

She swallowed, apparently deciding to trust them. "And reverse engineering kaxan? Why bother when the Empire already mass produces them?"

"Once we understand it, we may be able to build something better or exploit its weaknesses." The Colonel stared her down. "That won't be a problem, will it?"

"I don't think so." Katorin shrunk in on herself. "Basic transportation technologies are older than the Kemtewet species. Most of us don't remember why it works."

Marshall sighed, disappointed. "Fine. Just teach us how to use it. Translate the interfaces."

"This is quite a full-time job." Stokely scribbled madly. "Now, I know this is going to come up. Should the liaison be compensated?"

"They usually are by their native government, right?" Rockefeller studied Katorin thoughtfully.

Her eyes widened. "We need most of our funds to set up covers."

"Besides," Stokely added, "how are you going to set up an exchange rate for the currency of a state you want to ruin?"

"Well, the liaison can stay on the base," Rockefeller answered. "He won't need extra funds. He'll be needed here anyway."

"What if it's Sarah?" Stokely eyed him.

The whole point was that Sarah was supposed to go home to fix a household that had to be missing her.

"I don't think we need to worry about that," Katorin answered.

"Because you're not really going to send her?" he snapped back.

She brushed a tear from her cheek. "Were it up to me, I would station her here in a heartbeat. She's my little sister and my best friend; I want her to be safe as much as you do. But the reality is that we couldn't have sent her on a more dangerous mission. It's a sign of desperation that we even tried. If it succeeds, the payoff will be everything we could ever hope for. And if it doesn't, if she fails like the others before her, she'll be one more body in the Kem Empire's bloody trail."

Closing her eyes and breathing deeply, Katorin folded her knobby hands, collecting herself. "All the liaison needs is food and shelter. A stipend won't be necessary. At home— on our bases—we rotate through domestic duties. We can assist in those here, too."

Rockefeller nodded absently. She sounded so certain. Write off Sarah as dead, and by extension, Maggie. Gone forever. Not worth planning for.

As good as dead.

She and the Colonel compared "domestic duties," but he couldn't listen anymore.

His excursion brought back the chance of an alliance to severely reinforce the local defenses and capabilities, but at what cost? Two girls with their entire futures ahead of them. Two girls for the planet.

Was it worth it?

In the House, he'd make that decision in a moment with the clarity of knowing two lives couldn't outweigh billions.

But now?

They'd better get something else out of this Mephisthophelean deal.

"We can have someone type this and add some verbiage to make it official." Stokely motioned with his notepad to an invisible assistant.

"I prefer them as they are. Our council may add provisions as it sees fit." Her fingers fidgeted on the tabletop. "You will permit Kitchell to return with me, won't you?"

No one answered her.

"It will be difficult explaining your earnest and peaceful intentions otherwise."

"Of course." Rockefeller crossed his arms. "But the Kemtewet stays."

"Hasn't he done you enough harm?"

"That's not the point." Colonel Marshall crossed her arms, too. "The airman he possessed belongs here. He's one of us. No one's taking him away like he has no rights. He stays." She glanced away, and her voice darkened. "Besides, we need a study subject."

Katorin froze. Then, she forced herself to move, jerkily, uncertain. "I see. To find weaknesses."

"Naturally."

"I'm sure a liaison could provide insights. Especially if she's intact."

Rockefeller forced a smile. "We look forward to her insights."

"Sarah?"

Her heart pounded, railing against the images in her mind, the persecution, the slow death.

"Sarah!"

This time, she recognized Maggie's voice and opened her eyes, starting at the sight of the wide-open ballroom drenched in red, from crimson drapery to glistening ruby chandeliers hanging over pearly marble. Blood and bone.

She gagged on a memory of Vinnet having her teeth pulled out one by one, choking on her own blood.

"Sarah!"

Finding she couldn't move her head, she moved her eyes as far as she could to the side and glimpsed dark curls. "Maggie?"

"Good. You're awake. Now what?"

Awake? But plasma stunners shocked; they didn't knock people out. Why... Because she hadn't been asleep but reliving Vinnet's nightmarish memories. She swallowed against the restriction on her neck and studied the room. While the decor differed, the layout precisely matched that of the ballroom in Banebdjedet's mothership, but a lord couldn't have retrieved them from the ISC. That's why Vinnet was freaking out.

It had to be someone more powerful, someone Vinnet felt vulnerable to.

Vinnet wasn't supposed to be vulnerable; she was supposed to protect Sarah. Save the world. Get a body, then have everything else handled.

She didn't.

Sarah's stomach clenched. That left her alone, again, in the hands of people who wanted to hurt her. They'd succeeded in implanting something the first time. After that, what could they escalate to?

Vinnet knew.

They had to get out. But how?

"Do you know whose ship we're on?" Even as she asked, her voice trembling, she realized Maggie might not know. After all, she didn't have an alien operative in her head deciphering things.

"It's the guy you stood with this afternoon."

The Green Flame. Another king like the one Vinnet remembered. Would he rip out her teeth for no greater crime than hosting a Ger? The symbiont thought so. This wasn't fair!

"Is that bad?"

Sarah studied the people passing through, hoping to catch the Green Flame's approach before he surprised her. Most seemed to be maids servicing the adjoining chambers, but one, a woman in light armor, stood beside a support pillar, glaring at them. *Who's that?*

Vinnet didn't respond.

"This is bad." Sarah answered Maggie as softly as she could, trying not to move her lips too much. Why was the woman here, on a king's ship? She had to be a Kemtewet. A queen?

That caught Vinnet's attention. *No, they wouldn't let another queen out after us.*

Sarah's breath hitched in her tight throat. *Neith in a new body?*

Her heart pounded frantically while Vinnet studied the woman. *Too alone. It's probably one of the Green Flame's assistants.*

Just a drone. Whew. *So, it's just like the Green Flame?*

It might one day become the Green Flame. One more titled tyrant in a long, bloody succession.

Sarah ground her teeth. *A long succession we're going to end.*

Sure, that's what Vinnet had said all along, but this time was different. Sarah wasn't just going to break free; she'd get payback for them taking her, for them killing the three women, for them thinking they could pluck people up from Earth, use them, and move on to the next vassal. One way or another, she wouldn't let them keep her here. *How do we get out?*

In an instant's dim flash, another figure appeared in the empty yards between Sarah and the Kemtewet drone. His thick arms ended in clenched, meaty hands, and his shadowed olive robes set off the lighter green of the ballroom's drapery.

Wait, wasn't that red?

She and Vinnet both saw his face's vibrant flush against

the room drenched in green and sepia. *Teni*. The drapery and chandeliers warmed to match the hue of his face. Then their minds replayed the sound of crackling cartilage, the agony of broken and then severed fingers, and the taste of a throat screamed raw.

The next thing Sarah knew, he stood nose-to-nose with her, his foul breath playing hot and putrid across her face. "—is Anjedet?"

She shook. Had she blacked out again?

"Tell me, dredge-dweller. Where is Anjedet?"

"S-she's dead." Her shallow breaths could eke out only one word at a time.

"I don't believe you."

Vinnet's mind flitted between memories of dying and swimming in a warm pool against a long, floating carcass: Anjedet. "She's dead. I saw her body floating in gel at Banebdjedet's palace."

Wait, she hadn't seen that. That was before she met Vinnet, but she remembered it anyway.

The Green Flame eased back, frowning as he thought.

Was that it? Had she spewed out her usefulness that quickly? Was he ready to kill them? Maybe, if he had nothing else he wanted to know, he wouldn't drag it out like Vinnet expected.

There she went, hoping for a quick death again.

He crossed his arms. "That's what I'd expect you to say if you lied. You would need her alive to provide you with her personality, habits, and procedures. Unless you knew about the doppelgänger."

Had she? Sarah blinked. He said it like he'd kill her for that knowledge alone. If she'd known, that'd mean...what? That Anjedet meant for a spy to take her place? That the Kemtewet queen had sold out to the Gertewet? Not flippin' likely. Or that the Gertewet had an in through a human who had successfully pushed Anjedet into her risky escape. Again, not likely.

"The doppelgänger was part of your plan."

"No, the first time I heard of her was when Benny-J said she'd died."

"Then you must have kept Anjedet alive. Is she on Earth?"

"Why would she be?"

He swept out a hand, taking in both her and Maggie; they were from Earth. And Neith already had plans to conquer it.

"What? No! Leave Earth alone. Anjedet never went there! Banebdjedet came and got us."

"Did he?" The Green Flame turned to his assistant. "Remind me to have him killed."

The assistant bowed.

He'd do that so casually to his own guy? Benny-J had it coming, but still. Would his death be as gruesome as the ones he'd ordered?

"Where are you hiding Anjedet on Earth?"

And where did he come up with that notion? If he went looking for her, would he break into the Atlanta Underground or Kennywood amusement park or station his mothership's giant mass over Pittsburgh's incline until he found some suspicious cranny to send his search parties into?

And how many other people's lives would he screw up while he was there?

"You go to Earth, and the Air Force will blow you out of the sky!" Like they did Kitchell's kaxan, she realized, and like they would have Benny-J's if his hadn't been cloaked.

"What Air Force? Is that a Ger alliance?"

Even without Vinnet's active attention, the symbiont's

knowledge unfolded. Kitchell and Mr. Marshall—curse them—kept in touch with Marshall's old Air Force buddies, but that rocky relationship wasn't an alliance—or anything the Kem needed to know. Ever.

"Humans don't need aliens to know how to blow them up."

Scoffing, he stepped back to confer with his lieutenant.

"What's going on?" Maggie asked. Oh, yeah, she was here, too. "What's he want with Earth?"

"We can't do anything about it as long as we're strapped down like this." But no king would let a Gertewet go. He'd keep Sarah trapped here until he killed her. Vinnet was certain. But... But you never knew what might happen if something changed a little. "We have to get you free."

"With him standing right there?"

With or without him nearby, Sarah couldn't see how they could get out. The clamps around their necks, wrists, hips, and knees were too firm. Unless... "Maybe we can get him to let you out."

"Are you kidding?"

Sarah took a deep breath, her heart pounding in her ears in time with flashes of Vinnet's memories. This was a bad idea. "Hey, Green Flame!"

He turned his back more completely to her.

"I'll tell you where Anjedet is." She waited for him to turn back. "If you let the human go."

He stepped closer, so he hardly had to raise his voice to be heard. "Should I extract your companion, so it can't talk? This is not my first appointment."

The scanners at the exit of the queen's quarters could have detected Maggie's lack of symbiont. "You have scanners here, too," she realized, "in the medical bay. You can prove she's only human."

"Then why drag her all this way? Gertewet senti-mentality?"

She's my friend! Sarah held her tongue and borrowed from Vinnet's cover. She was a spy now; she'd better act like it. "Even Gertewet might need a spare." She spoke casually, but even as she said it, the idea sunk in: using a spare meant the symbiont moved to somebody else. She couldn't lose Vinnet already!

No! You're too young! Vinnet insisted to the long-dead host in her memories.

No, ignore her. It was just the king and Maggie and Sarah.

The Green Flame's wide hands engulfed the backboard on either side of Maggie's elbow clamps and leaned close. "Tell me about your master, vassal."

The room fell abruptly silent, except for the passing maids' brisk footfalls. Sarah couldn't see Maggie's face, only the maids' curious glances and the lieutenant's intent stare.

The stillness let Vinnet focus out of her nightmares, and the colors in Sarah's vision sharpened to olive greens and emerald chandeliers. *Where are we?*

"Sarah?" Maggie asked at last.

"Tell me," the king insisted, "about your master."

Finally, listening to him again, Sarah grasped the prob-lem: Maggie didn't understand him. How had she gone so long without noticing what languages he spoke? She could fix that. "She's human. She doesn't speak anything but English."

Oh, the Green Flame. Vinnet's focus threatened to tilt back into her memories and her predictions about the torture to come.

Sarah gritted her teeth. *No, you pay attention! That is not going to happen again. We're getting out. First, we have to get Maggie free.*

It isn't possible.

I'd rather die thinking it's possible and be proven wrong. She grimaced. *Shut up. You're not helping.*

The king asked his question again, this time in inconsistently accented English.

When Maggie didn't answer immediately, Sarah clarified, "He thinks I'm your master." That earned her another of the king's glares.

Maggie kept her voice low and tentative. "She's from Earth, from the United States, I think. She's about my age. Uh…"

Was that all Maggie knew about her? The days since she left home had blurred together without clear beginnings and ends, but it seemed like a lot. In that time, she and Maggie had been through much, but they hadn't talked about home, had they?

Everything had happened so fast.

It doesn't matter. Your friendship will end when he kills us.

I refuse to believe that; it's just getting started.

Maggie continued, "At the last place, she helped me get up when I tripped and hurt my leg."

"Who is she?"

"I don't know. She's a girl."

"What was her mission?"

Don't tell him. Don't tell him. Don't tell him.

Maggie mumbled, "She had to replace Anjedet."

"What next?"

"Uh…" She drew the tone out, stalling for time. "I don't know. Protect Earth?"

"From what? No one is attacking Earth!" the Green Flame growled.

"I don't know!"

He drove his fist toward her with brutal strength, but instead of the thud of flesh-to-flesh impact, metal unlatched, and the neck clamp swung into view. The Green Flame did something to Maggie's neck.

"Don't hurt her!" Sarah yelled.

He grunted and moved over to Sarah, smacking open her neck clamp with a latch on the back side. Before she could enjoy a single unrestricted breath, he wrapped his giant hands around the back of her neck and pinched.

Vinnet twinged under his fingers, trying to get away, and Sarah screamed in surprise.

He latched the clamp as abruptly as he'd removed it, stepped back, and thought.

The color of the drapes in Sarah's vision warmed. *No, stop! Vinnet, it's okay. It's working. He knows I'm telling the truth about Maggie being human.*

How can you be sure?

Staring at her, Teni motioned his assistant forward, and the Kemtewet woman stopped at his side. "That one knows nothing. Have someone take it down to Receiving."

It worked!

The lieutenant bowed and marched away. She returned a minute later with the king's steward in tow, who Sarah recognized because of his fashionable dress and rank pins. The steward unclamped Maggie, then steered her away with a firm hand on her shoulder. As they passed, Maggie's wide eyes met Sarah's, and she tried to muster a smile. Then she reached the end of the ballroom and was gone.

"Gertewet sentimentality," the Green Flame muttered.

Sarah rolled her eyes. She could do this.

"Now, tell me, where is Anjedet?"

THE MAN PUSHED Maggie out of the ballroom into the narrow room full of linens, work tables, and storage cabinets. And no one else.

It was perfect.

Like she'd practiced in the studio, Maggie elbowed him in the stomach, broke free of his grip, and turned to hit him in the side of his knee. He didn't move quickly once he hit the floor, but he did still try to push himself back up.

Was he an alien? Her kick to the back of his head was sloppy enough to slam down on his neck, too, where she'd seen the marks on Sarah. Alien or not, that did the trick. Unconscious or not, he stopped moving.

Now what?

She needed to get away from the still body in case someone came by. More importantly, she needed to get Sarah out. Whatever Sarah was thinking, Maggie couldn't fly herself home.

Watch it turn out there's a space subway to Earth.

Should she take the door back to the ballroom or the one that led to the sleeping quarters? Where after that? She could end up somewhere better, but she'd be useless if she got lost now.

Holding her breath, she inched toward the ballroom and prepared to run when she folded open the accordion-style doors. No one noticed; the alien and his sidekick focused exclusively on Sarah.

Maggie followed the path she'd watched the servants take along the room's perimeter.

All they had to do was turn their heads, and they'd see she wasn't where she was supposed to be. Then what?

Would they clamp her back up and try to ask her more questions?

Even as she wondered, the alien's deep voice snapped out another question at Sarah in the alien language. So much for listening in.

She caught Sarah's answer across the distance. "Seriously? What do you think it was?"

Wrong answer. Maggie heard the sound of his strike right before she ducked into one of the rooms she'd seen maids carry linens into.

As she'd hoped, it was empty, but it wasn't a bedroom with handy disguises. Instead, it matched the living room she'd been left in on the last mothership. Maybe, like hotel suites, the layouts were all similar. She ventured through the back doors into the bedroom and from there into a walk-in closet. If she had to guess, she'd say all the clothes inside were men's, but they weren't remotely consistent sizes. She found some pants and a shirt in the back corner that fit closely enough. Even if they were shiny jungle-green satin, the pants helped her feel normal.

More importantly, they weren't the gray shift the aliens expected her to wear. It was like the opposite of all her "What to do if you're lost or kidnapped" lectures. On Earth, keep the same clothes on, so authorities could find you with the clothes you were last seen in. Somehow, she didn't think the police would find her here.

Hoping the aliens wouldn't go far into the closet, Maggie sat on the floor in the back corner to collect her thoughts.

Her mom would have a fit if she knew Maggie had kicked someone's butt and stolen a boy's clothes.

It made her homesick. What would her big sisters think? That she'd finally proven herself or that she was still a dork? What about her dad? How had he found her?

She rubbed her eyes. If she didn't focus, Sarah would stay locked up all day, and they'd never leave. What if they moved her?

Panicked, Maggie shot to her feet and bolted to the suite's outer door, bowling into another maid. As Maggie steadied herself, the maid bowed.

Now what?

The maid seemed to think her important, maybe because of the clothes, and Maggie had only one thing she needed. Maybe she could use her mistaken identity. "Tell the King the Empress wants to talk to him." She held her breath.

The maid rattled off a response ending in "*Steward,*" then dipped her head again and slipped out the door.

Did she even understand? Maggie would have to hear what was happening to find out. She stepped up to the door, planning what to do once she went through.

Those big columns had to be good for something.

32

STILL BREATHING

S arah tried to lean her head toward the side where the neck clamp hurt less, but she couldn't decide which side that was. Her mind reeled with the effects of the Green Flame's strikes. Until today, she'd always thought slapping was a weak way of hitting someone. Apparently not.

The room stayed red in her vision, and the longer the interrogation continued, the more she'd swear the Green Flame had a pointy beard and a narrow chin like the Eater of Blood used to.

The king repeated himself. "What is your mission?"

Vinnet? Nothing from the symbiont made sense. *I'm going to tell him.*

Was that a sense of concurrence?

"It was..." What was the question again? Oh, right. "It was to kill you."

"Me?"

Was it really that hard to believe? Sarah knew the plan was more complicated than that, but she didn't care.

A new servant stepped up to the Kem woman's side to confer with her.

"What would that gain you?" the Green Flame demanded.

Maybe if she tilted her head back... Nope. *Vinnet, help!* Useless.

Sarah took a deep breath. "You suck. Your lord took us off Earth for no good reason and killed three people, just because he was mad. You should all die."

The Green Flame opened his mouth to respond, but the assistant interrupted. "My liege, the Empress has recalled the prisoners."

"What? My time isn't up." He glanced between Sarah and the woman then stormed off toward the door Vinnet's memories pegged as the route to the control room. He grabbed the messenger by the shirt, grumbling, "Who are you? Why didn't my steward report this?"

"I'm your Deputy King's Steward, my lord."

He carried on until he left the ballroom. Sarah took deeper breaths, ignoring the lieutenant and hoping her head would clear. *Vinnet, you've got to snap out of this. I need you.*

There's nothing else I can do.

Something clattered in front of her, and two images competed for her attention. In the first, the Eater of Blood showed off a grotesque feast he would share for information. In the second, Maggie held a brass pot over the assistant's collapsed body. Maggie's image ran forward and triggered the latches for Sarah's restraining clamps. With nothing holding her, Sarah staggered away from the backboard and collapsed against Maggie.

"Let's get out of here." Maggie turned the direction she'd been taken before and hesitated. "Which way?"

"To the crew quarters through the napery."

"Where's that?"

"Door to the right."

Walking into the napery made Sarah's skin crawl. The clean linens smelled fresh, but Vinnet's memories said that on the other side of the wall was the mothership's control room, where the Green Flame was. Sarah couldn't remember if it had a back door up ahead, but it seemed like it should.

They had to step over the King's Steward's prone body. Wow, had Maggie done that? *Remind me not to tick her off.*

Vinnet didn't answer.

The next threshold opened to a Kemtewet-style lavatory, its pots visible to each other and the hall. Some of the faces looked familiar: maids who were servicing the chambers around the ballroom. Others were uniformed crew members or brawny, armored types.

One of the voices rose over the others. "Those are the prisoners!"

"Go!" Sarah pushed Maggie through the far door before the muscle finished pulling up their pants.

The girls burst into one of the ship's barracks.

Maggie froze, but Sarah jerked her out of the main aisle and ran between the wall and a line of bunks. People shouted behind them, but the crew members were slow to rise.

Sarah juked between two beds and cut across to the opposite wall, where a kaxan hatch stood open. She dove through, trusting Vinnet's memories and the shift in gravity to drop her on the soft padding instead of the shock walls. Maggie fell in after.

Sarah scrambled to the controls and tried unlocking the screen.

"Enter password or do not touch."

"They're coming!" Maggie braced herself and stomped on the intruders.

Sarah tried again. No luck. "Pull the hatch!"

Maggie stomped again then leaned out and closed the hatch.

Sarah reached into the metal web holding the control screen and found the tiny power button.

The lights dimmed.

"What was that?" Maggie looked ready to kick ninjas.

"Power's off. They can't get in." Until they got into another kaxan and teleported in. Those were Kem crew members; they didn't have a control system language barrier like Benny-J's crew.

Sarah collapsed on the padding, gasping. *Wake up, Vinnet! We're almost free.*

We'll never be free.

"What's wrong? Why aren't we going?" Maggie asked.

"PTSD. Hang on." Sarah took a moment to focus on calming down. Whatever Vinnet felt, her host's anxiety couldn't help. The muscle outside could be ready to teleport in at any moment, but Vinnet had only to undock and enter new coordinates. Why hadn't her symbiont caught on?

Memories trickled into Sarah's mind. Another Gertewet had saved her from the Eater of Blood, the Ger who had worked on the cleaning robots. At the time, Vinnet had been a sobbing mess, but she'd been trying to hold onto hope in her metaphorical heart—only to have it ground out when her host died after all.

Sarah brushed her bruised cheek, trying not to wince too much. *Vinnet, I'm going to be fine. Please help me.*

It's no use. I can't help.

Fine. Real quick, put some coordinates in the kaxan. Sarah powered it back on.

Listlessly, Vinnet traced through how to set a destination, and Sarah followed along. They entered the simplest coordinates they could:

Earth's.

VINNET SAT UP, shielding her head from the blow to come. When it didn't land, she checked to see where her assailant had gone.

Gentle swells rocked the gel wall of the kaxan's symbiont environment.

She spun around, taking in the entire white cabin, where Maggie slept peacefully. No other feet interrupted the clear, padded floor. No shadowy figures clung to the ceiling. No one could hide here. The executioner must have been part of a dream.

Vinnet, I'm tired. Let's go back to sleep.

But you'll die. After all the torture, Vinnet could do nothing more for her host.

I'm fine. Let's sleep.

Something was wrong about the other girl in the kaxan. A Gertewet had rescued her, and the girl wasn't a host, was she?

She's human. We got you out.

Then her host died.

Sarah's groggy, tired mind cleared as she woke up. *Vinnet, I'm not going anywhere. Chill out.*

Vinnet studied her bare human legs. Despite the abnormally light skin tone, they seemed to have sufficient blood flow. The bones ran straight, unmarred by signs of new or old breaks. Ten fingers moved, and they all felt the texture and oil as she ran them through long, even hair. Her scalp had no sore spots where hair had been ripped out, and her tongue found no tooth-sized gaps. Her face and neck ached, but that would heal.

See? I told you I'm fine.

Fine? How? When the ISC captured them, she'd have sworn they were finished.

Sarah caught her up on the details, and at the end, Vinnet sat stunned, gazing in wonder at the sleeping teenager beside her.

Two human girls had saved her from one of the Kemtewet kings. As a Gertewet, she'd done much in the name of protecting humans, but even she had never thought them so capable.

Well, yeah, but even though you'd checked out, we couldn't have done it without you. We wouldn't have known how to leave.

Vinnet nodded absently. She'd failed. Not just her mission. Oh, Mute! Her mission! Anjedet's rebellion was a lucky break; with significantly more work, they could have started with any of the fealty. Since the Kem had discovered her—and the Empress had to know by now—could they try this with any others, or was the entire plan forfeit?

You took out two queens. That has to count for something.

Insomuch as it will slow Kem population growth temporarily. Vinnet rubbed her burning eyes. *With fast medical aid, Serket might be able to be revived. I don't think they could reattach Faces' tail. She's castrated.*

Not that it made much difference. Neith would spawn new queens. Maybe the Gertewet could try again, but not for years, not until the Kem relaxed their guard after this. Not until the Kem wouldn't expect it, and the Gertewet might die out before then.

She'd still failed her host within their first week together.

What? No, I'm fine.

You needed me at my best, and I did nothing. Worse than nothing. I hindered you. It was irresponsible and unforgivable. Vinnet reclined on the padded floor and stared at the diodes and air vents in the ceiling.

You gave us everything we needed.

You must understand. She balled her fists and pressed them against the floor. *I owed you my life the moment you let me in, regardless of the pretenses under which you consented. Even when working toward ending the Kemtewet, my duty is to protect you when I can. I failed.*

Any trip to Sais would have been dangerous.

Sarah, I put you in greater danger by not paying attention and not planning an escape, which you proved was possible. I gave up and... Vinnet wiped tears from her host's eyes, then sat up to turn her back to Maggie. *And I would have let you...*

A hand rested on Sarah's back, and Maggie rubbed her shoulders. "What's wrong? We're out now."

Vinnet shook her head. *If I'd killed Maggie fast enough, we wouldn't have landed in this mess.*

You don't really believe that, do you?

Her presence aided our insertion, but she blew our cover. If we'd stopped the queens from using her and stopped her from saying anything, we'd still be there now. It could have worked.

Maggie pulled her hand back. "I thought you were going to kill me."

How does she know that? Vinnet, she can't hear us, can she?

Even she could see the logic of it.

"When the queens took me. They wanted a body from Earth, and I thought... I thought you were going to kill me."

But we wouldn't, right? We'd never hurt her now.

Vinnet sighed. "*Never*" never took in all the possible circumstances. "You're going home. The Kemtewet won't interfere with you again."

"What about Sarah?"

Vinnet turned around and found Maggie close. "As my host, she's an enemy of the Empire, and it is as much her duty as mine to try to end it. We must return to our base, report in, and help the others plan how to continue from here."

So, we're not going to stop by my house?

Only briefly. Usually, Vinnet waited longer before visiting her hosts' families, but as long as they returned soon enough to keep her support operatives from deploying for a failed mission, a short side trip wouldn't hurt.

MAGGIE BLINKED her eyes open at the little lights in the ceiling, the same ones she'd stared at for hours before arriving at the lord guy's palace. Those lights meant something bad was about to happen. Maybe they'd zap into another place and watch more people get slaughtered like Susan, Sophia, and Judy. Maybe something would start living in her, like it had in Sarah.

Something scraped across the padded floor, and she caught Sarah turning away, her shoulders shuddering and breath hitching softly.

Maggie scooted over and rubbed her back. "What's wrong? We're out now."

In fact, before they'd fallen asleep, Sarah had said she'd set the ship to fly to Earth. It was supposed to be over, so why was Sarah crying?

Maggie froze when a new thought struck her. Maybe Vinnet had to kill her.

It made sense. Maybe Vinnet wasn't as noble as she seemed at first.

Maggie withdrew her hand, thinking back. Her mind flashed to an image of Sarah jumping into the pool, sword arcing through the air, too fast and too close. "I thought you were going to kill me." Sarah's eyes had focused on her. Maggie had seen how the sword tip just cleared her. It had changed mid-swing. "When the queens took me. They wanted a body from Earth, and I thought..." Without a head, she'd be useless to them. "I thought you would kill me."

"You're going home. The Kemtewet won't interfere with you again." Some answer.

Something else didn't sound right about that. "What about Sarah?"

"As my host, she's an enemy of the Empire, and it is as much her duty as mine to try to end it. We must return to our base, report in, and help the others plan how to continue from here."

It wasn't fair! Why should she go home when Sarah couldn't? Why did Sarah have to go back out where people thought watching animals tear someone apart was entertainment? Where they killed people to suit their moods, and where they kept people around to live in?

Not that Maggie would take her place, but she didn't want her new friend to have to go through all that again.

What if, someday, Sarah was the one watching a swinging sword and wondering whether it would land in her neck?

Maggie lay back down and rolled onto her side, trying to get a better image stuck in her head. But until she fell back asleep, all her new worst memories replayed themselves.

33

DO SOMETHING

"Unidentified kaxan, state your name, passengers, and intent."

Sarah rubbed her eyes and reached for the screen, fumbling through the video interface under Vinnet's direction until the image appeared: a young man in uniform matching Lieutenant Fairfeld. Oh, it was just the Air Force.

Another interruption. After all they'd been through, the blood and murder and politics and relived torture, couldn't they be done? Couldn't she lie down here in the kaxan and let the world spin by itself?

If we did, they might destroy our... Vinnet's memory meshed with Sarah's, re-synching. *You told the Green Flame that Earth would "blow his kaxan out of the sky?"*

She amused her symbiont. Good. Her eyelids drooped cozily closed.

They know we're here. We must answer them.

But I'm tired.

It's only a little longer. Only so they don't blow us out of the sky, too.

Sarah sent her image back. "This is Sarah and Maggie. We're from Earth. We're trying to go home."

The man's eyes grew wide, and he leaned in close to the camera. "Sarah *Anderson* and Maggie *Rockefeller*?"

She glanced at Maggie, who nodded. "That's right."

"And Vinnet?" he added.

How do they know... "Yeah."

"Awesome! Please cloak your kaxan. We need you to land in Montana. Check the transponders; we've got a bunch of kaxan here. Come on down and land inside the hangar. I'll have the doors open for you."

"O—"

The screen blinked clear as he signed off.

"—kay..."

One more thing keeping her from going home. Was the universe conspiring against her?

Maggie rested a hand on her shoulder. "They're waiting for us. My dad will be there."

But Sarah's wouldn't. What would he think of all this? What could she possibly tell him and her mom about where she'd been and why? Or about needing to go back out and keep fighting alien bad guys?

Because Vinnet was right: they had to do something. Not everyone could.

She followed Vinnet's guidance to cloak the kaxan and set the new destination, and the fragments of thoughts whirled through her mind: the kidnapping, the murders, the scrubbed mission, the fact that Maggie made it through alive. Or that Maggie's dad showed up and hers didn't or that Benny-J had kissed her or they'd killed queens or the Green Flame's intent to torture.

Or the symbiont now in her head.

Oh boy. That took the cake.

How could she explain leaving for the Gertewet? *"Bye, Mom, I'll be back in a few months."* Earth months or Sais months? Or would it be Sais years?

Once they find out you can work against the Kemtewet, they'll be amenable to it.

The Kemtewet? Sarah ran her hands through her hair. *They don't know about the Kem or aliens or spaceships or inter-planetary wars! They'll ask me why I'm not doing my homework and getting home on time.*

Do you still want to go?

Yes.

Sarah shivered. Yes, she still wanted to go home. She wanted all this to go away for a while and not keep peppering her with crises.

If she could just lie down and sleep for a week, that'd be a good start.

The ship settled next to all the other kaxan signals, and Vinnet showed her how to nudge it inside and land. The outside camera views showed men in uniform with matching guns lined up facing them.

Are they going to shoot us?

The man who'd directed them here waved to the others to lower their weapons.

They are trying not to.

That's something. Sarah released the hatch. *The sooner we get this over with, the sooner I can go home.*

They climbed down.

No one said anything when she and Maggie dropped to the concrete floor, but the guns quivered up, as if the men holding them didn't trust the girls. When security in the Central Palace had stunned her, it had burned and shocked, but somehow, she expected a bullet to feel worse.

She raised her empty hands.

"No, it's fine." The friendly man stepped forward, grinning, and the guns stayed down. "I'm Tech Sergeant John Bailey. We thought you weren't coming, but here you are! Everyone's on their way to see you. While we're waiting, can I check your necks?"

Sarah laced her fingers behind her neck, this time keeping the symbiont in, not out. "I have a Gertewet. Please don't touch me."

His smile faded. "Okay, Sarah. That's all I need to know."

Maggie let him check, but she shuddered at his touch.

Someone yelled at the far end of the hangar.

Trouble? Sergeant Bailey's grin returned full-force. "We're back here!"

The voice yelled again. "Maggie?"

This time, she recognized it with a pang.

"Dad?" Maggie whispered. Then she screamed it.

In moments, he bolted into view and engulfed Maggie: father and daughter reunited after Benny-J separated them against his queen's will. Well, good for them.

But if it weren't for this excursion, she could be hugging her own dad.

He whispered into Maggie's hair.

She nodded into his shoulder.

"Sarah." Before she could answer, Maggie's dad pulled her into a group hug. "You're okay."

"Yeah." Except for ruining the Gertewet's entire mission and making sure Neith had a chance to take over Earth. Sure. Okay. Whatever.

But his arm around her shoulders reminded her that she'd made it back to Earth, like Vinnet promised.

"Which one is the Gertewet?" Over Maggie's dad's shoulder, an older officer with her hair in a bun stepped out from between two kaxan. She looked pissed.

Sarah slid free. "I am."

The officer finished her once-over with a raised eyebrow, unimpressed. "So you're Vinnet."

"No."

Sometimes, a host-symbiont pair will go by the symbiont's name, Vinnet supplied, *but it's a little rude.*

Darn right it is. She straightened. "I'm her host, Sarah."

"Naturally." Her scowl turned to Maggie's dad. "Mr. Speaker, did you wait for them to get checked?"

"I was done," Sergeant Bailey answered. "Maggie's clean." He glanced at Sarah and corrected himself. "Just human."

What did that make Sarah? Dirty? More than human? Whoever the officer was, it'd be nice to not ever deal with her again. "What do you want with Vinnet?"

"I'm just minding what we've gotten ourselves into."

More people flowed out from between kaxan: Mr. Marshall and another old man. Katorin dodged around them and raced toward Sarah. "Vinnet!"

Katorin was alive?

Katorin tackled her like Maggie's dad had his daughter, and she squeezed like she'd found her lost puppy. It was weird. Sarah had only ever seen her once from a distance, but Vinnet knew her as a best friend.

Sarah couldn't help but be happy to see her. "I could've sworn they were going to catch you! But you're here! You're alive!"

"And you! Look at you—you're adorable! So young! That's going to be an adventure, isn't it?"

"I thought for sure the ISC was going to get you!"

"Nope. I had no problems!" Katorin pulled her closer and whispered into her ear. "You have to do something about these people. They're crazy, and they want to kill us all, but we need to be allies because—"

"Neith wants to take over Earth," they finished together.

Katorin knew? And she still escaped the capital without any problems?

Still holding his daughter, Maggie's dad stood and faced them. "Even if she didn't, we have to stop this from happening again. We have to get up to speed."

"We need a Gertewet stationed here." The officer looked like she had to chew the words before spitting them out.

Mr. Marshall was going to stay. She couldn't even look at him without Vinnet's sense of betrayal surging. Even if it was the other side of the country, this was too close.

Maggie's dad's smile turned predatory. "Welcome to Earth, Vinnet. I'm glad to meet our new liaison."

EPILOGUE

Khonsu swam into the new symbiont environment, hoping it was the last. Based on everything he'd overheard through the kaxan, it should be. Katorin and Kitchell had debated whether to bring him into Plains Base, since he (or, rather, the Gertewet named Khonsu) originated from Woods Base. They were supposed to be kept separate. In the end, they brought him in, because the base computer didn't have the planet's coordinates.

But the kaxan computer did.

In their excitement over the proposed treaty with Earth, they'd overlooked his access to the kaxan computer.

Neith would be pleased. Even more so than when she'd captured the Gertewet Khonsu and removed the symbiont while leaving the host intact. She had a special mission in mind.

She'd chosen him for the ISC before he'd chosen his own name or found a job to save up for his first vassal. She'd given him his first, a fighter retired from serving the first lord of the highest ranked king.

He had that vassal for a month before he got a new one, the Gertewet Khonsu's vassal. And Neith herself gave him his name, Khonsu.

He didn't know why she suspected the Gertewet would rescue him. But they had.

And he did know he'd do whatever he could to serve her. That would begin with informing her of two things: the location of Plains Base and the development of the treaty with Earth.

ACKNOWLEDGMENTS

I owe my deepest gratitude to the dozens who made this book possible, from Ann Cecil and Megan E., who gave me a chance, to my mom who suggested I redo this story.

From the "So... John" crew and the boys who squirmed in the cafeteria as we argued about Vinnet's future to Ella and my other wonderful betas.

From Ann Cecil, Urvi, Samara, and Jess, who gave me hard feedback I needed to hear; to Dr. Grimm and Pat, who pushed me to write better than I ever had before.

To Ike, who told me to "take this Rockefeller scene and put it at the beginning," and Pat, who told me to do it again with a later Rockefeller scene. And to R. Fendt for help with translations (but not all of them—mistakes are all mine).

From Molly F., Katti, Chrissy, and Nate, to Diane Turn-shek, Sean, and many, many others who have been relentlessly enthusiastic.

Rights of Use would never have made it without you all. Thank you.

ABOUT THE AUTHOR

 Shannon Eichorn is a science fiction writer and aerospace engineer in Cleveland, Ohio. She received her Bachelor of Science in Aerospace and Mechanical Engineering from Case Western Reserve University in 2012. During the day, she works in aerospace testing but has also written service instructions for turbofan engines, taught horseback riding at a summer camp, and supported supersonic wind tunnel testing.

She is a graduate of the Alpha Science Fiction, Fantasy, and Horror Workshop for Young Writers (2005).

If you enjoyed this book, please consider leaving a review on Amazon or Goodreads. To follow future releases, join the mailing list at blog.shannoneichorn.com

facebook.com/AuthorShannonEichorn

twitter.com/ShannonEichorn

goodreads.com/AuthorShannonEichorn

amazon.com/author/ShannonEichorn

THIS ALIEN SYMPATHY

A PROJECT BLACK BOOK SHORT STORY

Setira didn't see who took her to the clinic. She didn't notice when water started pumping into her body. She awoke to her mother's face.

"Setira?" A warm, wrinkled hand squeezed hers.

She blinked until the image focused. She knew the voice as well as the face, but no one ever came back from retirement. "Ma?"

The wrinkled hand brushed over her hair. "You're going to be all right. What did you do? Stop drinking?"

"You were gone. And Starlight and the baby. Why didn't you come visit to see the baby?"

Her mother's brow creased. "Of course I saw the baby, Setira. I delivered him." Glancing at something behind her, she let go of Setira's hand and walked away, her white doctor's robes swishing around her legs.

Doctor's robes? Her mother wasn't a doctor. And Doctor Mila delivered the baby.

Setira rubbed her burning eyes and looked again.

There stood the doctor, taking in the medical screens, finger tracing the details the way Doctor Mila had throughout Setira's pregnancy, the way Doctor Mila had when Setira had come to the clinic as a child.

Setira's mother had never worked at the clinic. She'd helped wash clothes for the village, same as Setira. But the doctor faced her and smiled with her mother's mouth, her mother's face. It was her mother's body, but it was Doctor Mila's mind.

Setira screamed.

Available on Amazon

OPEN INVITATION

The Project Black Book world is too large for one person to write alone. Coming in 2019, check AstraInvicta.com for details about writing for Project Black Book anthologies.

DRAMATIS PERSONÆ

As catalogued on wiki.projectblackbook.us:

Sarah Anderson - abducted Earth girl
Andrew Rockefeller - Speaker of the House
Joyce Rockefeller - Andrew's wife
Maggie Rockefeller - Andrew's abducted daughter

Project Black Book - A U.S. Air Force Undertaking
Col. Renee Marshall - Commander of Project Black Book
Maj. Joliene Patrick - an officer at Project Black Book
Lt. Kyle Fairfeld - an officer at Project Black Book
TSgt. John Bailey - Project Black Book personnel
Sgt. Rodriguez - Security Forces from Fairchild AFB
NFI-Com - A Congressional commission

Banebdjedet's Guard
Davon
Guerin
Kümmel

Gertewet (Ger)
body-possessing aliens against Kemtewet
("G is for good.")

Mute - the first Gertewet queen, deceased
Katorin (Beryl) - drone Gertewet, symbiont to Setira
Khonsu - drone Gertewet, missing at the Kemtewet capital
Kitchell - drone Gertewet, symbiont to Donn Marshall
Donn Marshall - former head of Black Book, host to Kitchell
Setira - non-Earth human, host to Katorin
Vinnet - drone Gertewet symbiont and operative
Coordinating Council - the governing body of the Gertewet

Kemtewet (Kem)
evil body-possessing aliens
("K is for kill.")

Neith - The Kemtewet Empress
Anjedet - Kemtewet queen entrusted to the Green Flame
Banebdjedet (Benny-J, four-armed man) - a Kemtewet lord
Cube Head (Paul) - a Kemtewet citizen
Doppelgänger - Anjedet's former host's twin
Teni - the new Green Flame
Uastschnesert - the former Green Flame

He With His Face Behind Him - Title of highest Kem king
Eater of Blood - Title of a Kemtewet king
Bone-Breaker - Title of a Kemtewet king
Green Flame - Title of a Kemtewet king
Eater of Ghosts - Title of the lowest-ranked Kemtewet king
Information Security Corps (ISC) - Kemtewet state security

Made in the USA
Middletown, DE
22 July 2019